Glamour,
It's no wonder people fall in love
with royals…

THE ROYAL
DUMONTS

**Three delicious, sensual stories by one
of your favourite bestselling authors**

We're proud to present

MILLS & BOON®

SPOTLIGHT

a chance to buy collections of bestselling
novels by favourite authors every month
— they're back by popular demand!

August 2007
In His Bed
Featuring
In Blackhawk's Bed by Barbara McCauley
In Bed with Boone by Linda Winstead Jones

The Royal Dumonts
by Leanne Banks
Featuring
Royal Dad, His Majesty, MD & Princess in His Bed

September 2007
Princess Brides
Featuring
The Princess is Pregnant! by Laurie Paige
The Princess and the Duke by Allison Leigh

Secrets
Featuring
Two Little Secrets by Linda Randall Wisdom
Taming Blackhawk by Barbara McCauley

THE ROYAL DUMONTS

by
LEANNE BANKS

Royal Dad
His Majesty, MD
Princess in His Bed

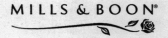

MILLS & BOON®

*This collection is first published in Great Britain 2007
Harlequin Mills & Boon Limited,
Eton House, 18-24 Paradise Road, Richmond, Surrey TW9 1SR*

THE ROYAL DUMONTS © Harlequin Books S.A. 2007

The publisher acknowledges the copyright holders of the
individual works, which have already been published in the UK
in single, separate volumes, as follows:

Royal Dad © Leanne Banks 2001
His Majesty, MD © Leanne Banks 2002
Princess in His Bed © Leanne Banks 2003

ISBN: 978 0 263 85682 8

064-0807

*Printed and bound in Spain
by Litografia Rosés S.A., Barcelona*

Royal Dad
LEANNE BANKS

LEANNE BANKS,

a bestselling author of romance, lives in her native Virginia, USA with her husband, son and daughter. Recognised for both her sensual and humorous writing with two Career Achievement Awards from *Romantic Times Magazine*, Leanne likes creating a story with a few grins, a generous kick of sensuality and characters that hang around after the book is finished. Leanne believes romance readers are the best readers in the world because they understand that love is the greatest miracle of all. Contact Leanne online at leannebbb@aol.com or write to her at PO Box 1442, Midlothian, VA 23113, USA. An SAE (with return postage) for a reply would be greatly appreciated.

Special acknowledgements to the
Lindamood-Bell Reading Clinic for their
creative and exciting techniques for helping
people learn to read.
This book is dedicated to all the special
education reading teachers who go the extra
mile to help non-readers become readers.
Thank you.

Prologue

He needed a wife.

The assignment was long overdue. Michel had put it off as long as possible. Leaning against his balcony rail, he looked at the private courtyard shimmering in moonlight. He knew the requirements for the position: discretion, grace, understanding and respect for his position. According to his advisors, a woman who provided a politically beneficial association would be a plus.

Michel's wife had passed away years ago, leaving him to parent his son by himself. With a dull pang, he remembered fragile Charisse. She had been a conscientious wife and loving mother. Although

Charisse had been chosen for him, or perhaps *because* she had been chosen for him, Michel had never felt more than a gentle fondness and protectiveness for his late wife. His son had suffered most from her death.

Even now, Michel's advisors had one list of requirements for the type of woman he should marry; Michel had another. He was older now and not as inclined to accept his advisors' choice as the final word for him. Whoever he married would love his son as if he were her own child.

If he were to place an order for a wife, he would say he preferred a woman with silky, long black hair and a body with well-proportioned curves. He preferred a woman with a quiet voice and a soft laugh and, most important, a biddable nature.

He moved his hand, and the moonlight reflected the gold ring on his finger that bore the royal crest of the House of Dumont. The ring was merely a symbol of a truth that had been with him since the womb. He was Prince Michel Charles Philippe, heir to the throne of Marceau. His father had passed away years ago, and Michel still missed him. Although his mother Queen Anna Catherine had given birth to seven children, she had always been more ruler than mother.

He knew he was envied for his wealth and power. He knew men dreamed of being in his position; of having the final say on any matter in his country.

Michel, however, had experienced the flip side of power, and he was humbled by the scope of his responsibility. For all his power, he couldn't stop the devastation a hurricane had wreaked on Marceau several years ago. Though he held the second-highest position in his country, he couldn't eliminate overnight long-standing social prejudice or ignorance. He couldn't solve all his country's problems in one day.

He might be the wealthiest man in Marceau, and he might be the highest-ranking male in his country, and he might have been trained from an early age to hold himself apart, but he was still just a man.

One

Early in the morning, Prince Michel walked through the hallway toward his office. His mind was divided between the myriad tasks and decisions waiting to greet him and the remnants of his thoughts from last night. He would need to marry soon. A quiet woman of breeding and grace, he thought. A woman who would bring peace and tranquility to the Royal House of Dumont. He continued down the hall, and the click of his heels on the gleaming marble floor did nothing to diminish the volume of loud voices.

"This way, mademoiselle," a man said in a loud, overly enunciated voice. "I will lead you to your quarters."

"Excuse me," a woman nearly shouted. "I'm sorry. What did you say?"

Francois, his son's assistant, was the man. And the woman? Michel took a detour and rounded the corner.

"Mademoiselle Gillian, do you require medication?" Francois asked in exasperation.

"I might," she replied. "I feel like I'm only hearing every other word you're saying."

Michel rounded another corner and caught sight of Francois and a young woman with a mane of curly, wild, red hair. She was dressed in jeans and a T-shirt advertising an American baseball team. Neither garment gave any indication of the shape of her body. Not that he was interested. This woman wouldn't know the meaning of quiet if it banged her on the head.

Francois glanced up and met Michel's gaze. Michel watched panic slice through the man's eyes. Francois immediately gave a quick bow. "Your Highness."

Distracted by the curious but bleary, green-eyed gaze of the woman, Michel gave an absent nod. "Who is our guest?"

"Prince Michel Charles Philipe, may I present Mademoiselle Maggie Gillian? She is here from the United States to tutor Prince Maximillian."

Michel felt an immediate twinge. His son had dyslexia, and learning had become such a chore for him that he avoided all books. Intervention was necessary, so Michel had arranged to import a highly recommended specialist. Mademoiselle Gillian faced the challenge of helping Max overcome his disability.

"Welcome to Marceau, Mademoiselle Gillian. We're pleased you're here to help Maximillian," Michel said.

"Thank you," Maggie shouted back at him. "I'm sorry, but I couldn't hear everything. I didn't catch your name."

Michel shot a quick glance at Francois, who looked slightly ill. "You may call him Your Highness," Francois enunciated so precisely that he nearly spit.

Maggie blinked and gave a vague nod. "Nice to meet you, Your Highness," she said, again too loudly.

Francois winced.

Michel cleared his throat. "Does she have a hearing problem?" he asked in a low voice.

"It's temporary, Your Highness. Apparently her ears were stopped up during the long flight."

Michel relaxed. "Very well. Show her to her quarters before you have to explain her to the guards."

"I'm trying," Francois muttered under his voice, then added, " Your Highness."

Michel left for his office and felt a twist of humor

as the sound of the woman's loud voice echoed down the hallway. Poor Francois.

Eight hours later Maggie awakened to a raging headache. Placing her hands on either side of her face to minimize the pain she was certain she would feel upon moving, she carefully slid from her bed, snatched the headache medicine from her cosmetic bag in the adjoining bathroom, and wrestled with the container. After she freed two pills, she tossed them into her mouth and gulped water directly from the faucet.

She was definitely going to have a *discussion* with her supervisor Carla Winfree when she got near a phone. Burned out from her teaching job at an inner-city public school in Washington, D.C., Maggie had desperately needed a break. Carla Winfree had gotten wind of a secret cushy assignment in the Mediterranean and put Maggie's name in the hat. Maggie had been chosen, but she'd been given very little information about her pupil or the job.

"Such as the fact that I'll be living in a palace," she said and dipped her head under the faucet for another gulp of water. "Such as I'll be teaching a seven-year-old prince. No way he can't be spoiled," she muttered. She splashed her face and wiped it with the hand towel. "Such as I have to deal with a smug, know-it-all pipsqueak by the name of Francois. And a prince, for heaven's sake." A tall, dark, handsome prince who was so stiff he probably had a steel pipe for a backbone. In the short time she'd met Francois and His Highness, she'd gotten the gist that these people were very big on appearances and decorum.

Maggie was not. She took a deep breath and counted to ten. She could deal with attitude. Heaven knows, she'd dealt with attitude from most of the kids she'd taught. But she had a tough time dealing with anyone who put on airs. If there was one thing she didn't like, it was smugness and superiority. Okay, they were two things, but they were related.

"I may not be the right girl for this job." She brushed her teeth and tried not to look at her reflection in the mirror. After a trip halfway round the world, she looked darn frightening.

A knock sounded at her bedroom door, and she eyed it, wishing for a peephole. "Who's there?" she asked.

A brief silence followed, and Maggie could almost feel the exasperation simmering from the other side of the door. "Francois," the irritating man said.

Maggie opened the door and saw Francois with a tray of tea and sandwiches. Her irritation faded slightly. Maybe he wasn't pompous after all. "Please come in," she said.

Relief flooded his face as he entered her room and set down the try. "Your ears are better? *Oui?*"

"Yes, they are. Thank you for the antihistamine and the food. I was starving."

"Not unusual for a trans-Atlantic flight. Your sleep patterns should adjust over the next few days. If you need a sleeping pill, let me know. In the meantime I will brief you on your duties."

Maggie felt the scratchy irritation return. She'd never responded well to an autocratic delivery of orders. "I think I understand my duties. I am to tutor Max because he has dyslexia and he's become so discouraged he no longer tries to learn." She reached for a sandwich and took a bite.

Francois tossed her a suspicious glance. "How did you know of his discouragement?"

"Because I work with these kids every day," she said, and mentally added, *because I've been through the same thing.* "These children bust their butts to keep up, but when they keep failing, they lose heart and hope. It's my job to give a little of that back." She paused. "It must have been tough for the family to come to grips with the fact that Prince Max wasn't perfect."

She took another bite of the sandwich and watched Francois stiffen. "Let me remind you that you are to discuss this with no one. You signed a privacy agreement. The prince's disability is a very delicate matter."

She waved aside his concern. "Well, it shouldn't be. Einstein had a learning disability, too, and he was smarter than anyone walking around this palace.''

Francois inhaled in barely controlled outrage.

Good thing there weren't any flies around or he would have swallowed one, Maggie thought.

''You are not to discuss the prince's disability with anyone besides Prince Michel or me.''

''I won't,'' she assured him. ''But I have to tell you I'm not sure I'm the right girl for this job. I didn't know I would be working with royalty, and I don't have a high tolerance for a lot of unnecessary, prissy protocol. Just in case you can't tell, I'm not a prissy girl.''

''That's quite clear,'' he said in a dry tone as he glanced at her T-shirt and jeans.

Maggie brushed aside the pinch of insult she felt. ''It takes a lot of creativity to get a learning disabled kid up and running, and that's where I keep my focus. I don't have time for unnecessary protocol. My whole goal is to help Prince Max find his joy of learning again, get him confident and reteach him how to read. I'll do whatever it takes to make that happen,'' she said, and silently added, *even though this kid might be so spoiled I can smell him from the other side of the palace.*

Francois gave her a look of guarded respect. ''After you have eaten and freshened up, I will introduce you to Prince Maximillian.''

Truce, Maggie thought. For now.

She finished her sandwich and toiled over what to wear, which was something she never did with her students back in the States. Maggie scowled, then pretended it was Parent Night and dressed in a blue cotton sheath and sandals.

Francois led her to the prince's schoolroom where the boy sat on a sofa watching *102 Dalmatians*.

"Your Highness, I present Mademoiselle Gillian," Francois said.

The boy stood, reluctantly tearing his gaze from the movie. Maggie noticed he was tall for his age. He was dressed in a suit, but his starched shirt was rumpled, and a shirttail hung out of his slacks. His hair was slicked down, but a cowlick on his crown rebelled, reminding her of Dennis the Menace. Maggie's heart softened. Since she'd stood in the shadow of her perfect brother her entire life, Maggie had a deep, abiding compassion for imperfection.

When Francois turned off the movie, she watched the little prince frown, then glance at her with wariness.

"Welcome to Marceau, Mademoiselle Gillian," Prince Maximillian said in a neutral tone.

"Thank you very much, Your Highness. It's a pleasure to meet you. Do you prefer Max or Maximillian?"

The little prince hesitated, and she quickly shot Francois a quelling glance. "Max," the boy finally said.

"Good," she said. "You may either call me Maggie or Miss Gillian."

Max nodded.

"I'm here to help you learn to read and write."

She saw his face immediately shut down. Funny, she thought, prince or pauper, that expression was universal among kids who'd experience too much failure.

"I don't like to read and write."

"I'm not surprised," she said, and wandered around the room eyeing shelves and shelves of unread books.

Max crossed his arms over his chest and looked at her with suspicion. "What do you mean?"

"I mean you've had a rotten experience trying to read and write and you've tried and tried. Trying has made you feel stupid even though you're quite smart."

"How do you know I'm not stupid?" he asked, and her heart broke a little at the doubt in his voice. The glint of defiance in his eyes held a world of pain. She remembered the years in her childhood when she'd felt stupid because she couldn't read.

"Because there are tests that measure learning and intelligence and you score high on the intelligence tests. You have had a problem reading, but I'm here to help you."

Max slid his gaze back to the television. "I would rather watch movies."

She smiled and bent down. "Watching movies can be fun for a while, but you're very smart and you will want to do other things."

He looked at her with a mixture of doubt and curiosity. "Are you American?"

"Yes," Maggie said.

"My father says American women often don't appreciate the importance of royal duty."

Maggie would bet there was a story behind that belief. "That may be true, because we don't have princes and princesses in America."

"My uncle married an American woman."

"What did you think of her?"

"She was nice. She showed me her computer and gave me a piece of chocolate."

Maggie took mental notes. Computers and chocolate. "What's your favorite animal?"

"Dog," Max said without missing a beat. "But I like lions a lot, too."

"Okay," she said, and cataloged the information. "We'll start tomorrow. Good night."

"Good night," Max said, then added, "Mademoiselle Gillian."

Maggie left the room, and Francois guided her down another hall. "Now you will meet with the prince."

Michel set aside thirty minutes to meet with the American tutor, then planned to retire to his quarters

with a glass of vintage Burgundy wine and sit in
complete and utter silence. It had been one hell of
a long day.

A knock sounded at the door. *"Entrez,"* Michel
said.

"Your Highness, Prince Michel, may I present
Mademoiselle Maggie Gillian."

Michel nodded. "Thank you Francois. You may
leave. Please join me, Mademoiselle Gillian," he
said, gesturing to the chair across from him.

"Thank you, Your Highness," the woman said
and stepped from behind Francois.

Michel blinked at the transformation of the
woman he'd met this morning. Although her hair
was wild as ever, her green eyes sparked with curiosity and intelligence. Her dress revealed feminine
curves and a distracting pair of legs. She moved with
a combination of purposefulness and sensuality. She
reminded him of a firecracker a palace guard had
quickly removed from his hands when he'd been a
teenager hell-bent on having fun.

Michel could barely remember the last time he'd
genuinely had fun. Between his father's death and
the responsibility of the throne that had been his
since birth, his life had been unrelentingly serious.
Fun was for other people, Michel told himself. He
had too many other important matters to manage.

"You have met my son," Michel said.

She nodded. "Yes, and I've read the folder on his

education and test scores. He's very intelligent, but discouraged. Not unusual for children with learning disabilities.''

Michel glanced away. He didn't like the term *learning disability* connected with his son. He still didn't like the idea that there was anything wrong with his son. ''Maximillian is not typical. As you've observed, he is quite intelligent and he will someday rule Marceau.''

She smiled, and her expression warmed him. ''Many parents go through a little grieving stage when they learn their child has a learning difficulty. It's the death of the dream of the perfect child, and it can be painful. That's part of it. But there's another part. I believe kids with learning disabilities are underrated. They view the world differently, and this can be an advantage. I'm sure I don't have to tell you that Einstein had learning problems.''

Michel blinked. He hadn't known. ''Einstein?''

''Oh, yes. His early-childhood teachers told his mother he would never amount to anything. Viewing the world differently can be a good thing. It's my challenge to help Max develop and learn and grow in confidence. I'll tell him that he needs to learn to read a little differently—''

''No—'' Michel began.

''Yes,'' she interrupted, surprising the daylights out of him. No one, save his mother, the queen, interrupted him. ''Prince or ghetto child, I try to be honest and positive with every child I teach,'' she said firmly. ''I'll tell him he can succeed because it's the truth.''

''Mademoiselle Gillian,'' he began.

''Please call me Maggie,'' she interrupted again. ''The formality is unnecessary with me.''

Unaccustomed to such a request, Michel paused, then chose to ignore it. He noticed her hands because she laced her fingers and slowly rubbed them back and forth. They were small yet capable looking, her nails unpainted, but something about the flow of her movements struck him as sensual. If she wasn't moving her hands, then she was expressing herself with a slight shrug that made her breasts sway, or she was touching her moist, full mouth. The word to describe her eluded him.

Michel caught himself and, reining in his wandering mind, he returned to the subject at hand. ''Maximillian has developed an aversion to books. He has lost all of his confidence.''

She nodded. ''I can see the aversion to books. He's lost a lot of confidence, but not all. Children are incredibly resilient. A little hope goes a long way.'' She grew serious. ''There is something else I need to discuss with you. I wasn't informed that I would be working in a palace, and I don't know anything about royal protocol. I didn't take any electives on how to curtsy, and—I'll be frank—as far as I'm concerned, it's clutter. I *was* informed that I would have a lot of latitude with this position, to accomplish my goals. If I'm not going to have that latitude, then I'm probably not the woman for this job," she said, and slowly stroked her throat.

The way she leaned toward him and kept her gaze on his suggested she was confiding in him, and created an odd sense of intimacy. Michel glanced at her slow-moving finger and his mind's eye traveled down the ivory skin of her neck to her chest. The sheath and whatever she wore beneath dissolved, and he imagined the sight of pale breasts and tight pink nipples. Lower still, he visualized her rib cage and belly button and a downy thatch of hair covering her femininity between her creamy thighs.

He had just mentally undressed his son's tutor, Michel realized and swallowed an oath. He clearly needed a glass of wine and his hour of solitude.

Michel had dealt with everything from foreign affairs to legislation today, but this woman was giving him a headache. "What do you have planned for Maximillian?"

"I'm going to help him rediscover his passion for learning."

Her mention of the word passion brushed over his nerve endings, reminding him of passions he'd long denied.

"We're going to do something very important."

"And what is that, Mademoiselle Gillian?" he asked.

"Maggie," she corrected with a sensual tilt of her lips. "Max and I are going to have fun."

A few sparse fun-filled memories from his childhood flashed through his mind. Michel wanted the fun for his son, but he also understood the responsibility Maximillian would one day face. "My son will one day rule. Preparing him requires years of training, and there's no way to escape the fact that it's serious business. As an American, you may not appreciate—"

"Oh, Max mentioned you didn't think much of American women."

Michel digested her words and felt a flicker of temper. "Mademoiselle, you've stated that you do not have an appreciation for royal protocol. Is it not considered rude in your country to interrupt when another is speaking?"

He watched her blink, then a look of chagrin crossed her face. She bit her lip. "I apologize. It's hard for me to restrain myself when I feel so passionately about something. You're right."

Michel was accustomed to deference from nearly everyone he met, but her apology and sincere acknowledgment of his point was a breath of fresh air. He nodded. "You'll have a great deal of latitude to accomplish what all of us want for Maximillian, however there are security and protocol factors. It's a fact of life. Francois is an excellent resource for any questions you may have. I'll want a weekly update on Maximillian's progress."

Maggie nodded thoughtfully. "Okay. Just one question please?"

"Yes."

"One of the things I ask the parents of the kids I work with is, do you read with your child?"

Michel felt a haunting sense of loss. "My late wife, Maximillian's mother, sometimes read to him. His nanny has read to him on occasion since then."

Maggie cocked her head to the side. "I'm sorry about your loss. I'm sure you're very busy, but it would help if you can squeeze in some reading every now and then."

"I spend time with my son, but I must delegate some responsibilities to others. That's part of the reason I hired you."

"But I'm a woman, and you're a man."

Silence followed. Her gaze held his, and a basic sensual awareness flashed between them.

Surprise and chagrin crossed her face before she glanced away. She cleared her throat. "This is a modeling issue." She paused when he didn't immediately respond. "Dr. Seuss is highly recommended for children with reading problems."

Michel had a vague recollection of reading a Dr. Seuss book when he was a child. "You want me to read *The Cat in the Hat*," he said, fighting a twinge of impatience. "Mademoiselle, I must teach my son to be a protector, a warrior. I teach him to fence."

She paused a moment. "Your Highness, in your lifetime, how many times have you used a sword to settle your differences or solve a problem?"

"Never," he admitted. "But the sport builds confidence." He held up his hand when she opened her mouth to speak. "I understand what you're saying. Maximillian will use words as a weapon and a bridge far more often than he'll use a sword."

She nodded slowly, and he felt an odd understanding pass between them. He saw a faint glimmer of respect in her eyes at the same time he felt a kick of challenge in his gut. The tutor from America was turning out to be more than he had bargained for.

TWO

He wasn't exactly what she'd expected, Maggie thought when the image of Prince Michel skimmed through her mind the next morning. If he had one iota of a sense of humor, he wouldn't be half-bad. She'd found the intelligence and banked emotion in his startling light-blue eyes distracting. His gaze gave hints that there were layers to this man. The notion made her curious. She wondered if he ever let down his guard. She wondered if he could.

He seemed like a man set apart, and something about that bothered her, which was silly, because Prince Michel was none of her concern. Max was. Although she'd struggled with a sliver of intimidation, she'd been determined to treat him just like she treated the parents of her other students.

His sense of honor emanated from him like the heat from the sun. The strength of his character was so rare to Maggie that she was fascinated.

But his confidence had emanated with the same strength as his honor. He seemed almost perfect. Heaven knows, she'd had to put up with enough of that quality from her father and brother. Lifting her hair in a ponytail, she pushed the complex Prince Michel from her thoughts. He was a puzzle best left in someone else's toy box.

She put a map to the palace grounds, a few cue cards and a mirror in a bucket and carried it with her as she headed for Max's personal classroom.

Dressed in perfectly creased slacks, a shirt with the shirttail once again hanging out and a lopsided tie, Max watched the television. Maggie made a mental note for her next conversation with Francois. Max's television time needed to be drastically reduced.

Max glanced up at her, noting her casual shorts and T-shirt with a confused expression.

Spotting the remote, Maggie turned off the TV. ''Do you have something special on your schedule today that I don't know about?'' she asked.

Max shook his head. ''Just school with you,'' he said, unable to hide his lack of enthusiasm.

''Why are you dressed that way?''

"I always dress this way," he said with just a hint of the same imperial attitude she'd glimpsed in his father.

She smiled. "Well you need to lose the shirt and tie, and change into shorts and tennis shoes, Your Highness."

He glanced at her with a combination of curiosity and suspicion. "What are we going to do?"

She pulled out the map and pointed to an area she'd circled with a red pen. "We're going on a quest to this pond," she told him. "We're going to try to find a frog."

Max's eyes lit up. "A frog?" he echoed with excitement. "I thought we were going to read and write."

"At the right time," she said.

"Bonjour, mademoiselle," Francois said from the doorway. He lifted his eyebrows in disapproval at her attire.

"Good morning, Francois. I was just telling Max to change his clothes. We're going outside today."

Francois immediately stiffened. "Where?"

"Here," she said, pointing to the map.

Francois shook his head. "No."

"Why not? I was told I could use the palace grounds at my discretion," she said.

"That is too far," he said.

"Says who?"

"The palace policy is that Prince Maximillian is

not to wander more than a half mile from the palace itself without an escort.''

She shrugged. "So I'm the escort."

"An official palace escort," he said in a snooty voice that grated on her.

Maggie counted to ten, then bared her teeth in a smile. "Okay. I'll share my sandwich with you. You're welcome to come along."

"Me!" Francois exclaimed. "I am not security. I—"

"But you're official, aren't you?"

"Yes, but—"

"And you're definitely from the palace?"

Francois frowned. "Yes, but—"

"And you want Max to get the best possible education, don't you?"

Appearing trapped, Francois narrowed his eyes at her in silence. After a long moment he sighed. "Very well, Mademoiselle Gillian."

Maggie glanced at Max, who was staring at her, wide-eyed. "Change your clothes, Prince Max. Time's a'wasting."

As soon as the boy left the room, Francois turned to her. "In the future, it would be best to notify me in advance."

"Fair," she said with a nod. "I'll need someone on standby every day for the next two weeks."

"But, mademoiselle—"

"Hey, you said you wanted notice."

Francois gazed at her with an expression of disbelief and disapproval. "But shouldn't you be teaching Prince Maximillian in the classroom?"

"Later." She glanced at Francois's formal dress. "You think you might need to change clothes, too?"

Francois sniffed. "Absolutely not."

"Suit yourself."

A few minutes later Maggie and Max led the way to the pond with Francois unhappily bringing up the rear. "We're going to be looking for tadpoles and frogs," she told Max as they neared the water.

They scoured the area, discussing the various plants and fish they found. When Maggie spotted some tadpoles, she and Max shucked their shoes and waded into the pond to catch them with the bucket. Francois warned her to remain near the edge.

"They're little, but fast swimmers," Max said, staring into the bucket.

"So they won't get gobbled up by the fish," she said with a smile. "We really need our frog now."

She and Max searched until he gave a cry of delight. "I found one!"

"Good job," she said, winding around a cluster of trees. Maggie noticed he didn't pick it up, so she took the frog in her hands and sat down and motioned for Max to join her.

"Okay, what do you notice about this guy compared to the tadpoles?" she asked.

"He's green and he jumps instead of swims, and he's a lot bigger."

The frog wriggled in her hands and made a croaking sound.

Max laughed. "And he's noisier."

"Yes, he is," she said. "Can you make the same sound he does?"

Max was silent for a long moment, then said, "Ribbit, ribbit."

Maggie smiled. "Sounds close to me. The word frog starts with *f*. What does that first sound feel like in your mouth?"

Max made the phonetic sound and gave a blank look.

"Make it again and think about how your teeth and tongue feel." She made the sound with him.

"I feel my teeth on my lips," he said and wrinkled his brow. "And I feel air."

"Excellent. We call that a lip cooler. That's what *f* feels like. Frog starts with *f* and the second letter is *r*. What does *r* feel like?"

Max made the sound. "Buzzy. A car engine in my mouth."

"Very good," she said, delighted and held up the mirror. "Where is your tongue?"

Max made the *r* sound and looked in the mirror. "It's hard to see, but the back of it goes up."

"That's right, and that is why we call an *r* a back

lifter. What about the *ah* sound? How does it feel?'' she asked.

He made an *ah*. "Open."

"Yes, and finally *g*," she said. "Where do you feel your tongue?"

"It's touching the roof of my mouth."

"Great," she said. "We call that a tongue scraper. Make that sound one more time, and put your hand on your vocal chords like this," she said, lifting her hand to her own throat.

Max followed her instructions.

"Now just for grins, make a *k* sound, but keep your hand on your vocal chords. And then make the *g* sound again."

He smiled. "When I make the *g* sound I feel it in my throat."

"Very good, now would you like to hold our new friend?"

Max's eyes widened, then he glanced at her cautiously. She saw more than a hint of interest on his face. "Yes," he said, and gingerly extended his hands.

Maggie continued the combination science/phonics lesson until a downpour of rain drenched them. Tossing the tadpoles into the pond, she grabbed Max's hand and they ran back to the palace with Francois.

As they burst through the palace door, she and Max were laughing, but Francois was not.

She glanced up just as three official-looking men rounded the corner with Prince Michel. She watched him pause at the sight of them.

"Oh, Your Highness," Francois said with abject misery as he bowed.

Three of the men gave a nod of deference to Max, then turned their attention to her. Maggie felt the weight of their gazes and was acutely aware of the trickle of water streaming down her back. Fighting an overwhelming feeling of intimidation, she shifted her feet. Her tennis shoes made a squishing sound. She looked like a drowned rat. The three men reminded her of a stuffy version of the Three Stooges. "Uh, hi, Your Highness," she said, and bent her knees slightly. "We got caught in the rain."

"So I see. Gentlemen, this is Mademoiselle Gillian. She is tutoring Maximillian this summer. Lessons outside today?" he asked her with a trace of doubt in his voice.

She felt his gaze take in every drenched detail of her. If she didn't know better, she would have thought his gaze actually lingered on her breasts. But surely that wasn't possible. He was a prince, after all. He probably only had sex for the pure purpose of procreation.

Maggie shook off her distracting thoughts. He'd asked about lessons. "Yes," she said. "Science and phonics."

At that moment the frog jumped out of Max's pocket.

Francois gasped. *"Mon dieu!"*

Maggie raced after the amphibian before he jumped on one of the prissy three men standing next to Prince Michel. "He won't hurt anyone," she said.

Prince Michel's hand closed over the frog just before she reached it. Maggie slowly lifted her gaze to his. "You brought back a visitor," he said.

Maggie's breath stopped in her throat. "Yes, but he's unarmed."

Michel's lips twitched. "Perhaps," he said, then offered the frog to his son. "But I believe he would be happier outside of the palace."

"Yes, Father," Max said, and ducked his head.

Michel paused a moment and ruffled his son's damp hair. "Change your clothes. Remember we have a fencing lesson this afternoon."

Maggie's heart tightened in her chest. It was such a human moment. She heard the combination of firm tenderness in Michel's tone. Michel glanced up at her, and she saw an odd mix of emotion in his eyes. "We shall talk later," he said, and walked away.

As she watched Michel leave, she heard Francois give a heavy sigh. He muttered something in French and shot her a look of pity. Maggie saw the same pity on Max's face.

"Why are you two looking at me that way?" she asked.

"Because my father said he would *talk* with you later," Max said glumly. "And you were such a fun tutor."

"*Were!* I'm still here." She chuckled. "It's not as if he'll send me to the guillotine for getting caught in the rain."

"It's true the guillotine hasn't been used in centuries. It's in the official museum." Francois shook his head. "But I'm afraid Prince Maximillian is correct. You will probably be deported within a day or so. The men accompanying Prince Michel were his advisors, and they looked extremely displeased."

"But the prince didn't seem too upset," she said, surprised at the alarm pinching her stomach. She suddenly wanted the opportunity to complete her work with Max. Although the royal rules and regulations got on her nerves, she wasn't ready to leave.

Francois lifted his chin. "His Highness has been well trained to control his emotions."

A little too well trained, in her opinion. Maggie frowned, then felt a shift in her emotion. "You're saying I'm toast because the advisors didn't like what they saw of me?" She felt a burning sensation flicker through her. "Well, if a little rainwater is going to get those guys' boxers in a twist, then someone needs to sit them down and talk some sense into them."

"Prince Michel's advisors are regarded as the most wise and intelligent men in all of Marceau."

"Then it appears to me that Marceau needs to import more than gasoline and tutors," she said, then turned to Max. "C'mon. If you can get cleaned up quickly, I'll read a book to you."

Max made a face. "I don't like books."

"Bet you'll like this one," she said, taking his hand.

"Bet I won't," he said under his breath as if he'd intended for her not to hear him.

"Bet you will," she retorted with a smile, and squeezed his hand when he looked up at her in surprise.

After cleanup, a Dr. Seuss book and Max's fencing lesson, Maggie was summoned for tea with Prince Michel. When she met him in the parlor, she gave a little dip, then sat in the chair opposite him. "Good afternoon, Your Highness. I appreciate your meeting with me because there is a matter with Max that I think needs immediate attention."

He lifted a dark eyebrow, then waved for the butler to serve the tea. "Thank you," he said after the man poured tea and coffee. "You may be dismissed." He turned to Maggie. "A matter concerning Max," he prompted.

"The television has got to go," she said.

"Max loves his movies."

"I know, but watching television isn't going to help him with his reading."

"Perhaps we could reduce his television time. Maximillian has such limited personal freedom," he said, as if he was well aware of the same limitations in his own life.

"The television shouldn't be in his quarters or his schoolroom. It needs to be inconvenient, at least for a while."

He took a sip of his coffee and regarded her over the edge of his cup. "You are a surprising combination, mademoiselle. You're tough about television but lenient about outdoor lessons."

Maggie had spent the better part of the day wondering if she would be deported, but she told herself she was merely curious. She was not worried. "I was told your advisors would advise you to fire me and that I might very well be leaving within the next day or two."

"But you don't agree," Michel said, surprising her with his perceptiveness.

Maggie looked at him and assessed him for the tenth time. She wondered how long it was going to take her to completely nail his character. "I have this sense that you've been told not to think for yourself for most of your life, and that may have worked for a long while. But you have a very strong mind of your own, and you don't necessarily accept the opinions of your advisors all the time. After all, how old are you? Forty-something?"

Prince Michel blinked, and Maggie had the awful

feeling she'd just stepped over another line. "Thirty-five," he said.

Oops. "Oh, well, I'm sure it's a maturity, responsibility thing. My point is that you strike me as a man who has been around long enough to respect his own opinions."

"My advisors are well informed and grounded in matters of royal tradition, responsibility, training and all issues concerning Marceau."

"I'm sure they are, and I'm sure you're cognizant of the need to not get entrenched."

"You're not afraid of getting *fired,* as you say," Prince Michel said, meeting her gaze dead-on.

Determined to be honest with him, she took a deep breath. "Maybe a little. But I don't really need this job. I'm more concerned about helping Max. We made progress today. If I stay," she told him, "I can't promise we won't get caught in the rain again. Did your advisors hassle the living daylights out of you? Do you ever just tell them to take a chill pill?"

"My sister and most of my four brothers have offered various colorful suggestions to the advisors, but since I work with them daily, I have a different way." He met her gaze as if he were confiding in her. "I tell them I will take their opinions under advisement."

She smiled slowly. "How very restrained and tactful," she said in honest admiration, but would have enjoyed seeing the man in full-fledged anger...or passion.

A knock sounded at the door. Michel gave a slight frown of impatience. *"Entrez,"* he said.

"Pardon me, Your Highness, but Prince Nicholas is here to see you."

Michel's face immediately cleared. "Send him in," he said and stood.

A tall man with shaggy hair, a five-o'clock shadow on his jaw, who was dressed in jeans and a T-shirt strode into the room wearing a crooked smile. He dipped his head, then embraced Michel. "How's the ruling business these days?"

"Busy as always," Michel said. "How is medicine? How long are you home?"

"Until the end of summer. I'm going back to the States for some additional training."

"But while you're here, you will provide consultation for the secretary for health and human services," Michel said.

Nicholas shook his head. "Of course. You're always trying to get me to take a desk job."

"It's natural that I would want the brightest and best for my administration," Michel said.

Nicholas shook his head again, and his expression softened. "You humble me. I'll always be grateful that you helped persuade Mother to allow me to study medicine."

Maggie had the odd feeling that she was observing something very personal. Although she was fascinated by the exchange between the two men, she didn't want to intrude. She stood and began to move toward the door.

"Who's this?" Nicholas asked.

"I should have introduced you," Michel said. "Prince Nicholas is my brother. He is also a medical doctor. This is Mademoiselle Maggie Gillian, Maximillian's summer tutor from the United States."

"It's nice to meet you, Your Highness," she said, uncertain which title she should use, then added, "Doctor."

Nicholas chuckled and lifted her hand to his lips. "Nicholas is fine. Your American accent is refreshing. I suspect the palace protocol is driving you mad."

"Either that or I am driving the protocol police mad," she said, feeling her gaze drawn to Michel.

"Perhaps Francois," Michel conceded.

"And the Three Stooges," she added under her breath.

Nicholas barked with laughter. "You've met the advisors," he said, then turned to Michel. "What a delightful woman. Where did you find her?"

"She's highly recommended in her field," he said. "We should celebrate your arrival tonight."

"This is one of the benefits of leaving the palace. They always throw a party when I return," Nicholas said, turning to Maggie. "You should come."

Reluctance shot through Maggie. It would be a perfect party with perfectly coifed people, and she would feel so out of place. "Oh, thank you, but I don't think so."

"Yes," Prince Michel said, surprising the daylights out of her. "You must come."

"But isn't there some rule about employees mixing with the royals?"

"Are you refusing my invitation?" Prince Michel asked her in the same silky voice she suspected he used when he told his advisors he would take their opinions under advisement.

She could almost have sworn she saw a flare of sexual challenge in his eyes. Her heart raced. Not possible, she told herself. She cleared her throat. "I get the impression it's a big no-no to refuse Your Highness's invitation."

"That would be correct," Prince Michel said.

She held her breath, certain the electricity she felt zinging between Michel and her was her imagination. "Then I guess that means I'm coming to a party tonight. Does this also mean I'm still employed as Max's tutor?"

"Of course," Michel said.

"Even though your wise counsel might have suggested otherwise," she said, unable to resist the slight taunt.

"The advisors offer advice. I make decisions," Michel said.

"There's a story here," Nicholas said, glancing from Maggie to Michel. "I can't wait to hear it."

"Later," Michel said, glancing at his watch. "I have an appointment with the prime minister in a few minutes. You can rest and decide if you want to demonstrate your rebellion with your hair and wannabe beard," he said to his brother with a wry grin. "Mother's out of the country, so it may not be as much fun for you."

Nicholas gave a mock sigh. "An advantage to being born third instead of first is that the only person who nags me when I don't shave is my mother. Michel is required to be perfect."

"Don't let Nicholas mislead you. He's no slouch. His academic performance has been stellar. He just likes to play the role of the unprince," Michel said, his pride in his brother obvious and appealing. "If I ever get a day off, I may skip shaving, too."

"I won't hold my breath," Nicholas said with a mix of humor and respect. "My brother is what you Americans call a type-A overachiever."

Michel rolled his eyes. "As enjoyable as this is, I must leave for my meeting. I'll see you both tonight," he said, then left the room.

"A man in demand," Nicholas mused. "He has been since he was born." He turned his curious gaze on Maggie. "You've impressed him."

Maggie made a face. "I think *disrupted* would be a more accurate description."

"A little disruption is good for him," Nicholas said. "What do you think of my brother?"

"I don't know him very well. I don't know him at all, really."

"But you have an opinion," Nicholas prodded.

"My opinion is just forming," she hedged, reluctant to share her thoughts with anyone.

"With the exception of my mother and sister, my brother is accustomed to women who agree with every breath he takes. I suspect you're not so agreeable."

"You suspect correctly," she said. Finding Michel's brother entirely too perceptive, she decided to leave. "It's a pleasure to have met you, Your Highness—Doctor. Please excuse me while I make the futile search for something appropriate to wear to your party tonight." She wondered if there was a way she could skip the event.

"You must attend," Nicholas reminded her, as if he could read her mind.

"Yes, I know," she muttered, still hoping for a way out. "Orders from His—" *High and Mightiness,* she added for her own benefit. "Orders from The Man. I'll see you tonight," she said, and headed for her room, her mind filled with thoughts of Michel.

So there was heart and determination behind the perfect facade. She felt herself surprisingly drawn to Michel. It was as if the lens through which she viewed him cleared a little more and she saw him in a different light. Another layer revealed. Her respect and fascination grew, as did her questions. As a teacher, Maggie knew the power of curiosity. She was also mature enough, however, to know that curiosity about a man could lead a woman down a treacherous path.

But the more she learned about Michel, the more she wanted to know.

Three

———

She laughed a little too loudly. Her dress was un-
suitably casual. Her hair was as impertinent as her
personality.

But every man in the room kept looking at her.

Michel knew he was no exception.

Irritated, he tried to focus on the lovely, soft-
spoken widowed countess who had been fawning
over him all evening. He nodded as she continued
to praise the wine selection. Michel considered telling her he'd had no part in that decision, but he
refrained. Barely.

His sister-in-law caught his eye and took pity on
him. Auguste's wife, Anjolie, walked toward him

and smiled at the countess. "We're delighted you could attend this evening, Countess Brevard. The royal palace has a beautiful selection of Renoir paintings in one of the parlors. I'd love to show you."

"Take a breather," Anjolie murmured for his ears only.

Michel nodded his silent gratitude and immediately headed for the balcony. The scent of flowers was sweet in the humid night air, the string quartet played a soothing refrain, and the lights from the cottages throughout the countryside glittered like a thousand candles.

He inhaled deeply. Before he had time to exhale, however, his moment of respite was invaded by a swirl of red hair and a groan as Maggie ducked into the balcony and leaned against the wall.

Michel watched her for a long moment before he spoke. Her skin glimmered in the moonlight, her lips shiny, her eyelids closing out the world.

"You don't like the party?" he ventured.

Her eyes flashed open in surprise. "Oh! I thought I was alone."

He lifted an eyebrow. "So did I."

"Sorry. I can look for a closet."

Unable to restrain a smile, he shook his head. "No. You can stay. But you didn't answer my question. You don't like our party?"

She met his gaze in the dark. "Do you want me to be tactful or truthful?"

"Truthful," he said immediately. He couldn't explain it, but he craved her particular brand of honesty.

"It's a little stiff. It needs something. Motown or Lenny Kravitz."

"A boombox blaring a remake of 'American Woman,'" he said, certain his ancestors would turn back flips in their graves.

She looked at him in surprise. "*You've* heard of Lenny Kravitz?"

Irritated, he recalled how she'd assessed his age as older. He shouldn't give a damn she viewed him that way, but he did. "You expected me to be familiar only with dead classical composers?"

She winced. "Well, I haven't heard those strings try any hip-hop. I guess I just thought the music would reflect your personality."

"And that is?" he asked, his tone clipped, to his own ears.

She hesitated. "I don't really know you well enough to judge."

"Exactly," he said.

"But if I had to say," she continued, "I would describe you as restrained, so I would expect your taste in music might reflect that quality." She studied him for a moment. "Do you ever yell?"

He felt like yelling *right now*. "The problem with

a man in my position yelling is the chain effect it causes. For example, if I had a screaming match with you right now, the guards would rush out here and haul you off to interrogate you. Even though you would be cleared of any hypothetical charges, you would be regarded with suspicion during the rest of your stay in Marceau.''

She looked at him with a combination of empathy and sympathy.

Irritation nicked through him again. ''I don't need your sympathy,'' he said.

Her eyes widened as if she were surprised he'd read her so easily. She met his gaze, then walked closer to him and shook her head. ''How can I not feel sorry for you? Your position can't help but make you incredibly lonely and isolated.''

''I'm surrounded by people every day.''

''Surrounded by people with whom you must measure every word, every gesture. Is there anyone you can trust enough to yell or cry or joke with?''

''I can joke with my sister and brothers,'' he said, then honesty forced him to add, ''at times.''

She shrugged. ''Call me crazy, but it looks to me as if you work damn hard for this country. I think you deserve to have someone looking out for your good.''

''I have many servants who make sure I am fed what pleases me and take care of my clothing. I have a palace doctor at my disposal.''

She shook her head and extended her hand as if she were going to touch him. At the last moment she pulled back as if she'd thought better of the action. Michel felt an odd sense of loss.

"I don't think you're getting it," she said. "Who worries about your personal happiness?"

Her question silenced him, echoing inside him. His happiness. What a novel concept. What an impossible concept. He brushed it aside. "My happiness isn't the top priority."

"Well it should be for somebody," she said. She hesitated a moment, then lifted her lips in a slow grin. "With your personal happiness in mind, I think I'll give you a few moments' peace. Excuse me," she said, and left him with the terrible sense that she had just found and opened his Pandora's box.

Later that night Michel couldn't sleep. He wandered the length of his bedchamber, thinking about what Maggie had said. The notion of his happiness had always been a forbidden area of thought for him, and he had avoided asking himself futile what-if questions. Sighing, he glanced outside a window and caught a flash of white in the courtyard. Narrowing his eyes, he took a closer look.

A woman dressed in a short nightgown wandered barefoot through the grass. His lips twitched. Maggie. He wondered if she'd remembered to prop the door to the palace open. If not, she was stuck and would have to pound on the door and wake up the guards.

Michel glanced at his phone. It would be easy to call a guard to let her in. He could punch the three-number extension, issue a one-sentence order and return to…ruminating and insomnia. He swore at the prospect.

Maggie sat down on the stone love seat and inhaled a breath of fresh air. She couldn't bear one more minute inside the palace. The walls felt as if they were closing in on her. When she'd laid down on her bed, she'd thought about Max and Michel. She wasn't worried about Max learning to compensate for his dyslexia. He was already responding to his lessons. She couldn't, however, help worrying about his future. He would one day rule, but would he ever be happy? Not if he followed in his father's footsteps. She frowned. What a suffocating life Prince Michel led. Someone should fix it, she thought, although she had no idea how. And, of course, it shouldn't be up to her to fix it; it was none of her business.

Her only concern was supposed to be Max's academics, but she would have to be a piece of wood not to respond to Max's thirst for adventure. Even though Prince Michel appeared disgustingly perfect, she thought and made a face, his sense of honor got to her.

Groaning, she stood, restlessly stomping over the grass. She'd come outside to *stop* thinking about Max and Michel. Mentally slamming the door on the two princes, she focused on the scent of the flowers.

"The next time you take an evening stroll, you might want to leave the door open," a voice said from behind her.

Startled, Maggie whirled around to see Prince Michel's shadow in the darkness. Her heart hammered in her chest. "Excuse me?"

He walked toward her, wearing a pair of lounging pants and an open shirt, looking moody and masculine in the moonlight. "The palace doors are locked every night at 9:00 p.m. You would have a tough time getting back in."

Off-balance, she gave an uncertain laugh. "I, uh, guess this wouldn't be a great time to ring the royal doorbell, huh?" She glanced at the door, which was now propped open, then back at Michel. She tried not to stare at his muscular chest. "Thank you for rescuing me."

He gave a slight dip of his head. "My pleasure."

An uncomfortable moment of silence passed. She folded her hands together in front of her. "I'm not ready to go in yet," she said.

"Neither am I," he said.

Was he was looking at her the way a man would look at a woman if he was interested? Her heart raced. That couldn't be, she told herself. It must have been a trick of the moonlight. She tore her gaze from his and wandered to a nearby tree. She touched the smooth, cool bark and tried to clear her head.

"Shouldn't you be sleeping?" she asked. "Don't you have at least three appointments tomorrow?"

"Six," he said, walking toward her. "I'll trade the fresh air for a few moments of sleep."

Her curiosity sprang up like a weed, and she glanced at him. "Do you ever sleep in?"

He paused, then laughed. "I can't remember the last time I slept late. Maybe college, after I stayed too long at a party. Feels like forever," he said, staring into the distance.

A forbidden urge to touch him sprang out of nowhere. She'd wanted to several times. Although he was clearly strong, his isolation bothered her. "Where did you go to college?"

"Oxford."

"How many wild oats did you sow there?"

He lifted his lips in a dangerous smile. "Not as many as I'd wanted to sow. And you?"

Surprise rushed through her. "Me? Wild oats?" She shook her head. "I didn't have time. I was too busy trying to keep my head above water with my studies."

He frowned, shaking his head. "Your résumé said you graduated cum laude."

"With a lot of thank-you, 'laude,' mixed in," she

muttered. "One of the reasons I wanted to teach kids with dyslexia was because I'm dyslexic."

His eyes widened and he arched his eyebrows. "Is that so?"

"Yep, it's not on my résumé, but the experience of being dyslexic probably contributes to my effectiveness with my students as much as my education does. I know what it feels like."

"What did it feel like?" he asked in a low voice.

"Horrible," she said. "I hated going to school. I would break out in a sweat whenever the teacher asked me to read. I spent a lot of time trying to hide my problems. I felt so stupid, and my brother was a perfect student. My parents didn't understand why I wasn't perfect, too."

"What changed things for you?"

"I had a teacher who was very persistent. She would stay after school to work with me. She told me I was smart. She believed in me, and she made it okay for me to be different."

"She gave you power," he concluded, perceptive again.

"Yes, she did," she said, pleased that he understood.

"And that's what you hope to give to Maximillian."

"That's what I'll help Max find in himself." She met his gaze, and his mere presence unsettled her. His unrelenting aura of strength got to her. Maggie was accustomed to the cubic zirconian version of strength, a superficial display of physical or financial muscle. Heaven knew, she'd had to put a brave face on a few bad situations herself. But she knew that when she looked at Michel, she was looking at the Hope diamond of strength—the real thing—and she was pretty darn sure Michel's power went deeper than his bones.

"You have always known you had power, haven't you?" she asked, her voice sounding husky to her own ears.

He nodded. "Always known it. But I haven't always understood it. That may take a lifetime."

She saw undercurrents of duty and curiosity in his light eyes, and the combination was incredibly appealing to her. *Who was she fooling?* The combination was sexy to her. It surprised the heck out of her.

"What are you thinking at this very moment?" he asked, his gaze searching hers as he moved closer. She instinctively backed against the tree.

A sliver of alarm shot through her, and she bit her lip. "Umm," she began, knowing she definitely needed to hedge, but her mind was too clouded. She sucked in a quick breath of air and inhaled his clean, masculine scent.

He lifted his hand to touch a strand of her hair. "Tell me," he ordered.

He spoke the words with such authority that she

felt compelled to do as he said. But she stopped herself. "Not in a million years," she whispered.

He went completely still. "Pardon?"

If you dare, she read in his gaze. She cleared her throat. "I'd prefer not to discuss what I'm thinking."

"I prefer you tell me," he said, again touching her hair.

Maggie was having a tough time breathing. "But it's my brain, so in this one situation, you don't rule. I do."

He paused a long moment. "In another time I could have had you thrown in the dungeon for defying me."

"You wouldn't have," she said, "even in another time."

He lifted an eyebrow. "I wouldn't?"

"You would have been too creative to use the dungeon routine. There are more effective ways of getting someone to talk."

His lips tilted in a sexy half-smile. "Such as?"

"I don't know. Take away my CDs, my baseball games. Promise me chocolate-dipped strawberries."

"The passions of Maggie Gillian," he said.

"Some of them," she said with a shrug, sinking into his light-blue gaze.

He gave her hair a gentle tug to get her attention. He clearly didn't know he'd never lost it. "For a moment,'' he said, in a voice like velvet, ''you looked at me as a man, not a prince.''

Her chest squeezed tight with an emotion she couldn't name. Closing her eyes, she tried to take a deep breath to dispel it.

''Didn't you?'' he asked.

He only touched a single strand of her hair, but her awareness of him suffused her. She swallowed. ''What if I did?'' she retorted, but the breathy sound in her voice diminished the punch of her words.

''Open your eyes,'' he told her.

She automatically did as he commanded, then frowned. ''You give a lot of orders.''

''Downside of the job,'' he said, not taking his gaze from hers. ''I want to kiss you.''

Before she could do more than stare in surprise, he slid his hand around the nape of her neck and took her mouth with his.

Her mind still frozen, she felt instinct take over. Her lips parted beneath the gentle pressure of his, and she felt him rub his mouth against hers in a slow, seductively exploring motion. She sensed this was a man who knew how to seduce a woman. A dozen protests sprang up in her mind, but the rapid hammering of her heart drowned them out.

His hard chest brushed her breasts, tempting, teasing, and she felt her nipples harden. She grasped for a millimeter of sanity. The edge of his tongue slid over her upper lip with just the right amount of pressure to make her curious what he would do next.

Pleasure taunted her. *It's just a kiss,* she told herself.

But he's a prince.

Not at this moment.

His low sound of approval disarmed her. His heat warmed, his mouth aroused. He kissed her as if she were a delicacy and he wanted to savor her. He slid his tongue over her tender inner bottom lip in an invitation she couldn't refuse. She caressed him in return, cupping her tongue around his, drawing him more deeply into her mouth.

The kiss went on, evolving into an erotic simulation of how his body would take hers, how her body would receive his. Maggie felt her nether regions grow swollen.

She heard a sensual moan of need slide through the thick air, and a full moment passed before she realized she'd made the sound. She wanted— Another moan escaped. She needed air. She needed sanity.

Maggie dragged her mouth from his and lowered her head to his chin. "Oh, wow. You're not supposed to kiss—" she drew a long breath "—like that."

He tangled his fingers in the back of her hair and skimmed his lips over her forehead. "How am I supposed to kiss?"

to Max. They'd just completed a lesson and she'd read a book by Dr. Seuss to him. The little prince gave a heavy sigh and looked longingly at the rain-splattered window, then the television.

"I want to watch a movie," he said.

"Another time," she said, standing and looking around the room. "Let's play a board game. What do you like?"

"Chess," he said, surprising her.

"Chess?" she echoed.

He nodded. "All the Dumont men play chess. It's tradition."

"What about the Dumont women?"

He shrugged. "I don't know. My cousins are girls, and they don't play."

His attitude ruffled her feminist side. "If it's a family tradition, then there's no reason the Dumont women can't learn."

"Do you know how to play?" he asked with a crafty expression on his face.

"No," she said. "But—"

"We can watch television."

"—but I can learn. You can teach me."

His eyes widened in surprise. "Me?"

"Why not?"

"You're the teacher."

"Yes, and I'm here to help you with your reading. But you're a very smart boy, and there are things I

can learn from you, too,'' she said. "Like chess."
She clapped her hands. "So let's get started."

A hint of pride lifted his chin as he rose from the
table. "I'll get my set."

After a few moments he returned and set up the
board. "These are the pawns," he said pointing to
the smallest playing pieces. "You can only move
them forward one space at a time, except the first
time when you can move them two spaces. And you
can move them diagonally to take out another piece.
The rooks look like castle towers and they move
forward, backward and sideways any number of
spaces. But they can't move diagonally. The knights
look like horses and they move in an *L* shape only.
Like two spaces up and one space over. The bishops
look like pawns, only they're taller and they move
only diagonally any number of spaces...."

Maggie's head began to swim. "Wait a minute.
Why did I think this game was just a glorified form
of checkers? Are there any more?"

"Just the queen and the king," Max said, and
lifted his lips in a smile reminiscent of his father.
"Don't worry. I'll let you go first."

Prince Michel checked his watch and frowned.
Max was late for his fencing lesson, and Max was
never late. Michel could have sent a palace assistant
to collect his son, but he thought better of it. He

would check Max's room himself. Who knows? He might run into Max's witchy teacher.

Michel checked Max's bedroom, then walked toward Max's classroom.

A shriek cut through the air. "My queen! You thief! You took my queen!"

Confused, Michel threw open the door. Maggie was pounding the table while Max gleefully held a chess piece in his hand. Michel couldn't remember seeing his son so animated. A warm feeling suffused him, invading his chest. He locked the moment in his mind, wanting more happy moments for his son.

Max glanced up, and his smile fell. His eyes widened and he gasped. He stood. "Oh, Father, I forgot my fencing lesson," he said, clearly appalled.

Michel took in the sight of half-eaten sandwiches and the expression on Maggie's face. She also stood. "It's my fault, Your Highness. I asked Max to teach me to play chess, and it appears I'm a slow learner," she said dryly.

"Oh, no," Max said. "You lasted much longer during this game. Besides, just because I got your queen doesn't mean I've won. You still have your king."

"I appreciate your kindness, Max, but you and I both know the king isn't worth squat without the queen." She turned back to Michel. "Your son cleaned my clock."

Michel watched Max beam and felt a rush of gratitude toward Maggie. His gaze dipped to her mouth and he remembered how she'd tasted. "It looks like you two have been at it for a while. Just curious. How many games have you played?"

"Four," Max said. "She was terrible during the first two, but she really was getting better during this last one."

"He's being kind again," Maggie said. "Look at all my pieces he's taken."

Michel's lips twitched with humor. "Good job, Max," he said. "We still have time for a short lesson. Get changed and meet me in the gym."

Max zoomed out of the room, and Michel turned to Maggie. "Thank you," he said.

She lifted her shoulders as if she didn't understand. "For what?"

"For playing chess with Max."

She smiled. "Your son is cool," she said. "A little sexist at times, but I imagine that's not his fault."

Michel raised his eyebrows. "Sexist?"

She nodded. "Oh, yes. He told me the Dumont *men* learn to play chess. He also said the Dumont *men* fence. I guess I'll have to ask him for fencing lessons next."

"Absolutely not," Michel said, feeling the slightest twinge of envy toward his son. God help him, that was ridiculous.

"Why not?"

"Maximillian isn't experienced enough to teach you to fence. If you learn to fence, you'll learn from me."

"Why does that sound like a royal decree?"

"Because you're American and you're not accustomed to being around a man who speaks with authority."

"Are you sure it doesn't have more to do with being bossy?"

"The only other person who has come close to suggesting I was bossy was my sister, Michelina."

"Isn't that interesting?" she murmured with a mock-innocent expression. "And she's not American, is she? She's just female. I wonder what that says."

Her defiance aroused the hell out of him. He wondered if she had any clue. Michel moved toward her. "I find your mouth exasperating."

She pressed her lips together tightly, an unsuccessful attempt at looking prim. Maggie couldn't be prim in a million years. Her generous mouth was made for pleasure. Her green gaze grew wary as if she were remembering the hot kiss they'd shared. "Are you sure you don't mean my opinions are exasperating?"

"Those, too," he said. "But your mouth is also—" he slowly lifted his gaze from her lips "—distracting.

"Really? Most people say that about my hair."

She glanced at her watch. "Don't let me keep you from the fencing lesson."

A tinge of irritation scraped through him. "Maximillian will need to put on additional equipment in the gym. Are you dismissing me?"

Her eyes widened, and she licked her lips nervously. "Oh, no," she said in an unconvincing voice. "I just know you're a busy man and your schedule is probably crammed."

"But you've told me I should make time for my own enjoyment."

"Yes," she agreed with a nod. "But not with me."

He dipped his head for further explanation and slowly backed her against the wall.

She winced as if she realized she was being backed against the wall verbally as well as physically. "I mean, I'm sure there are lots of other people you could enjoy more than me."

He wrapped his finger around one of her springy curls. "Are you saying you didn't like the way I kissed you last night?"

She bit her lip, and her gaze skittered away from his. "I, uh—" she cleared her throat "—I think I prefer to plead the fifth."

"We don't have the fifth in Marceau," he said.

"We already discussed this last night," she said. "I don't see why—"

"Exactly," he said in agreement, and took her

mouth with his. He tasted her gasp and dipped his tongue across the seam of her lips. Two seconds passed before she opened her mouth to his and tasted his tongue with hers. He felt the dark rush of arousal at her response to him. Her velvet, curious stroke made his blood rush through his veins, pooling in his crotch. It was so easy to imagine her sensual mouth on his naked skin, skimming over his abdomen and lower, where he grew hard with wanting. He felt more alive, more human than he could ever remember. Michel made a decision.

"Come to my room tonight," he said.

She gave a soft panicked moan. "Oh, no. That's not a good idea."

"Why not?"

"Because we don't know each other well enough."

"I know enough," he said. "I can take care of you."

Her eyes dark with arousal, she shivered slightly. "I don't know enough about you," she said, and pulled back. She laced her fingers together, then unlaced them as she began to pace. "I didn't come to Marceau to become your mistress. I'm really not mistress material," she told him.

"You'd rather be married," he said, knowing that prospect was impossible.

She looked at him in alarm. "Oh, Lord, no. There

are too many things I want to do, and a husband would really cramp my style.''

''Then you would be happy being my mistress,'' he said.

She wrinkled her brow. ''I'm happy being single and pursuing my interests.''

''And I am your interest,'' he said.

She shot him a look of consternation. ''Your ego is bigger than this palace.''

''Am I incorrect? Are you interested in me?'' he challenged.

She turned silent. ''No. You're not incorrect. You are interesting to me. That doesn't mean I should do anything about it.''

''But you will.''

She lifted her chin. ''Another order?''

''No,'' he said, because he felt a sense of fate about this woman. He would know her. He would take her. ''Fact. Now, I must leave for Maximillian's lesson. *Au revoir.*''

Maggie gaped after him. *''Au revoir,''* she mocked, not unlike one of her students. She gave a heavy sigh, blowing her hair out of her face.

What was she getting herself into?

Nothing, she told herself firmly. She could handle Max, and Max was the real reason she was here in Marceau, not his fascinating, surprisingly sexy father.

She wandered around Max's classroom, trailing her fingers over the solid wood furniture. She couldn't deny that she was drawn to Michel, but as far as Maggie was concerned, the man had danger signs flashing all around him. Although she was more adventurous than the average bear, she believed in being somewhat sensible. For example, even she knew and accepted the fact that there were some neighborhoods in Washington to avoid at night.

But when Michel looked at her with undivided attention, when he kissed her, her heart jumped. It sounded hokey, but when they talked something happened in the air between them and around them.

Maggie nibbled her index fingernail. And he'd suggested she become his mistress. She wrinkled her nose. The notion assaulted every independent fiber of her being. Besides that, it felt, well, icky.

She'd never taken much time for romance. There'd always been more important things to do, and she'd fought so hard to come out from behind the shadow of her brother and dominating father that she'd never wanted to put herself in such a position again.

And she didn't want to get involved now, she told herself firmly. At the same moment she couldn't help thinking what a powerful combination of a man Michel was. She wondered if she would ever meet a man like him again. She wondered if she truly wanted to let the opportunity to know this extraordinary man, his heart, mind and body slip through her fingers.

"Mademoiselle, this is the third time you have taken Prince Maximillian for one of your field trips," Francois said the following day as he mopped his brow with a handkerchief. "Isn't this excessive?"

"It's a reward," Maggie told him. "He has shown improvement already, and he worked hard this morning. Right, Max?" she said to the boy skipping slightly ahead.

He nodded as he swung the bucket. "You should have worn shorts, sir."

"Maybe you could roll up your pants," she suggested.

Francois looked down his nose at her. "I think not," he said. "And you should know Prince Michel is aware of all your activities. He asks for an accounting every day."

Maggie came to a dead stop. "Are you saying he's asked you to watch me?" she asked.

Francois seemed to grasp the slight pique in her tone. "Well, not in so many words."

"In exactly what words, then?"

She felt Max come to her side and glanced down at him. He looked at her and Francois and pulled at her hand. "My father does the same with me," Max said as if he wanted to placate her. "He doesn't have time to be with me all day every day, but he still wants to know about me every day. He always says if anything happens and he knows about it, then he can take care of me better."

Sometimes Max's sensitivity amazed her. "Take care of you how?"

Max shifted from one foot to the other. "The advisors and sometimes, Grandmother, the queen, can be, well, fussy."

"Prince Michel is quite protective," Francois said with pride.

"But I don't really need protecting," Maggie said.

Francois hesitated. "The advisors have opinions about almost everything," he said in a hushed voice as if he feared the butterflies fluttering nearby might repeat his words.

Realization hit her. "Oh, the advisors still don't like me."

"It's not so much a matter of liking as approving," Francois said, tugging at his collar, clearly uncomfortable with the discussion.

"Hmm," she said shortly with a sniff, then allowed Max to pull her forward. "They'll approve the results."

"That is what Prince Michel says," Francois said.

"And what Prince Michel says, goes," Maggie

said, remembering his assertion that they would be lovers.

"As it should," Francois said.

She could disagree, but she bit her lip and focused on helping Max enjoy the beautiful day. They caught more tadpoles and waded at the water's edge. Francois fussed if they waded more than a few feet from the edge of the pond. Ignoring him, Maggie talked about the life cycles of tadpoles and frogs. They nibbled on sandwiches and tossed a few crumbs to the fishes.

Max spotted a turtle on a rock farther out in the pond, and he was so excited Maggie would have thought he'd found the Holy Grail. Unable to resist the longing in his eyes, she waded out to the rock, getting wet up to her waist. She grabbed the turtle and returned. On the way, she stepped on something sharp.

"Ouch!"

"What is it?" Francois asked. "Did something bite you?"

"No, I stepped on something," she said, feeling her foot burn with pain.

"Are you okay?" Max asked. "Are you bleeding?"

The worried expression on his face tugged at her heart. "I'm sure it's just a scrape," she said, even though it hurt like the dickens. "Here, put the turtle in the bucket. You get to name him, but his name needs to start with a *T*."

"We're not taking that…that amphibian back to the palace," Francois said in an appalled voice.

"Reptile," she corrected. "We have to. We just got him and I think I could use a Band-Aid."

Max looked at her foot as she walked out of the pond. "You're bleeding," he said, and bit his lip.

"I'll be okay," she assured him. "I just need a Band-Aid." She sneaked a glance at the bottom of her foot and swallowed a wince at the dirty gash.

Francois pursed his lips, then opened his mouth, but Maggie cut him off with a shake of her head. "Sorry, but I think we need to get back. Let me put on my shoes."

During the walk to the palace, she helped Max think of names for the turtle. By the time they arrived, Maggie was grinding her teeth at the pain. "You go clean up," Maggie told Max. "And I'll do the same."

"But what about your foot?" he asked.

"I'll take care of it. You go on ahead. Okay?"

As soon as he disappeared down the hall, she turned to Francois. "Please get me a first aid kit."

"There's always a doctor on call for the palace."

"Not necessary," she said. "I'm going to take a shower. Please leave the kit on my bed."

She entered her room, stripped, turned the shower on hot and bit down on a washcloth while she cleaned her wound. Pulling on a big, fluffy terry cloth robe, she sat on the closed commode and looked at her foot. "A butterfly bandage," she murmured without much hope.

Sighing, she stood and opened the bathroom door. Prince Michel and Nicholas stood waiting for her. Her heart caught at the intense expression in Michel's gaze.

"We're here to see the foot," Nicholas said.

"Francois is such a busybody," she muttered, hopping forward. Before she could take a second hop, Michel scooped her up in his arms and carried her to her bed.

Nicholas immediately took her foot in his hands and made a clucking sound. "Stitches," he said.

"I was hoping a butterfly bandage," she began.

He shook his head. "Stitches and a tetanus shot."

"You're a regular messenger of joy," she said, and watched him pull a needle and sutures from his black bag.

"You shouldn't be careless with yourself," Michel admonished.

"I wasn't careless," she said. "Just a little adventurous. I had to get Tex."

"Tex?" Michel echoed.

"I'm surprised Francois didn't blab that part, too. Tex, the turtle, was on a rock out in the pond."

Nicholas chuckled and put a fat towel beneath her foot. "Something tells me Tex is no longer in the pond. Antibacterial antiseptic,'' he said, and spilled cool liquid from a bottle. "Cream for numbing," he said. "I'll stick you next."

"You waded into the pond for a damn turtle," Michel said.

"Max wanted it," she said. She felt the prick of the needle and winced.

"He could have lived without it," Michel said.

"It's not like it was a pony. It was just a turtle. It wouldn't have been that big a deal if I hadn't cut my foot. Don't you need to be meeting with some sort of ambassador or making legislation or something?"

"I can handle my schedule," he said in a too-soft voice of warning.

Despite her bravado, she felt a shiver of apprehension. She clamped her mouth shut while Nicholas worked on her foot. Michel paced beside her bed. The young doctor smiled gently when he finished, gave her a few instructions and squeezed her shoulder before he left.

Michel shoved his hands in his pockets and sighed impatiently. "You shouldn't be so careless."

"I told you I wasn't careless," she protested. The tension emanating from him made her stomach knot.

He sat down on the bed beside her and took her hand in his.

Maggie glanced down at the way his large, strong hand enveloped hers. The protective gesture tugged at something deep inside her. "I'm going to be okay," she said, meeting his gaze. "It's not as if I was attacked by a shark."

Michel groaned. "God forbid." He shook his head. "My son doesn't like to see you hurt."

Maggie's heart softened. "I know."

"Neither do I," Michel said, his gaze completely focused on her.

There was something beyond desire in his eyes. Tenderness. She saw it, and the effect slipped past her defenses like smoke through a keyhole.

Five

Michel listened to Nicholas's stories of his recent trip to America while the two brothers shared breakfast in Michel's office. One of his assistants interrupted with an expression of regret.

"Monsieur Faus wishes to see you briefly, sir."

Monsieur Faus was his least favorite advisor. As soon as Michel formally took the throne, he planned to retire Faus with honors. "After Nicholas and I finish breakfast," Michel told him.

The assistant gave a hesitant nod. "Yes, Your Highness. Monsieur Faus preferred to have a private word with you before the general meeting with the other advisors."

Michel frowned. Faus was going to make a fuss about something. He wondered what. "I'm sure he said it was an issue of grave concern."

The assistant nodded and gave a slight grimace. "Yes, sir."

"I don't mind. We're almost finished," Nicholas said. "I haven't had the pleasure of talking with Fausy in years. I'm surprised he's still around."

Michel resisted the urge to agree, then tossed his napkin on the table and nodded at the assistant. "Tell him I have five minutes."

Faus, a tall, self-important man with bulging eyes, was admitted to the office and gave a slight bow. "Your Highnesses."

Nicholas nodded. "Good morning."

Faus turned back to Michel. "I have an issue of grave concern to our country."

"Does this issue concern military, crime or famine?" Michel asked.

"No. It involves our future ruler, your son."

Michel tamped down the scratchy irritation he felt at the back of his neck.

"It has come to my attention that his American—" he said the word with disdain "—tutor endangered him during a trip to the pond."

"I don't know where you got your information," Michel said, his impatience with the man driving him to his feet. "But Prince Maximillian has remained on the palace grounds during his lessons. He was provided with a palace escort during his trip to the pond. His tutor has been protective of him. In fact, she injured her foot during the trip. More important, her methods have produced better results than I had hoped for. If the tutor should take Prince Maximillian beyond the palace grounds, I can assure you that security will accompany them.'' He nodded toward Faus. ''That should settle your concerns.''

Faus gave a slow nod. ''Yes, Your Highness. But I'm not sure it's appropriate for Prince Maximillian to be running barefoot on the grounds. This tutor does not appear to be a proper influence in terms of propriety.''

One of the things that irritated the hell out of Michel was the way everyone felt they should make decisions about how his son was raised. ''The tutor is providing Maximillian with invaluable tools that he will need throughout his life.''

''But propriety—''

''Propriety isn't always the top priority. Maximillian will have countless opportunities to focus on propriety. He's learning quickly, and he's happy.''

''Happiness is not a priority in Prince Maximillian's training.''

''I'm his father, and it's a priority for me. Maximillian is more productive when he's happy.''

''With all due respect, I understand your concern for Prince Maximillian as your son, but Prince Maximillian also belongs to the people.''

Michel felt his blood pressure climb. In the back of his mind he could imagine Maggie's response. *Butt out!* The thought calmed him, enabling him to speak his mind somewhat diplomatically. "It's my job as his father and his ruler to balance his future responsibilities with the development of his character. I appreciate your support of my judgment as I carry out both of these roles."

Faus gave a slow dip of his head and dismissed himself. As soon as he left, Nicholas rolled his eyes. "God, what a pain. Why don't you fire him?"

"It's not yet within my authority to get rid of him," Michel said, shoving his fist into his pocket. "While mother has passed on most of the responsibilities of the ruling position, I'm not officially *it*."

"So you've got all the work but not all the perks," Nicholas concluded. "Bummer. When do you think Mother, dear, will toss the crown in your direction?"

"I think she's waiting for me to marry again."

Nicholas made a face. "What a choice. Marry someone the advisors choose or put up with their endless yammering. I don't envy you, brother. How do you stand it?"

Michel knew that none of his brothers envied him, yet for all the frustration of his position, most days he wouldn't trade it for the world. He gave a wry chuckle. "How do I stand it? I care. I care about Marceau."

"We're damn lucky then that you're in charge," he said. He studied Michel. "Just curious, what's up between you and Max's tutor?"

Michel tensed. "Nothing. She's American. She's entirely inappropriate." *Even though he thought about her entirely too often,* Michel mentally added.

"She's not hard on the eyes," Nicholas said.

"Just hard on a man's patience," Michel muttered, and raked a hand through his hair.

"But real. So you won't mind if I spend some time with her," Nicholas said.

Michel didn't breathe for a half moment. He rolled through every response he should make. He shouldn't care if his brother spent time with Maggie. He shouldn't care if she laughed with him. Or kissed him. Everything inside him rebelled at the thought. He could tell Nicholas to leave Maggie alone so she wouldn't be distracted from her job, but he wouldn't. He met his brother's gaze. "I would mind."

Nicholas looked at him for a long, considering moment, then gave a slow smile of approval. "Okay."

"Join me for dinner," Michel said to Maggie.

Sitting on her bed, she put down her book. "It's nine o'clock. I've already eaten."

"Then you can eat dessert," he suggested.

"Rough day?" she asked, not immune to his weary expression.

"Will you or won't you join me for dinner?"

"I will," she said, rising gingerly to her feet. She'd gotten wind of a portion of his day, and she'd have to be heartless to shun him at the moment. "How could a girl resist such a charming invitation?"

"I used all my restraint with one of my advisors today."

"I heard," she said, and limped beside him down the hall.

Michel threw a sharp glance at her. "From whom?"

"Dr. Nick. He checked my bandage today."

Michel relaxed slightly, then glanced at her foot. "Perhaps I should carry you."

She put her hands in front of her. "Oh, no. I won't win any ballerina contests, but I can get wherever we're going under my own steam."

"Take my arm, then," he said, extending his arm. When she hesitated, he raised a dark eyebrow. "Or I can carry you."

"Pushy, pushy, pushy," she whispered under her breath and allowed him to lead the way. They traveled down one hall, took two turns, then climbed a short set of stairs. "Where are we going?" she asked as he opened the door.

"My quarters," he said, and Maggie almost

turned around. He must have sensed her apprehension. "Chocolate-covered strawberries for dessert," he said, and led her into a plush but masculine room with carved mahogany furniture. On the west end of the room a serving table stood in front of a door to a balcony.

"That looks nice," she admitted. "I'm surprised you don't have a server."

"By the end of many days, I'm in no mood for polite conversation."

"Then why did you invite me?" she asked, using the term *invite* loosely.

"I knew you wouldn't be polite," he said, and grinned.

Maggie laughed in spite of herself. "Okay. Are we sitting on the balcony?"

"We are. I have some port to go with your chocolate, and after I eat dinner, I may smoke a cigar," he said as they moved onto the balcony terrace.

"That's nasty," she said, pushing the wooden cart onto the terrace. When she lifted the tray, he took it from her and set it on the table.

"Pardon?"

"I said that's nasty. Cigars are nasty, but I won't keep you from smoking one if that's what floats your boat. Heaven knows, you don't have a lot of room for vices." She took in her surroundings, the wrought-iron table and chairs with cushions, the

bougainvillea and the view of the green garden below. "This is lovely."

"It's peaceful at the end of the day. Please sit,"
he said, gesturing to a chair, then he pulled his tie
loose and took his seat.

He lifted the sterling cover from the plate and
poured a glass of wine for both of them. On a china
plate sat three chilled chocolate-dipped strawberries.

"Now, those are beautiful strawberries."

"Enjoy," he said, and his voice held a tinge of
tantalizing seduction.

Unable to resist, she picked up one of the berries
and inhaled the aroma of dark chocolate. She took
a bite and closed her eyes at the delicious taste.

Sighing, she opened her eyes and caught Michel's
gaze on her mouth. Her lips burned. She cleared her
throat, tried to clear her mind and decided to broach
a subject she had considered lately. "I think it would
be a good idea for Max to learn to swim."

His fork stopped midmotion. "No," he said, simply, quietly.

"Why not? He's certainly old enough."

He swallowed another bite. "Safety issues."

"Safety?" she said. "You're teaching him to stab
people with a sharp object and you're concerned
about water safety?"

"That's different," he said.

"How?"

He sighed. "The swimming lessons have been delayed as a concession to my mother. One of my brothers drowned when he was three years old, and the family never really got over it.''

Maggie felt a stab of empathy. ''Oh, I'm sorry. That must have been terrible.''

''It was. My mother overreacts at the mention of swimming lessons. The situation is complicated by the fact that my mother is the queen. The time is soon coming, however, when she will yield on this issue.''

Maggie nodded, hearing the rock-hard resolution in his voice. ''A difficult predicament, but since Marceau is surrounded by water, it makes more sense for Max to be protected by learning than ignorance.''

''Agreed,'' Michel said, meeting her gaze, and she felt a connection resonate between them. When Michel looked at her, he really looked at her. She could almost swear he was searching her mind. The notion made her chest grow tight with an odd, unnamed emotion.

She took a sip of wine to break the intensity of the moment. ''I understand one of your advisors was a pain today.''

''Yes,'' he said, taking a bite of rice.

Her lips twitched. Even now he was reluctant to criticize the advisor. She found that both admirable and amusing. ''How did you learn to be so diplomatic?''

"It took years," he said, taking a sip of wine and leaning back in his chair. "There are practical reasons for being diplomatic. One, you get less press if you keep a low profile and don't throw temper tantrums. Two, people tend to magnify and exaggerate things I say."

"But don't you find it incredibly stifling?"

"Sometimes more than others. I don't dwell on it. Presenting a boring outward appearance reduces hassle."

"But you're not boring," she insisted.

"How do you know?" he asked, his gaze falling over her like a warm breeze.

Her heart flipped, but she tried to ignore it. "Because you just aren't. You're intelligent, you're multidimensional, and..." she said, hesitating.

"And?" he prompted.

"And you have a huge ego, so I probably shouldn't say anymore," she said with a grin.

"No," he said, leaning forward, studying her. "What were you about to say?"

Maggie took a moment to collect her thoughts. Her thoughts and feelings for Michel were far more complicated than they should be, but she sensed, more than anything, Michel needed her honesty. Crazy to think such a man would need anything from her, but she suspected that he did. "I think what makes a person interesting is passion, and although you may not be emotionally demonstrative,

I get the impression you're very passionate about Marceau and your son, and your family." She lifted her glass to him in a slight toast. "But we digress from my original subject about your advisor. I understand he was mean. Would you like me to beat him up?"

Michel leaned back his head and laughed, and the sound shivered down her nerve endings. He looked at her and shook his head. "The queen would not approve of you."

She tilted her head to one side, uncertain how she felt about that. "I guess it's a good thing I won't be around long enough to try to impress her."

His smile faded, and he took another sip of wine. "You have no wish to marry me, do you?"

She looked at him in consternation. "Absolutely not," she said. "It's nothing personal," she added hastily. "I mean, you're handsome and very intelligent. Your sense of humor needs a little work, and you're a bit bossy, but most men in your position would be. You don't appear to have any terrible habits, and I imagine you're great in the sack, but—"

He made a choking sound. "Pardon?"

She rolled her eyes. "Ego, ego, ego. Men are all alike," she muttered. "I said, I imagine you're great in the sack."

"What makes you say that?"

"Well, the way you kiss," she said, feeling a rush

of warmth at the memory of the kiss they'd shared. "You kiss like nobody's business," she said, feeling her cheeks heat because she'd run off at the mouth. "But there's a flip side, and it's your job. Your schedule is worse than a doctor's. On call twenty-four hours a day, 365 days a year with a thousand suffocating rules."

"Thank you for reminding me," he said in a dry tone.

"Sorry," she said. "Was I supposed to make you forget?"

"Yes," he said with a nod and an expression in his eyes that did strange things to her stomach.

"How was I supposed to do that?" she asked.

He reached across the table, took her hand and gently tugged. The pull was an invitation, not an order, and the gentle insistence of the gesture slid past her defenses.

He held her gaze as she rose from her chair to stand in front of him. His title did nothing for her, but the man drew her, in a deeply elemental way. Her defensiveness dipped still more. She bit her lip. "I'm all wrong for you," she warned him. "Your advisors would advise you to stay away from me."

"I've disagreed with the advisors more than once. They've been wrong more than once." His gaze hardened slightly, hinting at the dangerous steel his smooth exterior belied.

He lifted her hand to his lips, then turned it over

and brushed his mouth against the inside of her wrist.

Her heart stuttered. She felt as if she were in quicksand and sinking fast. *Help!* she begged her rational mind. A mixture of desperation and arousal clouded her mind. "I think I know what you need."

His gaze burned her inside and out. "What?"

"A chocolate-covered strawberry."

Six

Six

Without missing a beat, Michel said, "Then feed one to me."

Her mouth went dry. She hadn't been prepared for that response. Then again, her mind was so muddled she was doing well to plan her next breath.

"Feed one to me," he said, with just a hint of challenge.

Better the strawberry than her, she supposed. Tearing her gaze from his, she took a berry from the plate and gingerly lifted it to his lips.

He slid his tongue over the bottom and nipped the edge. The movement was so sensual she was sure her temperature rose three degrees. When he sucked a portion of the fruit into his mouth, she bit her lip. It was too easy to imagine his mouth doing the same kind of wicked things on her body. A piece of the chocolate cracked loose.

"You need to hurry or I'll drop it," she said.

"You're not close enough," he told her, and with a quick tug, Maggie found herself in his lap. He closed his hand around hers guiding the delicacy into his mouth in the same way she suspected he would guide her through lovemaking.

His gaze held hers as he took one last bite, then drew her finger into his mouth. The gesture was so blatantly sensual she closed her eyes.

"Look at me," he urged.

She opened her eyes to slits. "I'm trying very hard to stay rational here, and you're not helping."

"I find that when I keep hitting a wall, I need to try a different approach."

"I hesitate to heed your advice on this issue," she said, her voice wryly husky. "It's a little like taking Max's advice during a game of chess."

"Then I'll offer the same advice I think you would give me in this situation."

She was caught between extreme curiosity and arousal. "What would that be?"

"Forget rational," he said, and pulled her mouth closer.

"You are just too dangerous," she accused him

breathlessly. ''You give this impression of being totally rational and careful. Prince perfect.''

''So you know my secret. I'm a man with a man's
needs. And I want you,'' he told her, and took her
mouth. Splaying his fingers through her hair, he
guided her lips over his. She felt totally surrounded
by his warmth and strength, as if she sat in a sensual
cocoon that consisted of the way Michel felt, tasted
and smelled.

Still kissing her, he shifted her slightly so that she
straddled his lap. He pressed his hand against her
back until her belly was flush with his. Though they
were both clothed, she was acutely conscious of the
way her inner thighs hugged his hips.

He slid his hands down her arms, then to her hips.
He pressed his palms against the bare skin beneath
her shirt, and she shivered at the seductive sensation.
He boldly skimmed his hands up the sides of her
breasts.

Her heart hammered in her throat. ''What are you
doing?''

His eyes and hands did the talking, and they said
he was totally focused on her. His intense, undivided
attention did terrible things to her ability to think
and breathe. He released her bra and caressed her
breasts with his fingers.

''Come closer,'' he said, and the undertone of
need in his voice took down her defenses. He was
the most powerful, fascinating man she'd ever

known, yet he wanted her. Everything about him represented her most forbidden, seductive dare. He was a dark winding road that she couldn't pass by.

She kissed him while he stroked her nipples to taut little peaks of pleasure. Her breasts grew swollen, and a decadent need built inside her.

Lifting her shirt off, he moved his mouth from her lips to her breasts and shifted his hips for better access. As he licked her nipples, he rocked intimately against her. Through her shorts and his slacks, she felt his hardness stroking her, heating her, and it was all too easy to imagine sitting on his lap with nothing between them. It was all too easy to imagine his strong thighs supporting her while he pumped inside her.

She couldn't swallow her moan. He slid his hands beneath her shorts and gently squeezed her bottom while he moved her over him. She unbuttoned his shirt and filled her palms with the touch of his rock-hard muscles beneath smooth, hot skin. The scent of sensual madness filled the night air.

"I want more," he muttered, his hands restless, as if he couldn't get enough of her. He took her mouth in a carnal kiss, his tongue seducing and blatantly mimicking a more basic joining.

Maggie had never felt such a driving need, a want that hinted at desperation. She heard a ringing in her ears and wondered if she was going crazy. The ringing continued, and Michel pulled his mouth from hers.

Her vision hazy, she stared at Michel while their harsh breaths rent the air. His eyes were black with sexual want, his lips swollen. The expression on his face was so honest it knocked on her heart and plucked at every feminine nerve ending in her body.

The phone rang again and he swore viciously. "I'm sorry," he said. "I must answer this. The only calls I receive in my quarters at this hour are of utmost urgency."

Her legs feeling like gelatin, she slid from his lap and nearly fell when she stood. Michel's hands shot out to steady her. "Okay?" he asked, his gaze searching hers.

Feeling entirely too vulnerable, she waved her hands. "I'll be fine. I just need to catch my breath. Please get the phone." *Please leave me alone, so I can get myself together.*

He left, and she drew in slow, deliberate breaths. She locked her knees as she moved to the edge of the balcony. Her hands shook as she grasped the rail. She closed her eyes, thankful Michel couldn't see her.

Refastening her bra, she felt her cheeks heat at how quickly he'd aroused her. He had found his way around her body in no time, and he could have easily taken her on the patio table within moments.

Maggie was definitely out of her league.

The only thing she'd ever done on a patio table was eat cheeseburgers.

"There's been a rock slide on one of our major roads traveling to the other side of the island," he said, the phone still in his hand as he stepped in the doorway. "I need to make a few calls to authorize immediate intervention."

A cold chill raced through her. "Was anyone hurt?"

"Injuries, but no fatalities yet."

"Is there anything I can do?" she asked, then immediately answered her own question. "I can get out of here, so you can make the calls."

She tripped over the leg of one of the chairs. Michel reached out for her, but she jumped back so he wouldn't touch her.

"Oh, no," she said in a voice that sounded high-pitched to her own ears. Heaven help her, she needed a clear head. She bit back an oath. She wished she didn't feel so jittery.

"I'm sorry we were interrupted," he said.

"It was probably for the best," she said, avoiding his gaze as she moved past him in the doorway. "We went a little further than I, uh, think was wise."

He shook his head, put his hand on her arm and pulled her against him. "*Au contraire, chère,* I would have preferred we go much further. And we will," he said as if he were making a promise.

* * *

Max made terrific progress on his lessons during the next few days, but Maggie could see he was longing for another adventure. Her foot still wouldn't allow anything involving water, so she enlisted Francois's reticent help.

"Done," Max said as he completed his last worksheet for the day. He drummed his pencil against the desk and glanced out the window. "We still can't go to the pond, can we?" he asked glumly.

Maggie rubbed his cowlick and smiled. "No, but we can go for a drive."

Max looked at her in disbelief. "Security is going to let *you* drive *me?*"

She made a funny face at him. "No, but I'll have you know I'm an excellent driver. Especially in countries where cars are driven on the right side of the road," she insisted as she stood. "No, some guy named Hans is driving, and another guy is riding shotgun. Francois is coming along, too."

"This sounds like a lot of fun," Max said in a doubtful tone.

"Would you rather stay inside the palace?"

He met her gaze. "No."

"Then you can be my tour guide. I'll bring along a few books in case you get bored. Francois says you have to dress just in case someone sees you. I'll do the same and meet you in ten minutes." As she walked toward her room, Maggie wondered why

Francois felt she and Max needed three palace escorts for a little drive. Geez, did he think she would really cause an international incident?

A gleaming black Mercedes took them through colorful streets and past azure-blue waters. Max pointed out government buildings and the hospital that bore his late grandfather's name. As they drove past a road blocked off for construction work, Maggie studied the scene.

"Is this where the rock fall took place?" she asked, ducking to look up the winding road now mostly cleared.

Francois nodded. "Yes, it's a priority of Prince Michel to improve the island's infrastructure. The economy is changing."

"My father wants to try to find a way to bring in new businesses to make more jobs for people."

"Oh, looks like a clinic," Maggie said, taking in the small but lovely white building.

"Some of the children who were victims of the rock fall are recovering there," Francois said.

An idea sprouted in Maggie's head. "I'd like to stop," she said.

Hans slowed the vehicle.

"We cannot stop," Francois said. "A stop is not on our itinerary."

"Just for five minutes," she said. "I could give a few of these books to the children."

"I want to go, too," Max said.

Francois sputtered. "Absolutely not. It may not be safe."

Maggie shot him a look of disbelief. "A clinic? It's not as if it's a brothel."

"What's a brothel?" Max asked.

Francois glared at Maggie. "I knew this was going to be trouble. You promised."

Impatience stung her. "Oh, for Pete's sake, what can happen? The bodyguards can check out the place first, escort us in, and Max can learn a little lesson about charity. Do you really want to discourage His Highness from doing something good for the citizens of his country?"

Francois gave a heavy, unhappy sigh and continued to glare at her. He said something in another language to Hans, who then proceeded to pull the car into the tiny parking lot beside the clinic. Hans and Francois went into the clinic while Rolf sat in the car with Maggie and Max.

"Which books do you want to give away?" Maggie asked Max.

Max's face fell. "These are my favorites."

Maggie's heart swelled so tight she thought it could burst. Less than two weeks ago, Max had hated books. Now he had favorites. "Well, let's suppose I could replace all of them within a week, which would you like to donate?"

"You're sure you can get more?"

"Certain."

He shrugged. "Then I guess I can give away all of them."

She covered her heart. "You are growing to be such a fine man."

He was silent for a moment. "Think so?"

"Oh, I know so."

He sat up straighter and watched the window, squirming with excitement. Francois returned and opened the car door. "We will only stay for five minutes. We will visit no more than four patients. We will leave when I say. No arguments," he said, shooting a meaningful glance at Maggie.

Maggie nodded. She would have preferred a fifteen-minute visit, but since Francois was acting as if she'd asked for the crown jewels, she would be happy with five minutes. She bent down to Max and whispered in his ear, "Tuck in your shirt and be your nice self. They'll love you."

As soon as they entered, Maggie watched a line of nurses bow and murmur, "Your Highness." The excitement and curiosity on their faces was apparent.

"Thank you," Max said with a nod. "Good afternoon. I would like to meet some of the children who were hurt by the rock fall."

A nun stepped forward and bowed. "Please come this way," she said, and led the small entourage into a small room of girls with various injuries. Max shook hands with each of them and offered a book to the girls who could read. He made one last visit in another room where a little boy with a bandage wrapped around his head and another over his eye, lay in bed. "This is Ricardo. His family was in a truck when the rock fall took place."

"Your Highness," Ricardo said with excitement in his voice.

"It's a pleasure to meet you," Max said in his most proper voice. "Does your head hurt a lot?"

"It did, but it's better now, and they give us ice cream," the boy said with a smile.

"I get ice cream when I'm sick, too," Max said and extended a book to the boy. "Would you like a book? My teacher brought it from America. It's one of my favorites."

The little boy gaped in surprise.

"I hope you like it," Max said, then shot a grin at Maggie.

A camera flashed, and the bodyguard stepped in front of Max. "We must leave now," Francois said with a frown.

"Thank you, Your Highness," Ricardo said.

"*À bientôt,*" Max called as Francois hustled him out of the clinic.

"I knew something would go wrong," Francois fretted as he helped Max into the car.

Maggie shook her head. "What went wrong? Max was great."

"The photo," Francois said. "The prince will be furious."

"Which prince?" Maggie asked.

"Prince Michel," he said impatiently. "He doesn't like Max's photo taken without permission. It's a protective policy," he explained to Maggie.

"Oh," she said, understanding why Michel would want to guard Max's privacy, although in her opinion, Max had a little too much privacy and isolation. "Maybe it won't turn out," she said. "Or maybe the person who took it will save it for their grandchildren and not want to share."

The photo was on the front page of the evening paper. Maggie and Francois were summoned to Prince Michel's office.

Michel didn't look pleased as he stood and held the newspaper. His brother Nicholas sat on a love seat and shot Maggie a look of sympathy.

Michel held out the front page. "I want an explanation."

Maggie tilted her head and looked at the enlarged photo. The two boys were smiling from ear to ear. Her heart melted. Heaven help her, she was growing to love Max. "Those smiles are incredible, aren't they?"

Michel glanced at the photo and met her gaze. "That's not the point. I have a policy concerning photos taken of my son. Why was this policy ignored?"

"I'm sorry, Your Highness. I accept responsibility," Francois said in a martyred tone.

Maggie frowned. "It's not Francois's fault. I twisted his arm into letting us go for a drive because I could tell Max felt cooped up. When we saw the clinic, I thought it would be a great lesson for Max to visit the injured children, and I badgered Francois into doing that, too. We were in the clinic for a whopping five minutes with two bodyguards that looked like they belonged in the World Wrestling Federation. No one expected the photo. My fault. If you're going to tear a strip off someone, Your Highness, it should be me."

Michel paused, then turned back to Francois. "Mademoiselle Gillian was not familiar with my policy regarding photos of Prince Maximillian. You were."

"Yes, I was, Your Highness, and—"

Although Francois drove her nuts at times, Maggie couldn't bear for him to take the heat when it was rightfully hers. She stepped in front of Francois. "It's not his fault. Even if I'd known your policy about photos, I probably would have made the same decision. Max did something good and felt good about it. Besides, it's a terrific photo."

"What if it had been terrible and Maximillian had been forced to relive the viewing of it a hundred times through countless reprints throughout his life?"

Maggie's heart sank. "That wouldn't be much fun. I don't suppose you can issue an order about bad pictures, can you?"

"No," he said curtly. "I can't."

"So you try to limit his exposure with boring official palace photographs, right?"

She heard Francois give a sharp intake of breath at the same time Michel nodded.

"But the public will eat this up with a spoon," she said. She thought about all Michel had said, and felt a heavy sinking realization inside her. "I've been as bad as your advisors, trying to tell you how to raise your son. You have your reasons. I may not totally agree, but I would never want Max hurt. Never," she said, feeling tears sting her eyes. "I'm so sorry."

She saw a flash of warmth in his gaze, but he only nodded at her. He glanced over her shoulder at Francois. "Francois, Mademoiselle Gillian continues to present new opportunities for Max. I commend you for your creativity in balancing her ideas with palace security."

"Just one more thing," Maggie said, and heard Francois make a choking sound behind her. "I can see why the photo issue is a big deal, and I think it's wonderful that you want to protect Max, but I'd hate to think he can only go out at night because he's forbidden to have his photo taken. There's another way to protect him, and that would be cultivating a sense of humor.''

"Are you finished?" Michel said more than asked.

"I guess so," she said, feeling as if someone had let the air out of her balloon.

"I will take your suggestion under advisement," Michel said formally.

Her lips twitched as she remembered he used those same words when he didn't like the advice he received from the advisors. She was loath to be included in that category. She sighed. "I'd rather you were more direct and just tell me to stick it."

Nicholas snickered, and Michel gave her a long-suffering glance. "I will truly take your suggestion under advisement."

"Oh," she said, feeling a rush of surprised pleasure. "You're not just blowing me off. You mean it."

"Yes, I mean it," he said, his eyes glinting with masculine humor while his lips remained straight. She would have to ask him how he could make his eyes smile when his lips didn't. Later.

Seven

This time when Maggie sneaked out of the palace after ten o'clock, she propped the door open with a flip-flop. She wore the other rubber sandal on her healing foot. Nicholas had told her the stitches should dissolve within the next few days. She inhaled the breeze and stared at the full moon.

Michel had sent a message inviting her to his quarters for dessert and drinks, but she had demurred, saying she was tired. Actually, she was trying to be sensible. She was starting to care far too much for this royal dad and his son. Maggie could feel herself growing attached, and she knew she would be leaving in weeks. It was already going to be difficult to say goodbye to Michel and Max.

Her chest felt tight with those ''missing'' feelings she knew she was going to have. She breathed deeply and tried to allow the serenity of the evening to settle her.

''I thought you said you were tired,'' a male voice from behind her said, making her jump.

She reeled around. ''You walk very quietly for a prince,'' she accused, taking in the sight of his chest beneath his unbuttoned shirt.

''How is a prince supposed to walk?''

''With a loud, arrogant stomp so everyone knows he's coming. So if they're complaining about him, they can stop before he sends them to the dungeon.''

''You weren't complaining. You were looking at the moon.''

She turned back around and tried to recover some of the serenity, but her heart was skipping like a stone on the water.

He moved just behind her so she could feel the heat of him. ''I see you remembered to prop open the door this time.''

''I'm a fairly fast learner about practical things,'' she said.

''Why didn't you come when I asked?''

Maggie felt her heart hammer in her chest. ''I felt bad about not respecting your wishes about your son.''

''Are we going to discuss the photo again?'' he asked in a weary voice.

"We don't have to," she said. "But I don't compartmentalize real well."

"That's not the only reason you didn't come," he said.

She wouldn't expect such a man to be able to look outside himself and practically read her mind, but he could. "You're right," she said, still staring at the moon. "I have a problem."

He put his hands on her shoulder and turned her to face him. "I can fix it," he said with entirely too much confidence.

"No. I think you might make it worse."

He dipped his head in disbelief.

"Don't tell anyone, but I think I might be starting to like you and Max too much," she finally whispered.

His gaze softened and he lifted his hand to her cheek. "Oh, Maggie, that's no problem."

"Maybe not for you," she said. "But it is for me. I'm going away in a few weeks and I'm going to miss the devil out of you two."

"You think we won't miss you?" he asked.

"Not like I'll miss you," she confessed, voicing a forbidden fear.

"You're wrong. Besides you could stay."

"My assignment will be over—"

"It doesn't have to be over," he said, his gaze dark with secret emotion. "Your assignment can be extended. I can take care of you."

Mistress. "But that's so sleazy," she said.

"Pardon?" he said in disbelief.

"The mistress, kept-woman thing. I'd rather be your friend. I'd rather be someone you can be yourself with. The biggest, best gift you can give me is to be real with me. To laugh when you're amused, to yell when you're angry."

"I don't yell very often. A lack of restraint shows a lack of power."

"Power shmower," she said. "This isn't about being princely. It's about what you really, truly feel."

He stood silently for a long moment. "I really truly want to make love to you all night long," he said in a low, urgent voice that tied her in knots at the same time it undid her.

Her breath left her lungs. "I'm going to have to think about this," she said. "When my brain works again."

"When will that be?" he asked with an edge to his voice.

"When you're not within twenty feet of me."

He looked deeply into her eyes and shook his head. "I'll find a way for you to stay," he said. "I'll find a way to make you want to stay."

"The last one isn't the tough one," she said, and gave into the silent demand in his gaze and kissed him.

* * *

Two mornings later Michel heard a tap at his door, then his assistant announced Maggie. Michel nodded, and she rushed into the room like sunshine. His heart lifted at the sight of her, although he suspected she might not like his news.

"Good morning, Your Highness," she said with a bright smile. "You rang? No wait, I want to show you something first." She extended a sheet of paper for him to view. "Max's signature. Isn't it great? I'm so pleased with his improvement."

Surprised and pleased, Michel studied the paper. "Max hates to write."

"Hated," she said. "Past tense. I made a little game of it. I told him that since he was going to be very famous, everyone was going to want his autograph, so he needed to start practicing so he would have a dynamite signature."

"Clever. No surprise," he said.

"Thanks," she said, her gaze holding his. "Your Highness, may I invade your space?"

A mix of curiosity and excitement clicked through him. The woman had invaded his mind. Hell, she might as well invade his space. "Yes," he said.

Maggie stepped forward and put her arms around him, then looked up at him and pressed her warm soft lips to his. He felt as if something inside him sighed with relief and pleasure. She felt so right in his arms.

She pulled back. "You looked like you needed that."

He couldn't deny it, but it didn't make what he was about to tell her any easier. "I called you to my office for a reason. I have a visitor coming this afternoon and I didn't want to take you by surprise."

She shrugged. "You have visitors all the time, don't you?"

"Frequently," he said with a nod. "But not quite like this one. We're having a party tonight in honor of her visit."

"Oh, I know. Max has asked me to come with him, so I borrowed a dress from one of the administrative assistants' daughters."

Michel ruthlessly pushed aside the seed of regret growing in his belly. "This is the daughter of an Italian count. Her father is highly influential in the government, and he is also an astute businessman. The advisors are quite impressed with her. She was educated in Swiss boarding schools and can speak three languages fluently. She's poised and even-tempered." He paused. "She is being considered as a wife for me."

Her eyes widened, and her jaw dropped. "Oh," was all she said aloud, but he could practically see the wheels in her brain spinning so fast they smoked. She turned away, and that small gesture sliced at him. He watched her take a breath as if to compose herself, then turn back to him.

''I just really hope you'll make sure she likes
Max. He's such a terrific kid he deserves people who
see that,'' she said.

''This is not a fait accompli. Isabella is a prospect,'' Michel told her. ''But she will be a guest this
weekend, and I thought it fair to inform you.''

She nodded vigorously ''Very fair,'' she said.
''So I won't be expecting to spend time with you.''

''You don't have to attend the party tonight,'' he
said.

''Yes, I do. I told Max I would join him. But I'll
be okay. It's not as if you can really pay a lot of
attention to me in public, anyway. I mean, our relationship hasn't been and won't be public.''

Michel wondered why his gut was clenching.
''You need to understand that this is a political duty.
There is no emotion involved.''

She pressed her lips together, and her eyes turned
sad. ''Well, that's a darn shame. You do what you
need to do, and I'll be okay,'' she said, and even
though she stood mere feet from him, she could have
been a million miles away. ''Thank you for telling
me.''

He wanted to tell her that the visit had nothing to
do with his feelings for Maggie, but he wasn't accustomed to having to explain himself in this kind
of situation. ''You're very welcome.''

She nodded and walked to the door, then looked

over her shoulder as she was leaving. "I hope she makes you laugh."

That night Maggie put on her full armor. Full-length strapless turquoise dress with a slit, sexy sandals, mascara, eye shadow, blush, lipstick and perfume.

She felt like an amateur compared to the Italian visitor, Isabella. The woman wore a wispy chiffon, had a body that made Maggie rue the chocolate croissant she'd eaten for breakfast, and she moved like a cloud.

Maggie plodded. As she danced with Max on the balcony, Maggie told herself it didn't matter. She would never be a prospect for the position of wife to Prince Michel Dumont, and she didn't want to be. If there was one job she was ill suited for, it was the job of a prince's wife.

"One-two-three, one-two-three," Max said, moving in a surprisingly smooth waltz as he held on to Maggie's hands.

"You're doing great. Are you sure you haven't done this before?"

Max shook his head vehemently. "Nobody made me but you."

Maggie felt a tap on her shoulder.

"May I?" a male voice asked.

She turned to face Nicholas and felt a whisper of

relief. Maggie smiled despite her inner turmoil. "Did you want Max or me?"

Nicholas laughed. "You. I want to see how your foot acts under pressure."

"It's almost completely healed. Max, do you mind if I dance with your uncle?"

Max shook his head and pulled at his collar. "I'm gonna get a brownie," he said, and raced away from the balcony.

Maggie lifted her arms.

Nicholas took her arm and gestured toward the ballroom. "In the ballroom."

Maggie's heart sank. "Do we have to?"

He nodded firmly. "Yes." He led her nearly to the center of the floor, and they began to waltz.

"Is there a reason we couldn't stay toward the back of the room?"

"Yes, there is," Nicholas said. "I want him to see you."

"Who is him?" she asked innocently.

"My brother."

"Which one?" she persisted.

He shot her a look of disbelief. "Michel."

"You're not trying to cause trouble, are you?"

He shook his head. "No, but I think you're good for him. I don't want him to forget it."

Maggie looked past Nicholas's shoulder to the beautiful Isabella. "It would certainly be understandable if he did forget me. She's amazing, almost perfect.''

''Dull,'' he said. ''She's had everything interesting drilled out of her. Michel would die of boredom. You're an excellent dancer. Everything about you sparkles tonight,'' he said. ''Except your eyes.''

Maggie tilted her head. ''Are all of the Dumonts perceptive?''

''For the most part. In a position of authority it can be necessary for survival. Speaking of authority, did you know that although the queen has handed over most of the responsibilities to Michel, she has not given him the crown?''

Maggie shrugged and tried not to look at Michel. ''No. Why should I?''

''No reason. She's waiting for him to marry again.''

Maggie digested that fact. ''Is there that much difference between being the official ruler and the unofficial ruler?''

Nicholas nodded. ''When Michel takes the throne, he gets to choose his own advisors and set his own policies. Until then, he walks a tightrope between the queen's wishes and his own vision.''

''Sounds challenging,'' she murmured, and her gaze caught Michel's. Her heart leaped and she looked away. Although she'd been carrying around a silly secret ache all evening, she hated that he felt pressured to marry. He led such a complicated life. "Why are you telling me all this?"

"Just making conversation."

The dance ended and the crowd applauded. An attractive man in military uniform approached Nicholas. "Your Highness, it's great to have you back."

Nicholas grinned. "John, it's good to see you. How is my brother treating you?"

"Working us like dogs," John said, glancing curiously at Maggie.

Nicholas raised his eyebrows. "Pardon my manners. Colonel John Bonaire, this is Mademoiselle Maggie Gillian from the United States. She's tutoring Maximillian. Maggie, John and I were friends in our teens. We both attended boarding school."

"*Enchanté,* mademoiselle," John said, taking her hand and brushing his lips over it.

"Thank you," she said. "It's nice to meet you," she said, then turned back to Nicholas. "What did you mean about how your brother was treating the colonel?"

"Ah, my second-oldest brother, Auguste. You haven't met him yet, but I'm sure you will. He's second in command of Marceau's military. He has a twin named Jean-Marc who is a special diplomat to Japan. Of course, my youngest brother, Alexander, is married and operates a yachting business. He spends most of his time in the States. And then there's Michelina, she's the baby."

Maggie's head swam with all the names. "I don't know if I can keep all this straight."

"When you get lost, just use 'Your Highness' and that will keep you out of trouble," John said with a smile. The music started again. "Would you care to dance?"

Maggie opened her mouth to say no thank you, but Nicholas interrupted. "Of course. She's a lovely dancer. Both of you enjoy."

Maggie shot him a dark look, but took a breath and danced with the colonel. A dance with the colonel turned into three, then two other men approached her. She finally begged off and headed straight for one of the men carrying trays of champagne. She was tempted to grab two glasses, but thought better of it and instead went in search of Max. She found him beside the dessert table.

"I'm afraid to ask how many treats you've eaten," Maggie said as she brushed the crumbs off his flushed cheeks.

"Just a few," he said, but gave a slight wince. "My tummy doesn't feel good."

"Oops, that sounds like more than a few," she said, gently urging him to his feet.

Hearing a slight commotion behind her, she turned.

"Oh, look, Prince Michel is introducing Isabella Garbanza. Aren't they the perfect couple?" the bystander said.

Her stomach twisted, but she pushed the sensation aside at the sound of Michel's voice.

"Ladies and gentleman, it is my great pleasure to introduce to you our honored guest from Italy, Isabella Garbanza."

The crowd applauded and Isabella smiled regally and nodded. "Definite princess material," Maggie muttered under her breath.

"What did you say?" Max asked.

Looking at his sweet face, she was struck by an idea. "Nothing, but there's one thing I want you to do before we leave."

His face brightened. "We're leaving?"

"Definitely," she said. "Have you met Mademoiselle Garbanza yet?"

He shook his head.

"I think you should go meet her."

Max looked at the long receiving line and made a face. "That's a long line."

She knelt down in front of him and looked into his eyes. "Usually you should take your turn like everyone else. That's the fair thing to do. But since your tummy hurts, we can make an exception."

"I can butt in?"

"Just this once. Be brief and whatever you do, don't heave on her dress."

Prince Michel was grinding his teeth so much his dentist was going to give him hell. Speaking of hell, where was the red-haired siren tutor who had danced with nearly every man at the party *except* him? He surveyed the crowd as he nodded absently at the people in the receiving line as they filed past him and Isabella.

Michel was just as irritated with himself as he was with Maggie. Isabella was beautiful, with impeccable manners and a soft-spoken voice. Her posture and carriage were perfect, she clearly understood European men, and she gave the impression she would be an undemanding mate. She was exactly what he'd wanted.

One month ago.

It was the party, he told himself. His entire point of view would change when he had time alone with her tomorrow. He nodded at another well-wisher in the receiving line, and suddenly he saw his son before him.

"Maximillian," he said in surprise.

Max bowed. "Hello, Father, good evening, Mademoiselle Garbanza. We are honored by your fine presence. Welcome to Marceau."

Michel's chest swelled with pride. "My son, Maximillian," he said to Isabella.

She dipped her head and gave a perfect smile. "Thank you for your kind welcome, Your Highness. It's a pleasure to meet you. Aren't you up a bit late?"

"Oh, I'm getting ready to leave. Mademoiselle

Maggie told me to greet you. She's leaving with me. Good night," he said, and ran through the crowd.

Michel stared after him and found Maggie. Her gaze met his across the crowded room. She smiled, imperfectly but sincerely. When Max caught up with her, she bent down and hugged him. He could well imagine her words of praise. An odd emptiness gnawed at him.

"Your Highness," said Isabella in her dulcet tones. "May I ask who is Mademoiselle Maggie?"

"Maximillian's tutor."

She smiled, again perfectly. "How broad-minded of you to include the help."

By the time Maggie read five books to Max, his tummy ache was gone and he fell right to sleep. When Maggie turned out her own light and lay down, every time she closed her eyes, the image of Michel and Isabella standing together and smiling appeared. They had looked so perfect together they could have modeled as figurines for the top of a wedding cake.

She tried to blot out the image and concentrate on the fragrant breeze, but her sheets felt scratchy. She felt restless and irritated. Another image of Michel and Isabella popped up. A knot formed in her chest. Would Michel tell Isabella his secrets? His true feelings? Maggie felt jealous and inferior and she was angry with herself for feeling that way.

Michel would never be hers. He never should be hers. Fighting the terrible, stupid feeling of loss, she tossed and turned for hours until she drifted into a restless sleep.

The following day Maggie was determined not to sit and mope. Max was scheduled to play with his cousins, so Maggie visited the market, then popped into an adult reading class at a library. The teacher welcomed her with embarrassing gratitude, but Maggie soon sat down to work with two of the adults learning to read. After the class, Maggie agreed to send along some educational materials before she departed Marceau.

She left the library feeling more in control of herself. The class had provided a welcome distraction. Still not inclined to return to the palace, she took a cab to the beach and walked along the shore. She sat on the sand and watched the sunset, then enjoyed an early dinner alone in an Italian restaurant. The host took pity on her and made conversation while she ate. He was an older man who spoke in broken English, but his kindness felt like a warm salve to the ache she'd been trying to escape.

By the time she returned to the palace it was nearly ten o'clock and she was tired. It took some doing to get past the guards, but she finally succeeded and trudged through the halls to her room. She opened the door to find the silhouette of Michel standing in front of her bed.

*   *   *

"What on earth are you doing here?" she asked.

"Where have you been?" he demanded, relieved as hell that she was okay, but angry that she'd worried him.

"To the market, library, beach and dinner," she told him. "You still haven't answered my question."

"With whom?" he asked, ignoring her questions.

Confusion crossed her face. "With whom what?"

"You went to dinner with whom?"

She lifted her chin. "With myself. Who did you have dinner with?"

"Myself," he said, anger oozing through him. "Isabella's visit was a failure."

Her eyes widened in surprise. "Why? She's beautiful."

"Yes," he said curtly, running a hand through his hair.

"She's perfect."

"Not exactly," he said, pacing the length of her small bedroom. "She's a snob."

Maggie winced. "Oh, sorry."

"But that wasn't her worst crime," he said.

"What was?"

"She wasn't you."

Eight

She wasn't you.

Maggie's heart felt as if it had stopped. She tried to breathe but couldn't. "What are you saying?"

He moved closer to her and touched her cheek. "That you have ruined me, *chère*," he said in a dark, sensual voice.

Maggie swallowed over a lump in her throat. "Should I apologize?"

"I couldn't even kiss her."

A wicked relief rushed through her. She bit her lip. "How terrible," she said, unable to keep the joy from her voice.

He shook his head and drew her forehead against

his. "Then you made it worse by disappearing to-day."

"I told Francois some of my plans."

Michel frowned. "He didn't mention them to me."

"I couldn't stay here. All I would have done was mope." She closed her eyes. "I hate being jealous."

"I couldn't tell you were jealous, especially when you sent Maximillian to greet Isabella."

"If you married her, I wanted her to love him, too," she said, stepping into his arms.

"I'm not marrying her," he said, and immediately unzipped her dress and pushed it to the floor. Swearing under his breath, he unfastened her bra.

Maggie shivered at the scalding speed. "Fast," she said through a tight throat.

"Overdue," he muttered, and took her mouth. His lips consumed hers in a kiss that made her blood roar through her veins. He suckled, nibbled and licked at her lips at the same time his hands slid over her breasts with taunting familiarity. As if he knew how sensitive her nipples were, he barely brushed them with his fingers, then moved away until she was aching for more.

The scent of unspent passion hung in the air, and Maggie was rocked by the power that vibrated between them. He slid his hard thigh between her legs, a sensual masculine invasion that made her pulse beat faster.

It was a calm night outside, but she felt thunder and lightning inside her. There was a possessiveness in Michel's eyes that burned her to her soul. Something inside her, something older than time, pushed her toward him. She unbuttoned his shirt and pushed it from his shoulders. While he ate at her mouth, she skimmed her hands over his bare skin and felt his chest gently abrade her nipples.

She allowed her hands to travel over his hard abdomen and lower, to his hips and thighs. He stood very still as she drew her hand closer to the part of him that throbbed with arousal. She brushed her hand over him, once, twice and drank in the sound of his groan.

She unfastened his slacks and slid her hand down the front of his briefs. He was hard, and touching him so intimately made her dizzy.

Michel picked her up and laid her down on the bed. Standing before her with the moonlight playing over him, he stripped. The strength of his muscles made her feel protected. And the sight of his arousal jutting out proudly made her buzz in all her secret places. But the honest need in his eyes melted her defenses.

Something about him compelled her to give him everything she could. Although a part of her was afraid, she could not have turned away from him if she'd tried. He tossed a couple of packets of protection on the beside table, then joined her on the bed.

He lowered his head to taste her nipples and she gasped. He pushed her panties out of the way and began to fondle her intimately.

Maggie grew wet and restless with need.

"I love the sounds you make," he told her. "I love the way you move." He slid his finger inside, and she gasped again. He gave her a French kiss that obliterated everything but him from her consciousness.

Then he made a path of sensual destruction down her throat, to each of her breasts. He skimmed his tongue over her belly and rubbed his cheek over her femininity and placed a kiss on the inside of her thigh.

Maggie couldn't swallow, couldn't breathe.

With agonizing slowness he found her most sensitive place and rubbed his tongue over her. Maggie felt herself grow so swollen she feared she would burst. Then she did, shattering over the edge. She thought she was done, but he took her with his mouth again.

When she began to shake, he pulled on protection and pushed her legs apart. "Look at me," he demanded in a husky, rough voice. Holding her gaze, he entered her inch by excruciating inch.

She bit her lip at his size.

His eyes closed to slits of pleasure, and his nostrils flared. "*Ma chère,* you are so small."

"Not very experienced," she murmured, holding her breath and waiting to adjust to him.

His gaze moved over her possessively. "I'm glad." He squeezed her bottom, and she relaxed.

He plunged deeper, and she gulped.

"You're mine," he told her in a voice that sounded as if it could travel through universes and across seas. "Now you're mine."

He began the age-old rhythm. His passion was so fierce she needed some reassurance, some measure of tenderness. She reached for his hand, and he lifted hers to his lips, and her heart was lost.

She clung to him as he shook with release, and something told her she would never be the same.

The sunlight streaming through the window awakened Maggie early the next morning. Lifting her hand to cover her eyes, she squinted around the room. Her senses awakened slowly. She was naked beneath her white cotton sheet, and when she shifted her legs, her thighs and breasts felt tender. She inhaled deeply, recalling the way Michel had made love to her. She wondered when he'd left her and fought a stab of abandonment. She looked beside her on the bed. If she didn't smell just a hint of his masculine spicy scent, she could almost believe she had dreamed that he had been in her bed.

Maggie sat up and wrapped her arms around her knees. The morning was peaceful, but her heart was in an uproar. Well, she'd gone and done it this time. Made love with a prince. How was she ever going to get him out of her system now?

Maggie bit her lip, and her gaze snagged on a wall calendar. The date she would be returning to the States was circled in red, and it wasn't far away.

Her stomach clenched. Maggie had often grown attached to her students, but this was different. Too restless to remain still, she stood and pulled a robe around her. There were so many things she wanted to teach Max, so many things she wanted to make sure he experienced.

And Michel. She closed her eyes at the clench inside her. Maggie wanted to know everything about him, but she knew that would take more than a few weeks. It would take a lifetime. She thought of his position and the proper bride he must someday wed. Her heart sank at the thought, and she castigated herself for her feelings. She had no right. She was temporary to him. He was temporary to her.

Why had their lovemaking felt timeless?

She looked at the calendar again. It would take a lifetime to know him. How could she fit a lifetime into two weeks? What would be left of her heart if she did?

"Thank you very much, but no thank you," Maggie said as she set the satin-lined jeweler's box firmly on the table in Michel's private den.

Michel looked at her in surprise, trying to understand the hurt and anger shimmering in her green eyes. He opened the box and looked at the diamond bracelet inside. "You didn't like it?"

She pressed her lips together in a frown. "Let's just say it's not me."

"Would you prefer a different stone than diamonds, or a necklace?"

She sighed. "I appreciate the thought, but I really don't want jewelry from you."

Michel couldn't fathom a woman who didn't want jewelry. "Why ever not?"

She crossed her arms under her chest. "Aside from the fact that I'm not a big jewelry person, I don't want you giving me jewelry. If you want to give me something, then give me—" She broke off and shrugged.

"Then give you what?" he asked, stepping closer, determined to eliminate the distance she was putting between them. He wanted her wrapped around him the way she'd been last night.

"I just don't want jewelry," she said in a low voice after a long pause.

A ray of recognition broke through his confusion. "You felt I was paying you for making love with me," he said, feeling his temperature rise. "You don't want me to give you gifts."

She looked at him warily. "Not...not...jewelry."

"I wasn't paying you for making love to me," he

told her as he ground his teeth. "If I want to give you a token of my feelings for you, then I damn well should be able to do it."

Her gaze softened, and she lifted her hand to his cheek. "When I go home to the States, I don't want to take tokens back with me, Michel. I want to take enough memories to keep me forever."

His chest squeezed tight, and he covered her hand with his. "It's not necessary for you to return so soon," he said, and when she opened her mouth to argue, he shook his head. "I'll help you to see things differently."

She stared at him, then her lips twitched. "Oh, really, and how do you plan to do that?"

The dare in her eyes was a delicious tease he couldn't resist. "Just because you may not have a weakness for diamond bracelets doesn't mean you don't have a weakness for other things," he said, and guided her forefinger to his lips. He encircled the tip with his tongue and watched her bite her lip.

She cleared her throat. "Such as?"

"Chocolate strawberries," he said, drawing her finger into his mouth. She closed her eyes, fighting the arousal, but not winning, he noticed with a rush of gratification.

"And me." He picked her up in his arms and walked toward his bedroom. He had dreamed of seeing her there, her wild, red hair spilling over his pillow, her body naked on top of his sheets. Michel had never felt so possessive about a woman before, not even his wife. That thought could have bothered him, but not now. Now Maggie was in his arms, lifting her lips to his, and soon she would be his again, in the most elemental way.

Hours later she curled against him, both of them replete with lovemaking. He felt her nuzzle his throat, and he smiled. An exquisite contentment seeped through him.

"Tell me the story of Marceau," she said.

"Which story?"

She groaned. "The story of why your family got the job as rulers."

"Hundreds of years ago the Dumonts didn't rule. The Dumonts were cousins of the ruling family of Rocher. To make a long story short, the Rochers were not good money managers, and they often squabbled among themselves. Somebody was always trying to steal someone else's wife. There was a duel between the heirs to the throne and both were killed. The Dumonts protested the chaos the Rochers had created and threatened a takeover. The Rochers didn't want to lose everything, so they made a deal. Dumonts would take Marceau, and the Rochers would take the Gantos Islands."

She raised up on her elbow and looked at him in confusion. "But I thought the Gantos Islands belonged to France."

"They do. The Rochers took the Gantos Islands,

but they still had money problems, so after a time, they ended up being forced out for a chest of gold French coins that has never been accounted for.''

She widened her eyes. ''Whew, missing gold coins, wife stealing, political plots.'' She shook her head. ''And I thought my family was dysfunctional.''

He chuckled, thinking he liked the sight of her naked in his bed, with her wild hair spilling over her shoulders. ''Yes, but the Dumonts prevailed. What about your family?''

She made a face. ''We don't have any gold or political plots. I had a perfect brother who was the apple of my father's eye. My parents have been separated for some time, but they haven't divorced. I think they can't give up torturing each other. Even though I had problems in school, as I grew older, they turned to me to mediate and *fix* things. Not a fun job.''

''I can see not,'' he said, glimpsing a trace of pain and frustration in her eyes. ''You're not close to them now,'' he concluded.

''No. I keep in touch and visit on holidays and birthdays.''

''So it wouldn't be difficult for you to be away from them if you decided to stay on Marceau,'' he said, planting the thought the same way a farmer in his country would plant a vegetable crop. He had observed that Maggie responded well to planting.

She looked at him sideways. "Yes, but I have other reasons for going back to the States," she said. "I like being an American."

"You can have dual citizenship. We're very liberal in that way."

Her lips turned upward in a slow, but brilliant smile. "If you keep this up, I'm going to start thinking you really want me to stay."

"You could have a wonderful life in Marceau," he said. "I can make it happen."

She shivered, distracting him with the slight jiggle of her breasts. He loved the way her aureole felt in his mouth. Michel felt his body respond. It didn't matter that he'd just made love to her. He wanted her again.

"You're tempting," she said in a low voice. "But what happens when you decide you're in the mood for something different from a red-haired American woman who is not into jewelry?"

"That would take a damn long time," he said.

"And in the meantime I would have fallen desperately in love with you. And you would have to find a discreet way to ditch me. Then I would return to America and try to put my career and myself back together." She skimmed her hand over his jaw. "I think it would be very foolish to count on a relationship you and I might have."

Irritation nicked through him. "It would be foolish for you to underestimate my power in this."

"Your Highness, you have my utmost admiration and respect, and I know you have all kinds of power, but I have to continue to count on me, not you. In the end it's going to be just me."

His chest grew tight at her words. He wanted her to count on him. He wanted to be her protector. He wanted, and as much as she was giving herself to him, he wanted more. He ran his thumb over her kiss-swollen lower lip. "You have a lot to learn about me, but we have time."

She darted her tongue out over his thumb, surprising him with her sexual mischief. "Tell me what else I have to learn about the mighty Michel."

"That I'm not fickle," he said, meeting her gaze dead-on. "And I like to win."

"Max must have gotten the same qualities from you. He's not fickle. He wanted a dog when I first met him, and he still wants one now. He likes to win, and whenever I play chess with him, he does."

"The desire to win will help him with some of his royal duties. In just a few weeks he'll be expected to address the people on National Citizenship Day."

Maggie did a double take. "Address the people, how?"

"It's tradition," he said, still distracted by her breasts. "All seven-year-old heirs to the throne make an address on National Citizenship Day. He will read a brief speech which will be recorded for radio and television."

"Wait. Wait just a minute. Max is making terrific progress, but I wouldn't want to put him in front of a TV camera and tell him to read."

"You won't. You will just prepare him for it."

She pulled back and frowned. "Do you have any idea how difficult it can be for a dyslexic to read in front of a large group?"

"You do it all the time."

"Yes, but I know the tricks."

"You can teach them to Max."

"I think you should reschedule this for next year."

Michel laughed. "Even I can't reschedule Citizenship Day."

Clearly distressed, she made a sound of frustration. "But you don't have to make him do this."

"The people expect it. Max's appearance is not optional," he said gently, firmly. A part of him was deeply touched by her protectiveness of Max, but he also knew she would need to bend this time. "He will do fine with your help. It's part of the reason I hired you."

As if she knew she was batting against a stone wall, she sighed. "It's one of those royal-appearance duty things, isn't it?"

"More," he said. "Seeing Maximillian say his brief words gives the citizens of Marceau a sense of pride and assurance in the future. I don't agree with everything the advisors say, but Max will have many opportunities because of his position. He will also be required to perform duties because of his position."

"To whom much is given, much is required," she quoted and turned silent for a long moment. She eased back down to the crook of his arm as if she were mulling over her thoughts. "I think I wouldn't be a very good mother," she said.

He stared at her. "Why in heaven's name would you say that?"

"Because I think I would do just about anything to keep my child from hurting, and sometimes we all have to hurt a little in order to grow."

"You're very tenderhearted, *ma chère,* but you're also very strong. Your child would have your strength, too."

She gave a heavy sigh. "I should probably leave," she said, but didn't move.

Michel vehemently disagreed. "No," he said.

"Unlike you, I'm likely to fall asleep and not wake up. You'll have to kick me out of bed, and I'll end up getting my feelings hurt."

Realization echoed inside him. "You were hurt when I left last night," he said.

"Not really." She must've read the disbelief on his face. "Well, maybe just a little bit. A very little bit."

"I didn't want you to have to face the gossip from the palace employees," he told her.

Her gaze softened, and she swallowed hard, as if she were fighting a knot of emotion. "I hate to feed your ego, but you're right," she said with a lightness at odds with the intensity in her eyes. "There's a lot I don't know about you."

He pulled her face to his. "Stay and learn."

Nine

Two weeks! Two blinkin' weeks!

Maggie did her best to hide her dismay and frustration when she learned she had two weeks to help Max prepare for his public presentation. When she'd reminded him of the event, he'd gotten a sick look on his face. But Maggie was determined to make this a successful experience for Max, and in a way for Michel, even if it killed her.

Or even if Michel killed her when he learned the latest thing she'd done. He would probably need to get in line behind Francois and all the advisors, and the queen, too, if she were here.

She received the planned speech from the palace

PR people. It was three pages long with words in-appropriate for a seven-year-old, so Maggie gently *edited* it.

Okay, she hacked it. It was now one and a half pages long. She rewrote it on a different computer and printed it off in a huge font on colored paper so it would be easy for him to read.

"This looks different from the first one they sent over," Max said, looking at the paper.

Maggie decided not to address the issue. "I think what we're going to do is have you memorize the speech."

Max's eyes widened in alarm. "The whole thing!"

Maggie nodded. "Don't worry. You have excel-lent memorization skills, and we're just going to do it in little chunks, two or three times a day."

Max gave a heavy sigh. "I'm going to be cooped up in this room for the next two weeks trying to memorize this."

"No, you won't," she assured him. "You and I are going to have a picnic by the pond today and we're taking the speech with us. You can think of it as eating one cookie twice a day, instead of eating the whole jar and getting sick."

"It's more like taking cough medicine," he grum-bled.

She couldn't disagree. "Besides, I have ordered

a very special reward for you after you have finished memorizing the speech.''

Max perked up. ''What kind of reward?''

''It's very special. It's a surprise.'' *To everyone except me,* she thought, and fought a little attack of nerves.

He studied her with curiosity. ''Is it from America?''

She nodded. ''Yes.''

''Is it books?''

She shook her head. ''No. It's something you've never had before. And I'm not going to tell you any more, so don't ask.''

''Is it videos?'' he asked slyly.

''Absolutely not,'' she said, shooting him a dark look. Max knew she didn't approve of vegetating in front of the television. ''If you don't start memorizing, you'll never find out what it is because you'll never get it.''

He gave a heavy sigh. ''Is it—''

She held up the speech. ''Don't ask.''

Every night Michel insisted she join him in his private quarters. They made love, but they also talked of his dreams for Max and Marceau, and of his memories of childhood. He asked about her life in Washington, D.C., and was appalled when she casually referred to crime in the schools.

"If you insist on returning, I'll send a guard with you," he said, his light eyes blazing.

Maggie chuckled as she sat cross-legged across from him on the sofa. "I don't think Hans would go over very well with second-graders. Plus he probably wouldn't appreciate the assignment when the kids spill milk on him and smear him with peanut butter."

"Or you could decide to stay in Marceau and function as the national literacy representative."

Curious, Maggie met his gaze. "I've never heard of a national literacy representative," she said.

"It's a newly-created position. The literacy representative will work with the royal education advisor to facilitate literacy programs for both children and adults."

"Just out of curiosity, how new is this position?" she asked.

His eyes glimmered with humor and intelligence. "It was approved today."

Maggie looked at him, feeling a rush of emotion and frustration. What a power play to create a job to lure her to stay. On the other hand, how could she not fall for the man when he was creating a dream job for her in such a beautiful setting?

She crawled onto his lap. "You're making it very difficult for me to leave."

"That is my purpose," he said, his expression so sensual she found it hard to breathe.

"Why?"

"You would be very good for Marceau. I'm confident our literacy rate would increase exponentially."

"And that's the whole reason," she said. "Because I could do wonders for literacy. There's nothing personal at all."

His gaze darkened, and he lifted her hand to his lips. "I didn't say that. I want you close by." He slid his other hand behind her neck and took her mouth in a kiss that whispered secrets—secrets Maggie was afraid to believe. He tasted her and tempted her like a man determined to keep her. *He didn't just want her,* he needed her. The seductive possibility alternately thrilled and terrified her. How would her life be if she stayed? How much more of Michel would she grow to know and love? Wouldn't it be harder than ever for her to leave then?

The ghost of Maggie's future rang a warning bell. She kissed him with all the passion in her, but her heart was heavy. How could this possibly end well?

"On Citizenship Day, we celebrate the strength and determination of our ancestors who have kept Marceau at peace for over two centuries. We celebrate the commitment of our government to ensure that no one in Marceau should go hungry. We also celebrate the bright future to which each citizen contributes. I'm grateful and proud to be a part of this country where the people have such strength and heart. God bless Her Majesty, Queen Anna Catherine, His Highness, Prince Michel, and every citizen.''

Maggie's eyes filled with tears and she put her hand to her heart. She and Francois sat among the crowd of stuffed animals she'd created as pretend spectators for Max's performance. She began to applaud. ''Bravo!'' she yelled. ''Bravo!''

Francois began to clap, too, and she heard him sniff. *''Magnifique!''*

Max beamed with pride and pleasure. ''I did well, didn't I?''

Maggie went to hug his sturdy frame. ''Oh…you *rock*,'' she said.

''What does *rock* mean?'' Francois asked.

Max nodded. ''It means you're the best.''

Francois sniffed again. ''Your father will be so proud. The queen,'' he said, his voice catching. *''Mon dieu,* the queen will be beside herself. The PR department outdid themselves with the speech.''

''Oh, well, Mademoiselle Maggie helped—''

''But Max's delivery was what really made it all work,'' she said, not wanting to get into a snit fest with Francois over her revision of the speech. She had a veritable smorgasbord of snit fests to face in the coming twenty-four hours.

Max tugged at her arm. ''When do I get my reward?''

"Very soon," she said. "I'm picking it up for you later."

"It has arrived from the States?" he asked, moving from foot to foot in excitement.

"What reward?" Francois asked warily.

"Oh, it's a surprise I promised Max when we first started working on the speech."

"What is this surprise?" he asked, his wariness turning to suspicion.

And rightfully so, Maggie thought, uneasiness twisting in her belly. "If I tell, it won't be a surprise," she said giving a meaningful sideways glance at Max. Heaven help her, she was the worst at subterfuge and evasion. "Very soon," she said, patting Max's cowlick.

Michel joined his advisors after dinner for an evening meeting in anticipation of the extended holiday before Citizenship Day. They had covered just about everything on the agenda when he heard a strange noise down the hall. The meeting continued, but so did the noise that he couldn't quite identify. He tossed a questioning glance at the male assistant standing by the door, and the assistant gave a nod and opened the door.

To a yipping sound that strongly resembled the sound a *dog* would make.

One of the advisors turned to him with a look of

surprise on his face. "Your Highness, is there a *dog* in the palace?"

Michel wondered who on earth would bring a dog to the palace, and his mind didn't have to travel far. *Maggie.*

"I'd like to call the meeting to a close and allow you gentlemen to begin your holiday. We've covered all the pressing matters. I do appreciate your attendance so late in the evening, and I look forward to your presence at the Citizenship Day celebration."

"Prince Maximillian will be speaking, won't he?" one of the advisors asked.

"Yes, of course, and I understand from his assistant that he's very well prepared." Prince Michel smiled. "We will all be proud." He stood, inviting no further questions. "Good night, all," he said, and left the room.

His assistant met him halfway down the hall where Michel heard raised voices. "Your Highness, there is a problem."

"I got that impression," he said, drawing closer to the recreation room. The dog's howling, along with the voices grew louder as he opened the door.

A beagle puppy, yipping and howling, sat cowering at Maggie's feet as she shook her finger at a red-faced Francois.

"Dogs are not allowed in the palace. They are forbidden by the queen," Francois shouted.

"It's too late to send him back," Maggie retorted. "I promised Max a reward for learning his speech, and the puppy is his reward."

"You should not have made that promise without consulting the palace authorities. You have really done it this time, Mademoiselle Gillian. The dog must go," Francois said, moving toward the puppy.

Her eyes glinting with sparks, Maggie raised her chin and her hands as if she were ready to take him on. "You just try it."

Time to step in before a full-fledged brawl breaks out, Michel thought. "Francois is correct," he said. "The queen does not allow dogs in the palace."

Maggie jerked around to meet Michel's gaze. He saw her resolution sink for just a second before she recovered. "Given the fact that she gave birth to several children, I'm not exactly sure how she escaped with no pets, but that's beside the point. The queen won't have to take care of him. The queen is not a seven-year-old boy who wants a pet so badly he sneaks tadpoles into his room. It's not as if he has a dozen friends or siblings to play with," she said, then, as if she suddenly remembered a smidgen of protocol, she bent her knees in a pseudo curtsy. "Your Highness."

"Puppies are noisy and messy. They disturb palace life."

"Babies are noisy and messy, too," she said,

matching him argument for argument. "Are they forbidden from palace life?"

Michel struggled with an overload of frustration. "Of course not," he said. "You should not have brought that dog into the palace without permission. Max is going to be disappointed when the puppy is removed."

"If I may say, it's wrong, wrong, wrong for that puppy to be removed. That puppy will inspire Max to read how to take care of it and develop a sense of responsibility. That puppy will provide companionship and friendship especially after I—" She stopped, clearly faltering at the thought of leaving.

Michel's gut twisted.

"Having the puppy will give him invaluable qualities throughout his life."

"You were not invited to say so," he said firmly.

Through the corner of his eyes, Michel saw Max peek through the doorway. He watched his son bend down and clap his hands at the beagle. The beagle apparently recognized his protector and skittered across the floor into Max's arms. Max picked him up and was rewarded on the face with puppy licks.

"Sir," Max said, looking at his father with beseeching eyes. "I'll do anything to keep the dog."

Damn, Michel thought. At this moment there was nothing in the world he wanted more than to give his son this simple wish. The problem was that he had bigger issues to broach with the queen, one of which was nonnegotiable for him. Michel had learned not to overwhelm the queen with more than one battle at a time.

"Put the puppy in the basement," he said crisply.

"In the dungeon?" Maggie asked, appalled.

"We don't have a dungeon anymore," he told her impatiently. "It's been remodeled."

"May I sleep with him?" Max asked.

"Absolutely not," Michel said. "If I find you disobey me on this, the dog will go."

"But he's just a puppy," Max said. "He'll be lonely."

"Then I suggest you study mademoiselle's puppy books to learn how to help him successfully make the adjustment." He glanced at Francois. "You will help Max with this."

Francois blanched. "Me?" he echoed, his voice breaking. He cleared his throat. "Begging your pardon, Your Highness, I know nothing about dogs."

"Due to Mademoiselle Gillian, it appears we will all be learning about dogs, whether we wish to or not."

One of the assistants cleared his throat. "If I may offer my assistance, Your Highness," he said. "My family had several dogs during my growing-up years."

"Most normal families do," Maggie muttered under her breath.

Michel shot her a quelling glance. "Thank you.

This is to remain strictly confidential until further notice," he said, then turned full bore on Maggie. "Mademoiselle Gillian, meet me in my quarters."

"When?" she asked warily.

"Immediately," he said, and caught the faintest wince on her face as he strode out of the room toward his quarters. The anger roaring through his head drowned out any other sound.

As soon as he arrived at his door, he swung it open, waited for her to enter, then slammed it shut. Michel couldn't remember the last time he'd slammed a door. He was so angry he deliberately stood several feet from her. "Do not ever undermine my authority again," he said.

Maggie flinched at the steel in his tone. "I apologize, but I did it because I'll be leaving soon."

"That is not decided," he said, feeling his frustration grow exponentially.

"Whether I go next week, next month or next year," she said, "we both know I will eventually have to leave."

"We do not know that," he said in a crisp voice.

She looked up at the ceiling as if she were seeking help. "Listen…you can deny it until, well, in the States we say, until the cows come home. But when all is said and done and I return to my country for whatever reason at whatever time, nothing will change for you, but everything will change for me. So I can't be the queen of denial."

She sighed and moved closer, tentatively reaching out to him. Michel didn't trust himself to let her touch him.

She dropped her hand to her side, and his heart felt as if it shrank.

"If I had it to do all over again, I would still get Max the dog. I'm sorry, but I just don't understand why a beagle needs to be a state secret or cause an international incident. I just don't get it, and this is why it will never work out for me to be here. When it comes down to a choice between protocol and what is going to make you and Max happy, I will always look after your hearts. Always," she said. "And that means I will always cause trouble."

Michel felt as if he walked a fraying tightrope. The rope would not hold much longer. His relationship with his mother had always been more professional than personal. Now was no different. At the same time the clock was running out for Maggie. Selfishly he refused to accept her departure. He might have sacrificed many other things for the sake of the crown, but he refused to let her go so easily. He needed time to collect his thoughts.

"The queen returns day after tomorrow. I will use the time to prepare for my meeting with her."

Maggie's gaze was warm with concern. "You have a lot on your mind."

It was strange as hell, but even though she'd just

complicated matters, her presence calmed him. "Yes," he said simply.

"Would you like me to leave?" she asked.

"No," he said immediately.

"Then what can I do? I knew there might be a few objections to the puppy, but I didn't want it to make things worse for you. Is there anything I can do to make things better?"

The longing in her voice to make it all better scored his heart and tempted him terribly. "Is it possible for you to follow instructions without arguing?"

Affronted, she shot him a dark look. "Yes, I can follow instructions without arguing."

He pulled his jacket off, then discarded his shirt. "Follow me," he said as he headed for his bedroom. "You can rub my shoulders," he said.

Maggie still had mixed feelings about his imperious tone, though the sight of his bare strong back had distracted her. She truly didn't want to cause trouble for Michel, and it appeared she had. If giving him a back rub would make him feel a little better, then she certainly wanted to do it.

He lay down on his bed and gave a heavy sigh as if the weight of the day had been great. Maggie suspected it had. Her heart squeezed at the thought. This was the man behind the crown, and he was tired and frustrated.

Amazing that she had the power to make him feel better. "Do you have any lotion?" she asked.

"I just want your hands," he said, and her heart gave a little jump.

She started with his neck, gently kneading his tensely corded muscles. Moving to his shoulders, she massaged, thinking that in many ways he carried a huge weight every day. She rubbed her way thoroughly down to his lower back. Slowly up again, she moved her hands to his shoulders and neck to his scalp.

He gave a murmur of approval when she moved her fingertips over his scalp. Maggie continued until she was certain he had fallen asleep.

Instead, he rolled over and met her gaze. "Take off your blouse," he said.

Confused, she searched his expression. "But I thought—"

"Are you arguing?"

Follow directions without arguing, she remembered, and took off her blouse.

"Now your bra."

She did, feeling slightly self-conscious. Her breasts reacted to the sensation of his gaze. "Touch my chest," he told her.

Leaning forward, she ran her hands over his muscular chest. The assignment was no hardship. His chest was beautifully masculine. She caressed him and slid her fingers through the soft hair in the center of his chest. With each touch she saw his breath deepened. The atmosphere changed. He might be giving the directions, but she felt a heady sense of feminine power.

He was becoming aroused.

So was she.

She skimmed her hand down to his belly and stole a glance at him. Lower and lower she trailed her fingers to just below the top of his slacks. Emboldened by the desire steeping in his eyes, she unfastened his belt and slowly unzipped. If she didn't know better she would swear Michel was holding his breath.

Part of her wanted to make love to him. Another part wanted to tease.

''Oops,'' she said, lifting her hand away. ''I'm not following instructions.''

''Yes, you are,'' he said, and his gaze melted her.

He looked at her breasts again, and his gaze felt like a seductive stroke. She lowered her mouth to his throat and kissed him. Her breasts meshed with his rib cage, and he gave a sigh of pleasure.

She pressed openmouthed kisses over his chest, sliding her tongue over his nipples, then French kissing his abdomen.

He removed his slacks and underwear, revealing his full arousal. He reached for her, but she dodged him.

"Maggie," he said, and the dark sexual need in his voice mirrored her own.

She shook her head and lowered her mouth to kiss the inside of his thigh. "I'm following your instructions."

"I haven't given you any," he said, plunging his hands through her hair.

"Your body has," she said, and rubbed her thumb from the base of his shaft to the tip.

"Maggie," he said again, this time his voice ragged around the edges.

Following a forbidden instinct, she replaced her thumb with her mouth and drew her lips up the length of him.

He swore and tangled his fingers more deeply in her hair.

Reveling in the sensation of his thighs against her bare breasts, she moved her head from side to side, rubbing her cheek over him, taking her time. Then she took him into her mouth, and he made the sexiest masculine sound she'd ever heard.

She felt herself grow moist between her thighs. She stroked him with her lips and tongue. The tip of his manhood turned shiny with the honey of his arousal.

Meshing her gaze with his, she lowered her head once more and swirled her tongue over him.

He swore as if the sight was too much for him.

It must have been. Before she knew it, he flipped

her over on her back and took her mouth. "I can taste me on you," he said as if it were an unbearable arousing experience, and he kissed her again. He played with the aching tips of her breasts and skimmed his hand down between her legs to find her wet and wanting.

"You feel so good," he told her. "So good," he said and lowered his mouth to her nipples. The sensation was excruciatingly wonderful.

Unable to hide her arousal, she arched against his mouth. He continued to touch her femininity as if he were stroking the petals of a rose. "I always want to take you too fast," he muttered, and took a deep breath.

Turning her on her side, he stroked her so that she felt his hardness rubbing against her bottom. With one hand, he stroked her nipple and the other, then he slid his finger inside her. She felt the strength of his chest at her back and the combination was oddly erotic. She undulated against him, and he groaned.

"I can't go slow if you're not still," he told her.

Maggie felt the heat inside her grow. Her body felt like a flower ready to bloom. She wanted him in every way.

"I don't want you to go slow," she said, and undulated again.

He groaned, and with one smooth, slick movement, he entered her femininity from behind.

She caught her breath at the exquisite pleasure. She wiggled and he slowly pumped, still touching her most sensitive spot. The combination was too much. She clenched around him and soared.

He thrust once more, deep inside her, and she felt his body shudder with pleasure. After several moments of trying to catch her breath, Maggie rolled over to face him.

His gaze was so intently possessive it took her breath again. "I like the way you give a back rub," he said, his voice rife with every intimate implication. "I like the way your hands and mouth feel. I like the way your breasts feel." He slid his hand over her waist. "I like the way you feel when you take me inside," he said, and kissed her.

Maggie felt as if she were utterly under his spell. Whatever he asked of her she wanted to do. She had never felt like that about a man, and feared it could be a dangerous situation. Her brain was too full of him at the moment to contemplate a way out, though. She was compelled to find a way to show Michel the depth of her emotion for him.

"I keep trying to find the perfect way to show you how I feel," she confided as she lifted her hand to his cheek.

"You're on the right track," he said, his eyes full of seduction. "Keep trying."

Ten

Before she'd left Michel last night, he'd instructed her to stay out of trouble for the next two days. He'd said it as if he'd thought that might be setting a new record.

In her attempt to be boring, Maggie joined Max as he brought the puppy up from the basement to take him for a walk outdoors. As they turned down a hallway, she and Max stopped at the sound of two women having a heated conversation.

"You're not old enough to go out with a man unchaperoned," a woman said.

"As far as you're concerned, I'll be eighty before you think I'm old enough," a younger woman retorted.

"It may well take you that long to mature," the other woman said. "I thought you would be pleased to join me on this diplomatic tour to America."

"I was," said the younger woman. "Thank you very much. Now I would like to return without an entourage."

Max's eyes rounded. "It's Queen Anna Catherine," he whispered. "And Princess Michelina. They're always arguing."

Panic sliced through her. "But she wasn't supposed to return until tomorrow," Maggie said.

Max shrugged his shoulders helplessly.

The voices drew nearer and Maggie glanced around, desperately seeking an escape. Spotting a closet, she hustled Max and the puppy inside and pulled the door shut behind them. "Please be quiet," she said to the puppy. "Please be quiet."

But it was dark, and the dog began to whine. "I'll hold his mouth together," Max whispered as the queen and her daughter drew nearer.

The dog let out a yelp, then another, and Maggie cringed.

"Is that a dog I hear?" the queen asked in disbelief.

The puppy barked again. Maggie glared at him. "You must have a death wish," she whispered, but the puppy just wagged his tail and barked again.

The door flew open, and Maggie found herself staring into two pairs of the trademark Dumont

light-blue eyes. The older woman was the epitome
of poise. Maggie suspected the woman's spine knew
no other position than stick straight. She was beautiful in an intimidating way. The princess, equally
beautiful, wore an expression of mild amusement,
but the man standing behind the women was fully
disapproving.

The beagle dashed out of the closet and immediately puddled on the marble floor, and Maggie
knew she was toast.

"What is a dog doing in the palace, Monsier
Faus?" the queen asked the man behind her. "The
palace does not allow pets."

Maggie's heart stopped at the man's name. This
was the advisor who had been a royal pain to
Michel.

Monsieur continued to look on with disapproval.
"Several events outside palace protocol have taken
place during your absence. I feel it is my responsibility to inform you."

Maggie fought the urge to bite the man's leg. She
shot to her feet, then quickly bowed. "Your Majesty, I'm responsible for the dog. I gave it to Prince
Maximillian as a reward for his preparation for Marceau's Citizenship Day. The prince did not approve.
In fact, he fired me," she invented, determined to
protect Michel. She searched for the appropriate
word. "For—"

"Insubordination. No surprise there," Michelina

said, and Maggie blessed the woman a thousand times over for filling in her blank. She bent down to pet the puppy. "Cute dog. I always wanted one, but *my mother* wouldn't allow it."

"Your Highness, about the other violations of protocol," Faus began.

Violations. Maggie gulped. What a strong word to describe a frog, a turtle and a photo op. "Your Majesty, I'm certain your son is eager to be the first to greet you and meet with you. He is, after all, your heir," she said with an edge directed at Faus. "Marceau's heir."

The queen gave Maggie a hard look. "Your name and position," she demanded, more than asked, but Maggie was growing accustomed to the routine.

"Maggie Gillian. I am," she said, then corrected herself. "I was Prince Maximillian's summer tutor."

"From America," the queen said.

"Yes, Your Majesty."

"Why am I not surprised," she murmured with a sigh.

"I can read now," Max said in a still, small voice.

The queen's eyes softened just a shade. "You can?"

He nodded and bowed. "Yes, ma'am. I can read now. I couldn't before," he confessed.

Maggie bit her lip at his courage. She was so proud of him she couldn't speak.

"If you've done such a good job with Maximillian, then why is Prince Michel firing you?" she demanded of Maggie.

"The puppy," Maggie reminded the woman. "But it's time for me to go back to America."

"I want her to stay," Max said.

The queen raised her eyebrows. "That is for Prince Michel to decide. Now you and your tutor must clean up the dog's mess while I talk to Prince Michel."

"Your Majesty," Faus began.

"Later," the queen said, and left the rest of them in her wake.

Michel answered the queen's summons and dipped his head as he entered her office. "Welcome home, Your Majesty," he said.

"Thank you," she said. "Faus met me at the door and was eager to give me a report, but Michelina and I happened upon a dog on the way to our quarters."

Michel tensed.

"A dog who puddled on the floor, plus your son and a red-haired woman with the worst curtsy I've ever witnessed. She said you fired her for insubordination, and when Faus said he wanted to give me a report, she had the cheek to advise me that the proper course would be to meet with my son." The queen gave an indignant huff. "This had better be good."

Michel couldn't stop a rush of warmth toward Maggie. She would sacrifice herself to protect him. The knowledge gave him strength. "Which would you like me to address first?"

"The palace does not permit dogs," she said with implacable firmness. "The dog must go."

Round one. "Elvis sleeps in the basement, and Maximillian will be responsible for his care."

The queen blinked. "Elvis," she echoed in disbelief.

Michel bit the inside of his cheek to keep from laughing. "Maximillian named the dog."

"Elvis," she repeated. "You must not have heard me. The dog must go."

"The dog will stay," Michel said calmly.

The queen turned deadly silent. "Are you defying my authority?"

"No. I'm merely exercising my authority as a father, as any father in Marceau has the right to do," he said meeting her gaze head-on.

He watched his mother digest his words. "Michel, may I speak frankly?"

"Yes, ma'am."

"I'm getting too old for this. I don't want to rule anymore. I want to be a grandmother. I want to step down, but I want you to be married first. How was the visit with Isabella?"

Round two. "Isabella is a lovely woman, but we aren't well suited."

"But I thought—" The queen broke off and frowned. "Didn't you find her attractive?"

"She's beautiful," he said.

"Did she offend you in some way?"

"Not at all," he said, thinking of how many times Maggie had disagreed with him. "We simply are not well-suited. I'm not a twenty-year-old anymore. I've grown more opinionated about this matter."

"Picky," she said and sighed. Her weariness and age suddenly showed to Michel. "I'll have to think on this. In the meantime, is Maximillian prepared for Citizenship Day?"

"Yes."

"Good. If this tutor has been so successful with Maximillian, perhaps you should reconsider firing her." She winced. "It would appear that she has good intentions if not always sound judgment. Anything else I should know?"

"There was a rock slide on the road to the north," he said.

The queen tensed. "Injuries?"

"Yes, but no fatalities."

She eased slightly. "Good."

"Nicholas helped attend to the injuries. He used an assumed name."

She closed her eyes for a moment. "He's home."

"Temporarily," Michel said. "And he got a haircut."

She opened her eyes and smiled slightly. "Crumbs from heaven."

"Prince Maximillian paid a brief visit to the clinic housing some of the victims and gave away a few books. A photograph was taken and published in the newspaper. The palace PR department was ecstatic."

"But you weren't," she said. "Anything else?"

Round three. "I'd like to offer Faus an ambassadorship to Switzerland," he said. Actually he preferred sending Faus to Antarctica, but was trying to honor the man's years of service.

The queen did a double take. "I'll take that under advisement. You should remember that a thorn in one's side keeps one humble," she said, and narrowed her eyes. "I suspect there's more."

Round four. "Prince Maximillian will begin swimming lessons next week after Citizenship Day."

The queen's face hardened. "Absolutely not."

"Again," he said as gently as he could, "as a father, I must make wise choices for my son."

"I cannot permit this," she said, her eyes full of fear.

"You must."

She took a breath. "As a leader how can you

make this choice? How can you allow your son to be placed in danger?''

''As a leader, I cannot allow my heir to be ruled by fear or ignorance.''

She took another breath. ''Tell me there's nothing else.''

Final round. ''There is a woman I am considering marrying.''

The queen's eyes rounded. ''Oh really. Who is this? Have I met her? Tell me she's European.''

''You've met her, but she's not European. She is Mademoiselle Maggie Gillian,'' he said, and felt a flood of freedom flow through his veins at the announcement.

The queen gaped at him. ''God save me. The tutor,'' she said. ''The fired tutor responsible for the dog in the palace. The American tutor with the terrible curtsy.'' She sucked in a breath of shocked disbelief. ''Absolutely not. Over my dead body.''

Michel swallowed a smile. ''You have time to think about it. Perhaps after you have an opportunity to rest.'' He hadn't seen his mother this rattled in a very long time. He felt a wave of pity for her. ''How was Michelina?''

The queen pressed her lips together as if to stifle a sigh. ''Hellacious,'' she said. ''Your sister is impossible. When you take the throne, you must also take control of her.''

In your dreams, Michel thought, and felt an impulse he hadn't had in years. He could almost hear Maggie hounding him to follow his instincts. "Mother," he said, and she glanced at him in surprise, "welcome home." And he kissed her cheek.

The following afternoon Maggie found an unobtrusive place toward the front of the crowd waiting for Prince Maximillian's appearance. With a mixture of pride in Max and heartache at the knowledge that she would be leaving the next day, she stood with the citizens of Marceau.

The queen, decked out in robe and crown, offered a brief greeting to the warm crowd. Maggie sensed a great affection and respect for the queen. There was, after all, a lot to admire. The woman had given birth to seven children and survived the loss of a child and her husband. She'd ruled under the threat of war and economic devastation and somehow managed to keep her country at peace.

Maggie caught sight of Michel's brother, Auguste, standing to the side, the military second in command. His wife and two little girls sat behind him.

Michel approached the microphone, and the crowd erupted in applause. Her heart clenched at the sight of him. He emanated power and strength in public and private. In private, though, she had seen and loved another side of him.

Her throat grew tight with emotion. She wished

things were different. She wished she could stay even though it would be foolish for her future. Francois, however, had confided to her just this morning that rumors about her and Michel had begun to swirl around the palace. Pretty soon there would be a leak, and the press would find out, and Michel would lose his precious privacy.

Her eyes stung with unshed tears. She couldn't be a part of hurting him. She wouldn't be. That was the reason she would finish packing her clothes this afternoon and be gone tomorrow. She had given what she could, not near enough to last a lifetime, but she couldn't stay any longer without causing damage.

"Good citizens of Marceau, it is my great honor to introduce Prince Maximillian, who will deliver a special message on this day set aside to honor the great citizens of Marceau."

Maggie watched Max approach the microphone and search the crowd. She smiled just in case he was looking for her and prayed that he would be okay.

He took a big breath and began to speak. He delivered the speech perfectly, and she let out a whoop of happiness at the end. She gave him a thumbs-up. He must have caught sight of her because he smiled and return the signal.

"Do you know the young prince?" a man in front of her asked as the crowd went wild.

"Kinda sorta," she said, beaming when the crowd started chanting, "Encore, encore!"

"Darn, we didn't plan for this," she muttered.

Max stepped in front of the microphone again and the crowd quieted. "The citizens of Marceau *rock!*"

Maggie laughed, and the crowd once again roared its approval. She gave another thumbs-up and the man in front of her snapped a picture. Max echoed the signal, and the man took his picture, too.

Fear knotted her stomach. She watched the man turn toward her, and she stumbled toward the back of the crowd. Michel would not be pleased, she thought, running as fast as she could. She could only pray her photo wouldn't turn out.

Two hours later Michel, thrilled with his son's success, entered Maggie's room. He picked her up and spun her around. "He was amazing, incredible. The queen still doesn't quite understand the term *rock,* but she's very pleased."

"I'm very glad," she said quietly. "I'm very, very glad for all of you."

Hearing her muted tone, he studied her. "I thought you would want to celebrate. This is a huge success for you, too."

"Max did the work," she said simply.

Confused, Michel glanced around her room and noticed her suitcase on the bed. His gut sank. "Why are you packing?"

She inhaled as if visibly trying to calm herself. "My flight leaves tomorrow."

"Absolutely not," he said.

"My assignment is complete."

"You cannot leave," he told her, struggling with an odd sensation that combined desperation and flat-out denial.

"I must leave," she told him. "Rumors have started about you and me. It's only a matter of time before people outside the palace hear. I can't allow that."

"I'm not afraid of rumors," he said, trying to identify the odd sensation he felt. *Sweating,* he realized in shock. He was sweating. No one made him sweat.

"Not only that, I got caught in another nonboring moment today, and I'm afraid the press will go for the jugular once the photo is out."

Michel paused. "Photo?"

"I was a bit demonstrative when Max gave his speech," she said, biting her lip. "After I screamed and whistled and gave the thumbs-up, a reporter snapped my picture and started asking questions. I ran away," she added quickly. "But..."

A plan came to mind. Michel looked into her green eyes and put his hands on her arms. "Will you do something for me if I ask you?"

He saw the fear in her eyes soften. "I'll do anything except stay," she said.

"Three more days," he said, willing her to agree.

She shook her head, and he began to sweat again. "Bad idea," she said. "I really should go."

"Three days," he repeated. "Is it so much to give out of your life?"

Her eyes grew shiny. "You don't know how hard this is for me," she whispered.

Michel ached for her. He hated seeing her in pain. "Three more days," he repeated.

She nodded. "No more than that," she said, her gaze full of warning. "Absolutely no more than three more days."

He kissed her firmly and pulled back. "Excuse me. I have a pressing meeting, but I want you to come to my quarters later."

Ignoring her protests, he headed down the hall to put the palace PR department to work. After an hour with his top three press aides, he knew he had laid the groundwork for his success. Family demands, however, continued to plague him. Michelina wanted to discuss a way to return to the States. His brother Nicholas was already leaving for a professional symposium. His other brother Jean-Marc had sent a fax requesting the assignment as Marceau's diplomatic representative to the United States.

Everyone wanted to go to America, Michel thought. His mother was going to flip.

The queen insisted on proudly showing pictures of her newest grandchild to all. She was pleased to give a full report on the parents, too: Michel's youngest brother, Alexander, and his wife, Sophia.

By the time he retired to his quarters, Maggie was nowhere in sight. Although he missed her, he knew tomorrow was going to be a very busy day for her. He had big plans for Maggie Gillian. She was damn well going to need her rest.

Eleven

As soon as the morning paper hit the front step, Michel ordered it brought to him. With satisfaction he read of his son's triumph. His heart swelled at the sight of the photos of Max giving the thumbs-up sign and at the sight of sweet Maggie, her love and joy emanating from her eyes.

He pored over the article praising Max and the other article, lower on the page, but still prominent, revealing the impact of Maggie's tutoring on Max. The article detailed her impressive academic credentials. The resourceful reporter had even managed to get quotes from some Marceau citizens who had met Maggie at the library's adult literacy program and the clinic Max had also visited.

Michel knew Max had once been viewed as a sad, lonely child after his mother had died. The people who had felt sorrow for him now shared in his victory. The woman who had helped make it happen was Maggie. Maggie Gillian had just become a national treasure.

Michel downed the last of his coffee and tucked the newspaper under his arm for his meeting with the queen.

The queen tossed him a sideways glance as he entered the room. "I've already read it," she said of the paper.

"Including the article about Maggie," he said.

She nodded regally. "Amazing how the press got access to all that information in such a short time."

"Not really," Michel said. "We have an excellent PR department."

"Michel, she's not right for the job of your wife. Your wife must be poised and self-controlled. She must defer to you and support you in all matters. She must be above reproach. She must respect royal protocol."

He stuck his hands in his pockets. "That's what the advisors have told me for years."

"And the advisors are correct."

"The problem is that the advisors don't have to marry my wife. I do."

The queen absorbed that comment. "I am not at all swayed," she told him. "But I am listening."

He nodded. "I didn't plan to love her and would never have chosen her for my wife."

"Then why do you choose her now?"

He searched for the words. How could he possibly explain this? "She is argumentative," he said, "but I've never met a woman deliver a more sincere apology than Maggie. She's impatient with protocol because she's impatient with anything that interferes with my happiness. She believes I deserve to be happy. She doesn't love me because I'm royalty. She loves me in spite of the fact that I am royalty. She loves Michel," he said, certain he was bungling this.

"She makes my worst day better," he said. "She takes the grind out of ruling. I'm a better man because of her."

The queen silently studied her folded hands. "Your father did that for me. I have missed him," she said, her voice quiet. She lifted her head to gaze at Michel. "I will see her this afternoon," she told him, and Michel knew he was halfway there.

"I still don't understand why your mother wants to see me," Maggie said as Michel led her toward a formal parlor. "She can't stand me."

"She's grateful for your work with Max," Michel said.

"Max did the hard part." She felt a sick feeling as she stopped just outside the parlor door. "Michel, I really don't want to talk to your mother. I'm only going to be here two more days. Can't I go to the beach or something instead?''

''Ma chère, this isn't optional,'' Michel told her as the assistant opened the door.

Maggie fought a slice of panic. ''I don't want to do this,'' she whispered desperately.

''You'll be fine,'' he told her, and kissed her.

Maggie tried to draw courage from his strength as she faced the parlor. Inhaling deeply, she told herself she would only have to face the woman once. At least this time she was doing it sans Elvis, the beagle.

She entered the room and dipped her knees in a curtsy. ''Your Majesty,'' she murmured, uncertain whether she was supposed to speak first or wait.

''Please be seated, Mademoiselle Gillian,'' the queen said waving to the chair opposite her. She nodded to the assistant to pour the tea.

''In the short time you've been here, you've made quite a dramatic impact on my son and grandson. Both sing your praises.''

''Prince Max has been a pleasure to work with. He's been an excellent student. He will be a terrific man,'' she said, knowing the warm spot in her heart for Max would never turn cold.

''Do you love my grandson?'' the queen asked bluntly.

''How could anyone not love Max?'' she answered with a shrug. ''He's smart and funny and curious. He's tough, but he's got a great heart.''

"You don't treat him like a prince," the queen observed.

"That's right. He's already got a gazillion people doing that, so I have just tried to treat him like a human being. I think everyone should have at least one person who loves them and treats them like a human being, don't you?"

The queen sipped her tea and appeared to consider her words. "But what of preparing him to rule?"

Maggie took a sip of her tea and set it down. "It depends on what kind of preparation you mean. There are others who can teach him protocol and Prince Michel will make sure Max fulfills tradition at the same time he learns character. Max is really fortunate to have Michel as a father. Michel will make sure Max gets what he needs."

"But what of your contribution to Maximillian?" the queen continued.

Maggie shrugged. "I helped him learn to read and let him see that learning can be fun. I like to think I helped him find some of his power. You see, I'm much more interested in building character than making a prince. Between you and Michel, Max has some pretty big shoes to fill. He will need to be a good human being if he is to be an effective ruler."

"And Prince Michel, how do you view his destiny as ruler of Marceau?"

Maggie found the queen's question odd, but the woman's attitude compelled her to answer. "It's a tough, lonely job with long hours. He's an incredibly intelligent man who is passionate about his vision. Marceau is lucky.'' She wanted to say, Can I go now?, but she bit her tongue.

"What I wish to know, Mademoiselle Gillian, is why you think you would be the best woman to be the wife of Prince Michel?''

Maggie blinked and felt light-headed. Surely she couldn't have heard correctly. "I'm sorry. Could you repeat the question?''

The queen patiently repeated her question word for word.

Maggie shook her head. "I would be a terrible wife for Michel,'' she said. "I don't know any of the protocol, and if I did, I'd probably forget it. I argue with him. I wouldn't mind having two or three children, but I'm not interested in having six, with all due respect,'' she said. "I am much more interested in Michel's happiness than I am interested in the fact that he's a prince. I'm interested in him as a man,'' she said, having trouble avoiding saying that she loved him. "Plus I would be a rotten princess. I don't know how to curtsy correctly—''

"I have observed,'' the queen said in a dry voice. "That can be learned. Thank you for coming. You may be excused.''

Maggie blinked at the abruptness. "Oh. Well, it was nice meeting you again, Your Majesty,'' she said, standing and giving another slight bob.

The queen nodded.

Maggie walked to the door. "Goodbye,'' she said.

"*À bientôt*, mademoiselle.''

Whatever that meant, Maggie thought as the door closed behind her. This was one weird family. She rounded the corner where Michel was leaning against the wall.

He looked at her expectantly. "How did it go?" he asked.

"With all due respect," Maggie said, "your mother is weird. She didn't really thank me for working with Max. She just asked me a lot of odd questions." She tried to shake off the strange conversation. "I think I'm going to the beach for a little while."

"I'll go with you," he said. "The car is waiting."

She searched his gaze. "Are you sure you have time?"

"Yes, of course," he said, as if he was a man of leisure. And Maggie knew he wasn't.

The black limo glided through Marceau's streets to a gated area that led to a private beach. "For security reasons my family uses a private beach on this side of the island."

Extending his hand to her, he guided her through a treed area to the deserted afternoon beach. Maggie inhaled the scent of salt and sea air. "This truly is a beautiful place," she said, thinking she would miss it for far more than its beauty. It was difficult to believe she'd arrived in Marceau just over six weeks ago. She gazed at Michel and memorized his profile with the wind ruffling his dark hair. He appeared deep in thought, yet peaceful. She wanted to seal this moment and every moment she'd shared with him forever in her mind.

The sand was packed down from the recent rain, so she kept her shoes on. "I'd like to take back a couple of shells," she told him, and walked to the edge of the water.

As she knelt to pick up three shells, she felt Michel's hands on her shoulders. "There's something I must discuss with you."

Her stomach turned a flip at his tone. She glanced up at him. His solemn expression seemed ominous. "Is something wrong?"

He nodded. "I have a problem and I need your help."

She immediately stood. "What is it?" she asked, unable to imagine him needing her advice for anything other than Max's education.

He touched a wild strand of her hair. "I'm preparing for an extremely high-level negotiation, and I find I don't have much to offer the other party."

"Are you negotiating for a special service or alliance, some sort of trade agreement?"

"Yes," he said.

"All three," she said, bemused. "Well, what do you want from the other party?"

"Everything," he said. "I want total commitment, loyalty and access."

"And you can't offer the same?"

"To a degree, but as you know, I was born with a prior commitment," he said with a wry grin.

Perplexed, Maggie shrugged. "It doesn't sound like a very equitable agreement."

"It won't always be," he agreed. "I could provide a monetary exchange."

"That might help," she said.

"But the other party isn't interested in money," he said, and his gaze was so compelling Maggie couldn't have looked away from him if her life depended on it. "Not interested in diamonds or titles."

Her heart pounded in her chest. Her mind slowly put two and two together, but she couldn't begin to speak.

"I could promise you jewels and wealth," he told her. "I could promise that people would bow to you, but none of that would win you," he said. "I can't promise that you'll be my top priority every minute of every day. As you've said, I have a job with terrible hours."

He raked a hand through his hair and swore. "I've never wanted a woman more in my life, and I'm totally botching this. Do you know that you are the only woman who has ever made me sweat?"

Maggie's head was spinning, but his last question got through. "I am?" she asked, biting her lip. "Little Maggie Gillian makes the mighty Prince Michel sweat?" she ventured, incredulous.

He looked more tense than a fully stretched bow. Although her own chest was tight with emotion and her mind was filled with confusion, she took his hand. "Maybe it would be better if you didn't treat this like a negotiation. Maybe it would be better if you just said what you feel. Because it sounds like the most important thing you're offering is your-self.''

''I love you,'' he said.

Maggie locked her suddenly liquid knees.

''You've been a haven I didn't know I needed. I want to be the same for you. I have many people who are paid to protect me. You would protect me without compensation. I can promise the same for you. You've given my son new life. You fill me up when I feel used up.'' He narrowed his eyes in con-centration as if the words were difficult to find. ''You're the one woman I want to know and who I want to know me. Please be my wife.''

Maggie grew light-headed. Tears filled her eyes, and she covered them with her hand. A sob welled up in her throat and she couldn't contain it. She hadn't dared to dream Michel would ask such a thing.

''Why are you crying?''

She shook her head helplessly. ''I...I...'' She sobbed again. ''I didn't know you felt that way about me. I want to be the woman for you.'' She sniffed. ''This is going to sound crazy. I want to take care of you, but you need a wife who is dif-ferent from me.''

Michel gently shook her shoulders. ''Don't you understand? No other woman has even thought she wanted to take care of me. You are more rare than the finest precious stone. There's no other woman who can help me be the best man I can be, the best ruler I can be.''

Maggie felt another storm of emotion rage inside her. She swiped at her cheeks and sniffed. ''Oh, God, but I would be such a lousy royal.''

''You wouldn't be the traditional royal wife. That's not necessarily bad. We can work that out.''

She shook her head, full of doubt, still afraid to hope. ''I don't know, Michel. If this were just about you and me, the answer would be easy.''

''Marriage is rarely just about two people. More is involved. Our life together will be a challenge,'' he said. ''But you are worth it to me. You must decide if I'm worth it to you.''

That night Michel's family was apparently holding a meeting. Maggie had no idea why. She had her own life crisis staring her in the face. Unable to sleep, she stole outside to the courtyard and drank in the peaceful darkness.

Moments later Michel joined her, still dressed.

She gave a questioning glance at his attire. ''Late family meeting,'' she said.

He nodded. ''We received some pretty amazing news. A letter with postmarks from about fifteen countries arrived for my mother today. It was forwarded from several places. It had to be over fifteen years old.''

''Wow. Do you know where it originated?''

He shook his head and stuck a fist in his pocket, his gaze full of turmoil. ''There are more unanswered than answered questions. There was a lock of hair and a button enclosed with the letter. The person who wrote the letter said my brother Jacques Simon did not drown when he was three.''

She gaped at him. ''What?''

''Jacques's body was never found. There's no signature on the letter. Whoever wrote it said that Jacques survived falling overboard during the storm, and he was picked up by a fisherman, a childless fisherman.''

Amazement warred with doubt and hope on Michel's face. ''Do you think he could still be alive?'' she asked.

''We don't know, but we have reason to hope. The hair has already gone to a special lab. My mother remembers the button from Jacques's coat.''

''How is she…your mother?''

''She fainted,'' he said in disbelief. ''I've never known her to faint. If Jacques is alive, we must find him.''

Michel appeared to want to go in search of him right this minute. ''But not tonight,'' she said, skimming her hand over his arm.

He met her gaze and took a deep breath. He nodded. ''Not tonight.''

She smiled. ''You've had a full day. Engineered the public relations miracle of turning me into a heroine,'' she began.

His eyes glinted with pleasure. ''You read the article.''

''You wrote it,'' she said.

"Not technically," he said. "I just provided a little guidance and a few leads."

"Uh-huh," she said at the understatement. "You also bulldozed your mother into approving me, proposed marriage and found out your dead brother may be alive."

His gaze asked the question, but he restrained himself from speaking it. She could spend a lifetime seducing that man past his restraint. "It occurred to me that we have never danced."

He glanced around the courtyard, then pulled her into his arms. She felt his heart beating against her cheek, she again heard his unvoiced question and closed her eyes.

Her heart was full and achy with the prospect of the decision she was about to make. "It also occurred to me that I've never been on a picnic with you. Or a boat for that matter. I've also never made love with you in your office."

He pulled his head back and gazed at her. "You're making me sweat again."

A thrill raced down her spine.

She swallowed over the lump in her throat and the tinge of fear that she was inadequate. "I think I want to make you sweat for a long time," she whispered.

"How long?"

"Forever."

Epilogue

Six months later, on a bright sunny morning, the minister of the official church of Marceau pronounced them husband and wife in front of five hundred of Michel's close friends and family along with Maggie's loved ones. This was the royal version of a small ceremony.

During the months of their engagement, Maggie's doubts had fallen, one by one, under Michel's steady love and determination. Surprisingly enough, Francois had become an advocate and friend, filling her in on proper protocol—some of which she followed and some of which she did not and never would.

Michel lowered his head and took her face in his

hands. "This is the happiest day of my life," he said, and kissed her.

With her husband's mouth on hers, she heard bells throughout the city begin to ring. Marceau was pleased.

After an elaborate six-hour reception, Maggie and Michel stole away to his yacht and left Marceau and Max in the caring hands of the queen. The queen planned to officially hand the throne to Michel soon.

Maggie stood in her husband's arms on the deck as the sun began its slow descent. She turned, sliding her arms around him and burying her face in his chest. He gave a rumble of approval. "Don't you want to watch the sunset?"

"I'd rather watch you," she said, looking up at him.

"How does it feel to be a princess?" he asked with a teasing light in his eyes.

"Oh, you're not going to start that already, are you?"

He chuckled. "But, Your Highness," he continued.

She swatted him. "Oh, shut up."

"Whatever pleases Her Highness," he said, and she groaned.

She met his gaze. "You know I've never made love to you on a yacht," she said.

His eyes darkened. "I can change that."

She nodded, feeling the anticipation inside her already begin to build. "The queen told me that you would always belong to the people."

With the wind whipping through his hair, he was thoughtful for a long moment, then a glint of sexy mischief crossed his eyes. "Parts of me will always belong exclusively to you."

"Oh, really," she said, unable to keep from smiling. She didn't think she'd stopped smiling all day. "What parts would those be?"

He picked her up in his arms and carried her toward the bedroom. "Let me show you." His eyes were full of promises she knew they both would keep.

* * * * *

His Majesty, MD
LEANNE BANKS

This book is dedicated to all the people who volunteered during and after the crisis of 9/11. You define the true meaning of heroism.

Prologue

"**I** want you to be nice to this one," Queen Anna Catherine said with an imperious tone that Nicholas believed had been genetically implanted. "This one has great potential."

He smothered a yawn as he joined his mother for tea in her favorite parlor in the palace. They all had great potential. His mother had been trying to find a wife for him since he'd slept in a cradle. She hadn't succeeded yet, and if he had anything to do with it, she never would. He would marry if and when and whom he damn well pleased.

"I'm serious, Nicholas. No shenanigans this time," she said with a warning glint in her eyes. "She could be important to Marceau."

Nicholas's gut knotted. Uh-oh. She was going to

pull the good of the country routine again. "How important?" he asked skeptically.

"Her father is Grant York. He's known as a business genius. He owns a conglomerate of luxury resorts all over the world."

Nicholas nodded with little enthusiasm. "Tourists," he said.

"Yes," his mother said, as if she too had struggled with the idea of their island country being invaded by hordes of outsiders. "A connection with York Enterprises would provide a boon for our economy. It's not in the best interest of our citizens to keep Marceau a secret."

"You know I'm not interested in getting married," he told her, hating the sharp poke of responsibility he felt.

"You don't have to marry Tara York. I just want you to be a kind escort during her stay here at the palace," his mother said. "However, it wouldn't hurt you to settle down."

"Yes, it would," Nicholas said, feeling a noose tighten around his neck. "I think what you meant to say is that it wouldn't hurt *you* if I settled down."

Queen Anna Catherine sighed. "You are undoubtedly the most blunt of your brothers."

Nicholas thought of his brothers and couldn't disagree. "It could be worse. Michel will rule. He needs to know how to be tactful in order to deal with the royal advisors. On the flip side, you get to refer to me as 'my son, the doctor,'" he said, with a sly grin because his mother had been against him going for his medical degree. His brother Michel's negotiation skills had smoothed the way, and for that, Nicholas would always be grateful. And for facilitating his medical career, he would also be indebted to both his brother *and* his mother.

Queen Anna's eyes lit with grudging admiration. "You've chosen a difficult path. To be a royal and a medical doctor will never be easy."

"But nothing else will do," he said and felt the truth echo in his bones. By luck he had been born a prince, but Nicholas knew his destiny had always been medicine. "Medicine is as demanding as a wife."

His mother raised his eyebrows. "Many men have both," she said. "But we can save that discussion for another day. Tara York will arrive tomorrow. Show her a good time for the sake of Marceau."

Nicholas rolled his eyes at his mother's melodramatic request, but nodded. "Always for the sake of country," he muttered, rising. He gave a brief bow of his head in respect, then headed for the door.

"A shave and a haircut wouldn't hurt, Nicholas," Queen Anna suggested.

Nicholas paused. His mother was nothing if not shrewd. She knew he'd deliberately discouraged more than a few of her matchmaking attempts by sporting shaggy hair and three-day stubble. Seeing the weariness on his mother's face, Nicholas bit back a retort. Although she had tried to hide it, the search for conclusive information on his long-lost brother was clearly wearing on her. His mother had seemed to age years during the last few months. She looked almost vulnerable. The knowledge grabbed at his gut, because Queen Anna Catherine had hitherto been known as The Iron Lady. ''For the sake of Marceau,'' he said wryly, running his hand over his stubbled chin.

One

"**I** think you've just been out-geeked," Nicholas's sister, Michelina, whispered in his ear as Tara York stumbled into the palace's grand entrance hall.

Nicholas blinked at the sight that beheld him. Tara York's brown hair was pulled back into an unbecoming bun, Coke-bottle lenses covered her eyes, and she wore a matronly dress he would expect to see on a woman twice her age.

"Quick," Michelina continued, sotto voce. "Let me call Fashion Emergency."

Although he couldn't disagree, Nicholas felt a ripple of irritation. "Not everyone feels compelled to look like an advertisement for *Vogue Paris* when they walk out the door. You may find it difficult to believe, but there are more important things in the world than choosing between Dior and Versace.''

''Perhaps I might have the opportunity to experience some of those choices if Mother wouldn't keep me trapped in the palace like Rapunzel,'' Michelina retorted. ''Either way, I think I can safely say that Miss York didn't choose that dress from Dior or Versace. You must admit, Mother has never sent you a prospect like this.''

''She's not a prospect. She's a guest,'' Nicholas said, and moved toward Tara as she stumbled again.

''Excuse me, Your Highness,'' Tara said, and gave a quick dutiful curtsey. ''I'm afraid the long flight has upset my equilibrium.''

He automatically reached out a hand to steady her, but she pulled back. ''I'm fine, thank you,'' she murmured.

''Miss York,'' Nicholas began.

''Please call me Tara,'' she said with a slight, tight smile that Nicholas thought he might like if it were just a bit wider and more sincere. She waved her hand to encompass Michelina. ''And you must also be Your Highness.''

His lips twitched. ''Not necessary. I'm Nicholas, and this is my sister, Michelina.''

Michelina dutifully stepped forward. ''We're so pleased you could visit our country, Tara. You must tell me if there is anything I can do to make your stay more comfortable.''

Tara adjusted her thick glasses. ''Thank you, Michelina. I need to make sure there's an Internet connection in my room.''

Michelina hesitated in surprise. ''An Internet connection?''

Nicholas watched a sliver of concern cross Tara's face. ''Yes, it's actually the only thing I require. You do have phone lines in the palace, don't you?''

Michelina nodded. ''Oh, of course we do. It's just that most of our visitors prefer to enjoy outdoor activities, especially our beautiful beaches.''

Tara shrugged. ''I'm sure they're beautiful, but I burn so easily,'' she confided, adjusting her glasses on her nose again. ''I'll be able to keep busy inside, thank you.''

Michelina gave a slow nod of wonder. ''As you wish, but if you should change your mind, please feel free to let Nicholas or me know.''

Baffled by the strange creature standing before him, Nicholas studied her. The thick glasses couldn't hide the intelligence in her eyes. Her courteous tone couldn't hide the fact that she didn't want to be here. ''I'll have your bags taken to your room. Would you like a snack before you freshen up? There will be a small dinner party held in your honor this evening.''

''A dinner party in my honor?'' Tara echoed in dismay. In fact, Nicholas might call it dread. He knew all about the emotion because he felt exactly the same way about most of the formal palace parties. ''That's not necessary,'' she said, a shade desperately.

Nicholas felt a twinge of sympathy for the woman. ''My mother, the queen, insists,'' he said.

Realization crossed her face, and she nodded with a sigh. She met his gaze and, despite her thick lenses, in that one moment, Nicholas felt an inexplicable understanding pass between them.

Tara averted her gaze. "If it's not too much trouble, I would appreciate some juice. And I'm sure a shower will do wonders. Thank you for your hospitality."

"Our pleasure," Nicholas said, curious despite himself. He introduced Tara to a palace aide and watched her walk down the hallway. He wasn't sure he'd seen a more hideous dress, but the ugly garment didn't conceal Tara's shapely calves. His curiosity was piqued.

His sister squeezed his shoulder. "You have my sympathy this time. Mother can't possibly be serious about a match with that woman."

"It doesn't matter if Mother is serious about her matchmaking attempts. I'm not," he said.

"But an Internet junkie. How in the world will you entertain her?"

Nicholas loved his sister, but he also knew Michelina tended to jump to conclusions. "Something tells me there's more here than what meets the eye," he said, and decided if he was going to be assigned the task of entertaining Tara York, he might as well satisfy his curiosity about her.

Tara ditched her glasses the second she entered her suite. Pacing the length of the large, elegant bedroom furnished with 18th-century antiques, she massaged her temples and sighed. She didn't need glasses, and they actually gave her a headache. The heavy lenses, however, had served—and would continue to serve— an important purpose. They, along with her dumpy clothing and her deliberate social ineptitude, kept the dogs after her father's fortune at bay.

Tara suspected Prince Nicholas might not appreciate being called a dog, and he was certainly better looking than a dog, but in her mind, all marital prospects presented by her father were dogs.

They all wanted her because of what her father could do for them, and no matter how much Tara argued with him, her father insisted marriage was in her best interest for his peace of mind and her own safety.

She bent down to toss her shoes into the closet, turned her head to the side and the room suddenly tilted. Struggling to steady herself, she stubbed her toe on the edge of the carpet and pitched forward. Swearing under her breath, she felt the sting of panic that came from being out of control. Standing perfectly still, she took a deep breath to calm herself.

Her clumsiness had been the bane of her existence. Ever since she'd been a child, Tara had fought a propensity for tripping over her own feet. It was one of those things that seemed to come and go with no advance notice. After a broken arm and a fractured ankle, her father had become overprotective. He always referred to it as her "little problem." Tara understood part of his uneasiness about her clumsiness.

She agreed it was best for her not to get behind the

wheel of an automobile, and she didn't attempt dancing for fear of injuring someone. She shuddered to think of the injury suits people would file against her and her father. She agreed that she was certainly more clumsy than the average person, but she did not agree that a husband was the answer to her "little problem."

More than anything, Tara craved a feeling of accomplishment and independence. She wanted to contribute. She didn't want to be that giant sucking sound her father heard just before he fell asleep at night. She had often feared she was a disappointment to her father—certainly a liability—and she wanted to prove herself, not just to him, but to herself as well.

Taking careful steps, she unpacked her laptop computer and carried it to the desk. After placing it on the desktop, she stroked the machine. Inside that computer lay the secrets to her progress and the promise of her future. So far, she'd earned two college degrees over the Internet, and she was currently working on her master's degree.

Nicholas Dumont's curious gaze flitted through her mind. Although he was handsome and she had to admire the fact that he'd earned his degree in medicine, Tara knew his family must want something from her father. On the other hand, her father probably loved the idea of the built-in security level that royals provided. He was no doubt quite prepared to give the Dumonts something they wanted if they gave him something he wanted—a husband for his daughter.

A bitter taste filled Tara's mouth. She didn't want

a husband, royal or otherwise. She glanced at the array of ugly dresses the palace aide had hung for her in the closet, then back at her computer. She wanted freedom, and she knew how to get it. She also knew how to be the opposite of alluring and seductive.

Nicholas was probably more intelligent than most of the men she sent packing, but he was still a man, and no man in his right mind would want her, with her thick glasses, lack of style and ''little problem.'' Tara knew she was completely resistible.

After sitting through five courses and politely answering more than a dozen questions about her father while she evaded questions about herself, Tara wished she could disappear. The calories from the chocolate mousse alone, she reminded herself dryly, would ensure she wouldn't be disappearing any time soon. She glanced around the table and concluded that with the exception of royal blood and position, the Dumonts were like most families—a combination of functional and dysfunctional.

Throughout the meal, she felt Nicholas's curious gaze on her, but tried to ignore him. She hadn't been at all successful. She couldn't help noticing his hands as he cut the beef burgundy and lifted the glass of red wine to his mouth. They were strong and masculine, but something made her think they were also gentle. When his mother complimented him, she heard his muffled long-suffering sigh. She wondered how appalled he was at the thought of being paired with her and hid her smile of amusement behind her wineglass.

She sensed Queen Anna's offspring viewed their mother with a mixture of emotions; love and protectiveness interspersed with impatience at her attempts to orchestrate their lives. Michelina was quiet and appeared to be brooding. The heir, Michel, seemed to bite his tongue more than once. His American wife, Maggie, divided her attention between distracting Michel from his annoyance, talking to Michel's son, Max and trying to put Tara at ease. The love between the three of them was palpable.

True love mystified her. Her parents had not been in love, and she'd rarely had an opportunity to observe the real thing. Tara felt a tiny dart of longing as she watched them, but she refused to examine the emotion too closely. Marriage was not for her. She didn't want to transfer her dependence from one man to another.

"We're all quite proud of Nicholas," Queen Anna said to Tara. "He graduated at the top of his class."

"Pushing, pushing," Nicholas muttered under his breath, and took a sip of wine.

"And he's an excellent swordsman," Queen Anna continued. "I'm sure he's too modest to tell you he has represented Marceau and won many competitions. It's all Nicholas can do to dodge the magazines featuring royal bachelors. He's always a favorite."

"Stick a fork in me. I'm done," he muttered, then cleared his throat. "Mother," he said. "After Ms. York's long flight, I'm sure she would enjoy some fresh air." He turned his gaze toward Tara. "May I show you the balcony?"

Escape! Tara's heart raced with the anticipation of leaving the endless dinner. "Yes. I'd like that very much, thank you," she said, and quickly stood, nearly knocking her chair to the floor in her haste.

Nicholas grabbed the chair and righted it, then stood and offered his arm. "Excuse us," he said, and led her from the room.

As soon as they rounded the corner to the balcony, Tara removed her hand from his arm. She felt a shiver of relief when he stepped away at the same time she did. He clearly was not attracted to her.

She moved to the railing and inhaled the sweetly scented air. A combination of moonlight and strategically placed floodlights illuminated the beautiful gardens below. No matter what city she'd visited during her father's mandatory find-a-groom tour during the last six months, Tara had been too busy with her studies to enjoy the moonlight. The greenery and blooming flowers had a soothing effect on her.

"You'll have to forgive my mother. Subtlety isn't her strong suit," Nicholas said in a deep confiding tone.

Tara turned and allowed herself a moment to study him. Tall with broad shoulders, he gazed down at her with an inviting glint in his light blue eyes. One side of his lips cocked upward in a half grin. Dressed in a dark suit, he wore the clothing with masculine carelessness. She suspected he would be much happier with his sleeves pushed up his arms. Nicholas emanated an intellectual toughness combined with a social ease that drew her. He wasn't pushy or predatory like some of the other men her father had urged her toward. In another situation, she might even find him appealing.

She tensed at the thought and mentally slammed on the brakes. ''It's nice that your mother is proud of you, and it sounds as if your accomplishments warrant her pride. I think everyone wants that feeling of accomplishment.''

He lifted a dark eyebrow and nodded. ''And you?''

''Of course,'' she said automatically.

''What would you like to accomplish?'' he probed.

Tara's throat tightened at the question though, she knew he was sincere. At least, he appeared sincere. But she hadn't revealed her personal goals to anyone, she didn't want others making fun of her. By the kindness in Nicholas's eyes, she suspected he wouldn't make fun. Still, she thought it would be easier to disclose her bra size than her personal dreams, and she was pretty sure he wasn't interested in her bra size.

''My goals are currently under construction,'' she said.

He nodded. ''Fair enough. Mine are too, but your answer tells me nothing about you. It's my job to entertain you, and I can't do that unless I know what's important to you. Or at least what you like and don't like.''

''No, you don't,'' she said, looking away from him and inhaling a draft of vanilla-scented air. She felt him move closer, and an odd frisson of awareness shimmied down her nerve endings.

"No, I don't what?"

"You don't need to entertain me," she said, forcing herself to meet his gaze dead-on. "I can entertain myself."

He blinked in surprise, then cocked his head to one side. "What if I *want* to entertain you?"

"I can't imagine why. I don't think we have much in common," she said, even though a part of her wondered.

"We don't know what we have in common unless we get to know each other."

True, but Tara knew everything she needed to know. Her father wanted her to marry this man, and she didn't want to marry anyone. She struggled with the desire to rip away the polite social veneer covering the awkward situation. She wanted to say *I don't want to marry you, you don't want to marry me—so let's bag the pretense.*

"I appreciate your hospitality, but I'm quite an introvert, so I'll be perfectly content to spend time alone in my room and explore the palace and its grounds...by myself. Please feel free to carry on with your regular schedule."

Tick-tock, tick-tock. Her thesis was calling her, and she needed to rest to get over her jet lag. She wondered how she was going to maintain her schedule on her thesis without becoming a total recluse during her stay in Marceau.

"There must be something we can offer you," Nicholas said. "Do you ride horses?"

With her lack of coordination? she thought wryly. "I'm sorry. No."

"Speed boat?"

Tara had learned long ago that putting herself behind the controls of anything with an engine was a prescription for disaster. She shook her head.

"Bicycle riding?"

"No, thank you. What can I say? I lead a quiet, boring life." *I promise I would bore you to tears,* she wanted to say. "Speaking of quiet, I think jet lag is kicking in. You wouldn't mind if I retire to my room, would you?"

Frowning, he shook his head. "No. I'll walk you to your room."

Tara wanted to tell him it wasn't necessary, but bit her tongue. She didn't need to be a shrew—she just needed to be firm. "Thank you." He escorted her down three long hallways, and although they didn't talk, Tara felt hypersensitive in his presence. When she glimpsed her room, a rush of relief raced through her.

"Thank you again for your hospitality," she said, grasping the doorknob as if it were a lifeline. If she hurried, she wouldn't have to meet Nicholas's unsettling curious gaze again.

He stopped her with a hand on her shoulder. He took her hand, and stopped her breath and heart at the same time. She watched in amazement as he lifted her hand and brushed his lips over it. "Welcome to Marceau, Tara," he said. "If there is anything you need, call me."

A hot, sensual thought stole across her mind. Nicholas gave the impression he could take care of all of a woman's needs. Needs she'd decided to put off for at least the next decade, she reminded herself. She swallowed. "I can't think of a thing at the moment." *Truer words were never spoken,* she thought, chiding herself for her muddled mental state. "But thank you," she managed, and removed her hand from his. "Good night."

"*A bientôt, chérie.*"

Biting her lip, Tara entered her room and closed the door and Nicholas Dumont behind her. If she weren't careful, she could like him, and that wouldn't be a good idea at all.

Nicholas glanced at the clock on his nightstand and swore. 3:00 a.m. He threw back the sheets and headed for the small refrigerator in the parlor of his suite. He usually slept like the dead.

There was no good reason for his insomnia except perhaps his distraction with his brother Jacques, who had been missing for over twenty years. The family had only recently learned that Jacques might be alive. A team of investigators had been hired to scour the globe for Jacques, but every once in a while Nicholas wondered what had become of his youngest brother after the accident.

Nicholas rolled his shoulders as he glanced inside the small refrigerator. Beer, but no water. He frowned and shrugged, deciding to go down to the kitchen and grab a bottle. It wasn't as if he had anything else to do. He pulled on a pair of shorts and walked out of his suite.

Another thing that weighed heavily on his mind was that he was trying to find a way to make his medical training of use to the people of Marceau. His oldest brother, Michel, the heir apparent, made no secret of his wish for Nicholas to become official medical consulate, but Nicholas himself craved a more direct, healing role.

Finally, there was Tara York, he thought as he glanced down the hallway to the room where she slept. The woman wasn't at all what he'd expected, and she seemed to be doing her level best to discourage his attention. He should be whooping with joy that he wouldn't be forced to entertain her or endure any real or pseudo-crushes, but she reminded him of a brainteaser he wanted to solve.

Waving at a guard, Nicholas ambled the rest of the way to the kitchen, grabbed a couple bottles of water and made the return trip. He paused at the hallway to Tara's room and followed an itchy sensation that led to her doorway. Light shone from underneath the door.

He raised his eyebrows. Why would Miss York be awake at 3:00 a.m.? He leaned closer to the door and heard her voice, then an electronic beep, followed by an oath.

Unable to stifle his curiosity, he tapped on the door. "Miss York," he said.

He heard the patter of her feet on the floor and a thump, followed by another oath.

Ouch. Nicholas winced. Sounded like a stubbed toe.

She cracked the door open and one blue eye peeked out at him. "What do you want?"

"I was up getting some bottled water, saw the light under your door and wondered if you needed some help."

"I'm fine," she said, still keeping the door minutely cracked.

"Is your toe bleeding?" he asked.

She paused, then he saw her hair cover his view of her. "Just a little," she admitted.

"Let me see," he said.

"It's not necessary," she said, a tinge of panic leaking into her voice.

"I'll make that determination. I'm a medical doctor, remember?"

"But—"

Nicholas gently but firmly pushed open the door.

Tara gave a muffled squeak of protest before she jumped out of the way.

Nicholas immediately glanced at her bleeding toe, then bent down and wrapped his hand around her ankle. Tara grabbed the dresser for balance.

"It doesn't look like it will need stitches," he said. "Nasty bruise, though."

Still holding her ankle, he allowed his gaze to travel up her shapely bare legs to the inviting hint of creamy thighs exposed by the high hem of her nightshirt. The nightshirt gave just a few hints of the female form beneath: the curve of her hip and the imprint of her nipples against the pink material.

Farther up, he took in the nervous swallow of her bare throat, then rosebud lips that somehow managed to look like a combination of innocence and sin. Her hair fell over her shoulders like rich cognac.

He looked into her blue eyes, then glanced at the desk where the computer sat with its cursor blinking. No glasses next to the computer. He looked at the bedside table. No glasses.

Suspicion and curiosity vied for supremacy in his mind. Just as he'd thought, Tara York wasn't exactly what she seemed.

Tara bit her lip and pointed at her toe. "See? No big deal. I've got oodles of bandages in my toiletry kit. Are you satisfied?"

Not by a long shot, Nicholas thought. But he would be.

Two

The man was kneeling at her foot and he was half-naked.

"You can let go of my ankle now," Tara said. *So I can think again.* Just the way his fingers looped around her ankle like a bracelet made her edgy. She'd felt his assessing gaze over every inch of her. It reminded her of the one time she'd sunbathed in the nude and gotten a whopper of a burn in tender places. There was no sun in sight at the moment, however, and she was clothed, so Nicholas shouldn't be affecting her tender places one iota.

He squeezed her ankle, then released it. Grabbing the water bottles he'd set on the floor, he stood. "Let's get a bandage on it."

Her heart pounding double time, she went to the

bathroom, foraged in her toiletry bag and grabbed one of her boxes of bandages. She pulled one out and returned to her bedroom.

Before she could apply the bandage, Nicholas snatched it from her fingers and took care of the task himself. ''There,'' he said, rising again and nodding toward her computer. ''Problems?''

''I'm having trouble connecting to the Internet,'' she admitted, relieved to have his attention pulled away from her. She wondered if he had any idea how distracting his bare chest was. ''I got the connection number for Marceau before I left home, but it doesn't seem to be working.''

''Let me see,'' he said, striding toward the desk. ''I know a few things about computers. Michelina's been calling me His Royal Geekness for years.''

That was difficult for Tara to imagine. Nicholas might be intelligent, but he seemed to have all the necessary social skills, and there was certainly nothing nerdlike about his appearance.

''Nice machine,'' he said, studying the screen. ''I see your problem. You don't have the entire prefix. Here,'' he said, entering two additional numbers. ''Try it now.''

Tara signed on and was immediately connected. Gratitude rushed through her. ''Thank you,'' she told Nicholas warmly. I've been wrestling with this all night,'' she said.

He nodded. ''No problem. Mind answering a question?''

She did mind, but since he'd solved her computer

dilemma, the least she could do was be polite. "No."

"Why do you wear glasses when you don't need them?"

He'd caught her. Tara felt heat rise to her cheeks. She looked away and took a careful breath. Darn, what could she do now?

"How do you know I don't need them?" she asked, stalling.

"You're not wearing them and they're nowhere in sight. As you say in America, the jig's up."

Tara frowned and looked at him hard. Except for the fact that he was half-nude, he appeared to be a reasonable man. She wondered if she could trust him. "I suppose you'd like the truth," she said reluctantly.

"And nothing but…so help you God as you Americans say." He said it playfully, but she knew he meant the words.

She sighed, irritated that Nicholas was obviously too smart to be taken in by her disguise. "I'm sure you know the purpose of my visit to Marceau is to make a match between you and me. My father wants me to get married. I don't."

"Why don't you?"

"Because I value my independence. I don't want anyone telling me what to do and when to do it," she said bluntly.

He nodded slowly. "Fair enough, but you still haven't told me why you wear glasses when you don't need them."

"I was trying to impress you with my homeliness."

Nicholas blinked, then his lips twitched with humor. "So, what you're telling me is that you deliberately made yourself less attractive so I wouldn't fall under your spell."

"Not exactly," Tara said. "Many men would be able to look past a lack of beauty in exchange for whatever they're hoping to gain from my father. So, I not only need to be unattractive physically, but also socially, I need to—"

"Bore the hell out of me," he finished for her.

"Exactly," she said, surprised that he understood.

He chuckled under his breath and shook his head. "So you really don't want to get married," he said, as much to himself as her.

"Not at all," she admitted.

"And the idea of marrying a prince—who happens to be a doctor—doesn't make the idea more appealing," he clarified.

Tara made a face. "Your royal title probably draws the press like flies at a picnic, and it seems to me that a doctor's wife would spend a lot of time alone."

He chuckled again and rubbed his square chin. "I knew there was something different about you the minute I saw you. My mother has tried to match me up with eleven different women, and I've pulled the same tricks you have. I don't shave and I wear a scruffy beard—and for good measure I discuss microbiology during mealtimes."

Amazement ran through her. "Eleven! Maybe you can give me some pointers. I'm only up to number eight." She took a second look at him, noting his haircut and shaven jaw. "But why did you cut your hair for me?"

"I didn't. I did it for my mother. She's had a tough time lately. A family matter. So I thought I should at least try to be outwardly cooperative."

"Weren't you afraid I might fall for you?"

"I was hoping to reason with you. It was a risk, of course. And if that didn't work, I would have treated you to my microbiology discussion."

"What does Marceau want from my father?"

"Now, that's a mixed bag. Many people in Marceau think it would be great for the economy if your father would build a resort here to attract tourists."

"But you don't agree?"

"I'm not crazy about the idea of a ton of tourists, but it might help the economy. Tourism isn't my area," he said with a shrug. "Medicine is."

Tara crossed her arms over her chest thoughtfully. "I can't claim to have a great deal of influence over my father, but I could certainly mention the possibility when I speak with him," she said and gave in to a little of her own curiosity. "Why don't *you* want to get married?"

"I don't want my attention divided right now. I have some important goals, and I don't want to be distracted by family responsibilities."

His candor lifted a weight from her chest. Tara took a deep breath and looked into Nicholas's honest light blue eyes. She could have sworn she felt a click snap between them. She felt it resonate inside her. "I think we understand each other," she said, unable to remember the last time someone had understood her. "We don't really have to pretend anymore."

"Not to each other," he agreed. "But we've both established that there are other interested parties."

Tara nodded. "My father, your mother. I could cut my visit short."

"And we both would get slammed with questions," he said.

"And I would probably be shipped out to number nine," she said, dreading that prospect.

"Or we could create the necessary illusions while you do your thing and I do mine. As long as we show up together every now and then, the situation could work to our advantage. If we give the impression that our parents have reason to hope they'll be successful in their matchmaking, they'll probably leave us alone."

Tara warmed to the idea, which held out the promise of freedom. "As long as we don't give them too much reason to hope."

"Exactly," Nicholas said. Giving a grin that made her stomach dance, he extended his hand. "Deal?"

She allowed his warm palm to enclose hers. "Deal."

He squeezed her hand, then released it. At the same time, Tara let out her breath. Had she been holding it?

He offered her a bottle of water. "We can drink to it."

She smiled. He was safe, she told herself even though her nerve endings were still jumping. After all, Nicholas Dumont offered a handshake and water, not kisses and champagne. So how could there possibly be any danger?

Three days later, Nicholas knocked on Tara's door again. He'd visited three clinics during the last few days and treated several patients. He had no idea what Tara had been doing except that she'd been taking all her meals in her room, which had drawn the attention of the queen.

Tara opened the door and her eyes lit with surprise. "Hi. What's up?"

"We need to talk," he said, and walked into Tara's room. "My mother has learned that you've been taking all your meals in your room, and she's concerned that you and I aren't spending enough time together."

Tara lifted her hair off the back of her neck and rolled her big blue eyes. Her face free of makeup, she wore a tank top designed to keep her cool and any normal man hot. Her shorts revealed slim shapely legs that brought to mind basic needs he hadn't addressed in ages. In her natural state, Tara York was damn easy on the eyes.

"So what do we need to do?"

"There's a charity ball being held at a hotel downtown. My mother insists we attend."

Tara wrinkled her nose with genuine displeasure. "A ball. When?"

"Tonight. We probably don't have to stay the entire time. A few dances and—"

"Dances! I can't dance. I can barely walk without

running into something. Plus, I need to study for—''
She broke off as if she'd revealed far more than she
intended.

"Study for?" he prompted.

"Nothing that would interest you," she said, and
began to pace. "The timing's terrible. If we absolutely have to go, then I'll go. But I can't dance."

Bemused by the degree of her anxiety, Nicholas
studied her. "It can't be that bad. I'm not big on
dancing, but I can waltz on demand."

She shook her head. "You don't understand. My
father calls it my "little problem." A nice person
would call it a coordination deficit. I call it dangerously clumsy. If you put me on the dance floor with
a lot of innocent people, then you'd better make sure
you're well insured, because somebody's bound to get
hurt, and when they learn who I am, they'll sue." She
met his gaze. "I'm not exaggerating. I don't even
drive a car because of it."

Nonplussed, Nicholas rubbed his jaw. "It's that
bad. Have you been checked by a neurologist?"

She waved her hand in dismissal. "I've been
clumsy since I was a child. No waltzing."

Nicholas searched for a solution that would satisfy
appearances and Tara's aversion to dancing. "You
wouldn't have to waltz. Just a slow dance or two. You
could just lean from side to side and I'll do the rest."

She shot him a doubtful look. "No twirling?"

"No twirling," he assured her. He glanced at the
computer. "What are you studying?"

"Nothing that would interest you," she said in a

cool voice that should have affected him like a door in his face. Instead, he grew more curious.

He walked to her desk and scanned the papers. She snatched them up, but not before he glimpsed the subject. ''You're studying psychology. The subject matter looks fairly advanced, not basic stuff.''

She cradled the papers to her chest protectively. ''It better be advanced. It's my thesis.''

Nicholas did a double take. She'd surprised him again. ''You're working on your master's degree?''

She gave a small nod.

''What university?''

''I'm getting it on the Internet,'' she said with great reluctance. ''I would appreciate you not telling anyone. My father doesn't know and—''

''Why not?''

She shrugged. ''My father is incredibly overprotective. He didn't want me to go to college, and to be perfectly honest, when I first started, I didn't have a lot of confidence. But I've done fine, and I know that if I continue to do well, I'll have more say over what I do with my life.''

Nicholas suspected she was playing down her success. ''What do you mean by doing fine?''

''I've successfully earned two undergraduate degrees, one in sociology, the other in psychology. I'm two-thirds of the way through my master's degree,'' she said slowly, as if her disclosure was as painful as pulling teeth.

''Why haven't you told your father?''

''It's not the right time,'' she said. ''Plus I don't

want any criticism or discouragement. I don't want to hear one disparaging word about my field of study, and I know him. He's a businessman, so he would tell me I'm training for a career where all I'll say is 'Do you want fries with that?' There may be some truth to his opinion, but I don't want to hear it right now. I feel better than ever about myself because of this. And I'm not going to let anyone take that away from me."

The combination of her passion and vulnerability resonated deeply with him. Nicholas had launched an uphill battle to study medicine. Such a thing 'just wasn't done' by members of the royal family, he'd been told over and over again ad nausem. "Your secret's safe with me. I took a lot of resistance from the royal advisors and the queen as I pursued my own goals. In the end, your father will probably come around. It took my mother a while to get used to the idea of her son becoming a doctor, but now she mentions it every chance she can," he added wryly.

Tara smiled. "My son, the doctor."

He nodded. "Yeah."

He looked into her blue eyes for a long moment and felt a strange sensation in his gut, rather as though he were just remembering he'd skipped a meal and were feeling hungry. He liked her smile, he liked her passion for independence and something about her made him want her to trust him and confide in him. Damned if he knew what it was, he thought ruefully, then returned his attention to the woman in front of him. "Eight o'clock, tonight then. In the foyer. Do you need to shop?"

She gave a mysterious smile and shook her head. "Oh, no, I brought the perfect dress."

At eight-fifteen, Nicholas paced the formal foyer. If Tara weren't in the palace, he'd halfway suspect he was being stood up. Although it was refreshing that he wasn't being chased, he felt a surprising poke at his masculine ego from Tara's complete lack of interest. The completely divergent emotions irritated the hell out of him. Ditching the waiting game, he told the escort and bodyguards to take a break while he checked on Tara.

He knocked on her door several times, but there was no answer. A ripple of concern oozed through him. He wondered if something was wrong. He pushed open the door. "Tara?"

The connecting bathroom door whipped open, and Tara walked out in a rush of steam, wearing only a towel.

Her hair was wet from the shower, and drops of water dotted the swells of her creamy breasts. Nicholas's mouth went dry.

Her eyes widened. "Oh! I'm so sorry. I was studying and I lost track of time. Unforgivably rude, but I hope you'll forgive me," she said, turning to pull a pair of silk bikini panties and a lace bra from her drawer. "I can probably be ready in ten minutes if I rush."

She appeared unaware of the fact that she was completely naked beneath that towel; Nicholas could think of nothing else. His body temperature cranked upward. He wondered if her nipples were pink or dusky-colored. He wondered how they would feel in his hands, in his mouth.

Her gaze met his. "Well," she said with a contrite expression. "Are you angry and offended?"

"No," he said. "Distracted" was a more accurate description of his mood. "I was just starting to wonder."

She gave a deep sigh of relief, drawing his gaze to her breasts. Nicholas couldn't help wishing the damn towel would slip. He transferred his gaze to her legs, and a steamy visual of settling himself between her thighs and— He mentally broke off the thought. He needed a drink. "We'll meet in the foyer in fifteen minutes. Although I've never met a woman who can get ready for a ball in that amount of time."

Tara's lips stretched in a smile with an edge of mischief. "Then I guess it's time you did."

Twelve minutes later, Tara lifted the hem of her yellow and brown gown as she made her way down the hall. The dress was both hideous and too big. Her ensemble felt like a burden tonight. Her glasses perched on her nose, and she felt a trickle of water running down her back from her braid. Although she knew her ruse was no longer necessary for Nicholas, she suspected it was best to continue her ugly duckling routine in public.

Turning a corner, she met Nicholas's gaze and felt

him dissect her appearance millimeter by millimeter. Her stomach took a crazy dip. If she didn't know better, she'd think he was mentally stripping the yellow and brown gown from her body. But that wasn't possible, she assured herself. Nicholas didn't view her as a sexually attractive woman, just as she didn't view him as a sexually attractive male.

The latter part of her thought process caused a discordant bell to clang inside her head, but she pushed it aside. "Under fifteen minutes," she said. "The only problem is my hair isn't dry, but that's a small price to pay for the extra study time. Are you ready to get this over with?" she asked gamely.

He shook his head. "Your transformation is amazing. Where did you find this…?" He pointed at the dress as if there were no words.

"Easy. I once had my colors done, and I was told which were the best colors for me to wear and which were the worst. This combination of yellow and brown is—"

"The worst," he finished for her.

Tara smiled. "Exactly."

He lifted his gaze from her dress to her eyes and she felt a strange tug in her stomach. Hunger, she told herself.

"Can you take the glasses off when we're alone?"

Her breath stopped in her throat. "Why?"

"Because I ask it."

The hint of regal authority in his voice amused her at the same time that his request unsettled her, but she couldn't really think of a good reason to refuse him. "Okay," she said with a shrug, and slipped her glasses from her face. She wondered how she could feel so naked when her body was covered from neck to toe.

Nicholas extended his arm to her. "The ball awaits."

Three

Tara had been dreading this moment the entire evening. Perhaps her entire life. Watching the swirl of evening dresses as tuxedo-dressed men spun their graceful partners around the ballroom, she felt her stomach twist and spin. She could feel a disaster coming. She shouldn't care that she was innately clumsy and that her feet seemed to have a will of their own, with the worst timing imaginable. She shouldn't care that she was probably going to step on Nicholas's well-shined black shoes and fall flat on her face. She shouldn't be embarrassed because she shouldn't care what Nicholas thought of her.

But she did. Just a little bit, Tara insisted to herself, and the reason she cared was because Nicholas wasn't like the others. He wasn't pretending to like her or to be attracted to her.

The music stopped and the orchestra eased into a slow, bluesy tune. Tara felt Nicholas's gaze on her, and her heart tripped.

"Ready?" he asked, sliding his hand down her arm to lace his fingers through hers.

The simple taking of her hand made something inside her jolt. She took a deep breath. "I guess," she said.

Nicholas gently tugged her toward the dance floor. "Smile. You look like you're headed for the guillotine. It's just a dance."

"Easy for you to say," she muttered under her breath, as she moved into dance position. Left hand on his broad shoulder, her right hand captured in his. She felt his other hand at her back, securely drawing her closer.

He began to sway. "Just lean into me. I'll do the work."

Tara lifted her gaze above Nicholas's strong chin, and the light from the chandeliers danced in her peripheral vision, creating an aura behind Nicholas's head. Feeling her equilibrium start to slip, she tightened her fingers on his shoulder and quickly shifted her focus to Nicholas's eyes.

"Problem?" he asked, pulling her closer.

Her chest tightened, making it difficult for her to breathe. "Just a little dizzy," she said, willing the sensation to leave her alone. "You have quite extraordinary eyes. They're so light, they look almost silver.''

''Family characteristic. How long have you had the problem with balance?''

''Since I was about eleven or twelve.''

''Do you experience nausea with it?''

''No. When I was younger, I remember often feeling as if someone were moving things like the floor or the steps,'' she said, smiling wryly.

He chuckled, a low, deep sound that skittered down her nerve endings. ''Broken bones?''

''A few. My father couldn't handle me getting hurt. I think he gave the bodyguards instructions to protect me from myself as much as anyone else. If you're trying to find a medical condition in this, you're going to be sorry. It's a very simple diagnosis. Clumsiness. It's inconvenient, but not terminal as long as I'm careful.''

Uncomfortable with his undivided attention so focused on her ''little problem,'' Tara looked away from Nicholas's intent gaze. ''How much longer do we need to do this?''

''Just until the song ends. Are you afraid I'll let you fall?''

''No,'' she said in a low voice. Tara knew he wouldn't let her fall, but she couldn't deny her uneasiness about other things, such as the subtle but delicious scent of his aftershave. He was holding her too closely, she thought, but she knew his motivation was protective, not sexual. That didn't change the fact that she was too aware of her breasts pressed against his chest and his hips brushing intimately against her.

The sensation of Nicholas surrounding her with his body and arms kicked up a riot of new and disconcerting feelings inside her. Her breasts felt swollen and her thighs trembled.

Frowning, Tara tried to make sense of it all. She jerked the wrong way and tried to steady herself. Her foot slammed down smartly on his shoe.

Aghast, she looked into his face and caught the slight wince of pain. Misery and embarrassment shot though her. "I'm so sorry, but I did warn you."

He shook his head. "It was nothing."

Tara's stomach knotted. "Yes, it was. Don't lie. The chivalrous routine is totally unnecessary with me."

"I'm not being chivalrous. I'm telling the truth," he insisted, drawing her stiff body against him. "Now, it might have been a different story if you'd been wearing heels. In that case, I might need stitches." His lips twitched. "And perhaps a tetanus shot. If you hit an artery, I might need a blood transfusion. The worst case scenario is if I were to develop a septic infection and need to have the foot amputated or die," he said without a blink. "I think I'll live."

Torn between amusement and her lingering embarrassment, she stared at him for a long moment. "You have an odd sense of humor, Nicholas."

"It distracted you, though, didn't it? You're not holding up your end very well," he told her.

"My end of what? I told you I couldn't dance."

"You're supposed to look like you're enjoying yourself, Tara. Instead, you look as if I'm torturing you."

"Aren't you?" she asked, but couldn't hold back a smile.

His gaze darkened mysteriously, almost sensually, she thought, but told herself the latter was impossible.

"There's a thin line between pleasure and pain. If I were going to torture you, I'd choose a more private setting. Relax," he coaxed. "You're as stiff as a board."

She groaned and deliberately tried to soften her stance. "It's tough to relax when you're talking about pleasure and pain while a hundred people are waiting to watch me fall on my face."

"You're majoring in psychology. Use a mind trick. Pretend I'm your dream man."

Tara's mind went completely blank. "I don't think I have a dream man."

Nicholas made a tsking sound. "Sounds like a bad case of denial."

"Okay, then who is your dream woman?"

"My dream woman is one who doesn't want to marry me and who won't prevent me from pursuing my interests."

"That could be your sister," Tara said.

It was Nicholas's turn to groan. "Add passion, intelligence and great legs."

"You want a great lover," Tara clarified, feeling a mixture of relief and the faintest pinch of inadequacy. She was completely sexually inexperienced, so that put her out of the running for Nicholas's dream woman. That was good, she told herself, and thanked the heavens when the music finally stopped. She immediately pulled away, wanting to rub away his disturbing effect on her. "Duty accomplished," she said, fighting breathlessness. "We can leave now."

Two hours later, Tara was safely situated in her room with her textbook on advanced bio-psychology preparing for an all-nighter of study. Nicholas would prefer a different kind of all-nighter with his so-called dream woman, she thought. An image of heat, nakedness and need slithered through her mind, and she shook her head.

Tara forced her mind to focus on the subject at hand. Before she knew it, another two hours passed, and then there was a knock at her door. Her heart hammered in surprise. She padded toward the door and wrapped her hand around the knob. "Who is it?"

"Nicholas. With sustenance," he added. "I couldn't sleep, and I saw the light under your door when I went to the kitchen."

She opened the door, prepared to send him on his way. The tray of sandwiches, cookies and coffee he carried, however, reminded her that she'd never eaten dinner. She told herself she would eat and send him away, and she absolutely would not look at his bare chest or legs. Geez, didn't the man own a robe or something?

"Thank you," she said. "I forgot I was hungry until now."

"No problem," he said, setting the tray down on a table by the bed. "I was awake."

"Do you suffer from insomnia frequently?" she asked.

"Just when I have unsolved mysteries on my mind," he said, grabbing half a sandwich and taking a bite as he sank onto her bed.

Tara took a half sandwich for herself. "What sort of unsolved mysteries?"

He swallowed and shrugged. "How to fund the free clinics I want to start for some of the more remote areas of Marceau. I think I can recruit volunteer physicians to donate time on a monthly or bimonthly basis, but supplies and treatment will require funding. Since I'm royalty, it wouldn't look right if I got the money from the government. Plus there would be too many strings attached."

"You probably need to set up some sort of charitable foundation or find a sponsor," Tara suggested.

He nodded. "And that's not my area. Medicine is."

She took a bite and returned to her spot on the bed. "You said *mysteries*. Is there more than one?"

He nodded again, his face turning serious. "Can you keep a secret?"

"Yes. Why?"

"We don't want to get the press involved yet."

"I avoid the press."

He took another bite and swallowed it. "This is about my brother."

"Which one?"

He gave a faint smile. "Good question. My youngest brother died in a boating accident when he was three years old.''

Tara felt an instant surge of sympathy. ''That's terrible. I didn't know.''

''It's not something my family has spent a lot of time discussing. Freud would have a field day with it,'' he said wryly. ''But that's for another day. We have reason to believe that he didn't actually die in the boating accident.''

Tara did a double take. ''Why?''

''We received a letter with a lock of his hair and a button from the jacket he was wearing at the time he fell overboard. We were taking a family vacation in Bermuda. My uncle took a few of us out one afternoon on his sailboat, and a terrible storm came up out of nowhere. We couldn't get back in time and were stuck out there half the night. The boat nearly tipped over. My brother fell overboard. There were massive searches, but he was never found. It nearly destroyed my parents.''

Tara shook her head. ''What an amazing story. Do you have any idea what could have happened to him?''

''Some ideas, but nothing solid. We've got detectives on it. The DNA from the hair matches the Dumonts'.''

Tara tried to imagine losing a child, then being teased with the prospect of regaining him. ''Your mother must be…''

Nicholas nodded. ''She's putting up a good front, but she's fragile. Even when my father died, she remained strong in front of us. I saw her hands tremble once on the day we buried him. And now, there's a little desperation I see in her eyes every now and then.''

''That's why you shaved,'' she said, liking Nicholas more than ever. ''And why you're willing to play along with the idea of entertaining me as a marital prospect.''

''For the time being,'' he said, narrowing his eyes. ''It helps that you're as uninterested in getting married as I am. You sure as hell aren't high maintenance. I have to practically drag you out of your room to *entertain* you. What are you studying?'' he asked, reaching for her textbook. ''Bio-psychology. My area. I can help you study.''

''Thanks, but no thanks,'' Tara said, reaching for the book. She suspected her concentration would go straight down the toilet if he helped her.

He snatched the book to his chest and wagged his finger at her. ''One moment, *chérie*. I'm going to check your knowledge.''

Tara sighed. ''That's what the test is designed to do.''

He cracked open the book. ''What is dopamine?''

''A substance that transmits messages between nerve cells in the brain. The absence of dopamine has been associated with lack of attention issues and impulsivity.''

''Very good,'' he said. ''Dopamine also controls the secretion of growth hormone.''

''Show-off,'' she muttered.

He glanced up at her for a long moment and smiled. "No one has ever called me a show-off before this."

"They were probably afraid they would get their heads chopped off."

"And you're not?" he asked with a hint of sexual challenge in his eyes.

"No, but if it will make you feel better," she said with a mock respectful dip of her head, "show-off, Your Highness."

He chuckled, then glanced back at the book. "Hyperthyroidism," he said.

She couldn't dodge the commanding note in his voice. It was so natural, she wondered if he was aware of it. "Excessive secretion of the thyroid gland that produces accelerated metabolic rate, extreme apprehension and excitability."

"Another thyroid disorder created by underactivity of the thyroid gland is—"

"My—" Tara closed her eyes. The word was on the tip of her tongue. "Myx—"

"Close enough. Myxoedema. Patients are frequently slow and tired—"

"—and overly sensitive to cold. They exhibit a slow pulse and reflexes."

He met her gaze with a glint of respect. She felt a heady rush at his expression. For her, respect had come in small, stingy doses, and she craved more. "Next," she said, lifting her chin in challenge, sensing that generating the glint of respect in Nicholas's striking eyes could become addicting.

Nicholas continued to quiz her for the next hour and a half, and her ability to answer his onslaught built up her confidence.

"Androgens," he said with a sly sideways glance. She rolled her eyes at his choice. "Sex hormones."

"Testosterone," he prompted.

"The chemical that causes grown men to fight like little boys," she joked, punchy from the late hour and Nicholas's relentless quizzing. "You ought to know."

He set the book down. "How do you know I got into fights?"

"With all those brothers, the testosterone must've run rampant. It's a wonder you didn't kill each other. Besides, your affinity for fencing gives you away.

"Testosterone is the most potent of the naturally occurring androgens. It plays a significant role in dominance and aggression. I appreciate your tutoring," she said. "But you have been dominating my bed for the last couple of hours, and since it's after three in the morning, it's my turn to dominate my own bed."

His gaze fell over her in a wholly masculine way, and Tara had the odd sensation of how Nicholas might look at her if she were a fencing partner. Or bed partner. The notion shimmied down her nerve endings like an electrical current.

He dropped the book beside him and leaned forward. "I think it would be fascinating to watch you dominate in bed."

Alarm and forbidden excitement raced through her.

She cleared her throat and tried to clear her mind. "Not fascinating at all," she said, lifting her hand as if she were on the witness stand. "I promise it would be boring. Just me in my nightshirt under the covers, breathing evenly, getting my REM sleep, with my eyes closed. See?" she said, growing increasingly nervous with each movement as he drew closer to her. "Boring. Very boring," she said, wishing she didn't sound so breathless.

He lifted his hand to her chin and rubbed his thumb over her throat.

She swallowed at the seductive gesture. "What are you doing?" she whispered.

"Just looking," he said, his eyes a kaleidoscope of predatory sensuality.

"You're not just looking," she told him in a voice that could have used a lot more conviction. "You're touching."

"So I am," he said, sliding his thumb over her chin, then slowly across her lips. "You're not at all what I expected."

She wasn't sure if that was good or bad. She only knew her brain felt as if it were turning to sludge while he stroked her lips with his thumb. His gaze slid over her lips like a hot French kiss, then he looked into her eyes. "I think we should get engaged," he said.

Four

Tara's heart and brain felt as if they had just slammed into a brick wall. She gaped at him, searching for her breath and *his* sanity. She pulled back from his hand and glanced at him suspiciously. "Exactly how long have you been taking mind-altering medication, Your Highness?"

His lips tilted in a crooked grin and he rose from the bed. "My brain is as clear as a bell. This idea is a stroke of genius."

"Which lies very close to madness," she muttered.

"No, it's *genius*," he insisted. "If you and I become engaged, my mother will get off my back, and I can do what I want to do. Your father will stop husband-shopping for you, and you can do what *you* want to do."

Tara frowned. "Yes, but I think you're forgetting that an engagement normally precedes a wedding, and neither you nor I want to be married."

"Which is solved by an extended engagement," Nicholas said.

"An extended engagement is still followed by a wedding and a marriage," she said, rising from the bed to face him.

"Not necessarily," he said. "Engagements can be broken."

Tara blinked. "Broken," she echoed.

"Of course. After a few years, you can dump my royal ass," he said, warming to the idea as he explained it. "This would be perfect. It would take me off the marriageable bachelor market, which would get the press out of my hair. I would be able to focus on getting my clinics running without distractions."

She shook her head. "I don't think you've thought this all the way through. The engagement itself will cause a media feeding frenzy, and we would be pestered for a wedding date. We would also be forced to make public appearances. It's terrible timing for me."

Nicholas looked down into the alarmed blue-eyed gaze of the woman whom he was certain possessed the intelligence and independence to carry off the charade. "What's your alternative?"

She stared at him for a long moment and sighed. "Prospect number nine," she grumbled. "I could probably delay it with a bad cold or pneumonia. Or I could break another toe. That would be really inconvenient, though."

"An engagement *is* the answer," Nicholas assured her. "We tell my family to keep it secret for a while. Then, when it leaks to the press, we announce a wedding date two years away. When the families start to pressure, we postpone the ceremony for some to-be-determined reason. We might be able to get four or five years of freedom out of this."

"I don't know," she said, looking at him suspiciously. "What about when you meet someone you want to—" Her cheeks colored, and she broke off as if she were searching for the right words. "When you decide you need to—" She broke off again and cleared her throat.

He shook his head. "When I need to what?"

Tara exhaled in frustration, sending a strand of her bangs flying. "When your testosterone kicks in," she said, lifting her chin defiantly.

It occurred to him that in another time he could have demanded her submission in every possible way. The Dumonts weren't known for abusing their royal power, but Nicholas had an inkling that Tara York's independence could drive a man to take extraordinary measures to make her his. Not that he was driven in such a way, he told himself.

"My testosterone," he said. "You mean when I feel the need to fence or start a war for the purpose of world domination?"

She glowered at him. "You know what I mean. When you find someone you want to take as a lover."

His mind wandered, not for the first time, to the

tantalizing image of Tara in bed. Naked, passionate, giving and wanting. "What's the problem?"

"Well, if the press should learn you've taken a lover other than your fiancée, they'll be all over it."

"I can be discreet," he said. "What about you?"

Her eyes widened in surprise, as if the notion hadn't occurred to her. "Um, I—" She shook her head and ran a hand through her hair. "Taking a lover isn't really my top priority. There are other things that are much more important to me right now."

"But everyone has needs, Tara," he said.

She bit her lip and looked as if she'd rarely considered her sexual needs. Then her eyes darkened, as if with sensual secrets, arousing his curiosity. "I'll be discreet."

"Then it's settled," he said. "We're engaged."

Alarm crossed her face. "No, we're *not*. Nothing is settled. I'm not making this kind of decision in the middle of the night."

"It's a no-brainer, *chérie,*" he said, feeling oddly impatient with her reticence.

"Maybe for you," she said. "I need to sleep on this. I need to think about it."

"Why do you find me objectionable as a pretend fiancé?"

She crossed her arms over her chest. "I—I didn't say I found you objectionable. Not you personally, anyway. But I do find the idea of engagement and marriage horrifying."

"But *I* don't offend you with the way I look or act?" he probed.

"For the most part, no," she said slowly, with a great deal of wariness. "I'm sure you know you're good-looking, intelligent and charming when you want to be, Nicholas."

"Then why delay?"

"Because I want to," she said, lifting her chin again.

"That's not rational," he said.

"It's after three o'clock. A half-naked prince has just suggested I become engaged to him. I don't have to be rational."

"Would it help if I were dressed differently?"

"I don't know," she said, rubbing her forehead. "It would help if you left."

Nicholas touched the soft underside of her chin and tilted her head upward. She looked so distressed and lost that an odd tenderness immediately slid through him. He wanted to soothe away the confusion and discomfort he read on her face. He wanted her to trust him. It was a strange, overwhelming need that ate at him. In another century, he could have demanded her compliance. The notion came out of left field. He sure as hell had never considered demanding someone trust him.

"This is going to work out very well," he assured her, rubbing his thumb over her silky bottom lip. He felt a lick of arousal curl in his stomach. "In fact, it could be perfect."

"Nothing's perfect," she whispered, her eyes dark with a combination of wariness and a woman's need denied.

Her expression presented a challenge he couldn't ignore. Nicholas lowered his head. ''Have some faith, Tara. You could be surprised.''

He took her mouth with his and was surprised at the level of electricity that raced through him. Her lips were soft, warm and inviting. He rubbed his mouth against hers, absorbing every sensation…her delicious, shocked intake of breath, the hint of her sweet taste and the velvet softness of her sensitive inner lips. He couldn't resist sliding his tongue just inside her mouth and swallowing her sigh.

She instinctively curled her lips around his tongue, and he felt himself grow hard with mind-spinning speed. He pulled back and stared at her. ''This doesn't have to be all bad.''

She licked her lips, and it was all he could do not to groan. He watched her take a deep breath, as if to clear her head. She shook her head. ''This is crazy…and *you* are the devil.''

The following morning Tara couldn't bear the confinement of her lovely suite. She could hardly bear the confinement of her skin, so she took a walk around the palace grounds. She wondered if she'd dreamed Nicholas's crazy proposition. She prayed she'd dreamed his kiss, but she knew she hadn't.

She'd tossed and turned alternately dreaming of his sensual kiss and of an appalling royal wedding with her as the bride. Tara shuddered at the thought. Every time she imagined herself married, she felt trapped and suffocated. As appealing as Nicholas was, marriage to him would entail even more restrictions than marriage to the average man.

In the bright light of day, his pretend-engagement idea was insane, yet she could see a few benefits. If they could keep the engagement roller coaster from riding out of control into a full-blown marriage, it was possible that she and Nicholas might actually gain some relief from their family pressures. The idea of dealing with the press, however, turned Tara's stomach.

Voices calling in the distance interrupted her thoughts.

"Elvis! Elvis!"

Tara stared in the direction of the voices and saw Prince Michel's wife, Maggie, and son, Max, yelling. "Elvis!"

Elvis? Tara wondered if the entire family was demented. Perhaps there was something in the water?

Maggie waved toward Tara. "We're looking for Elvis," she said, rushing toward her. Max's face was full of distress.

"Elvis," Tara echoed, confused. "Elvis Presley. Isn't he…?"

"No!" Maggie said, her eyes wide with alarm. "Elvis is Max's beagle. Have you seen him?"

Tara shook her head. "No, but I've only been out here a few minutes. Can I help you look for him?"

"Please do. We'll try the pond," Maggie said. "If we don't find him soon, we'll have to enlist the help of the guards. That will get back to the queen."

"And she'll say 'I told you so,'" Max finished. "The queen doesn't like Elvis."

"I don't think she dislikes Elvis. I think his barking makes her nervous," Maggie said.

"And when he pees on the palace floor."

Maggie winced. "Yes, and when he chewed the leg of that sixteenth-century chair." She shrugged. "But puppies do these things."

Tara couldn't help smiling at the odd combination of normalcy and breech of royal protocol. "If I may ask, how did you manage to get the queen to agree to the puppy in the first place?"

"Maggie snookered him in after I memorized my speech for Citizenship Day," Max said proudly.

"Sneaked," Maggie corrected with a smile as she ruffled his cowlick. "Michel was the one who went to bat for us and stuck to his guns," she said, love for her husband glowing from her eyes. "Otherwise, we wouldn't be looking for Elvis right now. He would have been shipped back to the States."

"Elvis!" Max yelled.

Maggie winced. "The guards will be here any minute, but we can't *not* yell."

Wanting to help, Tara lifted her fingers to her lips and let out a loud whistle.

Max did a double take. "Wow."

A dog's bark sounded in the distance, and seconds later a beagle bounded out from the thickly wooded area in the distance.

"Elvis!" Max cried.

Maggie glanced at Tara and smiled. "You've saved

the day. How can we repay you? How about Nicholas on a silver platter with an apple in his mouth?'' she suggested with wicked humor in her eyes.

Tara felt a surge of heat at the mere mention of his name, and immediately shook her head. ''Oh, no. I don't—''

Maggie patted her shoulder. ''It's okay. It's common knowledge that Nicholas can be the most charming man on earth when it suits him. He can also be a major pain if he thinks that mode's in his best interest. Such as when Queen Anna gets matchmaking on the brain.''

Tara couldn't muster one appropriate word, so she moved her head in a noncommittal circle.

''Let's take Elvis back inside,'' Maggie called to Max as the little boy snapped a leash to the beagle's collar. She turned back to Tara as the three walked back toward the palace. ''I hope Nicholas hasn't been too difficult.''

''Not at all,'' Tara said, thinking ''difficult'' was far too mild a term to describe Nicholas. ''He's been a perfect host.''

Maggie looked skeptical.

Tara focused on keeping her balance on the uneven ground to keep from stumbling.

''Go ahead and take Elvis into the basement,'' Maggie told Max, slowing as they neared the palace door.

Max frowned. ''But I wanted to play with him.''

''You can in the basement,'' she said. ''I think we can all use a break from the hot sun.''

Tara glanced over at Maggie, surprised to see that the redhead's complexion had turned white as paper. Alarmed, she moved closer. "Do you need to sit down?"

Maggie gave a little shake of her head and lifted her finger to her lips in a quick secret gesture. "Make sure you give Elvis some water, Max. He's probably thirsty after his adventure. I'll join you in a few minutes, sweetie."

Max sped through the palace door, and Maggie sank to a stone bench just a few steps away. She lowered her head to her hands.

"Should I get Nicholas?" Tara asked, feeling helpless.

"Oh, no," Maggie said, shaking her head.

"Can I get you something to drink?"

Maggie shook her head again. "I just need to take a few deep breaths and cool down."

"Then we should go inside," Tara insisted, worried about the warm, sunny woman she'd so recently met.

"There will be questions and a fuss. I'm not ready for that, yet."

Tara stared down at Maggie in confusion. "Not if you come to my room."

Still pale, Maggie glanced up at her. "Good idea," she said and slowly stood. "Let's go."

It took only a couple of minutes to walk the short distance to Tara's room, but Tara broke into a cold sweat as Maggie leaned on her. She prayed she wouldn't lose her balance. When they arrived, Maggie immediately reclined on Tara's bed and closed her eyes.

"Are you sure I shouldn't get Nicholas?" Tara asked, wishing the color would return to Maggie's face.

"Very sure," she said, then sighed. "Can you keep a secret?"

Tara nodded. After all, her life was full of secrets. What was one more? "Yes," she said.

Maggie opened her eyes and smiled. "I'm pregnant," she whispered.

Even from three feet away, Tara could feel Maggie's warm joy. "How exciting. I'm sure Prince Michel is thrilled."

Maggie's smile dipped. "Well, he doesn't exactly know yet."

Tara blinked in disbelief. "He doesn't?"

Maggie's eyes darkened with a trace of guilt. "I'll tell him soon. As soon as I tell him, though, he'll monitor every move I make, every bite I eat. He's incredibly fussy about my health and safety. He gets upset when I get a splinter."

Tara felt a surprising twinge of longing to be loved so passionately, then wondered where the odd feeling had come from. "He obviously loves you very much."

"Yes, he does," Maggie said, her voice softening. "When we met, I wasn't in the market for a husband, let alone a husband who was going to be king, but he changed my mind." She glanced up at Tara. "The

Dumonts have a habit of changing other people's minds.''

Tara thought of Nicholas's ridiculous proposal and felt her stomach clench. *Not mine,* she told herself. ''Since Elvis is living at the palace, it sounds as if you've influenced things around here too.''

''A little,'' Maggie conceded. She glanced around the room, and her gaze landed on the desk. ''I see you brought your laptop. Do you work for your father?''

Tara couldn't suppress a laugh. ''Not likely. My father is very controlling, and he still views me as a ten-year-old.''

Maggie nodded understandingly and slowly sat up. ''He wants you to get married so you'll be safe and protected.''

Tara felt a knot of self-consciousness well up in her throat. ''He might as well take out a classified ad. I think everyone in the world knows that my father wants me to get married.''

Maggie's lips tilted in a wry smile. ''If it helps, you're not alone. Queen Anna wants all of her children married and producing heirs. Right now, Nicholas is numero uno on her hit list.''

A knock sounded on the bedroom door, and Tara opened it to Nicholas. Her heart jumped at the determination in his gaze. He took her hand and lifted it to his lips. ''So, *ma chérie,* have you decided to accept my proposal?''

Five

"My, oh, my. Nicholas works a lot faster than I would have imagined."

Tara heard Maggie's teasing voice over the roaring in her ears and cringed. She glared at Nicholas. "No," she said, pulling their joined hands away from his lips. "Nicholas isn't talking about that kind of proposal," she said, her eye twitching at the untruth. "He's talking about taking me on an outing. He wants to impress me with the island, so I'll encourage my father to build a resort here," she said, uncomfortably aware of the fact that she was fabricating and not doing it well. She squeezed his hand. "Right?"

He lifted an eyebrow and glanced at Maggie, then back to Tara. "Right. We're going to the Westwood Beach."

Tara tugged her hand away from his and rubbed it against her side as she turned to face Maggie. "That's right. Westwood Beach. We just need to arrange the time, and I need to make sure I have my sunscreen."

Maggie slid a skeptical glance over Nicholas. "Make sure you take plenty of sunscreen. Westwood is a topless beach."

Tara restrained herself from stepping on his foot. Instead, she worked at producing a smile. "I only brought a one-piece swimsuit with me."

"The palace has a selection of swimsuits—"

Tara tossed Nicholas a drop-dead look for his helpfulness.

He shrugged. "But you should wear whatever makes you most comfortable." He turned to Maggie. "I haven't seen you around much. You look a little pale. Everything okay?"

Annoyingly observant, Tara added to Nicholas's character description.

"I'm fine. I've just been busy with your brother and nephew," Maggie said, standing, and gazing back and forth at Nicholas and Tara. "Tara and I were just discussing what the two of you have in common."

"Oh, really. What's that?" he asked.

"Her father wants her to get married. Your mother wants you to get married."

"You left out the most important common denominator," Tara quickly added. "Neither Nicholas nor I want to get married."

Maggie nodded skeptically and walked toward the door. "Uh-huh. Well, I should get back to Max. I've enjoyed chatting with you, Tara. Don't be a stranger. It's nice having another American in the palace."

As soon as Maggie closed the door behind her, Tara rounded on Nicholas. "*Why* did you do that? Now, she's going to think something is going on between you and me, and nothing is."

"That could change." Nicholas's lips twitched. "Especially if we go to Westwood Beach."

Tara rolled her eyes. "We're not going to a nude beach," she told him.

"Westwood's only topless. If you prefer a nude beach, it's a little more of a drive, but—"

Tara wanted to scream. "I don't want to go to a nude beach! I don't want to go to any beach with you."

"Well, you have to now," Nicholas said.

"Why?"

"Because you told her we were going to the beach. We'll sit down to dinner, and Maggie will ask you how the beach was, and it will get deathly quiet while everyone waits for you to respond. If you say we didn't go, everyone will wonder why not." He inclined his head toward her. "It would have been a lot easier if you'd just told her we were getting engaged."

"Easier for whom?" Tara asked in disbelief.

"For both of us. See, if you said we're engaged, then everyone will be excited. They might ask you questions, but I could tell them you're overwhelmed with joy and they shouldn't badger you."

''How long have you been delusional?'' Tara asked dryly.

''I'm not delusional. I'm right. This is perfect.''

''But I don't want to marry you, and you don't want to marry me.''

He pointed his index finger at her. ''And that's why it's perfect. I won't get in your way. You won't get in mine.''

He made it all sound so practical, so logical, yet Tara knew the situation was fraught with complications. Plus, Nicholas made her nervous. She feared he had the ability to kiss the stuffing out of her with no emotional consequences to himself. She bit her lip. ''I just don't know you well enough to pretend to be engaged to you.''

He gave a long-suffering sigh and rubbed his hand through his hair. ''Okay. How about if I take you on a secret outing tomorrow? It will reveal more about me.''

''I'm not going to a nude beach with you.''

He chuckled. ''This isn't a nude beach. You have to wear clothes, and you have to pretend I'm not a Dumont.''

She felt intrigued, despite her reservations. ''Where would we go?''

''It's a surprise,'' he said firmly.

''I want to know,'' she returned just as firmly.

''And you will. Tomorrow.''

Tara tamped down her frustration. ''But how should I dress?''

''Casual,'' he said. ''How'd you do on your test?''

Tara blinked at the change in subject. "I haven't taken it yet."

"Why not?"

Tara resisted the urge to squirm beneath his intense gaze. *Because you rattled my brain so that I can't think straight.* "I just haven't."

"You know the material," he said, and his easy yet complete confidence in her knowledge took her breath away. No one had ever expressed such belief in her.

She couldn't speak for an entire moment. "Thank you," she finally managed.

He wrinkled his brow in confusion. "For what?"

She shrugged, not wanting to explain. "Just thank you. What time tomorrow?"

He shook his head as if he still didn't get it. "I'll never understand the way women think," he muttered. "Nine o'clock in the morning. It's a day trip. I'll ask the kitchen staff to pack a lunch for us."

Dismay shot through her. "A whole day?"

He chuckled at her lack of enthusiasm. "Be careful. Your excitement will make me think you're crazy about me."

"But the whole day," she repeated.

"Take your exam and get it out of the way," he advised her, then snagged her hand and lifted it to his lips.

Unnerved, she batted his hand aside. "You need to stop doing that."

"You need to get used to it, *ma chérie. A bientôt,*" he said.

"A bientôt," she echoed, making a face at the door. Under her breath, she muttered, *"Ma chérie*, my fanny. I am nobody's *chérie,* and least of all His Royal Sneakiness's *chérie."*

That evening at a formal family dinner, Tara endured another battery of questions from the queen. Maggie chimed in with the news that Nicholas was taking Tara to the beach. Michelina offered to take Tara swimsuit shopping.

Nicholas covered his chuckle with a cough. "Where were you thinking of taking Tara shopping?" he asked Michelina.

"I'm sure Tara would enjoy a quick trip to Paris," she said in wide-eyed innocence. "Or Beverly Hills."

Queen Anna shook her head in disapproval. "Absolutely not. We have several fine boutiques in Marceau. There's no reason to drag Miss York off the island for such a frivolous reason."

"Perhaps she would enjoy a little getaway," Michelina said, squaring off against her mother.

"Michelina, not everyone feels the necessity to escape Marceau. In fact, many people treasure the opportunity to visit our island."

Michelina lifted her chin. Nicholas could see trouble brewing with his sister. It wouldn't be long before some sort of explosion occurred between her and his mother.

"I think we should ask Tara what she thinks. After all, she is our guest," Michelina said. "Would you like a little getaway, Tara?"

Nicholas watched Tara's eyes round with dismay. It was clear that she was being placed square in the middle of a power play between the queen and Michelina. The room grew hushed with expectation. She looked from his mother to his sister and cleared her throat. "Marceau is a beautiful place, and it has so much to offer. I can see why someone would visit and never want to leave."

Her comments drew a smile of approval from the queen.

"On the other hand, it's quite natural for people who have spent their lives in one place to want to explore other places."

The queen's smile faded.

"I actually think it's a sign of good upbringing. It takes confidence to be willing to venture away from home."

Silence followed. Détente between his mother and Michelina. "Very well done," Nicholas murmured for her ears only. "Are you sure you don't have political aspirations?"

Tara gave him a sideways glance. She opened her mouth to speak, but a palace aide strode to her side. "Please forgive the interruption, Miss York, but you have a visitor in the west parlor."

Tara looked at the aide in surprise. "A visitor?"

"Yes. Mr. Richard Worthington III."

Chagrin and dismay covered her face. "Dickie?" she echoed weakly.

"Who is Dickie?" Nicholas couldn't help asking.

She met his gaze and gave a deep sigh. "Number seven," she whispered.

"I thought you were done with number seven."

"I thought I was too. He was especially persistent."

"What shall I tell Mr. Worthington?" the aide asked.

"Tell him to take a slow boat to Alaska," Nicholas suggested.

"No," she said, biting her lip. "He's traveled very far. The least I can do is see him. Tell him I'll be out in a few minutes." She turned to the rest of the dinner party. "Thank you for the lovely meal and company. Please excuse me. I need to leave."

No excuses. Just *I need to leave.* Nicholas admired her style. He watched her rise from her chair and immediately decided to join her. "Same with me," he said. "Thanks, I need to go."

Queen Anna arched an eyebrow. "Why?"

"Because my guest is leaving," he said. "Good night."

As soon as the two of them left the formal dining room, Tara turned to him. "You didn't need to come."

"I want to size up my competition," he said, tongue-in-cheek.

Tara rolled her eyes and groaned. "If my father were broke, this wouldn't be happening."

"But he's not, and it is," Nicholas reminded her cheerfully. "I've been dealing with the same kind of thing my entire life. No use whining."

"I wasn't whining," she said.

"No?"

"I was complaining."

His lips twitched. "Thanks for making that distinction."

She nodded and adjusted her thick glasses. "Do I look homely enough to discourage Dickie?"

Although her glasses annoyed the hell out of him, her hair was twisted in some kind of unattractive bun and her shapeless brown dress hid her curves, Nicholas couldn't forget what was behind her disguise. The eyes behind those glasses glinted with humor, intelligence and feminine secrets. When she wore her hair down, it begged for a man's touch. And her body could drive a man to distraction.

"Depends how astute he is," he finally said.

"What do you mean?"

"I mean you can put Godiva chocolates in a plain box, but when you take a bite, there's no hiding the fact that the chocolate's Godiva."

Tara frowned. "He's not getting close enough to take a bite out of me. Let's go and get this over with," she said, and they walked the short distance to the west parlor.

As soon as Tara entered the room, Dickie sprang from his seat on the couch and rushed toward her. Tara drew back, but Dickie didn't seem to notice as he enveloped her in an embrace. Nicholas didn't have experience assessing other men's appeal, but he suspected his sister might describe Dickie as a hunk.

Number seven was tall and muscular, with a handsome, if desperate, face.

"Oh, Tara, I've missed you terribly. I can't believe I let you get away."

"Your company's merger with one of my father's companies fell through."

Dickie's face fell and he drew back slightly. "Yes, but—"

Tara took advantage of the moment and took a giant step away from him. "I'm sorry. I did mention it to my father, but I've never had a great deal of influence with him when it comes to business," Tara said. "Please allow me to introduce His Highness, Nicholas Dumont."

Dickie reluctantly transferred his attention to Nicholas. He nodded. "Your Highness. Your country is lovely."

"Yes, it is. As is Tara," he said, sliding his arm around Tara's waist, ignoring her start of surprise. "She and I have become very close during her visit here."

Dickie narrowed his eyes. "I can understand that, she's easy to fall for. But Tara and I share a special history," he said with forced affection.

"Really?"

"We attended kindergarten together," Tara said, subtly trying to wiggle out of Nicholas's arm.

"How sweet," Nicholas said. "But as you can see, she's all grown-up now."

Dickie frowned. "Yes, and Tara and I have an understanding between ourselves."

"Really?" Nicholas repeated, his voice full of deliberate skepticism.

"Yes," Dickie said with challenge in his eyes. He nodded toward Tara. "Tell him about us, Tara."

"Tell him what?" she asked.

Dickie looked at her in surprise. "I know you haven't forgotten that I told you of my intention to marry you."

Nicholas heard the sound of footsteps entering the parlor.

"Hello," Maggie called. "I understand we have another Yank in the palace. Michel and I thought we'd pop in."

Nicholas glanced over his shoulder and saw curiosity on Maggie's face. His brother Michel looked as if he'd been dragged along. "Your Highness," he said to Michel.

Michel lifted a brow at Nicholas's formality.

"This is my brother, His Highness, Michel Dumont, heir to the throne, and his wife, Princess Maggie," Nicholas announced, and mentally added trumpets in the background. "Your Highness, this is one of Tara's friends from America, Dickie."

Dickie stretched his neck against his collar in discomfort, then gave a nod of respect. "Your Highnesses," he mumbled.

"It's a pleasure to meet one of Tara's friends," Maggie said.

Dickie nodded again. "Thank you," he said, then turned back to Nicholas and Tara. "As I was saying, Tara and I have an understanding."

"Strange," Nicholas said, tightening his arm slightly as he heard more footsteps enter the room. "Tara and I have more than an understanding."

She shot him a look of wary dismay.

"We're engaged to be married," Nicholas said.

Tara's gasp was overshadowed by the collective gasps of the other occupants of the room.

"That's incredible," he heard his sister, Michelina, say from behind him.

"God has answered my prayers," Queen Anna crowed.

Tara stared at Nicholas with a mixture of horror and anger.

Red with indignation, Dickie stretched his neck against his collar again. "Well, Tara, is this true?" he demanded in an injured voice that Nicholas hoped Tara wouldn't fall for. "I thought you and I had shared something special. Do you want this prince you've just met, or do you want me, a man you knew even when you were a child?"

Tara bit her lip, her gaze moving between Dickie and Nicholas as if she were trying to choose between two forms of torture. She looked as if she wanted to punch Nicholas.

Her moment of indecision stretched, and Nicholas began to sweat. That was strange, he thought. He and Tara would have a mutually beneficial arrangement, and he would love to take her to bed, but he wasn't capable of anything involving his emotions at the moment.

She gave a heavy sigh, still looking as if she were

choosing between two devils. ''Nicholas was correct. He and I are engaged.''

Nicholas felt a rush of victory with a tinge of primitive possessiveness he would examine later. Following instinct, he pulled her into his arms and took her mouth with his. He swallowed her gasp of surprise and lingered over her soft lips. He felt her clutch his arms as if she weren't sure whether to push him away or hang on for dear life.

''You've made me a happy man,'' he said, and saw the dual meaning registered in her eyes. He could tell she knew he was saying the words for the benefit of their audience. At the same time, he was delighted to get his mother off his back, even if only temporarily. He and Tara shared a secret, and it wrapped around them like a silken rope, binding them together.

She leaned closer as if to tuck her head into his shoulder for protection. ''If this turns out badly,'' she said in a sexy, intimate whisper, ''I will make your life a living hell.''

Six

"**A**nother wedding," Michelina said, sliding her hands together in delight.

Tara stiffened and looked at Nicholas's beautiful sister. She could see endless shopping and whirlwind makeover written all over Michelina's face.

"I'm so pleased, Nicholas," Queen Anna said, moving toward Nicholas and embracing him.

Tara blinked. It was the first time she'd seen Queen Anna give anyone a hug. Her uneasiness escalated to pure panic. Queen Anna must really want her son married off.

Tara cleared her throat and caught Nicholas's gaze with a sharp glare. She noticed that Dickie must have slid out of the room during Nicholas's mind-robbing kiss.

"We don't want to move too fast," he said, giving his mother a quick hug. "Tara is overwhelmed, and I promised her I would give her time to adjust to Marceau and my life before rushing into a wedding."

Michelina's face fell. The queen's followed. "How much adjustment time before you plan to set a date?" Queen Anna Catherine demanded.

"At least six months," he said, holding up his hand before she could protest. "And we plan to hold off telling the press."

"But why on earth would you wait that long before you set a date?" the queen asked.

"A spring wedding would be perfect," Michelina added. "I could escort her back to America."

Spring! Tara's stomach turned.

"Absolutely not. I won't allow you to rush Tara. It's not fair to expect her to adapt to us and everything that comes with us so quickly," he told them, talking over their protests as he pulled Tara against him. "I refuse to jeopardize this marriage for the sake of speed."

The queen immediately turned silent. She gave a quick regal sigh of discontent, but inclined her head. "As you wish." She turned to Tara and took her hand. "Welcome to our family," she said gravely.

Guilt wiggled through her like a poisonous snake. Tara swallowed the bitter taste in her mouth. "Thank you, Your Majesty."

Michelina stepped forward and hugged her. "Welcome to the Dumonts. You will be my new sister."

More guilt. Tara forced herself to smile. "You're so kind."

Maggie pushed forward and hugged Nicholas first, then Tara. "You almost had me fooled this morning," she scolded playfully. "If you need an American ear for anything, you always have mine."

Then Michel welcomed her into the family with equal warmth, and Tara had to bite her tongue to keep from saying, *Just kidding. Hell will freeze over before Nicholas and I get married.*

Nicholas must have sensed that she was on the edge. "This is nice, but I'd like a few moments alone with my fiancée. I'm taking her for a walk in the garden," he said, reaching for her hand and leading her down the marble hallway. He swept her out a side door into the moonlit night, and Tara gulped deep breaths of the tropical air.

"I already don't like this," she told him. "You shouldn't have forced the proposal."

"I got rid of number seven, didn't I?" he returned with a trace of smugness.

She waved her hand. "Dickie was just desperate because my father didn't come through on the merger."

Nicholas shot her a look of doubt. "The man traveled around the world to get to you."

"To try to get to my father," Tara corrected.

"I don't think so. I think he wanted you."

Tara gaped at him. "You're insane. Totally insane. Is that the reason you pushed the engagement? Because you actually thought Dickie was operating under some misguided passion for me? You must have forgotten that I wrote the book on being resistible.''

"In light of the fact that *Dickie* traveled around the world to see you, you might need to do some revisions on your book,'' he said, loosening his tie and pacing along the garden path. "If he's known you since you were in kindergarten, then he probably knows you have killer legs under those ugly dresses and that your eyes talk when you don't. If he has a millimeter of testosterone, he's curious what you would be like in bed.''

Tara's head began to spin. "Dickie probably doesn't even know what color my eyes are. He kissed me one time, and I made sure it was boring.''

Nicholas wheeled around and faced her with a dangerous glint in his gaze. "Well, I know your eyes are blue, and your mouth is anything but boring.''

Tara's heart stopped. A trickle of sexual excitement burned through her, quickly followed by confusion. "This is weird. We aren't supposed to be attracted to each other, remember?''

Shaking his head, he walked toward her. "I never said I wasn't attracted to you.''

Tara's breath hitched as he loomed over her. "But we don't want to get married.''

"Exactly,'' he said. "That's part of the attraction.''

She blinked, the meaning of his words slogging through her brain at the speed of snails.

As if sensing her confusion, he elaborated. "You don't want to tell me what to do. I don't want to tell you what to do. Neither of us wants the ties that bind, but that doesn't mean I wouldn't mind having you in my bed.''

The following morning, Tara checked the results of her exam. Ninety-eight percent. Relief and exhilaration filled her chest to bursting. It was just a number, but it gave Tara hope. Hope that she wasn't nearly as useless as she'd feared. Hope that she could live on her own and find a way to contribute to the world. She still wasn't exactly sure how she could do that. She knew she just wanted to, badly.

And she would, she told herself with grim determination. She heard a knock at the door and her heart skipped. *For no good reason.* Nicholas. The man was full of contradictions. It had taken her half the night to settle down after he'd told her he wanted her in bed. Her stomach fluttered at the thought. She brushed her hand over her forehead and took a mind-clearing breath.

An outing with Nicholas. ''Heaven help me,'' she muttered at the sound of a second knock.

She turned off her computer and slowly walked toward the door. Tara wondered why she had a strange sense of foreboding about this outing. ''Lack of sleep,'' she said and opened the door.

Nicholas stood before her wearing a cap pulled low over his forehead, a pair of sunglasses, a casual white cotton shirt and a pair of casual slacks and tennis shoes.

No royal paraphernalia in sight. On closer inspection, she saw a stethoscope sticking out of his pants pocket.

She met his gaze. "So you're going to play doctor today?"

He gave a slight cringe. "You'll see soon enough. Fred will drive us, and we'll be riding on some dirt roads. You sure you don't get motion sickness?"

"I don't ride roller coasters, but I don't get motion sickness from a car ride," she said, growing curious despite her wariness about him.

He lifted an eyebrow above the sunglasses and nodded. "Then let's go," he said, and took her by the hand.

Ninety minutes later, as Fred drove the Jeep up a steep, narrow road, Tara bent forward to grab the purse she'd dropped on the vehicle's floor and felt her equilibrium spin. A kaleidoscope of colors and textures swam before her eyes. Green trees and splashes of pink flowers ran together. She sighed, wishing the dizzy feeling would go away. Forever.

They finally drew to a stop in front of an old wooden one-story building where a line of people wound down the street. "This would be easier if you stayed in the car, Fred," Nicholas said. "You just don't look geeky enough to be a med student."

Tara glanced at the huge, muscular bodyguard. He looked exactly like what he was—professional security.

"I can sit in the corner of the room and I'll be as quiet as a mouse," Fred said. "But I go where you go."

Nicholas sighed. "Okay, go do your security thing while Tara and I wait."

Fred nodded, and left the vehicle. Tara met Nicholas's gaze. "Will the other medical personnel in the clinic know your true identity?"

Nicholas nodded. "It's a two-edged sword. If doctors know I'm willing to donate my time, then they're more willing to donate theirs. I'm generally assigned young children or the elderly, because the youngsters don't recognize me and the elderly want to be heard and treated. They're not so picky about the doctor who treats them as long as he shows respect and listens."

"Why do you do this? Wouldn't it be easier to take a medical consultant job with the government?"

"You sound like my brother, Michel. He's committed to the government. I'm committed to the patient." He glanced out the window. "There's Fred. If anyone asks, you're a medical records assistant."

"What shall I call you?"

He cracked a grin that made her heart stutter. "Doctor," he said. "Doctor Do."

Fred opened the car door and the three of them walked into the small building temporarily operating as a community clinic. A nurse was waiting for Nicholas as soon as he walked past the cramped receiving area full of patients waiting to be seen. The nurse offered him a file and appeared to fight the urge to curtsey. "Dr. Do-Your-High—"

Nicholas shook his head. "Dr. Do," he said firmly.

She nodded. "Three-year-old in number two, Doctor,'' she said, nodding toward the area divided by curtains. ''Fever and runny nose.''

Nicholas pulled off his sunglasses and motioned for Tara to follow. As she hurried after him, she couldn't help noticing the sense of purpose amidst the flurry of activity. She tripped over the uneven entrance into the partitioned area and barely managed to catch herself. Nicholas whipped around to steady her, his gaze meeting hers. ''Okay?'' he said, and his intensity made her feel as if the room was turning.

She nodded and carefully backed away. ''Okay.'' She glanced at the small child sitting on his mother's lap. ''Customer's waiting,'' she whispered.

For the next few minutes, she watched him perform a routine evaluation. Nicholas checked the child's pulse and throat, then listened to his chest and heart. Tara, however, caught the not-so-routine things Nicholas did that put the little boy at ease. She noticed that he talked to the child in a low, comforting voice and that his hands were gentle, yet firm.

It was clear that Nicholas was meant to be a physician. More than ever, she understood his single-minded intensity about his profession. Even in this brief instance with the three-year-old with an earache, Nicholas was making a difference, and she instinctively knew he was destined to make a huge difference in the lives of the people of Marceau. Watching him affected her in a strange way. She felt an odd, tight sensation in her chest and stomach.

Nicholas allowed the little boy to hold his stethoscope while he checked his ears. The little tike started to wail when Nicholas moved the tool for better viewing.

Nicholas nodded in sympathy. "You answered my question, big guy. Red and inflamed. All kinds of fluid in there." He wrote a prescription and passed it to Tara. "Get the people at the desk to fill this, along with providing some vitamins, while I talk to big guy's mom about his vaccinations."

It was a simple assignment. A child could have performed it, but Tara felt something she'd rarely felt during her entire life. Useful.

After that, she didn't seem to have time to stop. She was either collecting patient histories, fetching medication or vitamins or watching Nicholas as he examined patients and diagnosed illnesses.

At the end of the day nearly all of the other personnel had left when an elderly woman suffering from heat exhaustion was brought in. Delirious and pale, she batted away all attempts to give her water to drink or an IV, as she insisted she needed to find her children. Since any children she had would be middle-aged by now, she was clearly delusional. No one knew her name, her clothes were soiled and she looked as if she'd been wandering around for days. The woman wouldn't even allow Nicholas to examine her.

"We'll need to restrain her if she doesn't cooperate," Nicholas said.

The remaining lab technician and receptionist nodded in agreement. Fred stepped forward.

"Can I try to persuade her?" Tara asked impulsively, moved by the fear in the woman's eyes.

Nicholas glanced at her in surprise. "Okay, but we need to get some liquids into her immediately."

"Okay," Tara said, and filled three glasses with water, then closed the curtains in the room where the woman was pacing. Having reduced the light and insulated the patient from distraction, Tara sat down and took a sip from one of the glasses of water. "How many children do you have?" she addressed the woman.

The woman looked at Tara and frowned for a long moment. "Four," she said. "They're waiting at home for me to fix their dinner."

Tara nodded and patted the chair beside her. "You should leave soon, but it's very hot outside, isn't it? If you drink some water, maybe you won't get so hot when you go home."

The woman frowned at her again, but slowly sank into the chair beside her. Tara drew in a half breath of relief. One step at a time. She took another sip of water and offered one of the glasses to the woman.

"Do you have boys or girls?" Tara asked.

The woman took a drink of water. "Two boys, two girls. They keep me very busy."

Tara smiled and lifted her glass to her lips again. "I'm sure they do. If you're not feeding them or bathing them, I bet you're entertaining them."

"All the time," the woman said, taking several swallows of her own water. "My Henri can't stay out of the dirt."

Tara continued to talk and the woman continued to drink the water. As if her frantic energy drained from her, the woman grew drowsy. "I feel very tired."

"You look like you don't feel very well. Would you let the doctor examine you?" Tara asked.

The woman nodded and closed her eyes.

Nicholas immediately went to her side and took her pulse. In the course of listening to her heart, he lifted a necklace from beneath her blouse with a health alert medallion.

"Diabetes," he said. "Tell the med tech I need insulin and a saline IV."

Nicholas worked on the woman for several hours, stabilizing her until they could move her to the nearest residential clinic one hour away. The glazed look in the woman's eyes faded, and she was finally able to recall her name. Her frantic relatives were contacted and planned to visit her early the following morning.

Leaving the residential clinic, Tara didn't know what time it was as she stumbled over a stone and pitched forward to her knees. Pain shot through her. Gasping for breath, she felt Nicholas's arm wrap around her waist and pull her upright against him.

"Okay?" he asked, his deep voice sending a shiver down the back of her neck.

Tara tried to squeeze a smidgen of oxygen into her deprived lungs and brain. She nodded, drowning in a combination of embarrassment and hyperawareness of Nicholas's hard body at her back.

"Are you sure?" he asked, turning her in his arms. "Are you breathing yet?"

I would if you would stop touching me, she thought. Tara deliberately inhaled a deep breath of air. "Breathing," she said with a nervous smile. "See? I'm fine. The ground moved when I wasn't looking."

He frowned and glanced down at her legs. "Any scrapes?"

"I'm fine. Just tired and a little embarrassed," she insisted. "Could we please go back to the palace now?"

He glanced at his watch and nodded. "Of course. The queen will have my head for keeping you out so late. And if she knew I'd put you to work in a free health clinic—" He broke off and shook his head.

"I liked it," Tara said, still integrating everything she'd experienced today. She felt bone-tired but satisfied. In fact, she couldn't remember feeling this satisfied in her life. "Do you go every day?" she asked as Fred held open the door to the Jeep.

Before replying Nicholas murmured a thanks to the bodyguard, then climbed in beside Tara. Fred drove the vehicle down the winding mountain road. "Not every day. I have state and family functions I'm required to attend. I'd love to have my own practice, but this is the next best thing. The more often I work at the free clinics, the more effective I am when I ask other physicians to donate some of their time. Someday I may accept a more official position with the government, but I'll always want to practice medicine with actual patients."

"And you should," she said, remembering how effective and caring he'd been with his patients in the clinic today.

Curiosity flashed across his face. "I should what?"

Tara heard just a tinge of the royal surprise in his voice that she would dare tell him he "should" do anything. She smiled. "You should always practice medicine directly with people because you're very good."

He looked at her for a long moment, then gave a short, humorless chuckle. "I haven't heard that from anyone in my family."

"They obviously haven't seen you in action."

Pleasure crossed his face, and he held her gaze. "Speaking of action…how did you know what to do with Celia?"

Celia was the mother of four who'd been suffering from dehydration. Tara shook her head and shrugged. "Lucky guess. Instinct. Believe me, it was nothing I'd read. I just thought maybe we'd make a little more progress if we stopped fighting her and went along with her instead. She was so concerned about her children. I thought maybe if she talked about them, she might unwind a little bit."

He lifted his hand to push back a strand of her hair. "And you were right," he said, studying her as if she were a surprise to him. "You didn't complain about helping, either."

"It was fun," she told him, trying to remain unaffected by the sensual sensation of his fingers in her hair. "I'd like to go again sometime."

"Really?" he asked, his eyes widening in surprise.

"Really," she said.

"That could be arranged."

"I'd like that."

"In the meantime, we're stopping for a swim. Fred," he said to the driver, "pull over at Augustus Beach."

"A swim?" Alarm kicked through Tara. "But it's midnight."

He shrugged. "Not a problem. This is a private beach for the family."

"But I didn't bring a suit."

Nicholas chuckled, and Tara saw a dangerously devilish glint in his eyes. "Neither did I."

Seven

Nicholas ducked his head under the cool ocean water to bring down his body temperature. Sitting close to Tara in the Jeep with no distractions aroused a mother lode of carnal instincts. He couldn't explain it. He didn't know if it was the look in her eyes or the way she bit her lip or her sweet and spicy scent. All he knew was that during the drive he was thinking about talking her out of her clothes and ravaging her.

She would be appalled if she knew he was fixated on the idea of sliding between her silky white thighs and pushing himself inside her until they both exploded.

Nicholas swallowed a groan and dunked himself under the water once more. He couldn't stay under too long, because he knew he was being watched by

Fred. Fred knew the queen was twitchy on the subject of swimming. It all went back to when Nicholas's youngest brother fell overboard all those years ago. If Queen Anna had her way, none of her children or grandchildren would ever go swimming.

Nicholas had long ago chafed at his mother's restraints, and his bodyguards had learned to watch without interfering. Nicholas glanced at the shore and a full moon illuminated Tara's profile along the shore.

He grinned to himself. She was curious, though she'd sworn she wouldn't leave the car, let alone get in the ocean with him.

"Come on in. The water's great," he coaxed, despite the fact that the water temperature was a little on the chilly side.

"It looks cold," she called back.

"It's great! I wouldn't have taken you for a water wuss," he yelled, deliberately goading her.

Even with the short distance between them, he saw her chin snap up. "I'm not," she retorted.

"Prove it."

"I don't have to prove anything to you."

True, he thought, and decided to move to shore.

He watched her kick off her shoes, and he stopped in midstroke. She began to unbutton her shirt, and his heart stood still.

"Turn around!" she yelled at him.

It cost him dearly, but he yielded, turning toward the dark horizon. He knew the minute she hit the water from her yelp of accusation.

"You lied. It's freezing!"

"Invigorating," he corrected with a chuckle. He stole a glimpse over his shoulder, but to his frustration she was already covered by the water.

"Cold," she said, swimming toward him.

Treading water, Nicholas turned around to face her. "You must admit it feels good after such a long day at the clinic."

"Bracing," she conceded, swimming beside him. "But more than few minutes in here and you'll have to treat me for hypothermia."

He reached for her hand and tugged. "Shared body heat is an excellent prevention against hypothermia."

"So is staying out of cold water," she shot back, reluctantly allowing him to draw her against him.

He felt the brush of her tight nipples against his chest and her bare belly against his. Her thighs brushed his, and the carnal thoughts he'd held back ran through his brain like wildfire. Tara's hair was slicked back and the apples of her cheeks were dotted with drops of water.

"You look like a mermaid," he said.

"I can't look like a mermaid," she replied, her gaze intently curious, but wary. "No fins."

"Your face, your hair, your eyes. You look like a siren from the sea."

She leaned closer and bit her lip, driving him a little crazy with the gesture. "Do you always say wacky things when you've worked a long day?" she whispered.

Nicholas grinned. "No. Just when I've worked a long day with a mermaid. Quit biting your lip."

She frowned, her breasts brushing against him in tantalizing torture once again. "Why?"

"So I can kiss you," he said, and lowered his head as her eyes widened. Her lips were soft and tasted faintly salty from the water. He rubbed his mouth over all of hers, sucking on her lips, rubbing his tongue over the seam. She opened her mouth ever so slightly in invitation, and he plunged inside to where she was warm, wet and welcoming. Even with the cool water surrounding him, he felt himself grow warm. And when her tongue twined with his, he felt himself grow hard under the water.

Nicholas felt the raging, ripping desire to consume her totally, starting with her lips and stopping with her... Hell, and not stopping.

He slid his hands over her back, pressing her bare breasts against his chest. Good, but he wanted more. He slid one hand down to her buttocks to wind her legs around him. The slim barrier of cotton she wore made him groan. "I want you naked," he muttered against her mouth.

Clinging to his shoulders, she pulled back slightly and looked at him with eyes full of arousal and confusion. "Things are moving too fast. What are we doing? I thought we were just supposed to be pretending to be engaged."

"We are," he assured her. "I told you that doesn't mean I don't want you."

She shook her head. "You could have anybody. Why me? Because I'm safe? Or because I'm convenient?"

Nicholas hadn't thought more deeply about this than appeasing the need she stirred in him so easily. He hadn't wanted to think any more deeply, but she was forcing him to. "The words 'safe' or 'convenient' don't come to mind," he said, and pulled her against him again. "I want you because you see me as a man. I want the honesty I see in your eyes. I want the passion underneath your skin. I can feel it." He slid his hand over her breast and toyed with her nipple.

She gasped, and he took her mouth again. This time, she opened quickly, matching the strokes of his tongue with her own. He squeezed her bottom and she undulated against him. If not for the scrap of cotton between them, he could be inside her. The thought nearly drove him mad.

He felt her start to shiver and realized the cold was getting to her. He lingered over her lips, then carried her toward the beach. Her wet, nearly naked body slid down his as she stood in front of him. Her breasts still pressed against him, taunting him.

"This feels more than a little crazy to me," she whispered.

"It will keep feeling crazy until we do something about it," he told her.

Her eyes darkened. "I'm not sure that what you have in mind is really a solution."

"Do you have an alternative suggestion?" he challenged.

"I don't know," she said, and with a deep breath pulled away from him. She'd better come up with something and soon, because she felt he was pulling her into a vast, sensual vortex…and part of her was eager to be drawn in even farther.

Tara's sleep was filled with disturbing, tantalizing images of Nicholas kissing her, making love to her. Bowing to her weariness, she slept late the following morning. A knock on the door woke her, and she jerked upward. Big mistake. The room felt as if it turned. Tara automatically tilted her head to one side and counted.

Nicholas burst through the door with a breakfast tray in his hands. "Good morning, sleepyhead. Did I wake you?"

Tara continued to count.

He frowned when she didn't respond. He set the tray down on her bedside table and bent over her. "What's wrong?"

"Just waiting for the room to" —she blinked and slowly met his gaze— "stop moving. It did. And yes, you woke me, but breakfast looks good." She eased into a sitting position.

Nicholas reached out and cradled her head in his hands. Her heart raced until she saw that he was gazing at her with a look of professional scrutiny in his eyes. "How often do you experience vertigo?" he asked.

"I don't know. I haven't paid that much attention. Sometimes I go for months without the dizziness. Then it seems like I get hit with it every other day." She shrugged. "I'm sure it's nothing serious. Just a little equilibrium problem I've had since I was eleven.''

"Do you notice if it's brought on by sudden movements?"

Tara thought about the times she had lost her balance. "Maybe. I haven't paid that much attention to how I feel before I fall, because I'm usually spending more energy putting on Band-Aids afterward," she said wryly. "Why do you ask?"

"Because I'm taking you to visit a friend of mine," Nicholas said, still studying her eyes.

"When and where?" she asked, plucking his fingers from her head. Nicholas might be able to endure such close proximity to her without becoming rattled, but she couldn't say the same. She reached for a croissant from the breakfast tray and took a bite.

"Today. Paris."

Tara nearly choked on her roll. "Paris? Why?"

"He's a medical specialist. I want him to examine you."

Tara felt an odd mixture of hope and fear. Although her clumsiness had been the bane of her existence, she'd always assumed her problem was just that—terminal but simple clumsiness. What if there was a medical reason for her lack of coordination? What if it could be fixed? "Do you really think there's something wrong with me? Something medical?"

"Maybe. There are a lot of things you don't do because you don't want to fall. I think you owe it to yourself to find out."

Excitement rushed through her, and she threw back the covers of her bed. "When can we go?"

Nicholas chuckled. "I think you might want to get dressed."

Just two hours later, the royal jet carrying Nicholas and Tara landed in Paris, and they were whisked into a limousine which carried them through the busy streets to an office on the West Bank where Nicholas's associate, Dr. Antoine Bordeau, greeted both of them. Tara filled out an extensive questionnaire, then answered even more questions from the kindly but persistent Dr. Bordeau. After a thorough physical examination and lab work, he shook his head and muttered to himself in French.

"Tell me it's nothing serious," Tara said, curious to know if the doctor had learned anything or if the trip had been a wild-goose chase.

Dr. Bordeau smiled and shook his head. "'Serious' is a relative term. I believe your vertigo may be related to an inner ear problem."

"But don't people with inner ear problems usually get nauseous?"

"Often, but not always. I think you have learned to compensate for this problem over the years. Crystals form, and if they are displaced in the semicircular balance canals, they can stimulate the balance nerve inappropriately. From my examination, I believe it is your right ear. And you said you tend to fall toward your right? Yes?"

"Yes," she murmured, not knowing whether to be

relieved or dismayed that there was a physical reason for her lack of coordination.

"This is a very satisfying kind of condition to treat because the treatment is a repositioning procedure and it's ninety-five percent effective."

"You mean I might not be a klutz anymore after today?" she asked, amazed at the prospect.

"Let's see what happens," he said.

Forty-five minutes later, Tara walked out of the doctor's office with follow-up instructions for the next forty-eight hours. "That was too easy," Tara said, almost afraid to hope Dr. Bordeau had been right. "Too easy."

"Just follow Dr. Bordeau's instructions, and you should notice a difference pretty soon," Nicholas said.

"But why didn't my doctor back in the States catch this?" asked Tara, confused and a little angry, as Nicholas escorted her to the limo.

"I think it's like you said. Your doctor was usually focused on trying to repair the damage caused by the vertigo, and you're not much of a complainer."

She shot him a dark look. "Are you saying I should have been more of a whiner?"

Nicholas paused, then nodded. "Yes. If something was bothering you, if you felt dizzy, then you should have told someone."

"My father was already so disappointed in me, I didn't want to emphasize my shortcomings any more by complaining. I know he would have much preferred having a boy instead of a girl, especially after my mother died when I was seven." Tara felt a slice of pain mingled with embarrassment at what she'd revealed. She'd always known she didn't measure up to what her father had expected from her.

Nicholas gently tapped his finger on her nose. "You've gotten awfully quiet. What's the American expression? A penny for your thoughts?"

She gave a sad smile. "I think this is one of those times when I could pay a professional a lot of pennies to talk about my thoughts. I could hold a pity party about how much I wanted to please my father but couldn't. I was raised in luxury and given a fine private school education. I've never been hungry except by choice, and I have received material gifts other people could only dream of. I would be an ungrateful wretch to complain."

Nicholas looked into Tara's eyes and caught a glimpse of something rarer than diamonds—a pure heart. He took her hand. He understood exactly what Tara was saying because he too had been provided with every possible material gift. Unlike Tara, however, Nicholas had also been given the gift of family, and from his brother Michel, he'd received unwavering belief and support. If ever anyone deserved the same, it was Tara. He took her small hands in his. It bothered the hell out of him that she had missed so much, that she had hurt so much. "You're an interesting woman. You remind me of everything good I want to be."

She shook her head, and her eyes grew shiny with unshed tears. "I can't imagine how I do that, but if

Dr. Bordeau's treatment works, my life will be totally changed. And it will be because of you.''

Nicholas got a kick out of the expectant joy in her eyes. ''After your forty-eight hours is up, what's the first thing you want to do?''

Her eyes widened. ''Oh, ten things all at once. Dance, run, skip.'' Her face lit up like a Christmas tree. ''Drive a car.''

For Tara, the forty-eight hours passed at an excruciatingly slow pace. She followed Dr. Bordeau's instructions to the letter, and urged Nicholas to go visit the clinics. She slept upright and avoided any quick jarring movements. Five minutes before the end of her vigil, a knock sounded on her door.

Certain it was Nicholas, she opened the door. ''I have five more minutes,'' she said, and laughed nervously. She was so relieved to see him her hands trembled. She laced them together.

''Let's check for nystagmus,'' Nicholas said, and she would swear he was almost as eager as she was.

''What's that?'' she asked.

''Involuntary eye movements triggered by inner ear stimulation,'' he said, and performed a short examination similar to one Dr. Bordeau had performed.

He finished and met her gaze. ''Put on your dancing shoes. I'll pick you up at eight o'clock tonight.''

He gave her a quick kiss, then left her staring after him. It took a full moment before Tara realized the procedure had worked. She let out a whoop of joy and pinched herself. Her mind reeled with possibilities. Independence was possible for her now. Indeed, it was so close, she could practically taste it.

Moments later, another knock sounded on her door. Tara opened it to find Maggie staring at her with a worried but expectant expression. "Is everything okay?"

Michel's wife must have heard her shriek of joy. Barely able to contain her happiness, Tara bounced on her toes. "Everything is more than wonderful. I'm not going to be a klutz anymore! I've been cured."

Maggie's brow wrinkled in confusion. "Cured?" she echoed.

Tara told Maggie the long, somewhat sad story about her lack of coordination and vertigo and how Nicholas had taken her to Dr. Bordeau.

Maggie's eyes gleamed with approval. "What a story. So Nicholas is taking you dancing tonight. What are you going to wear?"

Tara thought about her wardrobe, and some of the air went out of her balloon. She made a face and looked into the closet. "Oh, good point. I only brought uglywear." She glanced at the clock. "Do you think some shops might still be open?"

Maggie nodded. "Yes, but this isn't my area of expertise."

"Michelina? Do you really think she'd want to go shopping with me?"

Maggie rolled her eyes. "Do fish swim?"

Within no time, Michelina made arrangements with four dress shops and two shoe stores, and she and

Tara were riding toward town in the armored Mercedes.

"The armor is overkill, but Mother won't allow me out without it," Michelina said with a long-suffering expression.

"Only daughter," Tara said. "You must be so important to her."

"She's protecting her investment. She's hoping I'll draw in a marriage partner who will do great things for Marceau."

"Surely there's more to it than that," Tara said. "I'm sure royal duty is always a given, and I know I'm an outsider looking in, but it appears that Queen Anna is very proud and protective of all of you."

"Yes," Michelina admitted. "But she's way too protective. You probably wouldn't understand, since you're planning to marry my brother, but I want nothing more than to be independent."

Tara felt a slice of guilt at her deception. She bit her lip. "I understand wanting to make your own decisions, wanting to find your own way instead of following someone else's direction," she said quietly.

Michelina tilted her well-coifed head, giving Tara an assessing glance. "My brother Nicholas has always had a talent for looking beneath the surface. From the beginning, Tara, he said there was more to you than what met the eye. You're different from the usual woman my mother parades in front of him." She smiled. "You must be very special for him to be so determined to marry you."

It was all Tara could do not to correct Michelina.

All she could do to keep from saying that what she and Nicholas shared was a deep, passionate desire *not* to get married. She opened her mouth, then closed it. "You're definitely right about me being different from his other marital prospects," she said as the limo drew to a stop in front of a boutique. "I bet I win the award for the ugliest clothing."

Michelina's eyes widened as if she were surprised that Tara was aware of how unattractive her clothes were. She patted her hand. "We're about to change that—and more."

"And more?" Tara echoed, unable to keep a note of distress from creeping into her voice.

"Not to worry. You're in good hands."

Three hours later, Tara and Michelina returned to the palace with three new outfits, matching shoes, and foundation garments so skimpy, merely thinking about them brought a blush to Tara's cheek. And just when Tara thought Michelina was done with her high-octane fashion makeover, Nicholas's sister led Tara to the palace salon, where a stylist awaited her.

Tara drew the line at a bikini wax, but Henri cut and styled her hair, then applied makeup.

Delighted with the result, Michelina threw her arms around Tara. *"Belle, belle!* I can't wait to see Nicholas's face when he sees you. He'll have to pick his jaw up off the floor."

"I don't know how to thank you," Tara said, catching a glimpse of her reflection in the mirror and barely recognizing herself. Part of her craved the safety of her pre-makeover self. That Tara wouldn't turn heads. This one… Well, she supposed she would find out if this version would turn Nicholas's head. Her stomach dipped at the thought.

"Oh, this was all my pleasure," Michelina said. "Believe me, you've saved me from another interminably boring day in the castle keep. Now go get dressed. I want to see the complete effect."

It didn't take Tara long to dress. She glanced at the mirror every now and then, but the image of herself combined with the prospect of dancing with Nicholas unsettled her more than words. Michelina raved over the transformation.

Eight o'clock arrived, but Nicholas didn't. Another hour passed and Michelina was steaming. "Medicine is like a mistress to Nicholas," she muttered, growing more offended by the moment. In fact, Tara thought Nicholas's sister was more offended than she herself was. Tara felt a strange combination of disappointment and relief.

Nicholas's sister was determined that all her hard work not go to waste.

"Well, there's no other solution," Michelina declared at last. You and I will go to the disco without him."

Eight

Tara wasn't exactly sure how she'd ended up in Marceau's loudest, most crowded disco dancing with two men at one time, but Michelina had a heck of a lot to do with it. Nicholas's sister had mowed Tara's protests flat to the ground, insisting that both Tara and Nicholas needed to learn a lesson from this situation. Nicholas needed to learn that Tara wasn't always going to sit at home waiting for him, and Tara needed to learn to entertain herself in his absence.

Under the watchful eye of two palace security men, Tara and Michelina gyrated to an old American disco tune rerecorded in French. One song blended into another, and Tara reveled in her newfound balance.

When the deejay put on a slow song, she thought she would take a break, but her dance partners thought differently.

Nicholas walked into the disco and worked at tamping down the odd tension he felt in his gut. When he'd arrived at the palace to learn that Michelina had taken Tara for a girls' night out, he'd immediately smelled trouble. Michelina had a zest for life and excitement that was fast turning his mother's hair gray. Tara was probably stuck in a corner of the disco longing for quiet.

Surveying the crowd, he easily spotted Michelina, but not Tara. Fred pointed to a woman with long brown hair who wore a black dress that revealed shapely legs and a curvy body. He noticed that the foreign minister's son was wrapped around her like an octopus.

Nicholas blinked and shook his head. Not Tara. The woman turned her head and he saw the shape of her cheek and her full mouth. His temperature shot through the roof.

Striding through the crowd, he tapped the foreign minister's son on the shoulder and in French curtly informed the young man that he was cutting in.

Tara's eyes lit up. "Nicholas."

Nicholas looked appraisingly at her before he pulled her into his arms. "I see my sister's handiwork," he said tightly.

"She's amazing, isn't she?"

"Yes, amazing. I apologize for being so late. There

was an emergency," he said, confused as hell by his possessive feelings.

Tara shrugged. "That's what I figured. I was all set to go to bed, but Michelina insisted I needed to learn to entertain myself if I was going to be married to a doctor." Tara rolled her eyes and lowered her voice. "I really hate deceiving your family."

Nicholas saw the tinge of guilt in her eyes, but his mind was fixated on the idea of Tara entertaining herself. "I see you met Roberto," he said.

"Michelina introduced me. He's been very kind to dance with me tonight," she said. "I'm such an amateur."

Nicholas bit back an oath. "I don't think 'kind' is the accurate word, considering he was wrapped around you so tightly I wondered if we would need the jaws of life to separate you."

Tara pulled back and looked at him. "You don't think he was really interested in me that way, do you?"

He felt his skin prickle with frustration. "Tara, with the way you look tonight, any man with a drop of testosterone would want to take you to bed."

She blinked at him as if it took a moment for her to digest his statement. Sensual awareness darkened her eyes to almost black. "Does that include you?"

Nicholas felt himself turn rock hard with arousal. He'd tried every trick in the book to deny it and push it aside by working, but he was tired, edgy and hungry. Sexually hungry. And unlike every other man in the room, he knew what was beneath Tara's fitted dress.

He'd lost any inclination to be sensible when he'd walked into the disco and found Tara in another man's arms. He drew her lower body against his and looked deeply into her eyes. "You sound curious."

She swallowed, but didn't move away from him. "I guess I am."

"I can answer all your questions," he said, guiding her to the side of the room. He knew they were being watched. Instinct, long drummed into him, reminded him to take care. Another part of him didn't give a damn.

She tentatively undulated against him in rhythm with the music. Nicholas had a completely carnal urge to rip off her clothes. Instead, he lowered his hands to her hips and nudged her chin up to kiss her.

She welcomed his tongue, sucking him deep into her mouth while he rocked between her thighs. Each stroke of her tongue, each movement of her pelvis against his, was like a double intimate stroke. His heart hammered in his chest and his skin turned hot.

Guiding her farther into the darkness of the room, he lowered his hand to the hem of her skirt and rubbed his fingers over her bare, silky skin. He couldn't resist the urge to skim his hand up her leg. When he learned by touch that she was wearing a thong, he nearly burst the front of his slacks.

"I have to take you out of here," he told her. "I need to be alone with you."

Nicholas swept Tara from the disco to a waiting limo. ''No Jeep?'' she said in surprise.

''The Mercedes affords more privacy,'' he replied, and his gaze scored her with heat.

From the minute she had seen Nicholas, Tara's heart had beat double time, and it showed no sign of slowing down. Her body felt flushed inside and out from the way he looked at her and touched her. She knew everything between them was about to change, and she couldn't find the power in herself to stop it.

Wisdom and restraint scattered to the wind with the sweeping force of a hurricane. Raging need, which she read on Nicholas's face and felt reverberating inside herself, wouldn't be denied.

As soon as he followed her into the car, Nicholas pushed a button, and the privacy window rose between the driver and the back seat. Nicholas immediately took her mouth in a kiss that left her breathless.

Tara felt herself sinking into a deep, warm pool of arousal where instinct ruled over inhibition. Nicholas devoured her mouth, and she drew his tongue into her mouth. He slid his hands over her body as if to learn every curve and indentation. He moved one hand up her rib cage with agonizing slowness to the underside of her breasts. Her nipple pebbled against the lace bra, and she shifted restlessly. Tara yearned for a full touch.

''What do you want?'' he asked, his voice smooth with sexual taunting. ''This?'' He closed his hand

over her breast and she couldn't hold back a sound
of satisfaction.

He groaned at the sound as if she were torturing
him. He slid his hand under the hem of her dress
between her thighs. He found the elastic band of her
panties and rubbed his thumb on the soft sensitive
skin underneath. Tara held her breath while a rush of
expectancy roared through her. She shifted to allow
him freer access and he began to swear.

"Damn it! I don't want to wait until we get back
to the palace." He looked deep into her eyes with a
gaze that rocked her to her core, then took her mouth
in a carnal kiss.

Tara had the sense that she had been waiting for
this moment her entire life. Nicholas pulled his head
away, and his nostrils flared as he pushed the intercom button. "Take the long way home," he ordered
to the driver.

Nicholas turned off the intercom, then returned his
undivided attention to Tara. "This dress has annoyed
me since the moment I saw you in it," he said, moving his hands to the back of her dress.

Surprise shot through her. "You don't like it?"

"I like it so much that I want it off," he said, and
lowered the zipper in one slow, competent movement.

Her breath stopped.

He didn't.

He pushed the dress down to her waist, drinking in
the sight of her bare torso and lace-covered breasts.
Without pausing a beat, he unhooked her bra and
bared her breasts. His eyelids heavy with sensual ap-

proval, he lifted his thumbs to her nipples, and the delicious sensation teased them to tight buds.

Tara felt the wanting inside her tighten. She arched toward Nicholas and he acknowledged her feminine invitation. Lowering his head, he drew a nipple into his mouth. She felt a corresponding tension in her lower regions. Unable to stop herself, she arched again and he groaned. The sound vibrated over her flesh, sending her nerve endings into a frenzy.

Turning his attention to her other nipple, he swirled his tongue around her until she began to squirm with pleasure.

"Good, *ma chérie?*" he muttered. "I'm just getting started."

He pushed her dress the rest of the way down her hips so that she was completely naked with the exception of the black satin thong and strappy black sandals.

She felt another rush of heat and desire rise to her head, making her vision hazy with arousal. Tara had never felt so many sensations at once. She tugged at Nicholas's shirt, eager to feel his naked skin against hers. His flesh burned with the same heat that throbbed inside her. She ran her hands over his chest and lower to his abdomen.

He sucked in a quick breath and narrowed his eyes. "Go on," he said, with a combination of challenge and need.

With trembling hands, Tara unfastened his slacks and eased the zipper down over the bulge of his masculinity. She slid her hands beneath his briefs to touch him intimately, to caress him.

He let out a long hiss of a sigh at her touch, then stilled her hand with his. "Later," he said, lowering his head to drop openmouthed kisses down her abdomen. He removed her little thong and pushed her legs apart to kiss her at the top of her thighs.

Tara stiffened at the shocking intimacy, but Nicholas was clearly determined. Reassuringly he caressed her thighs while he mesmerized her with his magic tongue in her most sensitive, secret feminine place.

With each delicious stroke against her femininity, she felt the tension inside her tighten like a bow. He drew her into his mouth as if to consume her, and the sensation was too much. She tumbled over the edge, calling out his name and free-falling into his arms.

With a combination of possessive satisfaction and unspent need stamped on his face, Nicholas shed his slacks and underwear and rose over her with purpose. He put on a condom and lifted her limp arms so that she clasped his shoulders. "Hold on," he told her and thrust inside her.

The overstretched sensation took her breath.

Nicholas looked at her in surprise and turned perfectly, rigidly still inside her. "You should have told me," he muttered.

Tara licked her dry lips and inhaled a shallow breath of air. "I, uh, my brain—" She broke off and shook her head, unable to form a complete thought except that she didn't want him to stop. "Don't stop," she whispered.

Something primitive flickered in his light blue eyes and he began to move in a slow rhythm that muddied her mind all over again. He filled her completely. In her mind, body and soul, there was only Nicholas, taking and giving, making her want to give him everything.

His breath grew short, his movements swift and his body gleamed with the promise of satisfaction. She saw the moment he climaxed, the pleasure in his eyes. She was filled with the heady knowledge that she had helped put that expression in his gaze, and Tara had never felt more complete.

Moments passed in which the only sound in the limo was their combined breaths. Then Nicholas rose slightly and brushed his lips over Tara's cheek. He pulled away, switching positions so that she lay on top of him.

Tara's heart was doing strange things. She felt glorious, but vulnerable. "I have a question," she finally managed. "Was this supposed to make our situation less crazy?"

Nicholas chuckled, looping his hand around the back of her neck and drawing her lips against his. "You're a psychology major. You should know that repression is bad for your mental health."

All too conscious of his muscular body beneath hers, Tara tried to rein in her brain. "Yes, but I don't feel less crazy. I mean, if making love with you once was supposed to clear my mind, then—"

"Once!" Nicholas said, looking at her as if s

lost her mind. "What made you think we were just going to make love once?"

"Well, if we made a habit of it when we're trying to convince everyone that we're going to get married when we're not going to get married, then—" She broke off in confusion. "Wouldn't that be just too weird?"

He shook his head. "No. It just means we have an understanding."

"Oh," Tara said, still confused. She made a face and tried to draw away from him in hopes that she could then think more clearly, but Nicholas tightened his arms around her. "Would you mind explaining this understanding?"

He met her gaze. "We understand each other. You understand that medicine is the most important thing to me and I understand that you getting your education is the most important thing to you. We are extremely attracted to each other," he said, skimming his hand down her arm. "But we don't want to get married. We will behave as if we're engaged because it suits our individual goals."

Tara felt a rush of conflicting emotions. "What if something goes wrong?"

"What could go wrong?"

"hat if we fall in love with each other?"

…las shook his head and smiled. "Won't hap-
…e both too focused. That's the beauty of it."

…queezed her derriere and rose to a sitting
…her in his lap. "It's a damn shame, but
…t dressed so we can go back to the

palace. We can have a midnight snack in my quarters, and you can stay with me.''

With his gaze hungry for her and his arms wrapped around her, it was hard for Tara to give voice to the little whispers of doubt in the back of her mind. Her options were staying with Nicholas or staying by herself. Her heart offered no choice in the matter. Trying to get a handle on the euphoria racing through her veins like a drug, she got dressed.

Her legs were unsteady as she walked with Nicholas into the palace, but her shaky balance had nothing to do with her inner ear problem. The man had blown her away, yet he seemed totally at ease, laughing and teasing her.

As promised, they ate a midnight snack of sandwiches and soda. Nicholas told her about the medical emergency that had made him late.

''I delivered a baby,'' he told her casually.

Tara felt a pang of disappointment. ''What a bummer!''

''Bummer?'' he said, clearly perplexed.

''I would have loved to have been there,'' she said. ''Was it fun?''

He smiled and drew her close to him on his big bed. ''Yeah.'' He shook his head. ''Not every woman would be so interested in what I do.''

''But what you do is fascinating. You make a big difference in a lot of people's lives. I wish I could do the same,'' she added wistfully.

He toyed with her hair thoughtfully. ''You may underestimate your impact.''

She shot him a skeptical look. "Nice of you to say, but I think not. One day, though, I will make a difference, some sort of contribution. It may not be as dramatic as what you do, but I'll find a way to do something."

"I'm sure you will," he said, his gaze sliding over her like a hot fire. "In the meantime, I can make a suggestion for how you can contribute," he said, taking her mouth in a kiss that made her head fuzzy all over again. "To me."

The following morning, Nicholas awakened to a glorious sunrise and the even more glorious sight of Tara, naked, in his bed. Impossible though it seemed, he felt himself grow hard with wanting. His response was disconcerting as hell considering the fact that they had made love throughout the night. He wanted her again, but she was inexperienced, and he didn't want to make her sore.

Her eyes fluttered open. He watched confusion, followed by recognition, then self-consciousness, flit through her eyes. Wanting to wipe the self-consciousness away, he gave her a quick kiss.

"What in hell are you doing naked in my bed this morning?" he asked in a mock-serious tone.

She hesitated, then gave a tiny shake of her head. "You invited me to your bed." A smile tugged the corners of her lips upward like the morning sun rising on the horizon. "Then, when I politely tried not to overstay my welcome, you trapped me with your big, heavy leg."

His lips twitched. "I don't recall hearing any complaints. In fact, I could swear I heard you say something like 'Oh, Nicholas, don't stop. Oh, Nicholas, you feel so good. Oh, Nicholas—'"

Tara covered his mouth with her hand and tossed him a dark glance. "It's incredibly impolite of you to tease me this way."

He lowered his head, so that his nose rubbed hers. "You don't arouse my polite feelings."

"No, I obviously arouse your baser emotions," she said in a delicious breathless voice that made him reconsider giving her some time to recover from their wild night of lovemaking.

It cost him, but he exercised restraint. "Since I was late for our dance date last night, I'd like to make up for it today. I need to make a few phone calls, then you name whatever you want to do today."

She pulled back slightly, and her gaze dipped and swayed over his body with sensual secrets.

Nicholas groaned. "Except that. I don't want to make you sore. Stop looking at me like that."

"Like what?"

"Like a she-devil bent on ravaging my body," he said.

Her mouth dropped open. "I've never been called a she-devil."

"That's because no other man knows what you're capable of in bed," he retorted, and it occurred to him that he didn't like the idea of any other man finding out what Tara was like in bed. "Stop distracting me," he said. "Tell me what you want to do today."

She paused a half beat, then met his gaze with the force of an oncoming truck. "I want you to teach me to drive."

Oh, hell.

Nine

"**G**ive it some gas. Let out the clutch," Nicholas said for what had to be the fiftieth time.

Not enough gas, too little clutch. The Jeep sputtered, choked and died. In the Mercedes parked a short distance away, Nicholas saw Fred lift the page of the newspaper he had rested on the steering wheel.

Tara sighed in deep discouragement. She thumped the steering wheel with her fist and frowned. "I thought I had left my lack of coordination behind with my inner ear problem."

"That doesn't mean you'll instantly know how to drive a vehicle with manual transmission. That requires technique and practice," Nicholas said, wondering if his teeth were loose or just felt that way.

"Human spark plugs would help," he muttered to himself.

"Pardon?" Tara said.

"Nothing. You know, you could start out with a vehicle with automatic transmission, and I bet you would be gliding down the highway in no time."

She pursed her mouth and shook her head. "No. It's got to be a Jeep. I want to be able to drive a Jeep when you let me go with you to another medical clinic."

Nicholas felt his heart squeeze tight in his chest at the earnest expression on Tara's face. "You don't have to drive, Tara. That's why I have Fred."

"But what if there's an emergency and he can't drive and you need to look after a patient? I should be able to drive a Jeep."

"I can't imagine that happening. Stop torturing yourself about learning to drive a Jeep, and let's kick Fred out of the Mercedes and take it for a spin."

Tara sighed again and looked out the window. "I don't want to be useless."

The pain in her voice sliced at him. He took her hand. "You're not useless."

"Oh, really? Then tell me all the useful things I've done since I arrived in Marceau," she challenged him.

Nicholas looked into her blue eyes full of doubt and hope and drew a blank. Biting back an oath, he raked his fingers through his hair. This was important, blast it. "Maggie told me you helped her and Max find Elvis."

"I whistled."

"It was useful. You appeared with me at the ball and kept me from getting nagged to death by my mother."

"I stepped on your foot," she reminded him.

"A technicality," he said. "You temporarily kept the peace between Michelina and the queen with your diplomacy."

"*Temporarily* is the operative word there. Those two are headed for World War Three."

He couldn't disagree. "You coaxed a delirious woman into accepting medical treatment. And you made me feel good about what I'm doing with the free medical clinics when everyone else at the palace would like me to do something else."

Tara was silent for a long moment. "I think you would have found a way to treat Cecile, and I know nothing will prevent you from practicing medicine. Nothing should."

Nicholas couldn't argue her point. How could he make her see that she was important, that she made things easier just by her presence?

"Let me try again," she said, putting the Jeep into neutral. "If I can get out of neutral three times without stalling, I'll take that as success."

It took the rest of the afternoon, but Tara finally succeeded. As soon as they returned to the palace, Nicholas surreptitiously took a headache pain reliever.

Tara sat beside him at the family dinner. She wore the hated glasses and another ugly dress. He wondered where she had found her wardrobe. He noticed that Michelina wore a disappointed but curious expression. His sister would demand an explanation. Later, Nicholas thought, his mind consumed with the woman beside him. She'd barely looked at him all evening. It was as if she feared everyone would know they'd been intimate if she paid him any attention.

Maggie and Michel seemed distracted. Max was squirmy, whispering to Maggie and Michel throughout the meal. The queen was having difficulty keeping the conversation going. She nodded toward one of the waiters. "You may serve dessert now please."

Maggie and Michel exchanged a secret glance. The love between them flowed like a river. Nicholas was glad his brother had found a woman who loved him for himself instead of his title. Michel's was a lonely, demanding job, but since Maggie had come into his life, Michel had never seemed happier and more complete. A stray thought about Tara flitted through Nicholas's mind, surprising him. He brushed it aside. He and Tara had a completely different arrangement, and that suited him just fine.

"Maximillian has an announcement," Michel said with pride and love in his eyes.

Everyone waited expectantly while the child lifted his chin with a happy, proud look on his face. It wasn't long ago that Max had been downcast and defeated after suffering from dyslexia. Since Maggie had come to the palace as his tutor, Max's outlook had changed from night to day.

"We're going to have a baby," he said.

The queen gasped with delight, Michelina and others made happy sounds. Nicholas glanced at Tara and caught her knowing smile. Something told him Maggie had confided in her.

"Congratulations," Nicholas said, lifting his glass of wine. "To the father, the mother and the big brother."

"How long have you known?" Queen Anna asked. "Are you taking your vitamins? Have you seen a doctor?"

Maggie laughed, and Michel put his arm around her shoulder in consolation. "She's known just a while. She hasn't seen a doctor, but she is taking her vitamins. Max and I had to persuade her to share the news with the family because she didn't want anyone fussing over her," he said, meeting his mother's gaze with a royal challenge. "I assured her that if anyone is going to fuss over her, it will be me."

Nicholas lifted his glass again in support. "Hear, hear," he said.

"Well said," Tara murmured and lifted her own glass. "Hear, hear. Congratulations."

The rest of the family toasted the pregnancy. Nicholas would have to thank his brother later for the timely distraction he had provided. With all the attention focused on Maggie and the baby, it was easy to sneak Tara away from dinner without any awkward questions.

He pulled her along beside him toward his quarters. As soon as he closed the door behind them, he took off her glasses and drew her into his arms.

"You barely said a word to me during the meal," he reproached her.

"I'm not sure how to act," she protested. "I'm supposed to be engaged, but I'm guessing we don't want everyone to know we've become intimate. I haven't figured this out yet." She looked at him in consternation. "I don't think Miss Manners has covered this one."

Nicholas laughed at the expression on her face. "Just follow my instructions."

Tara stared at him as if he were crazy. "Ha! In your dreams, Your Highness. You had me fooled for a while. I thought you didn't have any of that royal obey-me attitude, but you were just hiding it."

"Like you were hiding Maggie's secret?" Nicholas said, enjoying her flush of surprise.

"My lips are sealed," Tara said.

"Bet I can unseal them," Nicholas teased, fascinated with the prospect.

She tilted her head to one side, and the secret sensual glint flashed in her eyes. The same glint that made him want to take her against the wall. "You can try," she said, and the invitation hung between them for a microsecond before he did just that.

Tara kept him up half the night with her postvirginal curiosity. With her combination of innocence and sexuality, the woman might very well drive him mad. No sooner did he take her than he wanted her again. Nicholas had never experienced such a combination of mind-robbing fulfillment and need. They finally fell asleep in each other's arms, exhausted, but not quite sated.

The next morning, a loud knock at the door to his suite awakened them. Nicholas glanced at the clock, frowning at the early hour. He wondered if there'd been an emergency.

Rising from the bed, he grabbed a pair of shorts.

"Who is it?" Tara whispered.

"I don't know," Nicholas said, and another knock sounded.

"Your Highness, Jean Robert here by order of Her Majesty, the Queen," his mother's longtime palace assistant announced from the other side of the door.

"I'll be back in just a minute," he told Tara in a low voice. "Stay where you are." Nicholas walked from the bedroom through his den and opened the door.

"Your Highness, the queen requests your presence in her chamber immediately," Jean Robert said. "And also the presence of Miss York."

Nicholas got an uneasy feeling in his gut. "Why?"

"I am not privy to that information, sir," Jean Robert said with the discretion that had enabled him to keep his position for over thirty years. "When shall I tell her you will appear before her?"

"Give me an hour."

"As you wish, sir," Jean Robert said and bowed before he left.

Nicholas closed the door behind him and returned to Tara. She looked up at him expectantly. "What is it?"

"My mother wants you and me to appear in her chamber," Nicholas said, still mulling over what Queen Anna might want. "I told Jean Robert we would be there in an hour."

Tara's brow furrowed in confusion. "Is she always this formal?"

Nicholas nodded and shrugged. "I think it's a queen thing. Michel just picks up the phone. She doesn't usually send someone to my door at the crack of dawn, though."

"Do you think she knows we've been together?"

Nicholas rolled his eyes. "It makes no difference if she knows or doesn't. I'm a grown man. My mother may be the queen, but she sure as hell doesn't choose my lovers." He bent down to give Tara a reassuring kiss. "We can speculate forever, or we can get dressed and find out what's got her royal panties in a twist."

Tara's lips lifted in a half smile, but her eyes were full of concern.

"Don't worry. I'll take care of you," he said.

"It's not your job," she said, rising from the bed and pulling on her clothes.

Nicholas took in the proud tilt of her head and felt a rush of protectiveness. For the sake of time, he swallowed the urge to argue. It might not make sense, and Tara might disagree, but Nicholas knew it damn well was his job to take care of her.

Fifty minutes later, Tara and Nicholas were ushered into the queen's private chamber. She stood looking out a window as if she were deep in thought. As soon as she turned, Tara curtseyed. Nicholas gave a micro-bow.

Queen Anna acknowledged them and waved her hand toward the settee. "Please be seated. I must discuss with you a matter of great concern." She walked from the window to sit in a beautiful chair upholstered in a cream and burgundy tapestry.

Tara studied the queen as she appeared to collect herself. Although her classic features were still beautiful, she appeared weary and somehow older this morning. Tara thought of all the responsibility and grief the woman had carried on her slim shoulders and felt a surge of admiration and sympathy.

Queen Anna Catherine turned her gaze to Nicholas. "Miss York's father and I have spoken several times this morning. It appears that Mr. York has received some compromising photographs of you and Miss York during a late-night swim."

Tara gasped, feeling her blood drain to her feet. Nicholas covered her hand with his.

The queen paused, and her expression softened. "Would you like some tea, dear?" she asked Tara.

Tara couldn't imagine swallowing anything. She shook her head. "No, thank you, Your Majesty."

Queen Anna nodded, then turned back to Nicholas. "Mr. York is perfectly willing to pay the exorbitant sum to keep the photographs out of the media, but as we know, these pictures have a way of resurfacing. Mr. York is demanding that the two of you marry immediately, and I agree. A marriage will protect both your reputations.''

Marriage. Tara felt Nicholas's hand tighten around hers. The room began to move. Tara shook her head, and a thousand protests formed on the edge of her tongue, but she couldn't muster a sound.

''How soon can we do it?'' Nicholas asked.

Tara jerked her head to stare at him in shock. ''What!''

The queen ignored her. ''I believe the minimal necessary arrangements could be completed within three days.''

Three days! Panic roared through her. Tara's breath came in short gasps.

Nicholas glanced at her and frowned. ''She's hyperventilating. I need a paper bag.''

The room spun in circles, and her vision turned hazy. Suddenly a paper bag was pulled over her head. As if from a distance, Tara heard the voices of Nicholas and the queen.

''It will have to be a small, private affair,'' the queen said.

''I wouldn't have it any other way,'' Nicholas replied stoically.

Tara felt her cherished control of her life slipping away. She ripped the bag off her head. ''This is insane and unnecessary. The photographs can't be that bad.''

Nicholas met her gaze with eerie calm. ''Do you remember what we were wearing that night we went swimming?''

Tara's mind conjured a revealing visual. She had worn bikini panties and Nicholas had worn nothing. She felt her cheeks heat and bit her lip. "Okay, so the photographs might be embarrassing. What's the worst thing that could happen? They go into a rag sheet and are used to wrap fish and line bird cages the next day. Soon someone else is bound to offer a more enticing scandal, and this one will be history," she said breathlessly, hoping she wouldn't have to put the bag back over her head.

Nicholas turned to the queen. "Mother, she is clearly overwrought. I think it would help if I had a few moments alone with her."

The queen nodded. "Yes, but remember time is of the essence."

Nicholas shuttled Tara out the door before she could protest any further. "This is insane," she told him as he led her to his quarters. "Totally insane, and I'm not going to do it."

Nicholas shut the door behind him and pushed her into a chair. Turning his back on her as she enumerated the reasons why they shouldn't get married, he poured himself a shot glass of Scotch.

"And besides, you and I agreed that neither of us wanted to get married. You must not be too thrilled about it, either, if you're drinking Scotch before nine in the morning," she accused, wondering if she should ask him to pour her a drink too. On second thought, she'd better hold fast to her razor sharp edge of hysteria, or the queen and Nicholas would have her in front of a judge before she knew it.

He grimaced as if the liquor burned his throat. "I'm drinking because it's a special occasion."

Tara shot to her feet. "What a line! You're drinking because you know this whole thing is crazy and you don't want to marry me any more than I want to marry you. This is going to mess up all our plans."

"Not necessarily," Nicholas said. "I could be stuck with a far worse marriage partner than you, and you could be stuck with someone worse than me."

"That's a matter of opinion," she muttered.

Nicholas bared his teeth in a semblance of a smile. "Remember Dickie."

"Yes, but Dickie wasn't a prince susceptible to attacks of royal duty."

Nicholas took a calming breath and leveled his gaze at her. "You're reacting emotionally and irrationally. The best course of action for us and our respective families is for you and me to marry and do it quickly. It's my fault a photograph was taken of you with me when you were nearly naked."

Tara hated the guilt she heard in his voice. "Did you take the picture?" she asked, and shook her head. "No," she answered her own question, then asked another. "Did you force me to take off my clothes?"

"No, but I dared you and goaded you into it."

"It was my own decision."

"But I influenced you." He walked closer to her. "This is the right thing to do."

Panic sliced through her again. "How can it be right when both of us have been doing our best to avoid it?"

"There are worse possibilities," he said in that duty-bound voice she could hardly bear. "You and I understand each other, so we'll offer each other the space we need to accomplish our goals."

His words echoed in her brain like a terrible refrain. His attitude cut her to ribbons. "So I'm supposed to promise forever to you, knowing that you're thinking things could be worse?" She felt a horrible urge to cry. "This is sick. I'm calling my father," she said, and swept past him.

He caught her just as she reached the door. "Tara," he said in a low voice that got under her skin, "I do care for you."

She closed her eyes, willing the tears to wait. "You're a doctor. You care for everyone. For that matter, you care for Elvis," she said, and dashed out the door.

Tara spent the rest of the day voluntarily locked in her room while she held a series of tense, terse, emotional telephone calls with her father. She refused food, but drank four bottles of water as she paced her suite and argued with her father.

He was appalled by the photographs. She could handle his shock, but not his disappointment. He firmly agreed that the best way to neutralize the potential damage of the photographs was for her to marry Nicholas, and the sooner, the better.

Tara protested, and told her father about the medical procedure performed on her and the exciting improvement in her inner ear problem. He was cautiously hopeful, but still adamant about protecting her reputation. She even shared the fact that she'd secretly earned two college degrees on the Internet. Although he congratulated her, he obviously didn't yet believe she could take care of herself.

His lack of confidence in her was just one more blow on a day when she didn't know if she could take any more.

"Tara," her father said, "I think you're forgetting that you are not the only consideration. There are other people involved. Have you thought about how this will affect the entire Dumont family? Have you thought about how this kind of publicity could damage Nicholas? For Pete's sake, the man is a medical doctor. He's already swimming against the tide." Her father turned silent for a moment. "How would this kind of publicity affect his credibility?"

His question immediately took the fight out of her. She felt as if her father had delivered a knockout punch. Tara sank down onto her bed.

A heavy, swollen silence hummed over the telephone line, while a collage of visuals of Nicholas raced through Tara's mind. She recalled his gentleness with the little boy in the clinic. She remembered his persistence with Cecile. She pictured his determination and passion for improving medical treatment in Marceau. He craved his freedom so that he could better serve his people. The irony of the situation hurt so much, she felt as if someone were squeezing her heart in two. She hated the very idea of being the woman who could come between him and his goal.

The tears she'd been stoically holding back began to flow down her cheeks.

"Tara," her father said. "Are you still there?"

"Yes," she said quietly, swiping her cheeks with the back of her hand.

"I'm told the wedding will be held in three days. I'll be there," he told her. "Think about what I can give you as a wedding gift. Since you're not having a large ceremony, think big," he added with forced laughter, as if to cheer her up. Her father had never understood Tara's lack of interest in exploiting his wealth.

A practical but extravagant idea came to mind. "I already know," she said, and she would love to see the surprise on her father's face. If she and Nicholas were being forced into this appalling situation, then she might as well make the most of it for both of them. "I'd like two," she said.

"Two," he echoed, confusion and surprise emanating from his voice. "Two what?"

"Two million dollars."

Ten

The white wedding dress hanging on the outside of Tara's closet door mocked her. She could almost hear it say "Na-na-na." Her instinct had been to choose something black, and Michelina had enjoyed the idea of Tara making a trendy fashion statement, but both she and Maggie had eventually vetoed it.

"First wedding," Maggie had said. "Everyone will expect you to wear white."

Everyone would expect a lot of things from her, Tara was learning. Everything had happened so quickly during the last two days, she felt as if she'd been trapped in a microwave oven. It appeared that the entire population of Marceau was more excited about this wedding than she was.

Except, perhaps, Nicholas.

She didn't know much about what he was thinking because she'd barely had more than a few minutes with him, and those few minutes hadn't offered any privacy.

Tara stared at the beautifully simple white dress and felt the sinking sensation in the pit of her stomach again that suggested she was about to make the biggest mistake of her life.

"It's beautiful," Michelina said, standing beside the bed in a rose-colored Chanel sheath. "I'm glad you went with this design, Tara. The other was too fussy." She glanced at her watch. "Only an hour to go. Your hair and makeup look fabulous. You should go ahead and get dressed."

Tara immediately shook her head. "Not yet. I, uh, don't want to mess it up."

Maggie shot her a curious look. Tara looked away, fearing Michel's wife would guess her true feelings. She'd learned Maggie was entirely too intuitive.

Maggie drew closer and took Tara's hand. Her eyes widened. "Tara, your hands are as cold as ice. Pre-wedding jitters?" she asked sympathetically as she briskly rubbed Tara's hand between hers.

You have no idea, Tara thought. "Maybe a few," she said, lifting her lips in a small smile.

"It's natural," Maggie soothed her. "The Dumont family can be a bit intimidating."

"In many ways, we're like a lot of other families. Dysfunctional," Michelina said. "The big differences are that we rule, we have a lot of titles, people expect a lot of us, the press is interested in the most intimate details of our lives and—''

''Michelina,'' Maggie cut in with a smile that didn't hide her alarm. She patted Tara's shoulder. ''Tara needs reassurance right now. She needs to remember all the wonderful things about Nicholas. Tell Tara something good about Nicholas from your childhood.''

Michelina furrowed her brow in concentration and paused for a moment. Her expression softened. ''Okay, I have two perfect stories. When I was little, I played with dolls a lot. Sometimes they would get broken, and Nicholas would fix them. I remember he spent hours repairing my dolls. He was destined to be a people-fixer,'' she said with a smile. ''The second story is that Nicholas secretly taught me to fence for several months until my mother found out. There's this long-standing tradition among the Dumonts that the men learn to fence, but the Dumont women aren't allowed.''

''I wondered about that,'' Maggie said. ''Michel has evaded the issue when I've asked him about it.''

''It makes the men nervous,'' Michelina said. ''I can't figure out if they're afraid the women will impale them in their sleep or if the women will hurt themselves. My mother's objection was the latter,'' she said with a scowl. ''But Nicholas didn't see any reason why I couldn't learn. He's the least chauvinistic of my brothers, although Maggie is transforming Michel.'' Michelina shrugged. ''Nicholas has a talent for looking beneath the surface, and he won't try to order you around too much.''

But will he ever love me? Tara's heart shook at the question. Where had it come from? she wondered, biting her lip. Love wasn't a part of this equation. This marriage was an arrangement made for the sake of protecting reputations and personal goals. Her relationship with Nicholas was a mutually beneficial agreement created out of a need for a defense against their parents' matchmaking efforts and passion.

But what about love? Her pulse raced, and she struggled with the urge to run. This was the right thing to do, Tara told herself. Nicholas might think her reputation was in danger, but Tara knew that for once, Nicholas was the one who needed protecting. And she was the woman to do it. She glanced at the wedding dress and ignored the roiling of her stomach.

She took a deep breath and stood. ''Let's get this show on the road.''

Fifty-nine minutes later, Tara's father offered his arm to her just before she was to walk down the garden pathway to where the assembled guests sat and Nicholas waited. Tamping down the voice inside her that continued to scream at her to run the other way, Tara knew she was an idiot if she didn't believe that her life was about to change.

Her father must have read the unbridelike dread on her face. He squeezed her arm and smiled encouragingly. ''Smile, Tara. I have the check for two million in my pocket, and I made it payable to you. You can think of it as mad money.''

Mad was right, she thought. This entire situation was mad, insane, crazy, wacko... She broke off her unproductive thoughts and took another deep breath. "Thank you," she said. "It's very generous of you."

"Nothing is too good for my daughter. Look, you've roped yourself a prince," he said.

When he said "rope," she pictured a noose. She smiled, however, and resolved to hold her lips in that position for the next two hours. "Let's go," she said, and they began the long walk. Nicholas's many relatives turned to look at her with happy, dreamy expressions on their faces. The queen nodded in approval.

Afraid of what she might see on Nicholas's face, Tara looked everywhere but at her bridegroom. She distracted herself from her nervousness by identifying Nicholas's brothers. The youngest, Alexander, and his adorable wife, Sophie, had rushed over from the States and arrived just last night. Tara had been told that their toddler son would be keeping an aide busy in the palace. The second born, Auguste, Marceau's military commander, sat with his wife and well-behaved daughters. Auguste's twin, Jean Marc, had flown from Washington, D.C., since he was now Marceau's diplomatic representative to the United States.

Michel stood tall and proud next to the trellis dripping in white roses. Michelina beamed her encouragement from the other side. Since Maggie was still suffering from intermittent morning sickness, Michelina had been chosen as Tara's maid of honor. Next to her stood the minister who was to perform the nuptial rites, his balding head gleaming in the sunlight.

Tara felt the intensity of Nicholas's gaze so strongly he might as well have called her name. Unable to ignore the call, she finally looked at him. Dressed in a tuxedo, he emanated strength and intelligence. And commitment.

Tara's breath stopped at the expression in his eyes. She could almost believe he genuinely cared for her. She could almost believe he wanted this. If she didn't know better, she would think that Nicholas almost loved— Her heart palpitated and she took a quick breath. It wasn't possible, she told herself. He was just a very good actor. He might have hated all those years of making personal appearances in the name of royal duty, but today the practice was paying off in spades.

The closer she walked to Nicholas, the more the whole scene seemed to take on an otherworldly sensation. This was someone else's world, someone else's wedding. After the minister greeted the guests, asked who gives this bride, and her father joined her hand with Nicholas's, however, Tara was slammed back into reality. This was her world and her wedding.

The minister could have spoken in Greek for all she took in during the next few moments. She somehow managed to repeat her vows, and she noticed the concern on Nicholas's face. It was as if he knew she'd hike up her dress and run away if given half a chance. When he placed the diamond-encrusted band, clearly a family heirloom, on her finger, she was filled with guilt. This ring didn't belong to her. It belonged to the woman whom Nicholas would someday love.

The minister pronounced them man and wife, and Nicholas drew her into his arms and kissed her. She felt the promise in his caress, and the duty. The assault of a dozen different emotions nearly undid her. Her eyes filled with tears. Nicholas brushed his fingertip under her eye and bent his head close to hers.

"It will be okay," he whispered, but even though the diamonds in her ring were the best and most authentic, Tara felt like a fraud.

The reception passed in a blur. She wasn't sure how she did it, but she danced and smiled as expected. Hours later, Michelina hustled her into her going-away dress, and Nicholas guided her up the ramp to the royal yacht that would take them to the open seas for the next two days.

He slid his arm around her waist. "Wave and smile for the cameras. It's almost over."

"And then what?" Tara murmured to herself, but did as Nicholas suggested. The yacht left the dock long after her arm grew tired, and she felt her smile begin to droop. Then, with the exception of ten crew members, she and Nicholas were finally alone. Under other circumstances, the ocean breeze would have been refreshing, but Tara just felt numb.

"What do you want to do?" Nicholas asked. "Are you hungry? Do you want to change clothes?" The silence stretched between them, and he gave a wry chuckle. "Wanna go for a nude swim?"

Tara shot him a dark look. "I believe that's what got us into this predicament." She closed her eyes and sighed. "I think going to bed is a good idea."

Another long silence followed, and Tara felt her stomach tense. She opened her eyes to meet his gaze and saw a combination of curiosity and sexual intent. Her breath hitched in her throat, and she felt an attack of nerves. "Go to bed to rest," she clarified quickly. "To sleep. To take a nap."

He nodded slowly. "Okay, let me show you to the suite."

As he led her around the deck, Tara struggled with her trepidation about making love with Nicholas. After all, it wouldn't be the first time. But it somehow seemed very different now that they were married, she thought as she followed Nicholas into the spacious, lush suite.

The large bed drew her gaze like a magnet. She would share that bed with Nicholas as his wife. Anticipation, expectation, hung heavily in the air like humidity before a storm.

Pushing aside the feelings that tugged at her, she looked around the rest of the tastefully decorated suite. She caught sight of flowers, champagne in an ice bucket and, most important, her luggage. "Oh good," she said, striding across the room. "The luggage is here, so I'll just grab some comfortable clothes and change in the—"

Nicholas was by her side, picking up the suitcase just as she touched it. "A bride shouldn't be lifting luggage."

Tara blinked in surprise. "Thank you," she murmured as he placed the suitcase on a luggage stand.

"You're welcome." He studied her with an unreadable expression on his face, then he leaned forward and dipped his mouth over hers for a kiss that almost lingered. "Get some rest," he said, as if she would need plenty of stamina later, then walked out of the room.

Tara's heart hammered in her chest. Had his gaze oozed sexual intent? Or was that her imagination? And how did she feel about it? She groaned. Too many questions! The last few days had been such a whirlwind, she hadn't had time to answer those kinds of questions, and she didn't have the energy right now. Now, she was going to rest, she told herself firmly.

After unzipping her suitcase, she was greeted with another surprise. No cotton pajamas. She saw Michelina's fine hand in the choice of lingerie. Silk, satin, revealing, seductive. Perfect for someone else's honeymoon.

Hours later, Nicholas arranged for dinner to be brought to their suite. He was watching her as Tara awakened because the dinner cart wheel squeaked loudly.

She lifted her head from the satin pillow and pushed her hair from her face. Her eyes were sleepy, her hair tousled and whatever she was wearing looked slippery and sexy. Nicholas felt a surge of possessiveness. She was his wife. The marriage sure as hell hadn't been his first choice for the outcome of their relationship, but it hadn't dampened his desire for her either.

Her gaze connected with his, then skittered away. "I'm afraid to ask how long I've been asleep," she said, rising to a sitting position.

"Are you sure you're no relation to Rip van Winkle?" he teased, pulling the champagne bottle from the bucket. "Would you like some dinner?"

Tara covered a yawn and nodded.

The sheet dropped to her lap, and Nicholas got another teasing image of her blue silk chemise. The material must have shifted in her sleep. The shadow of one dusky nipple taunted him. Nicholas remembered how her breast felt in his hand. He remembered her sexy restlessness when he drew her nipple into his mouth. He remembered how wet and tight she felt around him. He felt himself turn hard.

Tara must have read his expression. She glanced down and quickly adjusted her gown. Biting her lip, she turned her attention to the dinner cart. "Oh, lobster," she said, licking her lips in anticipation.

Something uncivilized and primitive rippled through him. Nicholas struggled with the urge to tear off that scanty bit of silk and the veil of discomfort between them.

"I don't think I ate more than a bite of cake at the reception, and that was for the photographer." She slid out of bed and quickly grabbed a robe.

Nicholas would have preferred her completely naked beneath him, but he bided his time. "Champagne?" he asked, and pulled it from the bucket.

"No disagreement from me," she said, lifting their glasses to catch the liquid when he popped the bottle open.

Replacing the bottle in the bucket, he lifted his glass to hers in a toast. "To us—for surviving the last seventy-two hours."

Tara nodded as if she didn't totally agree, but took a sip anyway. He pulled out her chair, and she sat down at the table and took another swallow of champagne. She licked her lips afterward, and her robe gaped to reveal the swell of one breast.

Nicholas took a deep breath and a long swallow of the bubbly liquid for fortification. He watched Tara lift a bite of lobster to her lips, and as she sucked it gently inside, Nicholas prepared himself for an hour of torture.

Everything she ate made his blood pressure rise another notch. She licked hollandaise sauce from the asparagus before she took it into her mouth. She took intermittent bites of lobster dipped in butter, and he would swear she moaned every time. The sounds of her gastronomic pleasure made him so hard he could barely sit.

After she finished the lobster, she looked at the chocolate hazelnut torte and shook her head. "I know I can't eat all of that."

"We can share," he said, plunging his fork into a slice of the torte and lifting a bite to her lips.

She looked at him in surprise, but opened her

mouth. As the morsel melted in her mouth, she moaned.

The woman was going to kill him, he thought.

"That was so good."

"Better than the wedding cake," he acknowledged, taking a bite even though he was much more interested in sating a completely different appetite.

She turned silent, and her eyes darkened with sadness. He immediately sensed her tension and unhappiness.

"I'm sorry," she said, misery filling her voice.

"Sorry for what?"

"I'm sorry we had to get married."

She was too far away, he thought. She'd been too far away ever since they'd decided to marry. Nicholas rounded the table and picked her up in his arms.

She stiffened. "What are you doing?"

"I think that's obvious," he said, lowering her to the bed. "I'm putting you to bed." He grabbed their champagne glasses and joined her. "Stop feeling responsible. The photos were taken of both of us. As I told you before, there are far worse things than you and I getting married."

She frowned, but accepted the glass and took a sip. "Far worse things. That doesn't really help."

"Okay. Then how about saying that this arrangement has its compensations?"

Taking another sip, she met his gaze. Her eyes were both wary and sexy. She parted her lips.

"Don't lick them," he said.

Her eyes widened in surprise. "Why not?"

"Because I want to.

Eleven

Nicholas lowered his head and ran his tongue over her champagne-wet lips. Tara paused for a long moment as if she were undecided, then she tilted her mouth for better access.

The gesture of welcome shot heat through his groin like an intimate touch from her hand. Nicholas consumed her lips the same way he planned to consume her body. She opened her mouth, and he dipped his tongue inside to explore, to take, to mate.

He felt her fingers climb up the nape of his neck and deepened the kiss. She moaned, the same sensual sound of pleasure she'd made earlier. The sound vibrated throughout him, cranking his arousal up another notch.

She pulled back slightly and took a quick breath.

"How will I know when you're doing something because of duty and when you're not?" she asked breathlessly.

Nicholas gave a rough chuckle and set his glass of champagne on the nightstand. He undid the belt of her robe and took her glass. "There are some things a man can't hide, *chérie.*"

"But I—"

He rubbed her lips with his index finger. "Unbutton my shirt," he said in a low voice.

She paused a long moment, then did as he asked, skimming her hand down his chest. She went a step farther and pushed the shirt from his shoulders. Meeting his gaze, she slowly lowered her hands to the top of his slacks.

He rubbed his finger over her mouth again.

She darted her tongue over the tip, sending his temperature up ten degrees. Seeing the dare in her eyes, he pushed his finger in her mouth. Tara licked it the same way she would...

Nicholas's restraint ran thin. He took a gulp from her glass and felt her unfasten his slacks. Something inside him tore open. He pulled his finger from her decadent mouth, and in one motion, he pushed her robe and chemise down to her hips. There was just a little champagne left in the bottom of the flute. Following his instincts, he took her mouth and spilled the rest of the liquid over her breasts.

He caught her gasp with a French kiss, then lowered his lips to taste the heady combination of champagne and Tara's skin. He took the nipple that had taunted him earlier deep into his mouth, groaning at the sensation. ''I've been wanting to do that all night,'' he muttered, and looked into her eyes, which were darkening with desire.

She bit her lip and shifted restlessly, a little sign of arousal that excited him even more. Something about this woman made him want to learn all her secrets. He wanted to be the man to put her over the edge. He wanted to be the man in whom she confided. ''What else have you been wanting to do all night?'' she asked, and that was all the invitation he needed.

He rid himself of the rest of his clothes and devoted himself to learning every inch of her body. He found out that kissing her nipple then blowing on it made her wriggle with pleasure. He found out that open-mouthed kisses on her abdomen almost tickled her. He also learned that her femininity bloomed like a flower when he sank his fingers into her wetness and stroked and caressed her.

He learned that when Tara grew impatient, her kisses were so wild and hot he wondered if he could get scorched. Her hands were eager and bold on his arousal. Just when he thought he couldn't bear one more stroke from her taunting fingertips, she lifted a finger, damp with the honey of his desire, to her lips.

So aroused he thought he would explode, Nicholas rolled them both over so that she straddled his hips. ''Are you ready?''

Her lips swollen and her eyes hazy with passion,

she nodded. Grasping her hips with his hands, he lowered her onto his aching, straining shaft. She closed her eyes and expelled a sexy sigh at their joining.

She was wet and tight, gripping him like a velvet glove. She felt so good, he was pushed to the edge of reason. She began to undulate over him, and he guided her hips for maximum pleasure. He watched her breasts dip and sway with her movements, but it was the expression on her face that compelled him. She was totally focused on him, she was a part of him. Everything she felt was written in her eyes: trust, hope, passion and something deep and ageless.

He felt a rush of primitive possession and something tender he couldn't quite identify. So much of their marriage had been a pretense for the sake of others. But this was real.

Her breath shortened and her eyes dropped to half-mast. She accelerated her movements, and he felt the beginning of her completion with her tiny, intimate clenches. The sight and feel of her sent him flying, and his climax was so powerful it rolled through him like thunder.

Tara collapsed on his chest, and Nicholas tried to catch his breath and a sliver of sanity. In the most basic, elemental way, he had taken her as his wife. With the taking, though, he could have almost sworn he heard a door locking behind him. A whisper slipped through the keyhole. Everything would be different for both of them now. He fought the possibility, making a silent oath to himself and that disturbing whisper. He had made a previous commitment before Tara had come into his life, and that would never change.

The following morning, Tara awakened just as the sun began to peek through the curtains on the windows. Her body was turned toward Nicholas almost the same way a flower turned toward the sun. She indulged the secret opportunity to look at him while he slept. His hair was attractively sleep-tousled, his profile aristocratic. His lips were full and sensual, his chin stubborn. He was such a strong yet gentle man. He was the most mentally fierce man she'd ever met. It was amazing to her that he could be so voracious for her. Last night, it was as if he couldn't get enough of her. He had been determined to learn every part of her body, and he had made her so hot she hadn't known where she ended and he began. And she had been consumed with meeting his every need.

It was as if everything she felt she couldn't say aloud to him she could say with her body.

Tara's heart squeezed painfully in her chest. She was very afraid. What she felt for Nicholas was so powerful that it shook her. She was afraid she had done what she'd sworn she wouldn't do. She was afraid she had fallen in love with him.

She saw Nicholas's eyes blink open and shut several times. He turned his head and gazed at her with his penetrating light blue eyes. "How long have you been watching me?" he asked, and pulled her toward him.

The expression in his eyes made her heart turn over. "Just a couple of minutes. I was wondering if you might like some breakfast."

He slid his hand down her hip. "Afterward," he told her, and drove all thoughts of food from her head.

If Tara could choose a day to seal in a scrapbook forever, it would be this day. Later, she and Nicholas shared breakfast in bed, then took a swim in the ocean. Nicholas tried to talk her into a nude swim, but had to content himself with stealing her bathing suit top until it was time to climb back on the yacht. They laughed and joked with each other, temporarily shelving more weighty concerns.

They shared dinner on the deck and she sat in his arms as they watched the sun set. Tara had the nagging premonition that once they returned to Marceau and the palace tomorrow, everything would be different.

"You're quiet," Nicholas murmured, fanning his fingers through her hair.

"It's been such a fabulous day. I hate for it to end," she said, tucking her head into his throat and inhaling his clean, male scent.

"Can't play forever," he said.

"No. I hope the adjustments won't be too difficult."

"They shouldn't be," he said with a shrug. "I'm not the most visible royal. If the palace PR department tries to book up too much of your time for appearances, tell them to stuff it."

"I really do want to finish my thesis. I've had a

few distractions recently that have kept me from making any progress.''

''Distractions? You're kidding,'' he teased, squeezing her waist. ''A little thing like marrying me.''

She looked up at him and smiled. ''Oh, I would say you're plenty distracting.''

He brushed a kiss over her forehead. ''I'll be out of your way day after tomorrow. I'm headed back to a free clinic on the other side of the island.''

''I'd love to go with you,'' she said wistfully.

''Didn't you just say you wanted to complete your thesis?'' he asked, brushing her nose with his forefinger.

''Yes,'' she said reluctantly. ''But visiting a clinic with you is a fun distraction.'' She looked into his face and dreaded him leaving. How silly, she thought. She should be relieved. ''Do you worry about this turning out all right?''

''You mean our marriage,'' he said. ''I told you. It could end up being the best of two worlds. You'll stay out of my way so I can achieve my goals, and I'll do the same for you. We'll allow each other the independence we crave. We understand each other. We have passion without the complications of emotion. There are some distinct advantages to the fact that you and I didn't marry for love.''

Tara felt a cold chill run through her. Nicholas had assured her that she wouldn't fall in love with him, but she wasn't sure how to stop herself. She sensed it would really upset him if he knew her emotions were involved in a major way. Her heart twisted with the same fear she'd pushed aside this morning. She needed to find a way not to love him.

Within eighteen hours, Nicholas and Tara were waving at the paparazzi as the yacht pulled into shore. Whisked off to the palace, they attended another party planned to celebrate their marriage and homecoming.

Nicholas dutifully stood by Tara's side and accepted congratulations and teasing remarks about the end of his bachelor days. At last, the party ended, and he and Tara retreated to his quarters.

He looked at Tara as she sat in the middle of his bed wearing a silky gown and emotion in her eyes that both warmed him and disturbed him. He couldn't help feeling torn.

She scooted to the edge and crooked her finger for him to come closer. "What?" he asked, allowing himself to be lured for the moment.

She smiled and lifted her fingers to loosen his tie. "I'm going to help you get rid of your tie and shirt. Isn't that what good wives do?"

"It's not a bad start," he said, feeling arousal hum through him as she unbuttoned his shirt.

"The last few days have been so wonderful, I don't want them to end." She slid her finger down his chest to the top of his belt and looked up at him through the dark fringe of her eyelashes. "If you won't let me go with you tomorrow, will you tell me which clinic you'll be visiting?"

His heart gave an odd twist. "You are really interested in what I do, aren't you?"

She wrinkled her brow in confusion. "Of course I am. You make a difference in people's lives. You meet interesting people with problems and help solve them. How could I not be interested?"

Nicholas felt the twisting sensation again and lifted his hand to touch her silky hair. "Every other woman my mother has thrown at me has been bored to tears by my interest in medicine. Why are you different?"

She shrugged and chuckled. "Oops. I tried to warn you, but it's a little late now. You're married to a weirdo."

Weirdo. He damn well liked her kind of weird. He had never thought he would find a woman with whom he could share his passion for his work. Never. Tara was such a compelling mix of qualities. Her genuine interest and honesty were like pure oxygen to him. Nicholas couldn't help admiring her determination to get her education. It was more than admiration. He understood her need to become something different from what was expected of her. That same need echoed inside him.

He wanted to take her with him to the clinic tomorrow, but something stopped him. If he believed love and a conventional marriage wouldn't keep him from his goals, she would be an ideal wife except for the fact that she was damn distracting to him. Even now, he felt the same regret she'd just expressed about their honeymoon ending. She underestimated her appeal, he thought. She underestimated her power. She knew what was important. Her lack of absorption with her appearance only made her more seductive to

him. He wanted her laughter, her tears, her trust. He
could spend entirely too much time wanting her even
though he could have her in his bed every night.

Alarm tightened into a knot in his chest. He
couldn't be sidetracked. He could give Tara his affection, but his head and his heart were his own.

The following morning, Nicholas left their bed by
6:00 a.m. to travel to the other side of the island to
work in a free clinic. Tara scolded herself for missing
him and took her breakfast in her room. She turned
on her computer to delve back into her thesis. Just as
she began to make progress, a knock sounded at the
door. Tara opened the door to a young woman.

"Your Highness, I am Ana Reeves and I have been
assigned the great honor of being your palace aide."

This was news to Tara. She extended her hand.
"I'm pleased to meet you, Ana. I must confess I don't
expect to have the same schedule of duties the other
royal family members have, so I don't plan to give
you much work."

Ana shook her head. "Oh, no, ma'am. If you'll
pardon me for saying so, you're already scheduled
through next month."

Tara blinked. "Excuse me? No one told me I was
scheduled for anything."

Ana smiled. "That's my job, ma'am. You're in
great demand because you're the newest wife of a
Dumont. Prince Nicholas has always been a bit elu-
sive, so I imagine people feel that by meeting you,
they are, in a way, meeting him. I see you're already

dressed. Princess Maggie is feeling a bit under the weather from morning sickness, and she asked if you might consider taking her place at tea with a local women's club.''

Tara swallowed her dismay. She'd rather get a tooth pulled. ''I—I—I'm not sure I have anything to wear,'' she protested.

''I'm told Princess Michelina purchased some wardrobe additions in your absence. Have you checked your closet?''

''No,'' Tara said, confused. ''Just a second.'' She hurried to the large walk-in closet in Nicholas's bedroom. She'd been so busy since she set foot in the palace yesterday that she hadn't unpacked, and this morning, she'd pulled on shorts and a top from a dresser drawer. Tara flung open the closet door, flicked on the light and gazed at her side of the closet. She blinked, unable to find any of the garments she'd brought with her. Instead, more than two dozen new designer outfits hung in their place. Although she knew Michelina meant well, she felt a twinge of resentment.

Slowly she returned to her new aide. ''It appears Michelina has been shopping.''

''Yes. Her taste is exquisite. Shall I tell Princess Maggie's aide that you will attend the tea?''

Tara hesitated. She hadn't taken the time to decide how many royal duties she wanted to take on. On the other hand, she liked Maggie very much and wouldn't dream of letting her down. She sighed. ''I'll do it. Just this once,'' she said.

Ana beamed and clasped her hands together. "She'll be so grateful. Now let me get your appointment book."

After that, Tara felt as if she'd stepped on a motorized banana peel that never stopped. Inundated with invitations, Tara found her schedule packed to the brim. When asked questions about Nicholas, she quickly learned the art of saying something without revealing anything. The questions, however, reminded her that her marriage was in many ways a sham. There was so much she didn't know about the man she called husband.

She tried not to think about the fact that Nicholas was gone nearly every day, even on the weekends. The only time she saw him was during dinner with the family or at night when he physically reminded her of their vows by making love to her.

Craving more of him, she asked him about his day, and he told her stories about the children he treated, and the other doctors who contributed to the free clinics. Tara found herself envying his time away from palace protocol, and was appalled with herself. She knew those feelings were dangerous, because Nicholas had been straight about his priorities from the beginning and she'd accepted them. She desperately needed a change of pace.

One night after they'd made love, she curled against him. "Nicholas, let me go with you tomorrow."

He turned still and silent. "I won't be home until very late."

"That's okay. I just want to go with you for a change. I'll stay out of the way or help patients with their medical forms, but I really want to go."

"But, Tara, I thought you've been wanting to work on your thesis. I haven't heard you talk about it at all, lately."

His objections made her stomach knot, but she was determined. "I haven't had time because of all my royal obligations."

"Tell them to clear your schedule," he said, then ran his hand through her hair. "You're allowing me to accomplish the things that are important to me. I promised you I would do the same for you."

Tara sighed. She couldn't argue his point without revealing the fact that she simply wanted to spend time with him, and if she revealed that, he might guess that she loved him, and things between them would be even worse. Frustrated, she stayed awake, trying not to feel the way she felt.

Tell them to clear your schedule. Easier said than done. Everyone always wanted an explanation, and she couldn't provide one without revealing her goal of earning her master's degree. Even then, she doubted that her education would be considered a valid excuse if duty called.

Every night, Tara asked Nicholas if she could join him the following day, but he always had an excuse. After the fifth night, she was so hurt, she hid in the bathroom and cried. When Nicholas kissed her before he left the next morning, she pretended to be asleep. As soon as he left, she stared at the designer dress hanging outside the closet door. She was scheduled to wear that dress to several activities today where she would pretend to be Nicholas's happy wife.

The truth was, she didn't feel at all like Nicholas's wife, and she certainly didn't feel happy. She felt as if she were wearing someone else's clothes and living someone else's life. Tara felt as if she were drowning.

Was this how the rest of her life would be? Pretending not to love Nicholas, pretending to be someone else? The possibility terrified her so that she felt she could hardly breathe.

Willing herself to calm down, she knew she had to do something drastic. Soon.

Twelve

One week later, Nicholas checked the results on a strep test and wrote the prescription for his droopy ten-year-old female patient as he pulled a blanket around her. "She needs to start taking this immediately and finish all of it even after she starts to feel better," he said to the girl's mother.

"Thank you, Doctor," the woman murmured.

Just as she and her daughter left, Fred entered the makeshift examination room. Nicholas's bodyguard wore an expression of concern as he gave a quick nod. "Your Highness," he said.

"Problem?" Nicholas asked.

"It's your wife, sir," Fred said.

Nicholas's chest twisted like a vice. "Tara? What's wrong? Has there been an accident?"

"No accident has been reported, but she's missing."

"Missing?" Nicholas echoed, alarm slamming into him. "What do you mean, missing?"

"We don't know, but we thought you should be informed. Your wife canceled her scheduled appointments, made a trip to the bank, then stopped by a clothing shop. Her escort lost track of her after that."

Nicholas racked his brain for what could have happened to Tara. Every possibility raced through his mind. What if she'd been kidnapped? His blood ran cold. He rubbed his face. That would be the worst, he thought. He couldn't avoid a twist of discomfort over some of the things she'd told him recently. She'd felt overwhelmed by all the requests for her appearance at various functions, and she hadn't been pleased with her progress on her thesis. She'd repeatedly asked to join him and he'd refused. Nicholas's stomach turned. An unwelcome possibility slithered through his mind like a serpent. What if she'd left him?

He turned to Fred. "We're returning to the palace now."

During the drive home, Nicholas brooded over Tara. He'd been so determined to prove to himself that marriage wouldn't get in the way of his goal of jump-starting the free medical clinics that he'd ignored every warning flag she'd waved. How many times had he ducked her request to join him during one of his clinic days? A bitter taste filled his mouth. She didn't know how distracting he found her. She didn't know that he wasn't sure he would be able to keep his mind on the job if she was near. She didn't know because he sure hadn't told her. The knowledge scared the hell out of him.

He remembered the brief, odd conversation they'd shared this morning before he'd left. Her eyes still sleepy, she'd lifted her arms to embrace him. He remembered how tempted he'd been to crawl back into bed with her.

"Tell me what you like about me," she'd whispered.

An edgy discomfort had twisted through him. If he told her how many things he liked about her, they'd be there all day. Instead, he'd chuckled as he hugged her. "I like the honesty I see in your eyes," he'd said, inhaling her scent. "And I like the way your hair smells. Work on your thesis some today."

He'd left her, feeling as if she'd wanted more from him, needed more. If there'd been nothing inside him to give, he might have dismissed the feeling, but Nicholas felt far more for Tara than he'd been willing to admit, even to himself.

As soon as he arrived at the palace, he brushed past the queen's aide and Michel's inquiring gaze. He strode to the suite he'd shared with Tara for the last month and immediately spotted an envelope with his name on it propped on the bed where they'd made love.

Nicholas tore open the envelope and held his breath as he read Tara's message.

Dear Nicholas,

I've decided to take a sabbatical from palace duty. With each passing day, it seems I slide further and further from my goal of finishing my thesis, and I can't help feeling less of myself. I didn't want to burden you with this, so I made arrangements with the university sponsoring my online classes to spend the summer on campus. I'm hoping I can follow your example of achievement.

In the meantime, I've set up a charitable foundation for the free clinics. You should receive the information by courier this afternoon. Maybe you can think of it as my dowry. Please know you have my admiration and love. We can figure out what to do about our "arrangement" later.

Love,
Tara

Nicholas's chest physically hurt. A wrenching sensation tore through his gut. What if he'd lost her before he'd really even known he had her?

"Nicholas."

Nicholas heard Michel's voice from just a few steps away. "Is Tara okay?"

Nicholas paced the bedroom, looking for signs of her. It appeared she'd left most of her belongings. "Probably," he said, checking the closet. All her clothes hung there as if she would return any minute. "She didn't want anyone to know, but she's working on her master's degree. She hasn't been able to get anything done because of all the ceremonial appearances she's had to make." He went into the bathroom and saw some of her toiletries on the counter. Checking the shower, he saw her shampoo.

I love the way your hair smells. His words from this morning haunted him.

"Where is she?" Michel asked, standing just outside the bathroom door. "And for heaven's sake, what are you looking for?"

"I don't know what I'm looking for," Nicholas said. But deep inside he knew he was looking for a sign that she wasn't truly gone. "She left to attend summer session at a university."

"Which one?" Michel asked, exasperation creeping into his voice.

"I don't know." He felt like a caged animal.

Silence followed. "Your wife has left the country to attend a university and you don't know where it is?"

"I've been busy," he said, and knew the response was lame before it left his lips.

Michel lifted a dark brow. "Perhaps too busy."

Nicholas stiffened. "Perhaps," he conceded.

"What are you going to do?"

Nicholas swore. "I don't know. She kept asking to visit a clinic with me, and I wouldn't let her because I get distracted as hell around her. Plus, I've been damn determined to get the free clinic program off the ground."

"Did you tell her?"

"Tell her what?"

Michel's jaw clenched with stretched patience. Nicholas saw the warning signs, but at the moment he didn't care.

"Did you tell her *why* you didn't want her to visit a clinic with you?"

"No," he admitted, calling himself a fool. He sank down on the bed.

Michel sighed and walked to stand in front of him. "It's none of my business except for the fact that you're my brother, and I wouldn't call myself an expert on women, but Maggie tells me American women want show-and-tell. They want the words, the actions. They want it all. The flip side is they give everything in return."

He hadn't thought he wanted everything from Tara. In fact, he'd told himself and her he hadn't wanted much from her at all. "Ass," he called himself under his breath and raked his hand through his hair. "I didn't want to get emotionally involved with her."

"With *your wife?*" Michel asked in an incredulous tone.

"I didn't want to get sidetracked from getting the free clinic program off the ground."

"Oh," Michel said. "You thought you would have to choose between your passion for your woman and your passion for your career."

Surprised at his brother's understanding, he looked up. "Yes, how did you—" He broke off, recalling that his brother's position as future ruler of Marceau was just as consuming as Nicholas's. His brother was totally in love with his wife, and had in fact lightened up quite a bit since Maggie had come into his life. "So how did you do it?"

"I have never wanted a woman the way I wanted Maggie. Having her with me is the difference between living and just existing. She fulfills me as a man. I'm better because of her, and I will do anything to keep her."

That night when Nicholas went to bed alone and Tara wasn't there to question him about his day, Michel's words played through Nicholas's mind. Why had he fought this? he wondered, and knew it was fear. He hated seeing it in himself. He inhaled deeply, searching for a whiff of her scent on the pillow. An image of her smile floated through his tortured mind, her laughter echoed inside him. Her tenderness.

His chest twisted tight with a sense of loss. What had he done? She had been his for the taking, and that was all he'd done. Take. How in the world could he get her back?

Three days after she'd fled Marceau, Tara carried her two bags of groceries up the stairs to her second-floor apartment. A lot had happened during the last three days. After she'd made flight arrangements and set up the charitable foundation at the bank for the free clinics, she'd ditched her escort by exiting through the back door of a busy boutique and quickly gotten a taxi. Within an hour and a half, she'd taken a seat over the wing of a Boeing 747 jet armed with her laptop, which she'd stashed in a large purse, along with credit cards, passport and toothbrush.

Although Tara had tried not to look back, she had trouble falling asleep at night. She told herself it was the time zone change. It wasn't Nicholas. After all, she'd barely spent any time with him even if she had fallen in love with him.

She fumbled for her keys in her purse as she stopped in front of her door. Balancing both bags on her hips, she stuck the key in the door and was puzzled when the knob turned so easily. It was almost as if she'd forgotten to lock it, which was entirely possible, she supposed, not alarmed. The great thing about Groton Hills, Idaho, was the insulated nature of the small, college town.

She nudged the door open with her knee, then made a quick dash for the kitchen counter, colliding with an all-too-familiar male body. The impact took her breath and sent her groceries tumbling to the floor.

"Milk, eggs," she said desperately, unable to tear her gaze from the man who had filled her heart and mind even with half a world between them. Her heart pounded in her chest. "Nicholas, what are you doing here?"

At the same time, he said, "Why did you set up the foundation?"

He looked travel-weary, and she couldn't stop looking at him. Tara tried to muster some restraint, but she'd never imagined she could miss someone so much.

"I'm here to see you," he said, revealing nothing.

"But how did you get into my apartment?"

"Fred broke in for me. He's handy, that way." He nodded toward the back of the building. "I asked him to wait outside."

She nodded, still wondering why Nicholas was standing in front of her.

"Everyone was worried when you left," he said.

Tara took a careful breath and glanced downward, spotting the leaking milk container. Grateful for the distraction, she quickly scooped it up and put it in the sink. "I'm sorry. I didn't want anyone to worry, but I had to do it quickly, or I knew I wouldn't do it all. It was so easy to get drawn into the never-ending schedule of appointments, and—"

Nicholas slid his arm around her from behind. "Why did you leave me?"

Her heart stalled and she bit her lip. "I didn't leave you, per se. I left so I could finish my thesis."

He slowly turned her around. "Are you sure you didn't leave because I wasn't around more?"

She shook her head because she couldn't tell him the truth. Not this time. "No, I just—"

"Because I've been a fool," he said quietly with eyes so honest and intense she felt as if he were burning past her pretense with a blue flame.

"Fool?" she finally managed.

"When I was lying in bed the other night, I tried to pinpoint the moment you got into my heart. I wondered if it was after we came back from the honeymoon, when we lay in the dark and you would ask me questions. I was usually dead on my feet, but the sound of your voice and the feel of you in my arms gave me peace. Knowing you would be there made all the difference in the world,'' he said.

Tara's heart swelled in her chest, and a tiny seed of hope grew inside her. ''Why didn't you tell me this?''

He scowled. ''Because I was fighting it. I'd convinced myself that I couldn't devote myself to a woman and to launching the free clinic project at the same time. I couldn't divide myself that way. That was part of the reason I didn't want you to visit the clinics with me.''

Remembered hurt stabbed her. ''I don't understand,'' she said. ''You let me go with you once, and I didn't get in the way.''

Nicholas swore under his breath. ''You were never in the way, but my feelings for you grew. I couldn't be in the same room with you without wanting to focus my entire attention on you. All I wanted was to get you alone. I couldn't imagine attending to patients if you were anywhere near.''

Tara shook her head in disbelief. ''I can't believe I had that much of an effect on you. You were gone every day until late at night, even on the weekends.''

''Running,'' he said, lifting his hand to her cheek, ''from something so powerful it scared the hell out of me. I tried to tell myself that I just wanted you, but you didn't just get under my skin, Tara. You got into my heart. I can't let you go.''

A knot formed in her throat, and Tara's eyes burned with the threat of tears. She struggled with elation and fear. "I don't think I can go back to Marceau," she said. "I'll get in your way, and I can't bear the idea of keeping you from a goal you've had for so many years.

"Which brings up the question I asked you just a few moments ago. Why did you set up the charitable foundation?"

She shrugged. "It seemed like the right thing to do. My father asked me what I wanted as a wedding gift, and I told him two million dollars. I figured it would be a good start for you."

Nicholas shook his head. "A two-million-dollar wedding gift. In your letter you called it a dowry. What if I want the woman a lot more than the dowry? I want more than nights with you. I want a life with you."

Tears spilled over, and she began to tremble. She was still afraid to hope. "But what about your project?"

"I don't have to work seven days a week on it. I can't," he said, pulling her into his arms. "As important to me as this is, I can't do it by myself, and I've found some colleagues who are as committed to the project as I am. Two of them even agreed to handle the coordination while I'm away most of the summer."

Tara blinked in surprise and pulled back slightly to look at him. "Most of the summer?"

He met her gaze with dead-on commitment. "I plan to spend the summer with my wife while she finishes her master's degree."

Her heart stuttered. "Nicholas, you can't just sit here while I'm working on my thesis."

"You're right. There's a teaching medical center thirty miles from here. I plan to assist a colleague who specializes in gerontology three days a week. That will give you time to work on your thesis without me interrupting you," he said with a slight grin, then turned serious. "It will also give you and me time to stop pretending we don't love each other."

Tara bit her lip and blinked back another spate of tears.

"*Chérie,* you're killing me with your tears. Are you happy or sad?"

"Happy, I think," she said. "I couldn't even allow myself to hope that you would love me."

"You know you left your shampoo," he told her.

Tara blinked at the abrupt change in subject. "I left most of my things."

"I missed you so much when you left that I got up in the middle of the night to smell your shampoo. But it's just not the same as when its scent is on your hair. Tara, forgive me. Give me a chance to win you."

"Oh, Nicholas," she said, her heart so full she thought it might burst, "you won me a long time ago."

"Then give me a chance to spend my life winning you, and let me start now."

"Oh, yes," she said, feeling as if the stars were clicking into alignment as he dipped his head to kiss her.

He scooped her up into his arms and walked toward the back of the apartment. "It can't possibly get better than this," she murmured more to herself than him. "Not possibly."

"Yes, it can. When we return to Marceau, we're moving out of the palace. The palace was fine for my bachelor days, but I want more privacy for you and me now. Especially in the current emotional climate."

"What's wrong?" she asked, lifting her fingertip to the frown between his eyebrows. "Problems between Michelina and the queen?"

"World War Three," he said, setting her down on the bed. "My mother has been waiting none too patiently for more news from the private investigator about my brother Jacques."

"This is the one you all thought had drowned?"

He nodded, jerking loose his tie and unbuttoning his shirt. "My mother hasn't wanted to tell Michelina because my sister has been so flighty and temperamental lately, so she held a private meeting with the Dumont men and told us that the investigator believes Jacques may be living in the United States."

Although she was distracted by the sight of his muscular chest, Tara felt a sliver of surprise. "Wouldn't that be amazing if you could find him? Can you imagine what he's doing?"

"We don't know much except that his adoptive father was a fisherman in the Caribbean and they migrated to the United States."

"So why is Michelina upset?"

Nicholas made a face. "She found out about the

private meeting and popped a cork. My mother is afraid she's about to run away. When they're in the same room, they're either arguing with each other or not speaking at all," he said, diverting her attention as he started to unfasten his slacks. "One more reason we don't need to be at the palace 24/7." He pushed his slacks and briefs down his legs, and Tara was reminded again of what an impressive virile body he had.

"You're overdressed," he told her, joining her on the bed. He lifted her shirt over her head, then went to work on her jeans. "I need to be as close to you as I can get."

Tara felt a drumbeat start in her blood.

He buried his face in her hair and inhaled. "Oh, Tara you smell so good, feel so good," he said, running his hands over her bare skin as if to reassure himself that she was real and his.

"One more thing before I get too busy." He slid his fingertips over her breasts, then rubbed his thumbs over her nipples. She arched against him, thinking he'd already gotten busy.

"I've chosen who I want to head the charitable foundation," he said, lowering his lips to one of her already stiff nipples.

Tara struggled to concentrate. "Who?"

"You." He lifted his head and looked at her with such a powerful combination of passion, trust and love that she could hardly breathe.

"Me?" she squeaked.

"You. There's no one on this earth I trust more to

manage the foundation. There's no one I trust more with my life.''

Tara's heart squeezed tight. ''Oh, Nicholas, I don't know what to say.''

He dipped his mouth over hers for a lingering kiss. ''You don't have to say anything,'' he said, and his eyes glinted devilishly. ''Unless you want to moan or scream a little.''

By the time he finished with her, she'd done both.

Epilogue

Nicholas was so proud, he could have burst the buttons on his jacket. As his wife walked across the small wooden platform for her master's degree diploma, he gave a loud, distinctly unroyal whistle and clapped his hands.

Tara tossed a sideways glance in his direction, but she couldn't hide her joy. It shone in her eyes and the wide smile that stretched from ear to ear. Nicholas just thanked his lucky stars he could be a part of it all. He had never felt more complete than he had during the last ten weeks he and Tara had shared together while she finished her degree and he studied with a local physician specializing in gerontology.

Grant York, Tara's father, stood beside him in the back of the room and joined him as they applauded.

"She did this all on her own," Grant said with a mixture of pride and regret in his voice. "She sure didn't get any help from me."

"I don't know about that," Nicholas said. "She tells me her dad wrote the book on the power of determination."

Surprise glinted in Grant's eyes. "Really," he said, then nodded as if the notion pleased him. "I wouldn't have missed this for the world," Grant said. "I have to leave for Chicago right after the ceremony, but I'm glad she's finally getting her moment in the sun." He gave Nicholas an assessing glance. "You know she was hell-bent and determined not to marry you even after I received the photos," he said in a low voice.

Nicholas nodded, remembering how he'd sweated, wondering if Tara would ditch his royal butt at the altar. "I wasn't sure she would go through with it until I saw her walk down the aisle."

"Well, you have me to thank for it," Grant said.

Nicholas did a double take. He couldn't wait to hear this. "How is that, sir?"

"I spent four hours on the phone explaining to her how marriage was the only way to save her reputation. She wasn't having any of it until I asked her how those photos could affect you. That stopped her in her tracks."

Nicholas stared at Grant, then looked at Tara as she rejoined the other candidates for degrees. His heart turned inside out. He should be used to the sensation since it seemed Tara turned his head and heart on a regular basis. "She married me to protect my reputation," he muttered in amazement.

"She did," Grant said. "Like I said, you have me to thank for it, and you can thank me by keeping her barefoot and pregnant. I want grandchildren."

Nicholas met his father-in-law's cagey gaze. The man was just as pushy as Nicholas's mother. "You can rest assured that I'll expose Tara to the possibility of pregnancy at every opportunity, but there won't be any babies until we're ready," he said, even though the notion of a child had sneaked into Nicholas's brain a few times lately. He would have said he was the last man interested in any familial chains that bind, but damn if he didn't like the idea of Tara growing big with his baby.

The dean conferred the degrees to the small group of candidates, and Tara walked toward them.

"What do you mean when she's ready?" Grant asked.

"I mean Tara is going to be busy. She has accepted the position of Director of the Free Clinic Support Charity."

It was Grant's turn to give a double take. "Director?"

"Is there anyone else I could trust to do a better job?" Nicholas asked.

Grant hesitated a microsecond, then shook his head and smiled. "No one," he said, and opened his arms to Tara. "Congratulations, sweetheart. I couldn't be more proud."

Tara gave her father a big hug. "Thanks, Dad. It means so much that you could come."

Grant pulled back and Nicholas would almost swear he could see a tear in the tough tycoon's eye. "You know I believe you can do anything you want," Grant said in a gruff voice.

She smiled. "High praise coming from you."

"I mean it," her father said, rubbing her chin with his thumb. "And if you should decide you want children…"

Tara laughed, and the rich full sound filled up Nicholas's heart. "I'll let you know." She kissed her father on the cheek. "Thanks again for coming, Dad."

Grant gave a salute, then strode out of the room. His jet was waiting.

Still smiling, Tara turned to Nicholas and just looked at him, her eyes full of a dozen emotions.

He took her hand in his. "How does it feel?"

"Great," she said. "Kinda."

"Kinda?"

"A big part of the reason I was so determined to finish this degree was because I wanted to feel good enough for you. I'm happy and relieved that I finished, but I'm still just me."

"Just you," Nicholas said in disbelief, drawing her against him. "Silly woman, you have always been good enough. Don't ever forget that."

"That sounds like an order."

"It is," he said. "Now what does the graduate want to do?"

"Eat a quick bite and leave for Marceau," she said. "We're packed and ready to go. I want to see our new house."

He studied the faint blue circles beneath her eyes. He had noticed she'd seemed more tired during the last month and attributed it to her intense study schedule. It seemed she grabbed a nap at every opportunity. "Are you sure you don't want to go somewhere for a couple days of rest? You've earned it."

She shook her head, and her tassel bobbed. "I want to get to our house. The sooner, the better."

"As you wish, Your Highness," he said.

She swatted him. "I'm not sure I'll ever get used to the new title."

"Maybe if I start calling you Princess in bed," he said and tugged at the tassel on her mortarboard. "Speaking of which, this tassel gives me some ideas."

As promised, Tara and Nicholas ate a quick meal, then boarded a private jet for Marceau. Nicholas noticed she picked at her food, and as soon as the jet took off, Tara fell asleep. She slept the entire flight. He awakened her just as they prepared to land.

When she fell back asleep during the limo ride to their new house, he fought an undercurrent of concern. Her need for rest was natural, he told himself, but he couldn't help wondering if something else might be wrong. He searched his mind for symptoms she may have exhibited during the last few weeks.

Fatigue, poor appetite. He frowned, deciding to arrange for her to visit the palace doctor.

The limo pulled into the gated drive of the two-story stone villa his aide had chosen with the assistance of Maggie and Michelina.

Tara awakened and sheepishly covered a yawn. "I'm sorry," she murmured and looked outside the window. "We're here. It's beautiful."

Nicholas took her by the hand and led her to the front door where a housekeeper stood waiting. Just before they entered, he swooped her up in his arms to carry her into the house.

Tara gave a start of surprise.

"Since we married in a rush, we missed a few traditions."

"Like carrying the bride across the threshold," she said and met his gaze. "Are you trying to make me feel like a bride again?"

"I'm hoping I can talk you into doing something with that tassel. Second honeymoon," he said.

"I could have sworn you were antimarriage," she said.

"You changed my mind."

She bit her lip in a surprising show of nerves. "I hope so," she muttered.

Nicholas wondered where her doubts had come from. Despite her protests, he carried her to the master bedroom on the second floor. She looked around the room, nodding in approval at the blue and ivory décor. "Maggie and Michelina did a very nice job," Tara said. "But I want you to see another room."

Puzzled, he glanced at her and allowed her to slide to her feet. "What room?"

She inhaled and took his hand. "This way," she said, and walked with him down the hallway. They passed a bathroom and linen closet, then Tara pulled him into a freshly painted, but empty room. She pulled away from him.

"I need to tell you something, and I'm afraid," she said, biting her lip.

The fear in her eyes made his gut clench. "What is it? You can tell me anything."

Her expression full of uncertainty, she gave a nod that lacked conviction. "You know how I've been tired a lot lately?"

Nicholas's stomach turned, and he mentally clicked through a list of terminal diseases. "Have you been hiding something from me about your health?"

She wrung her hands together. "Kinda," she said and her eyes grew shiny with tears.

Alarm shot through him and he moved to take her in his arms. "Tara, what—"

She lifted her hand to keep him away. "This is difficult, so just let me finish. I know you didn't want to get married, but you did. I also know that even when you got married, you didn't plan to get so emotionally involved."

"But I did."

"Right. Well there's another thing I'm pretty sure you didn't plan."

"And that is?" he prompted over a hard knot in his throat.

She paused for a long moment, then met his gaze. "I'm pregnant," she said and her face crumpled. "That's why I brought you in here. This is going to be the nursery. I know you didn't really want to get married, and you probably didn't want to start a family for years, but—"

Relief coursed through him and he pulled her against him. "Why didn't you tell me?"

"I was afraid you'd be disappointed," she said, her voice cracking and breaking his heart. "A wife is enough baggage without adding another little person."

"Tara, how could you think that?"

She looked up and met his gaze. "I know what your goals are, and they don't include a baby."

He lifted his hand to her cheek, amazed at how she'd changed his point of view. "They didn't," he corrected. "Past tense. I didn't want to get married until I met you. You changed my mind. Don't you understand? I'm a better doctor by having you in my life. I'm a better man." He touched her still-flat abdomen with wonder and kissed her deeply. "I wonder if she'll have your smile."

"Who?"

"Our baby."

Tara searched his gaze as if she were afraid to hope. "I was hoping *he* would have your eyes," she said tentatively.

Nicholas grinned. "I was thinking *she* would have your determination."

"Or *he* might have your intelligence."

"Or *she* would have yours."

She looked at him with a mixture of surprise and faint exasperation. "I can't believe you've actually thought about having a baby with me."

"Believe it."

She swallowed. "What if we have a boy?"

"Then I will be proud as hell and love him," Nicholas said, then added slyly, "And we can try again."

Tara blinked. "Pardon me? Again?"

"And again. As many times as you're willing."

She laughed nervously. "Why do you want a girl?"

"Because I think you should be reproduced."

Her eyes softened. "That's funny. I thought the same thing about you. Every night during the last few weeks, I made a wish just before I fell asleep that you would be happy when I told you about the baby." She shook her head in wonder and her blue eyes filled with tears. "You made my wish come true."

Nicholas's chest felt tight as he took a deep breath. "Tara, I want to make all your wishes come true," he said. And she had every confidence he would succeed.

*   *   *   *   *

Princess in His Bed
LEANNE BANKS

This book is dedicated to all my royally
wonderful readers who wanted Michelina's story.
You're all princesses in my eyes.

Prologue

The wig was going to change her life.

Michelina could barely contain her excitement as she pulled off her tiara and covered her black hair with the dull brown wig. She'd already scrubbed her face free of her usual cosmetics and changed out of her chic designer dress into an unremarkable skirt and blouse she'd filched months ago from her new sister-in-law, Tara York Dumont.

Everyone had remarked on how Michelina had transformed Tara's wardrobe and sense of style. They didn't realize that all the while Michelina had been quietly taking lessons from Tara and observing the advantages of being a plain woman. Everyone noticed a glamorous, beautiful woman, but a plain woman disappeared, which was exactly what Michelina intended to do. Of course, Tara hadn't really been plain.

She'd just dressed herself unbecomingly to disrupt her father's matchmaking attempts. Michelina's brother Nicholas had seen straight through Tara's ploy, and the two of them had quickly learned they were soul mates.

Sweet, Michelina thought, rolling her eyes, but she had lots of life she wanted to live before her mother, queen of the island country of Marceau, succeeded in marrying her off to Count Ferrar of Italy.

Michelina made a face at the mirror in the powder room of her cousin's house in Paris. Music from the party vibrated off the walls. She put in the tinted contact lenses she'd ordered from the Internet along with her fake passport. Another observation from Tara. Amazing what a girl can order off the Internet to alter the color of her distinctive silver eyes to brown, and her heart raced at her reflection. She didn't even recognize herself!

Shoving her fake passport and the rest of her belongings into her reversible bag, Michelina took a deep breath, left the bathroom and wound through the throng of guests. Her bodyguards stood next to the front door. She knew their instructions were not only to protect her, but also to keep her from running away. Michelina had nearly bitten her tongue off at least a thousand times during the last month in order to persuade her mother to allow her to attend her cousin's party.

Reaching the front door, she leaned close to the housekeeper so she wouldn't be overheard. "I need some air," she said.

The housekeeper opened the door. "Of course, mademoiselle."

"Merci beaucoup," Micheline thanked her, and slipped out the door. Her heart hammering a mile a minute, she forced herself to walk down the hall, then down the stairs. Luck was in her favor. The doorman caught a cab for her right away. Her muscles pulled tighter than an overstretched rubber band, she knew she wasn't nearly free yet. At Charles de Gaulle Airport, she made the endless trek through security, her palms sweating all the while. What if they found out her passport was fake? What if they pulled off her wig?

But her fears proved unfounded, she finally boarded the jet and took her seat, her first time in coach. She thought of her brother Nicholas and his wife, Tara, her oldest brother Michel and his wife, Maggie, and felt a stab of guilt. They would worry. Then she remembered the secret they'd kept from her. Her anger and resolve flared like a wild fire.

They'd thought she couldn't handle the news that the brother they'd long believed dead was in fact alive in the United States. She would prove them wrong. She would go one better. She would find him and bring him back. She would prove once and for all that she wasn't Princess Useless.

The jet began to move faster, the engines roared and the force of the takeoff pushed her back against her seat. Euphoria shot through Princess Michelina Dumont. She had escaped.

Her mind was already in America. First stop: Wyoming.

One

Princess Michelina had bought herself a black Ford truck.

Exhilaration at her newfound freedom, however, was tempered with a sliver of uneasiness. She was somewhere in Wyoming, but she wasn't exactly sure where, and she had a sinking sensation she should have purchased a mobile Global Positioning System.

The skinny road wound through the darkness with a few token signs. It was bad enough that she didn't know where she was, but Michelina constantly had to fight the urge to veer to the left side of the road.

Why did Americans drive on the wrong side of the road, anyway?

She turned a corner, and her headlights flashed across a cow standing in the middle of the road. Panic sliced through her. She veered to the right and barreled through a fence. Before she could catch her breath or regain control of the truck, a barn loomed in front of her. With a cry of panic, Michelina slammed on the brakes.

Too late. She plowed into the barn. The last thing she saw was the steering wheel before her head slammed into it. Everything went black.

"Truck hit the barn! Truck hit the barn," Gary Ridenour yelled as he burst into the foyer of Jared McNeil's quiet home.

Jared kissed his chance for an hour of evening peace goodbye and stuffed the newspaper into the magazine holder as he stood. He fought an undertow of dread. "What do you mean, 'truck hit the barn'?"

Breathless from his sprint, Gary shrugged and waved his arms. "Some truck came out of nowhere and ran into Romeo's barn."

Alarm sliced through Jared and he immediately grabbed his keys and headed for the door. "Romeo!" Romeo was his prize bull, and raked in the bucks with stud fees. Jared stomped through the front door and down the steps with Gary at his heels. "What happened?"

Gary shrugged again. "I'm not sure. I thought about checking on Romeo, but decided I'd better come and get you first."

Jared nodded and climbed into his truck. "Damn, if anything happened to that bull, whoever ran into the barn is going to learn the meaning of the word *trouble.*"

Gary scooted into the truck just as Jared started the

engine, shooting his boss a wary look. Everyone knew how important Romeo was. "That bull's tough. Maybe he slept through the whole thing."

"Romeo's a big baby," Jared corrected, scowling as he turned onto a dirt road. "He's probably bawling his head off."

Jared didn't need this. Besides being the owner of the largest ranch in southeastern Wyoming, he was interim everything at the moment. The local mayor had quit ranching and retired to Florida, so Jared was filling in until someone's arm was twisted hard enough to persuade him or her to take on that position, and since his sister and her husband were recovering from a serious automobile accident, Jared was filling in as caretaker to his two young nieces. Rounding the curve in the road, he pulled to a sharp stop and stepped out of the truck.

The night was black as pitch, and the first sound Jared heard was a bull bawling for all he was worth. Just as he'd predicted. He scowled. "I guess that's a good sign. At least he's not dead," he muttered as Gary joined him and they walked into the barn.

Romeo was alternately pawing the ground and bawling as he lifted his head toward a black truck in the barn. Jared felt a sliver of relief that his prize animal appeared to be physically unharmed. Ready to tear a strip off the reckless driver who'd crashed into the barn, he walked toward the truck. "Hey, buddy!" he called. "You better have damn good insurance—" He broke off when he saw a woman slumped over the wheel. Swearing under his breath, he pulled the door open. "What the—"

Gary raced to his side. "What is it, Mr. McNeil? What…?" Gary gawked. "It's a lady."

Jared tentatively reached out to touch the woman, and she moaned, sending a trickle of relief through him. "She's alive," he murmured. "Miss?" he asked, reaching for her hand and patting it.

"Should we call 911?" Gary asked.

"Let's give it another minute or two," Jared said, still patting her hand.

She lifted her head slightly and moaned again. *"Mon dieu,"* she said under her breath.

Jared couldn't hold back a wince at the furrow of pain between her dark eyebrows. Her dark silky hair sweeping over her cheek couldn't conceal her finely sculpted bone structure and velvet-textured, tanned complexion. Her eyelids fluttered, her eyes slowly focusing on him.

The intense, light-gray, almost silver color of her eyes took his speech for a full moment. He blinked, and of its own volition, his gaze traveled down the rest of her. She wore a fitted T-shirt that emphasized her small, round breasts and didn't quite meet the top of the low-slung jeans that hugged her hips and long legs.

Her eyelids fluttered again, and her dark eyelashes provided a sexy peek-a-boo fringe that concealed her exotic eyes.

Jared inhaled and caught a whiff of a scent that combined French, forbidden and expensive. He had the uncomfortable feeling that this woman was going to be trouble.

"Are you okay?" he asked.

She nodded slightly, then winced. "I think so, but my head hurts like bloody hell."

Trying to place her accent, which had traces of French, British and American, he pointed his finger at her forehead. "You're going to have a goose egg."

She glanced past the steering wheel. "What about the damage? How bad is the damage?"

"I think the bull will be okay, but you knocked out most of this side of the barn."

"I was referring to my truck," she said in a regal tone.

Jared raised his eyebrows. "I haven't inspected your truck. As long as you have good insurance, you should be okay."

She looked at him with a blank gaze, and Jared felt his stomach sink. No insurance. He would bet half his acreage on it. He narrowed his eyes. He was done helping wealthy damsels in distress. If Miss Silver Eyes didn't have insurance, then she could fork over the money. "I'm Jared McNeil and this is my barn and my ranch. What's your name?"

"Mi—" She broke off, and a sliver of panic crossed her face.

"Mi—what?"

"Mimi," she said with conviction.

"Mimi what?"

She paused a half beat, her gaze flickering away from his. "Deer—" she looked at him again "—man. Deerman. Mimi Deerman. Please accept my apologies for running into your barn."

She said it with such smooth expectancy that he almost nodded and said of course. But he caught himself. "The insurance company can handle the official apology. Are you from around here? Is there someone we can call?" he asked, even though he already knew the answer.

She shook her head, wincing slightly again.

He felt a small measure of sympathy for her. It was dark, she was lost...without insurance. His blood pressure spiked, and he pushed the thought aside. "Do you want to go to the hospital?"

Her eyes widened in panic. "Oh, no. I'm fine," she said, slowly stepping from the truck. "I just need—" She broke off, and the color drained from her face.

Jared automatically caught her against him. "Are you sure you don't want to go to the hospital?"

"Absolutely," she insisted. "Maybe I could just sleep in the truck."

Gary made a clucking sound. "You can't let her sleep in the truck, not with a hurt head."

Jared swallowed a growl of frustration. "I've got an extra room. You can stay at the ranch. Just for the night," he said for everyone's benefit, including his own.

"I'm greatly indebted to you." She met his gaze and he felt the punch of emotional fire in his gut. Like heartburn. He wouldn't be a man if a vision of her expressing her gratitude in dark, forbidden ways didn't cross his mind.

He cleared his throat. "It's just a night's sleep. We'll settle the score on the insurance in the morning."

Her face paled again, and he lifted her off her feet.

"Gary, see what you can do about securing the barn for the night. Move Romeo to one of the other barns. We'll take care of this mess in the morning."

Carrying her soft, curvy body to his truck, he tried not to inhale her man-trapping scent, and steeled himself against the temptation to take another slow, leisurely glance down her lithe, inviting form. Once upon a time, his sister had diagnosed his problem with women, and Miss Mimi's collision into his life just proved the point. According to his sister, Gina, Jared was a chaos magnet. He attracted women bent on wreaking chaos on his world and the world at large. One look at Mimi Deerman, and he knew she would give new meaning to the term.

The sounds of shrieking demons vibrated inside Michelina. Squinting her eyes, she winced at the obscenely bright light filling the room. She put her hands over her ears and slid her aching head underneath the pillow. Who on earth was screaming? Her mother would lay a Fabergé egg at such a disruption in the palace.

Michelina rubbed her cheek against the pillow. Something about the texture felt different. She peeked out from under the pillow. She wasn't in the palace, she recalled, her head still pounding like a cannon firing a ceremonial salute. She was in Wyoming.

Excitement and apprehension knotted her stomach as the previous evening's events came back to her. Her truck, she thought, frowning. She needed to get it repaired so she could continue her search for

Jacques. Slowly rising, she thought of the man who had carried her to his home.

Obligatorily kind, attractive if a woman preferred the overbearing, alpha-male type. Which she didn't, she thought, rolling her eyes. Her family was full of overbearing males.

The door to her bedroom burst open, and two little girls raced through, with Jared McNeil and a barking dog on their heels.

"Don't! Katie! Lindsey!" He finally stopped them when he grabbed them by the backs of their nightgowns. "I told you—" He broke off when he caught sight of Michelina sitting up in bed.

"Who's she?" the older child asked.

"She's here—" he hesitated briefly, then went on "—because she had car trouble and she got stranded last night. She's leaving today."

Michelina raised her eyebrows at his muddy explanation. "Car trouble. My truck—"

"Mimi Deerman," he interrupted loudly, "meet Katie and Lindsey, my nieces. They're staying with me while my sister and her husband recover from injuries they received—"

"—in a real bad car crash," Katie said, with worry in her young eyes.

Realization hit her. Mr. McNeil's altering of the facts was his attempt to be sensitive to his little nieces' situation. Her estimation of him climbed a notch. "Oh," Michelina said. "It's my pleasure to meet you. I'm very sorry to hear of your parents' accident."

Katie looked up at Mr. McNeil. "She's pretty, but she talks kinda funny."

He shrugged in agreement, then steered the girls toward the door. "Helen has oatmeal waiting for you at the table. Come on, Leo," he said to the dog, and tossed a glance over his shoulder. "You and I can settle the insurance matter in a few minutes."

Michelina froze. *Insurance?* Catching Mr. McNeil's intent gaze, she smiled to hide her panic. "No problem. After all, how much can a barn wall cost?"

Thirty minutes later, Michelina nearly fell out of the leather chair on which she perched in Jared McNeil's home office. She shook her head in dismay. "A barn wall *can't* cost that much."

"That doesn't include the repairs to your truck."

"The repairs can't be very expensive. It's just the front of the truck."

He gave her a pitying glance. "You'd be amazed what bodywork costs."

She opened her mouth to protest, but Jared's two nieces burst through the door. "Helen fell and she says she can't walk on her ankle!" Katie said.

"Helen?" Michelina echoed.

"Helen's my housekeeper. She was asleep when I brought you in last night," Jared said as he stood. "Where is she?" he asked Katie.

"At the bottom of the basement stairs."

"We'll finish this in a few minutes," he said to Michelina. "Whoever said trouble comes in threes was wrong," he muttered as he left the room. "My troubles come in *tens*."

Michelina felt a modicum of sympathy for the man.

Between the responsibility of his nieces, Michelina's untimely entrance into his barn, and Helen's fall, she could see that things definitely weren't going his way. She, however, had her own concerns. Michelina had brought enough money to live comfortably for one month, and then the truck had cost a little more than she had planned. She couldn't draw additional money from her account because it would be traced to her, and her one shot at independence would be over before she'd experienced anything. She felt her confidence begin to deflate like a balloon. What if what they said was true? What if she was too flighty to take care of herself or anything of importance? What if she really was Princess Useless?

The questions stabbed at a secret part of her she kept hidden. A princess wasn't supposed to suffer a lack of self-confidence, and if she did, God forbid that she expose it. At the thought of returning to Marceau, Michelina's stomach began to knot and burn. It seemed as if it had been knotting and burning more frequently during the last year.

Closing her eyes, she took a deep breath and tried to assure herself. She'd just got started. Sure, she had hit a bump in the road, technically a barn, but that didn't mean she had to abandon her plan. She would just need to improvise.

Jared McNeil appeared in the doorway, raking his fingers through his thick dark hair. "Do you know anything about kids?" he asked doubtfully.

The skepticism in his dark gaze rubbed at a raw spot. She'd seen the same expression on her brothers' and mother's faces. "Of course I do," she said, and

rationalized that she did have nieces and a nephew...
and she had once been a child herself after all.

"I wouldn't normally do this, but I think Helen has
broken her ankle, and that means I've got to get her
to the clinic so it can be treated. I don't want to take
the girls," Jared explained.

"I can take care of them," she offered impulsively.
How hard could it be? His two nieces seemed like
sweet children.

"You're sure?"

"Quite sure," she said, irritation bleeding into her
tone as she stood to make herself feel more equal to
him. It didn't quite work since he was still at least
six inches taller. She lifted her chin to compensate.

"Well, I'm stuck, so you'll have to do. I'll give
you my cell phone number in case you run into trouble. You might have to fix their lunches."

Michelina blinked. The palace staff hadn't allowed
her near the kitchen since the cake she'd attempted
to bake had exploded in the oven.

He sighed as if he'd read her mind. "PBJ sandwiches will do."

She refused to allow him to believe she didn't
know what PBJ sandwiches were. "I'm sure they
will."

"Katie can help you if you get in a bind."

Michelina narrowed her eyes. Now that was *in-
sulting*. "How old is Katie?"

"Five, but she likes to help in the kitchen. Something tells me you haven't spent a lot of time there,"
he muttered, pulling a card from his desk and pointing

to a number printed on the business card. "Call if you have any problems at all."

"There won't be any," she assured him, reaching for the card.

"I want your word," he said, holding on to the card.

She met his gaze and felt indignation mingle with a strange desire to meet his challenge. Michelina sensed this man was everything she wasn't—confident in himself and his abilities, accomplished, successful. She envied him all those qualities and was determined to get the same for herself.

"I give you my word of honor," she said quietly, meeting his hard gaze without flinching.

She saw a snap of electricity flicker through his dark blue eyes, and it filled her with a heady sensation, like drinking one too many glasses of champagne. His sexual intensity caught her off guard, and she couldn't make herself look away.

He pressed the card into her hand, and the touch of his warm, calloused palm made her nerve endings jump. For a few seconds, she wondered if he would be just as confident as a lover. She had a sneaking sensual suspicion that Jared McNeil knew how to motivate a woman to take care of his needs and how to take care of hers with breath-robbing ease.

An internal warning bell clanged, and Michelina took a mental step back. That blow to her head must have affected her thinking ability. She would examine her response later, she thought, pushing aside a tinge of uneasiness. He was just a man, she told herself. She would watch over his nieces this morning, be on her way this afternoon and forget him by evening.

Two

She could speak four languages fluently and had graduated from college with honors. She had been taught the names of the heads of state for every country in the world.

Why hadn't anyone bothered to teach her how to change a diaper? The palace nursery aides had always taken care of that particular task.

Lindsey would celebrate her third birthday in six months, but she wasn't ready to leave the world of diapers. It was humiliating, but Katie coached Michelina through the task. She just hoped the diaper wouldn't fall off. In her effort to avoid making it fit too snugly, she might have erred too far in the other direction.

Lunch followed and Michelina scowled as she remembered Jared's suggestion that she might need help for that task, too. If he hadn't abbreviated the name of the sandwich, she wouldn't have had a problem. Even she could spread peanut butter and jelly on slices of bread.

After lunch, she read approximately eighteen books in hopes of coaxing the girls into taking a nap. No such luck. Desperate, she played dress-up with the girls, applying lipstick and nail polish, fixing their hair and allowing them to take turns wearing the tiara she'd stuffed into her bag at the party when she'd escaped.

When Jared walked through the door with Helen, a middle-aged woman wearing a cast and walking on crutches, Michelina was pleased that she had delivered on her promise.

He didn't look pleased at all.

"I can probably still cook," Helen was saying, "but I don't think I'll be able to keep up with the girls while I'm on crutches."

"No, you won't, and finding someone is going to be—" He broke off and raked his hand through his hair.

Helen glanced at Michelina and gave a weary smile. "I don't believe we've met. I'm Helen Crosby. Jared told me about you. Mimi, is it?"

"Yes, it is. A pleasure to meet you. I'm so sorry about your fall. Perhaps you should sit down and rest—you've had a terrible day."

Helen glanced at Jared. "She's lovely," she said in surprise, making Michelina suspect Jared hadn't described her in flattering terms.

She studied his face, but he'd plastered a blank

expression on his tough features. Michelina was no fool. She'd seen her brothers don the same expression too many times to count.

"Let's get you to your room," he said gruffly to Helen.

"Maybe," Helen began thoughtfully, "maybe Mimi would be willing to care for the children."

Jared and Michelina shook their heads with equal fervor.

"Oh, no," Michelina said.

"No chance," Jared said at the same time.

Although Michelina was in full agreement, his tone grated on her.

Helen shrugged. "Well, it's bound to take a week or more to get her truck fixed, so she's got to stay somewhere."

But not here, Michelina thought.

"Not here," Jared said aloud.

She frowned, annoyed again by his tone.

"And you mentioned there might be a problem with her insurance," Helen added gently. "Maybe you could work out the barn damage in trade."

"Trade!" Michelina echoed.

"I don't think she's qualified," Jared said flatly.

"I could supervise," Helen said, then sighed. "You were right, Mimi. I think I need to go lie down. I'm sure you two will settle this in everyone's best interest."

Michelina's mind turned upside down as Jared helped Helen to her bedroom. She paced the length of the den as she whispered to herself, "Child care? Trade? This is ridiculous. How am I supposed to be independent if I stay locked up here? Surely, it would be better to be captive on Marceau than—''

Jared strode back into the room and pinned her with a gaze that stopped her words and stretched her nerves. ''Do you have insurance or not?''

Michelina swallowed over a sudden knot in her throat. ''I had just purchased the truck and hadn't quite—''

''Just what I thought,'' he said, interrupting her. ''No insurance. How do you plan to pay for damages?''

She bit her lip as he moved toward her. She wasn't accustomed to people invading her personal space without her permission. ''Well, I can pay for the damages. Just not now.''

''When?''

She cleared her throat. ''Perhaps a month. Or two.''

He stared at her in amazement. ''You think I'm going to accept an IOU from *you?*''

Insulted, she opened her mouth to protest, then remembered she was operating under an assumed name. The man was, unfortunately, justified in not trusting her. ''I had hoped.''

His jaw hardened and he shook his head slowly. ''No way. I'm not taking it in the wallet again for a pretty face. We'll go with Helen's suggestion. You can work off your debt to me in trade. Helen will supervise you.''

Shock raced through her. *''Supervise me!''* she echoed, nearly bursting with indignation. ''I never—''

''I thought so,'' Jared said, interrupting her again.

"I thought you didn't have much child care experience. That's why Helen will supervise you."

Michelina shook her head. "This is insane."

"I agree. It didn't show great planning on your part not to get insurance."

The comment stung. Michelina rebelled at the idea that she couldn't take care of herself. She might not be acquainted with everyday matters, but she could learn. She lifted her chin. "What if I refuse?"

"Then you can go thumb a ride," he said, cocking his head toward the front door. "Your truck isn't drivable."

Fighting the suffocating sense that she was trapped, she searched for another solution and couldn't think of one.

"You don't have much of a choice," he said, his gaze holding a mix of emotions as he let out a long sigh. "Neither do I."

Michelina closed her eyes for a second in search of peace and sanity then opened them again to the man currently responsible for her insanity. She swallowed her pride. "How long?"

He shook his head in disgust and headed for the door. "As long as I need you. I'm going to check the stock. Make sure the girls get dinner and baths."

Michelina stood gaping after him long after she'd watched his fabulous backside leave the house. She was trying to come to terms with what had just taken place. She had somehow become employed—however, she wouldn't have any money to show for it. And she was, of all things, a nanny!

The realization began to set in. She could envision

her brothers howling with laughter at her circumstances. Her mother wouldn't be at all amused, she thought, shuddering at the image of her cold, disapproving response. Had Michelina really screwed things up already?

The answer to that question mocked her like her worst nightmare. A tug on her jeans distracted her from her distress. She looked down to see Katie and Lindsey, their precious faces beseeching hers. Her heart softened. They really were sweet little girls— active and demanding, but sweet. She felt touched that they had sought her out.

"Lindsey's diaper is dirty," Katie announced.

A sound awakened Jared at 2:00 a.m. Lifting his head from his pillow, he listened as he heard the sound of the stairs creaking. He hoped Helen wasn't trying to navigate them. Or one of the kids. Waiting, he heard more sounds. He was bone tired, but knew he wouldn't sleep unless he made sure the girls were in bed where they were supposed to be. Groaning, he rose from his bed, pulled on his jeans and headed downstairs.

He immediately noticed the kitchen light was on. Hoping Katie wasn't trying to raid the cookie jar again, he stopped short at the sight in front of him.

Mimi, dressed in some kind of short silky robe that was falling off one of her shoulders, was sipping water from a glass. Her hair was sexy and sleep mussed, her legs endless, and she looked like trouble waiting to happen.

He cleared his throat, startling her so that she

spilled water onto the robe. The dampness plastered the robe to her skin, drawing his attention to her breasts.

"What are you—"

"I heard a noise and wondered if it was the girls," he said, lifting his gaze from her breasts and steering his mind from…well, lust. By his own choice, it had been a while for Jared.

"I'm sorry I disturbed you," Mimi said, reaching for a napkin to dab at her robe. "I was thirsty and awake."

"I would have thought you'd have been dead tired after a full day with the kids."

"I was," she admitted with a shrug, drawing his attention again to her breasts. "But I woke up. Time zone changes, I guess."

He met her gaze. "How many time zones?"

Her eyelids lowered slightly as if to shield herself from his question. "I didn't count," she said lightly and smiled. "You can go back to bed."

He nodded, sliding his hands into his pockets. "What are you going to do?"

"I think I may sit in the den. Would you mind if I turn on the television if I keep the volume low?"

She asked in a stilted voice, as if she were unaccustomed to asking permission. She was the kind of woman who oozed sensual luxury. From her silky, shiny, well-tended hair to her well-modulated speech and sometimes overly formal tone all the way down to her painted toenails, she gave the impression of culture and affluence. Exquisitely well-bred, he suspected, but down on her luck.

A sour taste filled Jared's mouth at the memory of a similar woman who had entered his life; he'd played the foolish white knight only to have her leave. He'd ridden that merry-go-round before. Mimi might be a curious thing, but he suspected he'd do well to put aside any curious urges she aroused. He shrugged. "You can watch the television, but reading is better for insomnia."

"You speak from experience."

He felt her gaze drift over him in speculation and his skin heated. Irritated, he brushed the sensation aside. "Yes. Follow me," he said, heading down the hallway. "I have a library."

He opened the door, turned on the light and waved his hand. "This is the result of four generations of book lovers."

Her eyes widened as she walked to the floor-to-ceiling shelves. "Brilliant. You have a wide range of titles," she said, running her fingers over the books with a caressing hand. The movement of her fingers made him feel itchy.

Brilliant. A British classmate with whom he'd kept in touch over the years often used the same expression. "Are you from England?"

Still absorbed by the books, she shook her head. "No, but I've spent a little time there. Hmm. French poetry. I wouldn't have expected to find that on a cattle ranch in Wyoming." She opened the book and gave him another assessing glance. "The copyright for this edition is four years ago."

"I graduated from Princeton and took my share of liberal arts classes," he said.

She lifted her eyebrows as if impressed. "I wouldn't have expected that either."

"I'm a third-generation rancher, but my family insisted on an east-coast education. They wanted me to be well-rounded."

"And are you?" she asked, with a playful challenge in her eyes that reminded him again that it had been a while since he had taken a woman to bed.

Jared wasn't biting. "I'm too busy to be well-rounded. Help yourself."

"Thank you. I will."

He left the room and headed upstairs, banishing the image of Mimi's silky legs from his eyes and her silky voice from his ears. Jared wasn't a weak man, but he was human. Fate had disclosed a not-so-funny sense of humor by dumping a sexy, sultry woman in his lap after a long period of self-imposed abstinence. He could tell Mimi had secrets she wasn't sharing, secrets he shouldn't want to know.

He shouldn't want to know exactly where she'd gotten her accent and classy manners. He shouldn't want to know what had brought her to Wyoming. He shouldn't give a damn how many men's hearts she'd undoubtedly left abandoned after she'd got what she'd wanted from them.

His blood pressure rose at the very thought as he entered his bedroom. Although he knew he was making an assumption, he figured it was a safe one based on her manslayer looks. He took a deep breath and stared at his empty bed. An image of Mimi lying there in invitation invaded his mind with the stealth of a secret agent.

Swearing under his breath, he paced the floor. She was just a woman. She wouldn't be here very long. He wouldn't let her into his heart the way he had Jennifer. It wasn't going to happen. Chagrined at how worked up he'd become, he took another deep breath and continued to rationalize both his reaction to Mimi and his determination to avoid her. When he slid between the covers and turned out the light, he had successfully banished her from his mind.

The following morning, as usual, Jared awakened before everyone else did. After a shower, he walked downstairs to grab something to eat before he headed out the door. On the way to the kitchen, he noticed that the light in the library was still on. Muttering under his breath over Mimi's lack of consideration, he pushed open the door and stopped short at the sight of her asleep in an overstuffed chair with a book on parenting propped on her chest.

An odd mix of emotions meandered through his gut. Even in sleep, she looked exotic and seductive. The book on parenting provided a stark contrast to her black velvet eyelashes, pouty lips, silky hair and skin. He had the strangest urge to grab an afghan and cover her.

Shaking his head, he reached for the book. Her eyelids fluttered. She stared at him for a long, sleep-bleary moment.

"Tell me I'm dreaming and it's not morning," she whispered.

He chuckled. "Sorry, duchess. You're not dreaming and it *is* morning."

She pushed her hair from her face and sat up. "Duchess?" she echoed.

"It's a nickname," he said, thinking it would also be a reminder to himself that she was off-limits. "You seem like a woman accustomed to the finer things."

She stared at him for a long moment, then laughed. "Oh, that's brilliant. I can't wait to tell—" She broke off suddenly.

"Can't wait to tell who?" he asked, curious.

She paused a half beat. "The girls. They love to play pretend, so they'll love knowing Uncle Jared plays the same game."

A manufactured tale, he concluded instantly. He wondered why she was so secretive. What did Mimi have to hide? "Uh-huh," he said, but didn't try to keep the doubt from his voice. He ran his thumb under the title of the book she'd been reading. "On-the-job training?"

She smiled and stood regally. "Refresher course. What is the weather supposed to be?" she asked, changing the subject.

"Hot. You might want to pull out the sprinkler, or the girls will try to get you to take them swimming in the pond."

She stiffened. "Swimming?"

"Yes. It's when you paddle and kick in the water."

She shook her head. "We're not going swimming. Where is this sprinkler? How do you operate it?"

"There's a half dozen of them in the garage. You hook one up to the hose and turn on the spigot and let the kids run through it screaming."

"Why must they scream?"

Jared wondered if she was from Mars. How could she not know what a sprinkler was? "They scream because it's fun and the water feels cold." He studied her. "Are you afraid of water?"

"Absolutely not," she said, lifting her chin. "I drink it every day."

She'd deliberately twisted his words. "I meant swimming in it."

"It's not my first choice of exercise."

"Did you almost drown?"

"Not me," she said, then seemed to catch herself. "My brother nearly drowned when he was a toddler, so my mother never allowed us to swim without strict supervision after that."

"Where are you from?" he asked.

She met his gaze and sighed. "East of here," she replied vaguely. "Please excuse me. I should shower before the girls wake up," she said formally, and walked out of the room.

Jared walked after her, feeling dangerously curious. "Don't you want the book?" he asked.

She turned around and reached for it. "Oh, yes. Thank you."

Jared held the book and her gaze. "Why are you here in Wyoming?" he asked quietly.

She looked at him for a long moment, as if she might trust him enough to reveal at least one of her secrets. Suddenly he had the outrageous urge to want to learn *all* of them. "It's a long story," she said, then pulled the book from his grasp and left him hanging—the same way he suspected she'd kept dozens of other men hanging.

Michelina chased the girls during the morning, then—out of desperation—took them outside in the afternoon. She broke a nail hooking up the sprinkler, but it was well worth it to hear the girls' laughter and delight. An added bonus was that they were both so tired they went to bed early. Michelina liked the effects from the sprinkler so much that she repeated the routine for two days. The third day, however, the weather turned cooler, so she took the girls for a long walk instead.

That night, as Michelina tucked Lindsey into bed, the little girl couldn't settle down. "Want Tiki," she said.

Tiki was Lindsey's favorite stuffed animal. She dragged the oft-repaired droopy bird everywhere. Michelina, Katie and Lindsey searched the house, but couldn't find the toy anywhere.

Lindsey began to cry. Her howls wrenched at Michelina's heart. Helen was resting, Jared hadn't arrived home and Michelina had never felt so helpless.

"Mama told Lindsay that hugging Tiki would be like hugging her until she got out of the hospital."

"Oh, moppet," Michelina said, stroking Lindsey's head. "I tell you what. If you try to go to sleep, I'll stay wide-awake all night if that's what it takes to find Tiki."

Lindsey's lower lip trembled, but she stuck her thumb in her mouth, nodded, then lowered her head to her pillow.

The two-year-old's courage grabbed Michelina's heart and twisted. She stroked Lindsey's baby-fine hair and pressed a kiss to her forehead. "You're a brave girl. Now, go to sleep, and I'll go find Tiki."

Michelina searched the house again and faced the unpleasant likelihood that Lindsey had dropped Tiki during their long walk earlier in the afternoon. Grabbing an umbrella and a flashlight, she went out into the stormy night.

By the time Jared arrived home from the county planning meeting, all he wanted was to grab a sandwich and fall into bed. Serving as interim mayor tried his patience. The latest insanity was Clara Hancock's insistence on a huge do for the county's anniversary celebration, and the other members of the committee universally agreed that his ranch was the optimal location for the party.

Jared growled. He'd been invaded and interrupted so much lately that the last thing he wanted to do was party. He growled again when he noticed several lights on. Couldn't the duchess at least turn off a few lights every now and then? No one was up when he entered the kitchen, and he wished he wasn't awake either.

His black lab, Leo, gave a sleepy tail-wagging welcome, but didn't move from his spot from beneath the table. Slapping together a sandwich, Jared sank into a chair at the table ready to take a bite, when Katie appeared in the doorway rubbing her eyes.

"Hey, sweetheart, what are you doing up?"

"Did Mimi find Tiki yet?" Katie asked.

"Tiki," he echoed, vaguely recalling Lindsey's stuffed animal. "What happened to Tiki?"

"Lindsey lost him today. Mimi said she'd look all night if that's what it took." Katie rubbed her eyes again. "I wonder if Lindsey lost Tiki during our walk."

"What walk?" Jared asked.

"We went on a long, long walk today."

Jared got an itchy feeling at the back of his neck. "Where?"

Katie shrugged. "Everywhere." She sighed and climbed onto his lap. "She's not in her bed."

Jared's itchy sensation intensified. "Mimi didn't go looking outside for Tiki, did she?"

"I dunno," Katie said. "Prolly. She said she would look all night if she needed to."

Jared stifled an oath.

"Can I have a bite?" Katie asked.

He sighed and offered his niece half his sandwich. He stuffed the other half in his mouth. After swallowing it, he rose and urged Katie toward her room. "You go back to bed. I've got something I need to do."

The thought of Mimi wandering out in the rain on the ranch made his gut knot. The woman didn't give the impression that she was any Sacajawea.

He hustled Katie into bed after quizzing her a little more about their walk, then returned downstairs and grabbed a slicker. His favorite flashlight was missing from the kitchen, which could be a good sign. If the duchess didn't have enough sense to stay out of the rain on a stormy night, at least she had had enough sense to take a light with her. He stepped out of the door, and the rain immediately slapped him in the face. Helluva night.

Three

The barn door burst open with such force that Michelina nearly wet her pants. Jared stood in the doorway glaring at her, his long black duster flapping in the wind while water dripped from his black hat. For a second, she fought the wild fear that he was going to pull out a six-shooter.

Michelina raised her only weapon of defense—Tiki, Lindsey's stuffed bird.

"Hasn't anyone ever told you not to go looking for stuffed animals in the middle of the night in the dark when you're not familiar with the territory?" he asked, walking toward her.

Michelina's heart pounded in her throat. "I've been taught many rules," she said, thinking most of the rules she'd learned had pertained to royal etiquette. "But I don't recall learning that particular one."

"You could have been hurt," he pointed out, his jaw tightening.

Even though she'd gotten lost, she didn't like his implication that she couldn't take care of herself. "How? I wasn't going to freeze. I was just going to get wet."

"You could have fallen and hurt yourself."

Michelina refused to confess that she had, in fact, fallen, and would have a nasty bruise on her right thigh as a souvenir. "I'm wet, but fine."

"And every once in a while, wild, hungry animals pay visits," he added meaningfully.

She hadn't thought about that, but it hadn't taken place either. "I haven't seen any wild, hungry animals," she returned. Except for you, she added silently.

He clenched his jaw again, then nodded. "Okay, well, since you didn't have any problems and you're happy as a clam, I'll let you continue to enjoy your evening in the barn while I head back to the house. Make sure you get back in time to make breakfast for the girls in the morning, duchess," he said and turned away.

Panic and indignation flooded Michelina as she gaped after him. "You may not leave me!"

He stopped dead in his tracks and looked at her as if she had sprouted an extra head. "Excuse me?"

She worked her mouth, but nothing came out. A first for her. *Bloody hell.* She cleared her throat and took a deep swallow of pride. "I—uh—I meant to say I would very much appreciate it if you would direct me back to the house." She paused for a moment and took another bitter swallow of pride. "I appear to have lost my way."

He cocked his head to one side. "Lost? Did I hear you say you got lost going out in the middle of the night in the rain?"

In her country, she could have had him fired, if not deported, for using that tone with her. Michelina was all too aware she wasn't in her country or on her turf. "Yes, would you please direct me back to the house?"

He let out a long exhalation. "Do you know it was insane for you to go looking for that bird on this kind of night?"

"I agree that it would have been much easier during daylight. But Lindsey was very upset, and the only way I could persuade her to go to sleep was to assure her that I would look for Tiki all night if necessary. I found the bird," she said, lifting her chin. "Even in the dark."

His gaze gentled a fraction. "So you did. Are you ready to go back, or was there somewhere else you wanted to go?" he asked in a dry tone.

"The only place I want to go is to the bathtub."

His gaze slid over her like a hot breeze, then returned to her face. "That can be arranged. Ready?"

She nodded. "There's just one other thing."

"What's that?"

"I owe you an umbrella." She lifted up the tangled vinyl and metal and frowned at it. "The wind blew it upside down within five minutes of my leaving the house."

He chuckled. "That's our Wyoming wind for you.

We may be landlocked, but we get gale-force winds every winter, spring, summer and fall. If you're not careful, it'll shake your foundations. There's no such thing as a Wyoming wuss.''

Stealing a glance at the tall, forceful man guiding her back to his house, Michelina realized the wind wasn't the only thing rattling her foundations....

As they drew near the house, Jared noticed that Mimi seemed to be slowing down. He put his arm at her back and urged her forward. "Tired?''

She nodded. "And a little cold.''

He glanced down at her. "Your teeth are chattering.''

She gave a forced smile. "Silly, isn't it? The temperature can't be that cold.''

"But you're soaked through, and when the sun sets here, there's a big drop in temperature.''

She nodded again. Her stoic silence bothered him. He had the strangest sense that it was so important to her that others not think her helpless that she might end up not asking for help when she needed it most.

"Are you sure you're okay?''

She nodded again silently. She stumbled and Jared caught her against him. Her slim body trembled. Swearing, he picked her up to carry her.

"This isn't necessary,'' she protested. "I can walk. It's not that far.''

"We need to get you out of the rain,'' he said gruffly, inhaling a heady combination of rain and her perfume. "I can move faster than you can right now.''

"It's not at all good form to brag.''

He absorbed her look of disdain at the same time she seemed to melt into him. "I wasn't bragging, just stating a fact."

"You don't have to lord it over me."

"I'm not lording it over you. We all have our strengths. I have more stamina, and you have more—" He stalled for a moment, considering what in the world to say next.

"I have more what?" she prompted.

Sex appeal in your little fingernail than most women have in their entire bodies. "Longer hair," he finally said, knowing it was an unsubstantial response.

"Hair," she echoed with a scowl.

"Exactly. What did you think I was going to say?"

"Courtesy, manners—"

"Mouthiness," he said, unable to resist.

She gaped at him as if he'd said the most impertinent thing she'd ever heard. "I think we might be tied in the area of mouthiness."

He grinned, carrying her up the steps to the porch and through the doorway.

"You can put me down now."

"Not quite yet," he said, climbing the stairs to the bathroom. He set her down on the carpet and turned the water on full-force.

"Thank you very much for your assistance, but I can handle my own bath," she said in a prissy voice.

Jared didn't know if it was the late hour or her tone, but he couldn't resist teasing her. "Are you sure you won't need some help? I wouldn't want you to fall asleep and drown in the bathtub."

Her teeth chattered because she was clearly still

cold, but her eyes sparked with heat. "If this is your attempt at a seduction," she said in a voice smoother than honey, "you need to work on your approach."

"I'm sure you're more accustomed to champagne and diamonds."

"Not really. I'm more accustomed to manners and courtesy."

"And men who obey your every whim," he added.

Her lips parted and her eyes widened as if he'd scored a direct hit. The knowledge brought him little joy, but he found himself fighting the urge to lower his mouth to hers and satisfy his curiosity about how she would taste.

"You may leave now," she said in the regal tone that stuck in his craw.

"As you wish, duchess," he said, and walked from the bathroom.

She pushed the door shut less than a millisecond after he'd stepped into the hallway. Temper, temper, he thought, but his deep-seated, overdeveloped sense of responsibility kept him waiting in the hallway just in case she suddenly fainted.

Instead of hearing her hit the floor, he heard the sound of wet garments splatting onto the linoleum. His mind provided the visual that correlated with the sound effects. She would pull off the shirt that had been plastered to her round breasts first. He heard two thuds. Tennis shoes, he suspected, followed by socks. Jeans next. He could just imagine her wiggling her very attractive bottom to get free from the wet denim. Her long legs would be bare. He wondered what kind of underwear she wore. Silky bikinis, a thong... An unwelcome shot of arousal heated his groin.

He closed his eyes, but the wicked visuals continued. He would almost swear he heard the snap of her bra as she tossed it aside and released her breasts. The nipples would be stiff from the cold. He could warm them with his mouth.

Jared bit back a groan when he heard the splash of water as she stepped into the tub. Seconds later, he heard her let out a long sensual moan that impacted on him like an intimate stroke from her hand.

Feeling himself grow harder with each passing moment, he forced himself to stay there two more steamy, torturous minutes, then told himself he'd done all he could do, with the exception of taking her to his bed and warming up both of them. Swearing under his breath, he reminded himself that she was just like his ex-fiancée, Jennifer. But he couldn't shake the notion that his ex would never have braved a storm to collect a stuffed bird for his niece. The image of Mimi naked in that bathtub would torture him the rest of the night, but the image of her standing drenched in that barn holding Tiki would disturb him even longer.

Grumbling under his breath, Jared trudged down the hall to his bedroom and stripped out of his wet clothes. *Chaos magnet, chaos magnet.* He could hear his sister's taunting voice play through his mind and scowled at the words. He supposed he could have let the duchess spend the night in the rain. If he were a different man.

But no, his sense of responsibility had been drilled

into him at such an early age that it ran through his veins like blood. He'd been a sucker for a woman in need of a white knight too many times to count. Only thing about Mimi was that she didn't appear to be trying to use her feminine wiles to get him to do her bidding. That, along with the fact that she hadn't attempted to shirk her child care duties, had him scratching his head.

Jared hung his clothes to dry on a couple of hooks in the bathroom and stepped into the shower. A quick, hot one and he would go to bed. As the spray spilled over him, he couldn't help imagining how Mimi's wet, naked body would look. Scowling when his body immediately responded to the seductive image, he couldn't bring himself to finish with a bone-jarring dose of cold water. After he toweled off and pulled on a pair of lounging pants, he decided to go downstairs and pour himself a shot of twenty-five-year-old Macallan Scotch. The liquor burned a trail of fire down his throat.

Deciding this was a two-shot night, he poured a second and carried it upstairs. As he rounded the corner, the bathroom door swung open and Mimi stepped out in a cloud of steam wearing nothing but a towel. The towel showed him very little pity, but her body showed him less.

The skimpy bit of terry cloth dipped dangerously low over her breasts, and dangerously high on her thighs. Her skin glowed, and her wet hair looked nearly black. She glanced at the shot glass in his hand. "How thoughtful. Is that for me?"

He opened his mouth to say no, but the expression

on her face did something strange to his gut. He cleared his throat. "Sure."

"Scotch?" she asked, taking the glass from his hand.

He nodded and watched her tilt back her head and empty the glass in one swallow. She squinted her eyes, then blinked. "Very nice. Macallan. Twenty-five-year-old?"

He nodded in surprise. "How'd you know? You don't strike me as the hard-liquor type."

"One of my brothers' friends educated me."

"And how did your father feel about that?"

Her gaze softened. "My father is dead."

Jared felt an instant of connected grief. "Sorry. My parents have passed on, too."

"Well, my mother is very much alive. Some might even say a little too alive. And then there are my brothers." Mimi winced. "When Nicholas learned that his friend had educated me on the finer points of hard liquor, his friend was banished from the palace." She cleared her throat. "So to speak. From the house, you know."

"It sounds as if your mother rules the roost with an iron hand."

Mimi's mouth twitched. "That's fair to say." She licked her lips. "Very nice Scotch. Thank you again," she said, handing him the shot glass. Then she glanced down at her towel as if she'd just realized her lack of covering. "I suppose I should go. Good night, Mr. Mc—"

"Call me Jared," he interjected, impatient with the

formality when she stood before him just one brief
terry cloth away from nudity.

Her gaze met his, and he glimpsed a compelling
combination of seduction and secrets in her silver
eyes. He should keep his distance. She was chaos,
and he didn't need her, but she wasn't quite the
flighty, superficial, helpless and spoiled woman he'd
originally pegged her as. A woman willing to brave
a rainy Wyoming night for a child's missing stuffed
bird had to possess some heart and will. And fire, he
thought, suspecting that although Mimi couldn't cook
in the kitchen worth a damn, she would be able to
burn a man's resistance to cinders in the bedroom.
And make him like it all the while.

"Jared," she said, rolling his name around in her
mouth like a fine wine. "Good night." She turned,
but not before the towel dipped, flashing him a peek
of the side of her bare breast, a peek that made him
itch to see more. Torturing himself, he watched her
walk the rest of the way down the hallway, part of
him praying she'd drop that towel and part of him
beating himself up for giving in to the temptation of
watching her.

The following night, Michelina successfully tired
out the girls and got them to bed early. In no mood
for television, she perused Jared's library for a while,
but she couldn't fight the restless feeling building inside her. She had made zero progress finding her
brother, and although she adored Katie and Lindsey,
she couldn't take care of them indefinitely. There was
also the matter of Jared.

She frowned when she thought of him. She shouldn't care what he thought of her, but for some insane reason, she did. She couldn't bear the idea that he thought she was some useless bimbo.

Scowling, she left the library and meandered through the house. On impulse, she decided to explore the basement. In the first room, she found discarded sporting equipment, a bag of golf clubs, baseball bats, balls and gloves, a football, a Ping-Pong table and pool table. She thought of Jared's broad shoulders and could see how he might enjoy athletics. Pushing open a connecting door, she was surprised to find a mini wine cellar. Inspecting a few of the labels, she was even more surprised at the selection. Nothing approaching the palace's wine cellar, but impressive.

Returning to the recreation room, she spotted a door on the other side and walked inside. It took her a moment to find the light switch, but when she did, her heart stuttered.

The walls held competition foils. She saw a shelf with protective equipment. *A fencing room.* Who would have known? A memory of her brother secretly teaching her the basics slid through her mind. She remembered the adrenaline racing through her as she tried to master his every instruction. Michelina had craved the challenge, but when her mother had learned of the lessons, she'd put an end to them.

Moving closer to the wall, Michelina carefully removed one of the foils and slid her finger along the cold steel of the blade.

"Careful."

She started at the sound of Jared's voice, then took

a calming breath and glanced at him. "I haven't held a foil in my hand in over ten years," she said, turning to look at him.

He rested his large, well-formed hands on his lean hips, drawing her attention down his body. Amazing how the way he stood reminded her of his physical power. The first time she'd seen him, she'd made the mistake of seeing the brawn and not the brains. Now, the combination of his muscular frame and intelligence made her stomach dip and sway. How odd, she thought, and pushed the strange sensations aside as she returned her gaze to his face.

He raised his eyebrows. "What in the world were you doing with a foil ten years ago?"

"Learning to fence. My brother taught me until my mother found out."

"Not ladylike enough?"

Michelina shrugged. "Probably. I loved it. Chess with muscles."

He nodded. "Yeah, my father taught me. I haven't played much since he died, but I couldn't bring myself to remodel the room."

"It's a nice surprise." She studied his face. "Are you any good?"

He stared at her for a long moment, then chuckled and rubbed his chin. "I'm probably a little rusty, but I could hold my own in a competition."

"Teach me," she said, the words popping out of her mouth impulsively.

Jared cocked his head to one side. "That sounds like an order, duchess," he said in a velvet voice.

Impatience and something darker shimmered through

her. She couldn't explain the desire she'd had for years. "I apologize. I've always wanted to learn, and when my lessons were interrupted, it frustrated the devil out of me. This seems the perfect opportunity. Would you, please?"

He paused for a long, considering moment and shrugged. "I can work in a few lessons." He grabbed protective equipment and handed it to her. "First things first, and the lessons will be dry," he said, in contrast to the charged vests used in official competitions where competitors are wired and scoring is determined electronically.

Adrenaline rushed through Michelina as she donned the equipment. "That's fine. After I learn foil, perhaps you could teach me épée."

"Let's stick to foil first. Let me see your position," he said, nodding his head in approval. "Not bad," he said and began the lesson.

Michelina concentrated intently on his every instruction. After a while, he agreed to let her play. She thrust and parried. Michelina couldn't remember feeling this alive in a long, long time…if ever. Her heart pounded like thunder in her chest, and she could hear her breath as she tried to keep up with Jared. He was better than he'd led her to believe, but that didn't stop her from going after him.

"You're doing well. Don't thrust without protecting yourself."

He provided just the right amount of encouragement and training. "You're light on your feet for such a muscular—" He touched her chest with the tip of his foil, and she sighed. "You're an excellent teacher. You make me want to beat you."

He laughed, and the sound rippled through her blood like a surprising shockwave. "I think you would want to beat anyone."

She paused. "Why do you say that?"

"Strong competitive spirit," he said. "Nothing wrong with that."

"I never thought of myself as a competitor."

"Maybe you never had a chance. It's not a bad thing. Some people consider a strong competitive spirit a great quality."

"Even in a woman?" Michelina asked, thinking of all the advice she'd received about not challenging a man's ego.

He nodded.

Curious and full of a half dozen emotions pulling her in different directions, she pushed back her mask. "Does it bother you when a woman has a strong competitive spirit?"

"No," he said, pushing back his own mask, his eyes lit from their play. "It's sexy."

Her gaze collided with his, and she felt a charge race through her. In that moment, he was the most compelling man she'd ever met in her life. His strength, mental and physical, was irresistible. Her heart pounded as a forbidden thought raced through her head. If she were in the palace, she wouldn't have more than one unchaperoned, unsupervised moment with a man. But she wasn't in the palace. She was on her own, making her own decisions.

Her heart pumped even faster. She wondered how

Jared would react if she kissed him. She wondered if she had the nerve to find out.

Wyoming isn't for wusses.

Adrenaline from the swordplay still racing through her, she held his gaze, dropped her foil, took a step toward him, then another and another, until she stood directly in front of him. She rose up on tiptoe, but he was still too tall, still just out of reach.

"Bend down," she whispered.

His eyes darkened. "Sounds like another order, duchess."

The possibility that he might reject her made her chest tighten with fear. She automatically covered it with anger. "I won't beg."

Just as she turned her head, he caught her chin with his fingers. "No need," he said and took her mouth.

Four

Michelina braced herself for a carnal kiss that would take her by storm. The inviting, sensual brush of Jared's lips over hers took her by surprise. How could his mouth feel both hard and soft? Back and forth, he moved his lips in a mesmerizing motion that knocked the slats out from under her.

Just when she thought she could take a breath, he caught her lower lip between his and sucked it gently into his mouth. He slid his tongue past her lips, and she felt the room spin.

Michelina moved closer to him, but their protective chest coverings formed a frustrating barrier. Even that couldn't hide his strength, and it was his strength that fascinated her. He wasn't the kind of man who would ask permission, but he also wasn't a man who would push himself on anyone. The combination was oh, so seductive.

She deepened the kiss, sliding her tongue over his, and she tasted hunger and restraint. She wondered what happened when he lost that restraint. Tilting her head to the side, she opened her mouth wider to allow him more access. He immediately took it.

Distantly she heard the thud of his foil as it hit the mat. She felt one of his hands tangle in her hair while the other slid to her back to draw her lower body against his. His obvious arousal sent a slick thrill through her nether regions.

She'd been so supervised her entire life, she'd never indulged in much more than a few stolen heated sessions of intense foreplay. Her virginity had always been very important to her mother. After all, a virgin princess would be able to draw a prize groom, a groom who would contribute to the betterment of Marceau. Whether the groom contributed to Michelina's happiness or not was far down the list of priorities.

Michelina had felt ambivalent about her sexual inexperience. Embarrassed, but she'd yet to meet a man who made her want to change her status. She wasn't certain she wanted to change her status now, but she bloody well wanted the protective vests out of the way.

She pulled back slightly and shrugged out of her vest.

"What...?" Jared asked, his eyes dark with passion.

She tugged on his vest. "You're not close enough."

His nostrils flared, and he ditched his vest, then dragged her back against him. "I can fix that," he muttered, and tasted her mouth again as if she were made of honey.

As she felt her temperature rise, she realized that no chaperons or bodyguards were going to break in and interrupt. The knowledge left her conflicted. She was on her own and she could do whatever she wanted.

Whatever she wanted...

Sinking against Jared, she reveled in the sensation of his hard chest against her breasts. She felt her nipples tingle with excitement and relished the sensation of being deliciously consumed. Inhaling his clean, musky scent, she wanted more. She lifted her hands and sank her fingers into his silky hair.

He rotated his pelvis against her and her head grew cloudy. Soft hair. Hard man.

She felt one of his hands curve around her rib cage and slide upward toward her breast. Her breath stopped somewhere between her lungs and throat. His kiss went on and on, and she didn't want it to stop. She felt as if she were tumbling in a glorious free fall that had no end.

His thumb moved closer to her breast in a sensual stroking movement. He barely brushed the bottom of her breast, and she bit back a moan as he pulled it back. Heat and a raw need she'd never experienced roared through her. She wanted to rip open his shirt and crawl inside. She wanted to feel his bare skin against hers.

Faster. Faster. Faster…

Heat and blood pounding in her head, she tugged at the bottom of his shirt and slid her hand over his warm flat belly. Jared groaned in approval, and she skimmed her hand up toward his chest.

Abruptly she felt his hand cover hers. He pulled away his mouth from hers and muttered an oath. His eyes blazing fire and incredulity, he gazed down at her. "What in hell are you doing?"

Arousal still kicking through a maze of internal barriers inside her, she worked her mouth, but no sound came out. "I— I—" She closed her mouth in horror and swallowed. She *never* stuttered.

"If you think playing with me is—"

She shook her head and licked her lips, still tasting him there. "I wanted to kiss you," she said, her voice sounding husky to her own ears.

He shook his head in confusion and took a step backward. "I don't know what you're used to, duchess, but if you're looking for a boy toy—"

"You're a man," she said, unable to keep the words from slipping out of her mouth.

His gaze held hers, and a wholly primitive sexual reaction inside her shook her like an earthquake. It was so strong, she had to lock her knees.

Jared swore again and slid his fingers through his hair, shaking his head. "I don't know what your education or experience is, but we were headed for a helluva lot more than kissing right here on the mat."

Apprehension, quickly followed by powerful anticipation, flooded her. In an instant, Michelina knew what she wanted. Her mind might be muddy with passion, but she understood, with crystal clarity, her own desire. "I told you I wanted you to teach me."

He stopped dead. His nostrils flared slightly. *"Fencing,"* he said emphatically.

She took a mind-clearing breath, and nothing inside her changed. Something told her nothing was going to change her mind or her will on this matter, but she would have to think about how to proceed. She'd never conducted an all-out seduction before, and she wasn't certain how Jared would feel about her lack of experience. He was, after all, a man of honor, and he was the man with whom she wanted to have an affair. An affair to give her memories after she'd married some other man in a union her mother deemed necessary for the betterment of Marceau. It occurred to her that, although she hadn't known it, Jared McNeil was part of the reason she'd come to Wyoming. Jared McNeil and her brother. But for totally different reasons.

She tried to change the tone, to ease the intensity, of their encounter. Picking up both of the foils, she prayed he wouldn't see her hands trembling. "You didn't like kissing me?" she managed in a light tone.

"I warned you not to play with me."

"Au contraire," she said. "I think you work so hard, you probably need a little play." She returned the foils to their places on the walls. "But we don't need to argue. Thank you for the lesson. Oh, by the way, I keep intending to ask you if you've ever heard of a man who lives around here named Jack Raven."

Facing the wall, she counted during his silence. One—two—three—four—five—

"As a matter of fact, I have."

Michelina's heart squeezed tight. She resisted the urge to turn around. She didn't want Jared to see her face. She might be ready to share her body, but she wasn't ready to share her secrets.

"He owns the best seafood restaurant in Wyoming. Considering we're landlocked, that might not be saying much. His restaurant's about forty-five minutes west of here."

She nodded and slowly turned.

"Why do you ask?"

She smiled and shrugged. "I love seafood."

With a mission in mind, the following morning Michelina took the girls for a walk to her wrecked vehicle.

A kind ranch hand named Gary strolled over to chat with her and the girls, and during the course of the conversation, he offered to get Michelina's truck road-worthy during his off-hours. He estimated that he might be able to get the vehicle mechanically ready within just a few days. When Michelina told him he'd made her wish come true, Gary blushed a bright red.

Excited that she might be able to visit Jack Raven's seafood restaurant in just days, Michelina zipped through the day with an extra spring in her step. That night she visited the fencing room again, but Jared didn't appear. She told herself his presence didn't matter. She could practice her technique without him.

Two days later, Gary informed her that the vehicle should be ready by the following evening, but the paint would still be a mess. Michelina brushed aside Gary's concerns about the cosmetic appearance of the truck. All she wanted was transportation.

High on Gary's news, she expended her energy in the fencing room after the girls went to sleep. She concentrated intently on positioning herself correctly and being light on her feet.

"I can tell you've been practicing," Jared said from the doorway.

She turned at the sound of his voice, her heart rate picking up. Allowing her gaze to linger on him, she was surprised at how happy she was to see him. "Thank you. I'll take that as a compliment."

He strolled to the wall and selected a foil, then picked up the protective equipment. "Are you ready for another lesson?"

"I've been ready," she said.

He shot her a quick glance, as if he were trying to determine if she'd intended her comment as a double entendre. She hadn't, but it would have been appropriate. She had decided that she wanted to take Jared as her lover. He might very well represent the only opportunity she would get to choose. Seducing him could be challenging, but she was very determined.

"I was hoping I hadn't scared you away," she said with a smile.

He dipped his head in disbelief. "You thought I would be intimidated by your technique?"

"Or lack thereof," she retorted lightly. "I have an

enormous desire to learn and I'm willing to practice, but my level of experience is pitiful. I won't deny it.''

Jared looked into her witchy silver eyes and tried, with only partial success, to read her. Her tone was playfully seductive. It seemed to him that she wasn't just talking about fencing…she was talking about sex. Of course, that could just be the way his mind was working. After those scorching kisses they'd shared a few nights ago, he'd been forced to take a cold shower.

He could have been doing paperwork tonight, but knowing Mimi was downstairs had caused an itchy sensation inside him. He'd squelched the idea of another fencing lesson as long as he could, and finally given in to the distraction. And Mimi was nothing if she wasn't a distraction, he thought as he put on his protective vest. As long as he kept her from drawing him into whatever her secret drama or scheme was, he would be okay. In the meantime, she would serve as an amusement.

''Let's see if we can improve your experience then,'' he said, pulling his mask in place. ''*En garde, duchess.*''

He was surprised at how much he enjoyed sparring with her. The woman was incredibly intent. If she was half that intent in bed, she could put a man in the hospital, he thought wryly. He bested her in another timed round, and she stomped her foot and tossed aside her face mask.

''Damn you,'' she said, her eyes spitting sparks at him. ''Surely you must get tired of beating me so easily.''

Unable to swallow a chuckle, he shook his head, telling himself not to be swayed by her combination of beauty and kick-butt spirit. "You would be furious if you knew I gave you an inch unless you'd earned it."

She scowled and lifted her chin. "You could at least be a little more gracious about your superiority."

"You're the one who keeps mentioning my superiority."

"Yes, but you keep demonstrating it," she said in a dark voice that betrayed a smile and gave him that itchy sensation again.

"I can stop," he offered.

"No," she said. "Please don't."

The honesty in her eyes hit him like a surprise jab from her foil. She was a little too easy on the eyes, too easy to like. He should go before he took her up on the offer she seemed to be making.

Ditching his protective wear, he returned his foil to the wall. "I should go. I need to return a call about the damned county anniversary celebration everyone wants to hold on my property. I don't know anything about putting on a party for that many people."

"I could help," she said.

Her offer caught him off guard. He glanced at her. "What do you mean?"

"I mean I have some experience planning parties."

More curious than he ought to be, he strolled toward her. "What kind of parties?"

She shrugged her shoulders. "Any kind. I've helped with both large and small gatherings. I've even helped oversee a few weddings."

"Your own?" he couldn't resist asking.

She blinked, then looked affronted. "No. I haven't ever been married." She paused a half beat. "Have you?"

He shook his head slowly. "I got close once."

"What happened?"

"She didn't want to live in Wyoming."

"Well, I guess I can see how it could feel a bit isolated here to someone accustomed to living in a larger city."

"True. The secret to avoiding cabin fever is to take trips."

"I'm in total agreement," she said with a big nod of her head.

"So you know what it's like to feel a little confined?"

"Little doesn't begin to describe it," she said crisply.

"Where did you serve your time?" he asked.

She frowned. "What do you mean?"

"I mean where was it that you felt so confined?"

She waved her hand in a dismissive gesture. "Oh, I think it was more the situation than the setting."

"And it was?"

She shrugged and looked away. "My home."

The little breadcrumbs of information she dropped for him only served to make him more and more curious. "Is that where you planned parties? At your home?"

"Some," she hedged. "Why do you ask?"

"You offered your services. I thought it'd be a good idea to find out your experience." His lips twitched. "It might have something to do with the experience you said you had caring for children."

She lifted her head regally. "Are you implying that I've done a poor job caring for your nieces?"

"Not at all, duchess. But Katie doesn't keep secrets real well, and she told me she had to coach you through diaper changing 101 with Lindsey."

She lifted her chin again. "Which just proves the point that I learn quickly and am quite trustworthy." She turned on her heel. "But if you'd prefer to plan your own party, I don't need to—"

"Oh, no." He shook his head and slid his thumb and forefinger around her small wrist before she could escape. "You made an offer. You can't take it back now."

She looked at him as if he were crazy. "I believe you're confused. I can do what I want."

"Well, I don't know how *you* were raised, but my father always told me that a man of integrity never welshes on his word."

She opened her mouth as if to argue, then closed her lips together. She narrowed her eyes at him for a long moment. "That's one more thing I like about you," she said quietly, surprising the hell out of him.

"I didn't know you liked anything about me, duchess."

She rolled her eyes. "Come on, you're not that dense. You know I envy and admire your strength. I also like your intelligence. And I like that you're a man who wouldn't welsh on a deal."

He told himself not to let her compliments turn his head. This was how these conniving women reeled in the men. If the damsel in distress act didn't work, they tried flattery. It wasn't going to work with him. He'd made a deal with *himself,* and he refused to welsh on that one. He wasn't going to fall for any more pampered damsels in distress. No way. No how.

"And I'm sure you know you have a very sexy body," she said in the same casual tone he would expect her to use when she discussed the weather.

Jared felt himself harden involuntarily.

"It makes a woman wonder..."

He shouldn't bite, he told himself, curious. He absolutely shouldn't bite. Curiosity won. "Wonder what?"

She gave a sexy, careless little shrug. "Wonder lots of things."

She seemed bold and shy at the same time, which confused the hell out of him. If he didn't know better, he would say she was giving him a come-on, but he knew from experience that it was always more complicated than that. Unwillingly aroused, he ground his teeth in irritation. "Well, I'll give you a little lesson about wondering. Wondering about the wrong thing can get you into trouble," he told her, and left before she could respond...and before he could give in to the overwhelming urge to scoop her in his arms, place her down on that mat and... As he climbed the stairs and strode to his office, his body and mind taunted him. *Wondering could get him into trouble, too.*

Five

"**O**kay, okay. I can't say no to my ladies," Jared conceded, ruffling Katie's and Lindsey's hair as they ate their midmorning snack. "I'll take you swimming in the lake today."

The girls screamed in delight.

Jared grinned, then shot a glance at Michelina. "You can come along, too."

Her stomach knotted and she tensed, an automatic reaction drilled into her since birth. He always seemed to be challenging her. As determined as she was to make sure he didn't dismiss her, she wasn't sure she wanted to take him up on the dare this time. "I don't have a swimsuit with me."

"No problem," he said, stealing a cracker from Katie. "We keep several for guests."

"But, uh—"

He cocked his head to one side and looked at her. "It's safe. You can use a life jacket if you like."

Katie, intuitive to a fault, turned around in her chair and stared at Michelina. "Are you 'fraid of the water?"

Michelina detested the idea of her fear poisoning the girls' enjoyment of swimming. She swallowed a knot in her throat. "I'm not very experienced."

"Uncle Jared will take care of you. He's a very good swimmer. He yells if we do anything wrong."

Michelina took a careful breath and saw her fate written on the wall. "Will everyone be wearing a life jacket today?"

He nodded. "Everyone." He clapped his hands together. "You girls go get your suits while I find one for Mimi."

The girls scrambled out of their chairs and zipped out of the room. Michelina felt Jared's gaze on her.

"I won't let anybody drown," he said in a low voice.

She felt the hum between them that never seemed to go away, but tried not to focus on it. "I'm sure you won't. It's silly for me to feel afraid."

"Well, you said there'd been a drowning accident in your family, and it sounds like your mother got a little overprotective. Kids can smell fear a mile away."

"Too true," she said, remembering how she'd felt when she'd seen her mother's hands turn white with fear any time she or her brothers had gone swimming. The old anxiety suddenly felt like an unwelcome, unnecessary weight on her shoulders. She looked at

Jared. Who would have known a Wyoming rancher would offer her so many opportunities to come into her own and finish unfinished business? "I guess I need a suit."

"Coming right up," he said, the approval in his eyes doing crazy things to her breathing. "But I'll warn you. None of them are designer."

What an understatement, she thought thirty minutes later, after she'd helped the girls into their suits, pulled on her ugly brown maillot and slathered the three of them with sunscreen. Even her brothers would have called Fashion Emergency if they'd seen her in *this* suit.

After throwing together a few sandwiches, they joined Jared in the foyer, and he pointed at the grandfather clock. "I'm getting old waiting on you females. What took you so long?"

Katie lowered her plastic sunglasses and shook her finger at him. "Mimi says us women should always use sun protection, so we don't get crinkly too early. Did you put on sunscreen?"

"No, but I'm out in the sun all the time."

"I bet you're gonna get crinkly."

Michelina bit back a laugh at Katie's blunt assessment, but couldn't miss the dark glance Jared tossed her way. "You've been warned," she said.

"Yeah, yeah. Let's get to the lake before the sun goes down," he grumbled, and opened the door.

Michelina and Jared strapped the girls into car seats, then got into his truck. He drove down the paved driveway and onto a curving dirt road. A beautiful small lake came into view, and the blue water reminded Michelina of the ocean surrounding Marceau. "It's lovely," she said.

"Full of fish," he said. "And the temperature is like bath water."

"Really?"

"Yep, we always fish after we swim," he said getting out of the truck.

Oh, goody, Michelina thought, her mind filled with images of worms, hooks and slimy fish. She stiffened her back and reminded herself this would only last a few hours and she would be a better woman because of it.

When Jared pulled off his shirt and ditched his wind pants, she forgot all about becoming a better woman. She couldn't help but stare. His body was incredibly distracting. From his broad shoulders to his bare, muscular chest, flat abdomen and well-developed thighs, he was the picture of masculine power. Thank goodness she could hide her stare behind her sunglasses, or he would tease her mercilessly. She helped put life vests on the girls and smiled at their squeals as they jumped off the dock. Sitting on the edge, she procrastinated taking her own leap as long as she could.

"Your turn," Jared called. "Come on in before we start making chicken sounds."

Scooting forward, she bit her lip and scraped her legs on the dock as she took the plunge. The ice-cold water took her breath away. Jared immediately appeared by her side, steadying her with his hands. He looked disgustingly healthy and warm. She didn't see one goose bump, and his dark hair was slicked back from his head, while his mouth lifted in a broad grin.

"See? That wasn't so bad," he said, treading water beside her.

"It's freezing!" she said. "I can't believe you deliberately put those children in this cold water."

"They're not hothouse flowers, they can take it. Tough Wyoming born and bred," he said with another light of challenge in his eyes.

"You lied."

He chuckled, and the sound rippled over her. She still wanted to pound him.

"It's all a matter of perspective. I can tell you with absolute certainty that there are no icebergs in this lake."

"Except for me," she muttered, her teeth chattering. "And to think I got splinters for this!"

Jared frowned. "What splinters?"

"From the dock when I scooted—" Michelina felt a wave of embarrassment. "Oh, never mind."

Realization crossed his face. "Oh, on your—" He wiped a hand over his mouth, trying unsuccessfully to conceal a smile. "That's a damn shame, considering you have a mighty nice—"

He stopped as Katie dog-paddled between them. "She looks mad. What did you do?" the child asked Jared.

"I didn't do anything," he protested.

"Mighty nice what?" Michelina prompted, enjoying his discomfort. After all, he'd done his share of making *her* uncomfortable.

He paused only a half beat. "Kick," he said. "She's a good kicker like you and Lindsey."

Lindsey beamed, and the foursome spent the next thirty minutes playing in the water. Michelina liked the playful man Jared became with his nieces. He teased and laughed and chased and even had the nerve to dunk her a few times. The only previous time she'd been dunked, her brothers had gleefully done the job. All her other escorts had been too intimidated by her to play with her. Michelina tried to imagine telling her mother to include playfulness on the list of requirements for her husband and shook her head.

When Lindsey's lips turned blue, they called a halt to the swim. Katie climbed out first, followed by Michelina. With Lindsey in his arms, Jared brought up the rear.

"I got a look at those splinters when you climbed the ladder," Jared said. "They'll have to come out."

She felt self-conscious, but refused to give in to it. "Are you offering to help?" she asked, throwing down the gauntlet to him for a change.

He opened his mouth in surprise.

"Nothing to say? Does that mean we have a new contender for the poultry contest?" she asked, then turned to towel-dry Katie. Minutes later, all four of them wolfed down the peanut butter and jelly sandwiches and lemonade they'd packed before they left. All the while, Michelina felt the sizzle of Jared's gaze on her. She knew no one but she herself or a licensed practitioner was going to remove the splinters from her upper thighs, but it sure had felt good taunting him about it.

Jared collected two fishing poles and a tackle box from the back of his truck. "Let's see if we can coax dinner out of this lake."

"Let me! Let me!" Katie cried, racing toward Jared. Lindsey popped her thumb in her mouth and searched for Michelina's hand.

"I think one of us might be ready for a nap," Michelina said, cocking her head toward Lindsey. "If you two want to fish, I could drive her back to the house and pick you up later."

Jared looked at her and shook his head in consternation. "In *my* truck? You're talking about driving *my* truck?"

Insulted by his reaction to her offer, she lifted her chin. "It's not that far to the house."

"Far enough," he said, shaking his head. "I'll take you and Lindsey to the house, then Katie and I will come back."

"Wanna fish," Lindsey said around her thumb.

"But you're so tired, sweetie," Michelina said, stroking the tike's almost-dry hair.

"Wanna fish," Lindsey insisted.

Michelina sighed. "Okay, maybe we can watch for a little while."

She sat down on the dock and pulled Lindsey onto her lap. Stroking the little girl's head, she watched Jared help Katie bait a hook and drop a line in the water. After a few minutes, he glanced back at them, then nodded and moved beside Michelina. "You were right. She was ready for a nap."

"I'm right about driving again, too. Gary tells me

I'll be able to drive again very soon,'' she couldn't resist telling him.

He arched his eyebrows. "Gary? Why would Gary say that?"

"Because he's fixing my truck after work."

Jared stared at her for a full minute. "And how are you paying him?" he asked in a low voice.

She got an uneasy sensation at his tone. "I'm paying him for parts, but he said he would do the labor free." She smiled. "He also said not to expect it to look cosmetically pretty."

He wiped his hand over his face and nodded. "You know he's hoping for more than a kiss from you."

She gaped at him. "He's been nothing but a perfect gentleman."

"Yeah, but you gotta know how you affect—" he pointed at her and shrugged "—men."

If truth were told, she really *wasn't* sure how she affected men—she knew only how her title and family position affected men. The intensity of Jared's gaze made her feel hot and just a little bit like a bad girl. Michelina rather liked the feeling. The possibility that Jared could want her without knowing anything about her title was heady. She carefully leaned toward him and whispered, "Why don't you show me?"

"Show you what?" he asked.

"Why don't you show me how I affect a man?"

He narrowed his eyes and leaned away from her. "Any man can do that."

"I didn't ask *any* man."

His eyes flickered with white-hot fire. "Duchess, you're asking for trouble."

She saw his biceps flex with the same tension she felt. Just as her rattled mind tried to produce a pithy but seductive response, Katie let out a yelp of delight.

In an instant, Jared was beside her, helping his niece reel in the fish. Lindsey jerked awake, her little eyebrows furrowing at the commotion.

"It's okay," Michelina assured her. "Katie's excited because she's catching a fish."

Lindsey's eyes rounded, and she shifted in Michelina's lap to get a better view. After Katie and Jared successfully collected the fish, the foursome returned to the house. Tired from their outing, the girls immediately went down for a nap, and after a long, hot shower, Michelina attempted to remove the splinters from the back of her thigh. She managed to pull out two, but the position was awkward, so she decided to try again that evening. Taking advantage of the girls' nap time, she sought out Gary and learned the car wouldn't be ready for at least another day.

Tamping down her impatience to move on her search for her brother, she returned to the house and learned that Jared planned to take the girls to visit their parents at the physical rehabilitation center. His sister and brother-in-law were due to be released any day, and would gradually begin taking over the care of Katie and Lindsey over the next couple of weeks.

Soon, Michelina realized, there would be no reason for her to stay. The knowledge tugged her in different directions. On the one hand, she was glad to have the freedom to try to find her brother. On the other hand, she felt oddly reluctant to leave. The latter feeling was related to Jared. He bothered her.

He bothered her by the way he seemed to challenge her at every turn, and she not only wanted to meet his challenge, she wanted to surpass it. He bothered her by underestimating her. He bothered her because she spent a lot of time wondering what kind of lover he would be.

Needing a distraction, she went downstairs and practiced fencing with the target dummy. Two hours later, disgusted with her performance, she returned her foil to the wall and marched upstairs. When she reached for the doorknob, the door opened without her touching it.

Jared appeared in the doorway. "I wondered where you were." His gaze fell over her. "You don't look happy."

Enormously glad to see him, yet annoyed at how much he affected her, she let out a sigh. "I sparred with the target dummy."

"Yeah?"

She walked past him. "The dummy won."

He snickered. "That bad, huh?"

She frowned. "I was horrible. It was as if I'd never picked up a foil in my life."

"Maybe you're trying too hard. Try taking a day off."

She nodded, thinking that if everything worked out, she could visit her brother's restaurant tomorrow night. "I may do that. Where are the girls? I'll help put them—"

"Already done. They'd had a big day and practically fell into bed," he said.

Surprise darted through her. "I didn't even hear you arrive."

His lips twitched. "Too absorbed in beating the hell out of my target dummy."

She shrugged her shoulders, too frustrated by him and the condition of her truck and everything else to argue. "Thank you for putting the girls to bed. I think I'll—"

"I'm ready," he interjected.

Something in his tone snapped her head around. She looked at him closely, and the masculine intent in his eyes made her stomach dip. "Ready for what?" she dared to ask.

He moved closer and skimmed his fingers down a strand of her hair. "Ready to show you how you affect a man...how you affect me."

His voice was smoky-sexy, and she felt a sudden shot of apprehension. She had thought it would take longer to seduce him. Actually, she had wondered if she would *ever* get him to be her lover. Her heartbeat skipped. Was *she* ready for this? She looked at Jared's tall, muscular body and the hungry look in his eyes. Was she ready for him?

She heard a little voice inside her taunting: *wuss*. She stiffened her resolve. This might be her only chance to choose a lover. Her *only* chance. She held her breath.

"Unless you've changed your mind," he said, his voice full of challenge and possibilities.

Her mouth went dry. "I haven't changed my mind."

He nodded in approval and took her hand. "Come up to my bedroom."

Her heart in her throat, she allowed him to lead her up the stairs. Her mind and pulse were racing. Had she thought of everything? Was she sure? Halfway to his room, she turned to him, "I must ask. Do you have—" She couldn't think of a delicate way to put it. "Um—"

"What?" he asked, the motion of his thumb on the inside of her wrist providing a terrible distraction.

"Contraception," she blurted out.

"Yeah. I'll take care of you. Don't worry," he said, lifting her hand and kissing the same place on her wrist that he had rubbed.

She felt light-headed from excitement, and they hadn't even entered his room. He led her the rest of the way down the hall and through his door, immediately turning on two lights.

"Shouldn't we turn out at least one of those lights?" she asked as he drew her against his chest.

"I want to see."

She didn't think it possible, but her heart pounded against her rib cage even harder. Then he lowered his mouth and kissed her, and the room began to spin. He darted his tongue just inside her lower lip as if he were licking her, eating her. She felt her breasts grow heavy. Skimming his hand to the top of her jeans, he deepened the kiss as he toyed with the buttons on her jeans.

Arousal pooled between her thighs, and she felt the achy need to touch his skin. She slid her hands beneath his shirt to his belly, and he inhaled sharply, grabbing her hand. Confused, she looked up at his face.

"May I take off your jeans?" he asked, dropping a distracting kiss on her throat.

"Yes," she murmured. Yes, he could do anything he wanted.

Returning his mouth to hers, Jared slowly pushed her jeans down. She was impatient for him to take off his shirt, but she supposed she could wait. Another few seconds. The urgency coursing through her surprised her.

He dropped to his knees and untied her shoelaces, interspersing kisses on her belly and knees as he removed her shoes and helped her out of her jeans.

When he rose to his feet, she slid her hand up under his shirt again, and he gave a groan that made her feel wet and wicked. "Ah, duchess, you're something else. I'm supposed to be the one showing you."

"That doesn't mean I can't touch you, does it?"

He groaned again. "Guess not. But it's my turn first." He stayed her hands again and gave her a French kiss that made her feel as if she was riding the world's fastest roller coaster. "I want you to lie down on my bed."

"I can do that," she said, her knees soft as she melted onto his big bed. She looked up at him, wanting to seal this moment in her memory. He was going to be her first lover, her first and the only one she got to choose. She riveted her gaze on him and stared. His hair was sexily mussed, his eyes dark with want, his lips still damp from their kisses. She could feel his hunger even though he wasn't touching her.

"I want you to do one more thing, Mimi."

She would do anything he asked her in that half velvet, half husky voice.

"Roll over on your stomach," he whispered.

Six

Curious why he would want her on her stomach, Michelina turned over and held her breath. She felt as if every nerve ending was on high alert.

"I've got the tweezers right here. This shouldn't take but a couple of minutes."

His matter-of-fact words penetrated her dazed arousal. "Tweezers!" She started to turn back over, but Jared's heavy hand on her back pinned her to the mattress.

"Be still," he ordered.

Mortified, then furious, she kicked at him. And missed. Bloody hell. The jerk had led her to believe they were going to make love, that he was so aroused he couldn't bear for her to touch him, when all he really wanted was to pluck splinters out of her thighs.

He caught her ankles in a viselike grip. "Cut it out,

duchess. If we don't get these splinters out, then you could get an infection and it would be my bad luck to find out you didn't have health insurance."

She was so furious, she almost couldn't speak. "Let me go! I don't want you touching me."

"You didn't mind a minute ago," he reminded her in that now-infuriating velvet voice.

"That was different. Let me go!"

"I'm not letting you go until I take care of those splinters."

"This is abuse. There has to be a law against it," she said, wishing she could snap her fingers and transport this scenario to Marceau. Her bodyguards would kill him, or at the very least, hurt him badly.

"Sorry, duchess, if you want out of my clutches, you're going to have to let me get your splinters."

He had led her to believe he wanted something a lot different than her splinters just moments before, she thought darkly. She felt another hot wave of humiliation, but had the uneasy feeling that Jared would hold her in this position half the night if that was what he deemed necessary. A growl rumbled in her throat. "I hate you for this," she told him.

"Fine. Hate me," he told her. "Just hold still."

He released his grip from her ankles, and Michelina stiffly dropped her legs to the bed. She counted to one thousand as Jared performed his surgery and comforted herself with countless evil punishments for him. *Put him on a rack.* Too easy. *Behead him.* Too fast. *Make him get a bikini wax.* Blood-curdling screams of pain filled her mind. The fantasy gave her enormous satisfaction.

She felt a pinch and jumped. "Ouch!"

"Done," he said, quickly stepping away from the side of the bed as if he knew she wanted to rip the skin off his bones. "That last one was deeper than the others."

She scrambled off the bed and stared at him. "Did you enjoy making a fool of me?"

He held up a hand. "I wasn't trying to make a fool of you. I just knew it was going to be tricky getting you to let me take care of those splinters."

"You didn't even consider being direct?" she asked accusingly.

"For about half a minute. If you're honest with yourself, then you'll admit you wouldn't have let me if I'd asked you outright."

Her fury bubbled inside her again like a volcano ready to erupt. "You have a lot of room to talk about honesty." So upset she could barely think straight, she snatched up her jeans and went to the door. She wanted to blast him. She wanted to punch him. The nerve of him! Getting her half-undressed on the pretext that he would make love to her.

Her chest knotted with indignation. An idea slid through her haze of anger. She took a deep breath at the outrageous scheme that played through her mind. Did she have the guts? She thought again of how he had played with her emotions, with her passion. Bloody hell, she did.

Taking a calming breath, she opened the door a sliver then stopped abruptly. With her back to him, she pulled her shirt over her head and unsnapped her bra.

"What in hell are you doing?"

"Almost done," she said, pushing her panties down her thighs and hooking them with her fingers. She turned around, fully naked, clutching her jeans, shirt and bra in one hand and her panties in the other. She watched his gaze consume her from head to toe and fought an unwelcome rush of heat.

He took a step toward her and she held up her hand. "I just wanted you to see…" she said in a voice that sounded breathy to her own ears. The combination of anger and nerves made her heart pound a mile a minute. "…what you're not getting," she finished, and tossed her panties in his direction at the same time she walked out of his door.

Jared almost went after her. He was one millionth of a centimeter away from going after her, hauling that gorgeous body into his arms and showing her how she affected him in every possible way.

That last little stunt she'd pulled had shocked the hell out of him. The vision of her naked body and the way she'd responded to his kisses earlier played nonstop through his mind. His skin was on fire, and he had an erection that wasn't going to quit anytime soon. He wondered if a man could burn to cinders from the inside out.

She had kissed him like a woman determined to give as good as she got. The touch of her hand on his stomach had had him in knots. It had been so easy to imagine her skimming that delicate hand down to where he was hard and aching for her. When she'd kissed him, he'd had a vision of her avid, wicked mouth flowing over his entire body, driving him to distraction, then satisfaction.

He'd wanted to touch her breasts, to put his mouth over the dusky tips, but he'd known he didn't have enough self-control for that. As it was, he still wanted to beat down her door and take her. She'd given him a good look at her slim, luscious body from her creamy throat, breasts that reminded him of peaches, the delicate curve of her waist and the inviting swatch of curls covering her femininity between her silky thighs.

It was just too easy, too tantalizing, to imagine plunging inside her moist, welcoming secrets. A groan started in his gut and slid out of his throat. He rubbed his face and swore. He'd had the most sexy, passionate woman raring to go, right at his fingertips, and what had he done? He'd pulled splinters out of her thighs, instead of sinking between them.

The wounded, indignant look in her eyes had made him feel guilty, and it had taken every bit of his concentration to focus on her splinters instead of her rounded bottom.

The worst part was that this was about more than her body. The woman was getting under his skin. If he hadn't cared about her, then he wouldn't give a damn about her splinters. She was still too imperious for his taste, but he had to admit he'd underestimated her. She had entirely too many secrets, and he wanted to know them all.

That was dangerous as hell, but true. She wasn't cut from the same cloth as his ex-fiancée. He was certain she'd come from a pampered background, but she'd been willing to work.

He liked her drive. He liked the way she treated the girls. Her self-deprecating sense of humor had taken him completely by surprise.

He liked the way she'd been looking at him when she'd thought he didn't see her. He saw admiration and fire in her silver eyes. He'd liked the way she'd made her desire for him crystal clear. Honest. She might be hiding a truckload of secrets, but she'd been honest about wanting him.

More honest than he had been with her.

The knowledge filled him with a bitter taste. Balling his hands into fists, he glanced down at the little strip of silk she'd tossed at him just before she'd left. He could have had her in his arms tonight, burning up his bed.

Regret twisted inside him. Even though he knew it wasn't wise, he wanted her. He wanted the fire he saw in her eyes, the passion she emanated. He'd been cold a long time.

He rubbed his thumb over her panties and groaned. Still hard, he shook his head. He'd been cold a long time, but he was burning up now. Jared had the uncomfortable feeling that he would be taking cold showers even after Mimi left his ranch.

Two nights later, Michelina waited impatiently after she had picked at her meal at Jack Raven's Seafood Restaurant. She'd asked the waiter if she could speak to the owner. The restaurant was bustling with activity, clanging dishes and silverware, Greek music playing in the background and quick-footed waiters eager to earn their tips. It was hard to believe that such a momentous occasion was about to take place. She was going to see her brother for the first time. Her stomach danced in anticipation as the seconds crawled by.

A harried-looking dark-haired man strode from the kitchen. His gaze landed on her, and he smiled and nodded. Michelina felt her heart race. Was this her brother? This man looked closer to his mid-thirties than his late twenties. As soon as she saw his eyes, she would know.

He extended his hand as he moved next to her table. "Hello. I'm Jack Raven. We're delighted you could join us this evening. Your waiter said you asked for me." He glanced at her still-full plate and frowned. "You not like your food?"

She shook her head. "Oh, it was delicious. I'm too full. I wanted the opportunity to compliment you." She craned to see his eyes, but the light was dim. Giving into her curiosity, she stood. Brown eyes. Her heart sank. This man's eyes were brown. Her brother had the trademark Dumont light eyes.

He smiled at her kindly. "You are very nice to compliment my restaurant. Please do come again. By the way, your accent…you don't sound as if you are from here."

"Neither do you," she said, trying to hide her disappointment.

He laughed, big and hearty. "Excellent point. Miss?"

"Deerman," she said. "Mimi Deerman."

"Mimi Deerman," he echoed, looking more closely into her eyes. "You have very unusual eyes. Beautiful. Please visit us again. I will make sure the chef prepares something special for you."

"Thank you," she said, appreciating his warmth and wishing the man had been her brother. She wished it had been that easy. She watched him leave and sank into her seat with a sigh. Now what? Distracted, she paid the check when it arrived, calculated the gratuity and drove back to the ranch.

When she arrived, she parked a little distance away and looked up at the large house, reluctant to go inside. Jared would probably be there with either questions or taunts. Every time she thought about the way he'd treated her just two nights ago, she felt herself grow hot with humiliation. Her thoughts and feelings grew inside her, making her feel as if she couldn't breathe. She opened the window. The events of the last few weeks bombarded her, and Michelina felt like a complete failure. She'd escaped from security just over two weeks ago with a grand vision of grand accomplishments, and what did she have to show for herself?

On the plus side, she now knew how to change a diaper and make a peanut butter and jelly sandwich, and she'd managed to keep Jared's nieces alive while they were in her care. On the minus side, she had wrecked her truck, been blackmailed into being a temporary nanny and, given the opportunity to improve her fencing, had found her own performance underwhelming. She'd failed in finding her brother. She'd even failed in seducing Jared.

The terrible fear she hid deep inside her surfaced. What if she really couldn't accomplish anything of any substance? What if she couldn't take care of herself? What if she wasn't good for anything except photo ops and wearing her tiara with style?

The questions clawed at her, making her feel raw and sore when she already felt wounded. A lump formed in her throat, and pressure built behind her eyes. Giving in to her disappointment in herself, she leaned her head and arms on the steering wheel and began to weep.

You really are useless. Princess Useless. The words reverberated through her brain, stabbing at her most tender places. This was her one opportunity to prove herself, and she was botching everything.

"Was the fish dinner that bad?"

Michelina jumped at the sound of Jared's voice so close to her. She swung her head to look at him as he leaned against the window of her truck. So strong, so confident, so insufferable. The last person in the world she wanted to see. Embarrassed, she swiped at her tears. "What are you talking about? What are you doing here?"

"Your fish dinner at Jack Raven's Seafood Restaurant? Was it that bad?"

She rolled her eyes in disgust. "It was delicious. How did you know where I went?"

"Gary told me he gave you directions. Did you accomplish what you wanted?"

Discouragement stabbing at her again, she sighed. "Not really." She glanced at him, resenting him. "What are you doing out here?"

He cocked his head to one side. "Well, duchess, I was afraid your wailing was going to wake every animal and human in a ten-mile radius."

She dropped her jaw. "Wailing," she echoed in disbelief, embarrassment and indignation battling for dominance. "I was *not* wailing!"

"Sounded like wailing to—"

Disgusted with him and herself, she shook her head and started to roll up her window. "You're impossible. You're the most insensitive—"

He put his hand on the window, stopping the upward movement. "Got you to stop crying, didn't I?" he asked, with the familiar challenging glint in his eyes.

She stared at him for a long moment.

"I managed to distract you from whatever was making you cry like you'd lost your last best friend, didn't I?" He shrugged those powerful shoulders of his, providing yet another distraction. "So I've got to be good for something."

She shot him a dark look. "Well, maybe that's part of the problem. You're good for several things," she said, poking at his muscular chest. "Too many things to count. And I'm just trying to find one or two things to be good for."

"I could name a couple," he said, his gaze brimming with sensual suggestions she wasn't foolish enough to believe.

"Oh, but of course," she said in complete disbelief.

He opened the door of the truck. "Come on out."

Her resentment toward him built at his order. "What if I don't want to?"

"Then I'll drag you out. Come on. Let's take a walk," he said, snagging her arm and tugging.

She scowled at him, but didn't feel like getting into an embarrassing debate where she would again fail. "Has it not occurred to you that I don't want to be around you?"

He slid his arm to her back and guided her toward the path. "Yep, but sometimes when you're upset, you don't always know what's best for you."

"And you do?" She stepped away. "If you say one word about the splinters—"

He lifted his hands. "I was never going to mention the splinters again. You won that one hands-down."

"Not quite," she said, remembering lying on his bed as he pulled out the splinters.

He stopped and turned to her. "Did you take cold showers and get no sleep for two nights?"

The dark intensity in his eyes took her by surprise. She opened her mouth, but it took an extra few seconds to form words. "Uh, no."

"Then I'd say you won."

She swallowed over a strange knot of emotion. "Funny, I don't feel like I won, but that's nothing new," she muttered.

He lifted his hand to her chin and lifted it so she would meet his gaze. "What are you talking about?"

"You, of all people, wouldn't understand," she said, his touch making her heart race.

"Try me," he insisted.

"I did."

His gaze falling over her like a warm breeze, he rubbed his thumb across her mouth. "Try me again."

Her heart stuttered. Another challenge.

"Tell me what you were talking about."

She took a quick breath of relief edged with disappointment. He wanted into her head, not into her body. Shrugging, she stepped back and looked away. "I just feel like a failure, useless."

"That's crazy."

"No, it's not," she said hotly. "I told you that you wouldn't understand. I bet you're good at just about everything you do. And I—" She waved her hand. "I'm not really good at much of anything except maybe planning a party every now and then and wrecking a truck."

"You've done a good job taking care of the girls. You're pretty good at fencing for a beginner."

"I'm hopeless at fencing."

He sighed and reached out his hand to pull her against him. "You've just had some rough luck lately. It happens to everyone. It's not as clear-cut for us humans as it is animals."

Both disconcerted and comforted by the solid wall of his chest, she looked at him in confusion. "Why are you talking about animals?"

"To add some perspective," he said, guiding her up the path toward the house. "Take Romeo, my prize stud bull."

"Why would I want to take him?" she asked dryly.

He chuckled. "Romeo is successful. He does one thing, but he does it so well that he makes a mint."

"I don't see what impregnating cows has to do with my situation. You basically set him up with a cow and he does his thing and—"

''Not quite,'' Jared said. ''We do a lot of this in vitro.''

She stared at him in surprise. ''Oh my goodness,'' she murmured in dismay. ''So, what do you do—give him photos of hot cows?''

Jared chuckled again. ''It's a little more mechanical than that.''

She instinctively covered her ears. ''I don't think I want to know any more.''

He drew her hands away from her ears. ''The point is, he doesn't fight his purpose,'' Jared said, lowering his face to just inches from hers. ''Don't fight *your* purpose.''

Her chest tightened with anxiety, and she couldn't help hearing shades of her mother in his words. As far as Marceau was concerned, her purpose was to be pretty when the camera caught her and to marry a man who could bring wealth, political influence or commerce to the kingdom. Michelina chafed at that purpose. She always had. She wanted more, but she didn't exactly know what. Sinking into Jared's gaze, she saw something in his eyes that told her to look further and dig deeper than she had before.

''When are you gonna let me see the real you?''

Her breath hitched in her throat. ''I think you got a pretty good look at me the other night.''

''I mean what's going on in here,'' he said, skimming his fingers over her forehead.

Another challenge, and she just didn't have the fortitude for it. Nowhere, no how, no way. She felt weak, but if she was going to match wits with Jared, she needed to feel strong. Pulling back decisively, she replied, "Not tonight."

"Did anyone ever tell you that you're a damn frustrating woman?"

She could hear the dissatisfaction in his voice. It mirrored her own emotions so precisely that she had to laugh. "No one who wasn't related to me. What about you?"

He shot her an indignant look. "What do you mean?"

"I mean has anyone ever told you that you're a damn frustrating man?"

He opened his mouth, then clamped it shut and narrowed his eyes.

His response amused her. "That can only mean one thing. So many people have told you that you're damn frustrating, you can't even count all of them."

"You're pushing for trouble."

"I already pushed for trouble. I've got a headache tonight."

He flashed her a seductive grin. "Lady, I could make you forget your headache."

Seven

I could make you forget your headache.

Jared's velvet offer continued to dangle in front of Michelina like a forbidden dessert. After she'd turned him down the other night, she couldn't stop the feeling that she was waiting for the other shoe to drop. In this case, the shoe belonged to Jared. She'd done her best to seduce him and he'd embarrassed her, but now that she could have him, she wasn't certain she could successfully pull off the experienced temptress. She had the uncomfortable feeling that Jared would be able to see right through her.

She'd been instructed to skip the champagne when ordering supplies for the county celebration. Sitting in an overstuffed chair in the library with the door pulled closed, Michelina added lemonade to her mile-long list. The girls were spending the night with their parents with the understanding that they could call Jared if necessary. Restless and uncertain of what her next move should be, she tried to bury herself in party planning.

Out of the corner of her eye, she spotted the door swing open and her heart jumped. She'd avoided him ever since he'd caught her crying in the car.

"Haven't seen you in the fencing room lately." Jared leaned against the doorway and looked down at her. "Did you get bored?"

"No. I've been busy planning the county celebration."

He nodded. "Good. No champagne, right?"

"No champagne." *But I haven't ruled out caviar,* she thought, mentally adding it in a rebellious gesture.

"Since the girls are gone, I've got time to give you a fencing lesson. If you decide you're up to it, I'll be in the basement," he said and strolled away.

Up to it. Her temperature and ire immediately rose. Michelina stared after him. How did that man manage to get her going so easily? She should be able to dismiss him. She had dismissed plenty of other men. Her brothers had never seemed to have any problem enjoying then discarding women. Glancing down, she noticed she'd crumpled her list in her hand. She definitely needed some practice if she was going to pull off everything her brothers had done. Taking a breath, she smoothed out the paper and eyed the open door. She may as well take the bloody fencing lesson.

Walking down the steps, she prepared her ego for another beating. Jared was pulling the foils from the wall as she walked into the room.

"Have you thought about lifting weights?" he asked, as he handed her the chest protector and her glove.

"Why? I thought dexterity was more important in fencing."

"A little weight training will strengthen your hand so you won't tire quickly. There are some weights in the rec room, if you're interested." His gaze skimmed over her, then settled on her eyes. She felt something inside her crackle and pop.

"Let's warm up, then work on closing the line and the riposte today."

The plan suited her mood. In the past, he'd focused on defensive moves. The riposte was a swift return attack performed in one smooth motion after a parry. If she were lucky, she would spend the next hour poking the great Jared McNeil with her foil.

Forty-five minutes later, she was in the groove and she'd worked up a sweat. Every time Jared gave her an instruction, she made the adjustment almost before he said it. She read his body language and began to predict which way he would move.

"You're doing well," he said.

"Thanks. Do we have to stop?"

"Three bouts?"

She nodded, jumping up and down to keep her concentration up.

"Winner gets a round of truth or dare," he said, moving in position to salute.

Michelina automatically went through the motions of the salute. "Truth or dare?"

"Kids' game. Harmless," he said. *"En garde."*

She gave him a run for his money and even managed to win the first bout. She was so happy she was beside herself. Flushed with victory, she went at him again, but he soon put her on the defense and won. He was ahead by two touches, so she tried a move new to her. It took him by surprise, but not long enough. He recovered and took that bout, too.

He pushed back his mask and gave a low whistle. "You're getting better. Faster."

She pushed back her own mask, struggling with conflicting feelings. "You didn't let me win, did you?"

He stared at her for a long moment and started to laugh. "Throw a bout for the helpless female? Not my style, and you're not helpless."

She breathed easier. "Then I really did beat you?"

"In one match," he was quick to point out.

Exhilaration rolled through her. "Yes, but I still won."

"One bout," he repeated, then cracked a grin as he took her foil from her. "You like winning, don't you duchess?"

"Winning against you is a big deal. I don't think there's any need to stroke your enormous—" she paused deliberately "—enormous ego, but you know you're good."

"Good enough to win two out of three bouts, which means you owe me a round of Truth or Dare."

She waved her hand dismissively. "Whatever that is."

"So do you choose truth or dare?"

She felt a ripple of uneasiness at the predatory glint

in his eyes. She wasn't certain about the rules of this game, but she knew she didn't want to answer his questions, and she knew he had plenty of questions about her. "Dare."

He nodded and moved closer to her. "Kiss me," he said. "For five minutes."

She gaped at him. "Five minutes?" She would melt into a puddle in the middle of the floor. "And what if I choose truth?"

He shook his head. "Once you choose, you can't go back. But I'll let you this time. Who were you looking for that you didn't find at Jack Raven's Seafood Restaurant?"

Talk about choosing between the devil and the deep blue sea. She couldn't welsh, though. He probably expected that, and even though she couldn't kiss him and didn't want to reveal anything about her family to him, she was going to have to do something. She looked at his mouth. Her heart squeezed dangerously tight in her chest. Definitely not kissing.

Taking a deep breath, she told herself that she wouldn't be here long enough for Jared to cause any real damage. "My brother. I was looking for my brother."

He stood stock-still. She read the quick shock in his dark blue eyes, then she could practically see the vapor trail from how fast his mind was moving. "Which brother? How many brothers do you have?"

"Five, but I've never met one of them."

He moved closer to her, and every step closer he took made her feel more on edge one second, more relieved the next. "Does this have something to do with the one that almost drowned?"

She nodded. "Were you good with puzzles when you were a child?"

He shrugged. "Good enough."

An understatement, she suspected. Was there anything he couldn't do well?

"What's the rest of the story?"

"He was just a toddler at the time. My family was vacationing in Bermuda, and my father and one of his brothers took some of the kids sailing one afternoon. A terrible storm came up quickly, and Ja—" She corrected herself. He wasn't known as Jacques Dumont anymore. "Jack fell overboard. My uncle and father nearly drowned trying to find him, but it was as if he'd disappeared. There were search parties, but he was never found. We thought he was dead," she said. "Until last year when we received a lost letter with a lock of his hair and a button from the jacket he wore the day of the accident."

"That's why you're here in Wyoming," he said.

"Most of the reason," she admitted.

"I'm surprised your family let you take off on this search by yourself."

"I'm of age, even though they might forget that fact," she said stiffly. "Even though they may not think I can be trusted with the truth—"

Jared held up his hands. "Whoa. Whoa, there. What are you talking about?"

"It's the only-sister-youngest-child syndrome. They think I can't do anything, which is understandable because I can't do much," she said, hating the way her voice trembled. ''I don't know why I'm telling you all this, because you probably agree with them and—''

''Hey,'' he said, giving her shoulders a gentle shake. ''Don't talk about yourself that way. You haven't had much of a chance to prove yourself, but you're doing it now. I already told you that you've done a good job with the girls. And you just beat me in a fencing bout.'' He shook his head. ''Don't put yourself down, and don't let anyone else do it either.''

She felt as thought she'd just been struck by lightning. Stunned at the way he'd defended her, she stared at him, speechless. Countless bodyguards had defended her because of her title, but she couldn't remember ever feeling as if someone had defended her for herself. The strength in Jared's eyes called to something deep inside her. She felt stronger—she felt as if she were capable of anything. She felt everything but useless.

Jared slid one of his hands though her hair, tangling his fingers around it. His gaze lowered to her lips, and his mouth followed, taking hers. Desire and something deeper and more powerful crackled through her. She lifted her hands to his head, reveling in the texture of his hair in her fingers, urging his mouth against hers.

The passion between them burst like a fiery explosion, burning away reason, logic and fear. Michelina only knew she wanted to be as close to Jared as she could get. She wanted to feel the beat of his heart against her palm. She tugged at his protective chest covering, and he accurately read her silent request.

He pulled off his chest covering and hers, stealing kisses all the while.

She immediately pulled loose his shirt and slid her hands up to his chest.

Jared closed his eyes and let out a hissing sigh, then he opened his eyes, and the expression in them made her heart thud in anticipation. "I'm not stopping you this time," he said. "Even if it kills me."

A ripple of excitement coursed through her, and she slipped her palm up farther, to where his heart pounded. He took her mouth again in a scorching French kiss while she allowed herself to explore freely the muscular contours of his chest and belly.

He took her with deep, drugging kisses that left her mind muddy and aware only of him. The room faded from her consciousness. With his mouth still fastened to hers, she was dimly conscious of him undoing the buttons of her shirt. She held her breath and felt her bra loosen. She inhaled just one breath and found herself standing before him half-naked.

"I've wanted to do this too long," he muttered. He lowered his wet, open mouth down her throat to her chest, then he lifted her slightly and closed his lips around one of her nipples.

Heat flashed through her, and she felt her knees dip.

Jared caught her against him and placed her down on the floor. Following her down, he kissed her again and she arched against him, craving the sensation of his hard chest abrading her tender nipples.

"Too hot," he muttered against her mouth. "Damn, you've got me too hot."

Michelina felt herself grow swollen and restless. She wriggled against him, squeezing his biceps, sliding her fingers over him, reveling in the texture of his skin. Skimming her hands down his broad back, she encountered his jeans and frowned. ''Why are you still dressed?'' Stretching her arms, she slid her hands beneath the waistband of his pants to his bottom.

He swore under his breath. ''You're not helping me slow down.''

''I didn't know that was my purpose,'' she whispered, the edginess in her voice kicking her arousal up another notch.

Growling, he pulled back and ditched his jeans. Before she could blink, he had removed his briefs.

Michelina stared, transfixed by the sight of his potent masculinity. At first glance, his size intimidated her. She swallowed over a lump of emotion that mixed apprehension and excitement. That could hurt, she thought, and forced herself to take a deep breath. But she wanted this, she told herself. She couldn't let him know how inexperienced she was. Her worst fear was that he would stop.

She lifted her hands. ''You're too far away.''

He groaned, allowing her to pull him partially onto her as he rested on his elbows. She loved the weight of him, luxuriated in the sensation of being surrounded by him. It didn't last nearly long enough, though, before he moved his mouth down to her breasts, teasing the already tight tips into oversensitive buds. His wicked, attentive mouth tightened a coil inside her, and she felt herself stretching, reaching for more.

Reading her body like a book, he continued moving his mouth down her belly, creating sensual havoc inside her. He removed her jeans and she held her breath when he moved lower still, kissing the inside of her thigh. Then he pressed his mouth against the secret part of her that clamored with need.

He rubbed his tongue over her with mind-blowing repetition. She couldn't breathe, couldn't think. She rode the edge of pleasure and uneasiness at the carnal intimacy with which he took her. But he touched her body as if he'd known her pleasure points the moment he'd seen her. He knew what he was doing. She reacted purely out of instinct.

His tongue stroked her, and she shuddered. He groaned in approval. ''You taste so good, feel so good in my mouth.''

Desire and need bubbled from her body, sliding out of her throat. She couldn't stop the sounds. The tension inside tightened unbearably, and she arched against his wicked, wonderful mouth, seeking, needing, desperate. He drew the wellspring of her femininity into his mouth, and a spasm of pure pleasure rocked her. Michelina gasped at the strength of the sensations that ricocheted through her.

When she caught her breath, she met Jared's gaze. It was so hot, she felt as if she were burning alive. He pulled a foil packet from his discarded jeans, ripped it open and rolled the condom over his engorged masculinity. Wanting the rest of him, wanting to take him as he'd taken her, she leaned up to reach for him, but he shook his head and slid his thigh between hers. For a second, she noticed the rough texture of his thigh against hers, but then he was pressing against the opening to her innermost recesses. In one sure stroke, he thrust inside her.

The too-stretched burning sensation took her by surprise and she flinched, holding her breath.

He looked into her eyes, gazing at her in disbelief. "You're not—you couldn't be—"

He started to pull away, and panic sliced through her. She locked her legs around his buttocks. "You're not really planning to back out on me a second time, are you?"

"Are you a virgin?"

She couldn't resist the urge to squirm under his hard gaze.

He swore under his breath. "Stop moving."

"Stop looking at me as though you don't approve."

"Oh, I approve, all right. I approve so much, I could explode with approval. But you still haven't answered my question."

"I think I'm probably not," she said, thinking it wasn't very nice of him to embarrass her this first time.

"You *think?*" he asked incredulously. "I *think* that's something you ought to know."

"Okay, well, I'm certain I'm not now."

He hesitated a half beat. "What about five minutes ago?"

Michelina sighed. "I always heard this was a lot of fun, but now I'm starting to wonder."

"Five minutes ago?" he prompted, undeterred by her impatience.

''This isn't very flattering. First you made me strip and led me to believe you were going to make love to me, and then you pulled out my splinters instead. Now, you're grilling me—''

''If you would answer the question.''

''Do you promise not to stop?''

He stared at her in disbelief, then shook his head and gave a rough chuckle. ''I promise.''

''I was extremely inexperienced five minutes ago.''

''How inexperienced?''

''Not at all experienced. Now could we get on with this?'' she asked, hot with self-conciousness. ''Or maybe we'd better just forget—''

Still connected to her, he lowered himself to his elbows, his face inches from hers. ''Why didn't you tell me? I could have made it better for you.''

''You weren't doing half-bad until you started asking questions,'' she retorted, and shifted as her body began to adjust to his.

He closed his eyes as if in agony. ''Are you trying to make me completely lose control?''

Seeing the raw desire in his eyes sent a ripple of arousal and feminine satisfaction through her. ''Fair is fair. *You* made *me* lose control, didn't you?'' she said, undulating beneath him, liking the idea of making him lose control.

He fastened his hands over her hips like a vise and shook his head. ''Not this time. Not your first time.''

She made a futile effort to move. ''This isn't turning out to be as much fun as I thought—'' She broke off when he slid one of his hands between them and found the fountainhead of her femininity with unerring precision. "Ohhhh."

Rubbing his thumb against her, causing a riot of sensations, he slowly began to move. The combination of his hand on her most sensitive place and his masculinity pumping inside her was exquisite.

"Oh, that is soooo—" Michelina instinctively arched, and Jared groaned. He continued to pump and fondle her until she felt hot and restless.

"Having fun yet?" he taunted, touching her, filling her.

"It's—" He filled her again, and the sensation made her forget what she'd wanted to say. *Fun* was such a lame word for all she was feeling. Warm, intoxicated, safe, excited. She tasted the heady flavor of a freedom she'd never experienced. The air between them grew hot and steamy and the room seemed to fade away. She was filled with Jared, enjoying the ripple of his muscles as he leaned against his elbows and thrust slowly in and out of her. She was so hot she was perspiring, so bothered she didn't know if she could bear another minute.

She wiggled, reaching for what she needed. "I want—"

His eyes heavy-lidded with passion, he strained. "You're not the only one who wants," he muttered, and the rhythm between his body and hers increased, taking her breath away.

Faster, faster, she felt the earth slide away from her as her body rocked into orbit. She felt Jared stiffen in release and clung to him with all her strength. He dipped his head against her shoulder. Their passion-heavy breaths mingled with each other, and Michelina reveled in Jared's chest against her breasts, his hard belly against hers and the sensation of his thighs rubbing the inside of hers. She had never felt so close to another person in her life.

He lifted his head and looked into her eyes, his gaze simmering with emotion. The combination of erotic possessiveness, sensual satisfaction and something deeper, more tender, made her heart feel tight and achy. ''You okay?'' he asked, lifting his hand to stroke her cheek.

She nodded, still trying to catch her breath. ''Yes, but I want to do this again.''

He stopped, searching her gaze. ''When?''

''Now.''

He closed his eyes. ''You'll be sore.''

Michelina could have purred. ''I've gotten sore from fencing, and I like this a lot more than I like fencing.''

Eight

It had been a long time since Jared had shared his bed with a woman like Mimi. He thought of his ex-fiancée and mentally shook his head. He'd never *had* a woman like Mimi in his bed. The woman hummed with secrets. That was why he was staring at her at 5:00 a.m. after they'd spent the night burning up his bed.

Jared had covered every inch of her very fine body, but he still had questions. Her body told him stories. Her body told him what she liked. She liked a firm, sure touch. She liked to be teased, but only for a while. She liked long kisses that left her breathless and made him so hard he ached. She might have been a virgin, but she was a fast learner, and if he wasn't careful, she would be the death of him.

Her gaze and touch told him she liked his body and

she trusted him. Partly trusted him, he corrected. He could still feel her secrets brewing under her silky-soft skin. When she'd told him she was looking for her long-lost brother, she might as well have sent a laser through his wall of protection against her. When she'd told him she knew he didn't believe she was capable of much of anything, he'd known he would have to prove her wrong. He'd never seen anyone who needed someone to believe in her more than Mimi.

He knew she was from a wealthy, pampered background. She'd been sheltered so much, she felt lost in the real world. Given the protective family, he wondered if her lack of a practical education had been calculated. If she didn't know how to get into trouble, then she couldn't cause a lot of trouble. Yet it looked as if she was making up for lost time now.

But she wouldn't stay around here long.

He heard the internal warning loud and clear and planned to heed it. Just because he'd let Mimi into his bed didn't mean he had to let her into his heart. Sure, she'd brought light and fire into his home, and he would enjoy her for the moment. Without getting too involved, he might try to help her find her brother, and he wouldn't turn down the offer of her body.

When she left, she would keep her heart and he would keep his and they would both have nice memories. It was best that way.

The sun peeked through the curtain opening and the room glowed with the gentle light of dawn. Inhaling the floral scent of her hair, he glanced down at her and felt his gut twist. Her features were soft in slumber, and that busy mouth of hers was still, but swollen from kisses. She lay on her side, the sheet covering the tops of her breasts like a strapless white gown. She was the kind of woman a man wanted to dance with in the moonlight. He lifted a stray strand of midnight-colored hair from her forehead, and she shifted. Her movement sent the sheet south, revealing her dusky-pink nipples. Jared remembered how her breasts had felt in his hands, in his mouth. He remembered how responsive she had been.

He felt himself grow hard. Unwilling to wake her, but reluctant to leave her spell just yet, he moved next to her, positioning his chest against her back while he slid his hand around her waist. She nestled her bottom against his crotch, and Jared became reacquainted with the true meaning of torture.

He stayed stock-still, but he was hyperaware of every breath she took. Her bare bottom wiggled again, and Jared swallowed a groan. Maybe this hadn't been such a good idea after all. He felt her yawn and wondered if she was waking up. She slid her hand down over his and sighed, wiggling against his swollen erection again.

"You are the most wiggling woman I've ever met," he muttered.

"Good morning to you, too," she said in a sexy, sleep-husky voice. "Are you complaining?"

"Yes and no," he said darkly.

"Why yes and no?"

He sighed. "Yes, because it's torture every time you move against—"

"Against what?" she asked, wiggling as she turned

slightly. "Oh," she said, realization seeping into her tone.

"No, because there are some advantages to this position and your tendency to wiggle," he said, sliding his hand upward to her breasts.

"What kind of advantages?"

He found her nipple and toyed with it until it grew stiff. Mimi wiggled again. Jared pressed his face into the nape of her neck, inhaling her scent, letting himself sink into a well of desire. "Do you want me to *tell* you or *show* you?"

"Both," she said. "I like the sound of your voice."

"Okay," he obliged, although he found it hard to talk while being distracted by her incredible body. "One of the advantages is that I have a lot of freedom with my hand. I can touch your breasts and play with your nipples." He stretched his hand to cover both of her breasts and reveled in the way she arched against his palm. Once again, her body told him what she wanted. He rolled one of her nipples between his thumb and forefinger, and she moaned in pleasure.

"Good?"

"Yes, but—"

He knew what she wanted, and he damn well was going to give it to her. Sliding his hand down her belly and lower, between her legs, he searched and found her wet and waiting for him.

"Like that?" he asked, feeling her tiny, sensitive bud bloom under his caress.

"Oh, yesss." Her voice was practically a purr.

He dipped his finger inside her while he continued

to move his thumb against her hot spot. He felt her skin heat, and her breath came in shallow little sexy gasps. She slid her legs farther apart, and the invitation nearly sent him over the edge. The way she trusted him with her body was irresistible.

He felt his own skin heat up and had trouble breathing evenly. She made a soft, sultry keening sound, and her body arched in complete pleasure.

"Oh, you—that—oh—" She stopped and gasped as if she couldn't find the words. "That was wonderful, but I wanted you inside—"

Unable to deprive himself any longer, Jared shifted her derriere and slid inside her tight, wet feminine core.

She made a surprised sound and went still.

"Okay?" He hoped so, because he was about to explode.

She wiggled. He groaned.

"I didn't know," she said, wiggling again. "I didn't know you could do it this way. The only thing is that I want to kiss you."

"Hold that thought," he said, and began to pump inside her.

He thrust and she wiggled, and it didn't take much for her to fall apart again while he went spinning straight through the roof.

Over the next few days, Lindsey and Katie came to Jared's house less and less frequently. Michelina tried to occupy herself with plans for the party, but she missed the busy activity Jared's nieces had provided. What truly distressed her, however, was how much she missed Jared when he was gone during the day.

Rolling her eyes in disgust at herself, she stomped down to the fencing room and took up her foil against the target dummy. With her concentration in the toilet, she wasn't performing much better than the last time she'd faced off with the target dummy.

The disappointed, disapproving faces of her mother and brothers flashed through her mind over and over. She felt the poison of failure seep through her veins. She hadn't located Jacques. Her family wouldn't view her ability to change a diaper as particularly impressive, and there would be bloody hell to pay when they learned she'd managed to lose her virginity. And they would find out. As a royal, she had to let her body be dissected and inspected on a regular basis.

The prospect of returning to Marceau turned her stomach. Her mother would be furious. Her brothers would disapprove. She didn't want to go back, but she didn't have any idea where her long-lost brother was, and the money she'd brought with her wasn't going to last forever.

Being with Jared made her feel safe, wanted, almost normal. The physical intimacy they shared made her want to tell Jared everything, but she was scared spitless he would reject her if he knew who she really was. And the longer her deception continued, the more trapped she felt. She rammed her foil into the dummy in frustration.

"The goal is to tap her, not gut her like a fish," Jared said from behind her.

Michelina jumped at the sound of his voice. "Oh!

I didn't know you were there." She shook her head in confusion. "Did you say 'her'?"

"Jennifer," he said, his face turning dark with displeasure.

She raised her eyebrows. "What a pretty name for such an ugly dummy."

He grunted, shrugging his shoulders as he walked toward her.

"Does she have a human namesake?"

"Yes. My ex-fiancée. She came running to me when she got embroiled in a scandal that involved finances, then married her attorney instead."

Michelina blinked and glanced again at the target dummy. "I see the resemblance," she said, her lips twitching.

"How can you see the resemblance? You've never met the woman."

"I meant the resemblance in terms of intelligence. For her to leave you for an attorney, she had to be quite stupid."

He stared at her for a long moment, during which she saw a dozen emotions come and go in his eyes. "How do you know the attorney wasn't the better man?"

"Because I know you. And I haven't met a better man," she said, the truth of it hitting her fast and hard.

"Maybe you haven't met a lot of men," he ventured.

"I've met dozens. No, make that hundreds."

"Hundreds?" he asked, arching his eyebrow in disbelief.

"Hundreds," she said firmly. *If not thousands.* She thought of how many men's hands she'd shaken, how many she had joined in a dance, how many she had entertained at dinners and formal events.

"Why were you so intent on destroying Jennifer?"

She shrugged. "Just working off some of my frustration."

"What's got you frustrated?" he asked, lifting his hand to chuck her chin.

His closeness muddled her mind. She looked away so she could think straight. "I've been thinking about my brother."

"Which one?"

"All of them," she reluctantly revealed. "But mostly Ja—" She cleared her throat to cover the French pronunciation of Jacques. "Jack." She pulled off her glove. "This is going to sound silly, but now that the girls are gone, the house feels terribly empty."

He chuckled. "Don't tell me you've got too much time on your hands. The county celebration is in just a few days."

She waved her hand in a dismissive gesture. "I've got all that covered."

"The library could use some help."

Her curiosity immediately piqued, she looked up at him. "What kind of help?"

"A lot of the books are falling apart in the county library and we haven't had anyone step up to boost the inventory."

"What about that Clara person you mentioned?

The one who insisted on holding the county celebration on your property?''

Jared shook his head. ''She runs the volunteer station at the hospital.''

''But this would be so easy. All it would take is a book drive. Ask people to donate the cost of a book and insert a bookplate with their name in recognition of their donation. For that matter, you could set up a table at the county celebration and jump-start the donations then.''

''So when are you going to get started?'' he asked.

Michelina gave a double take at the challenge she heard in his voice. ''I would need some assistance, some names.''

''I could help you out with that.''

''I can't make a long-term commitment,'' she told him, and she was talking about more than the book fair. She couldn't stay here in Wyoming with Jared indefinitely. She kept reminding herself that she was going to have to face her responsibilities, lame though they seemed, in Marceau sometime. Her stomach clenched. Most likely sometime soon.

His gaze grew hooded and unreadable. ''No one is expecting you to make a long-term commitment, duchess,'' he said in a too-smooth voice that chilled her.

Her heart clenched at his remote air. ''I wasn't saying that I'm incapable of making a long-term commitment. It's just that I know I'll have to return—''

''Where?'' he asked with an edge in his voice.

''Home,'' she said, nervous at the intensity humming from him. She didn't want him asking too many questions, because she still wasn't ready to answer them. "If you can supply me with some names of people willing to help, I'll organize the book drive."

"Good," he said, and took the foil from her hand. He hung it on the wall and turned back to her. "You should have told me you felt frustrated, Mimi. I could have helped you with that."

Even though they had made love several times, the dark sexual expression in his eyes made her heart race with jittery excitement. She laughed, trying to lighten the atmosphere, which was thickly layered with opposing emotions. "Are you saying you could have helped increase my frustration? I think you've already done that," she joked.

"Me?" he asked, his innocent tone belying the way he backed her against the wall. "I'm just a simple Wyoming rancher. How could I frustrate a duchess?"

"Simple," she scoffed, trying to keep a clear head even as Jared lowered his mouth toward hers. "You and Romeo have a lot in common. You're both full of bull."

"You're entirely too mouthy, but shutting you up is a helluva lot of fun for both of us," he said, then took her mouth in a hot French kiss that made the room spin. She tasted passion and a mirrored frustration in his kiss, and felt the desire to absorb as much of him as she could in the short time she was allowed. The more she learned about Jared, the more certain she grew that she would never meet another man like him. The uneasy suspicion that she would never feel this way about another man jabbed at tender places inside her with the precision of an accomplished fencer.

Michelina closed her mind to everything but him. She couldn't think about tomorrow. Tomorrow would be slapping her in the face soon enough. Just for now, she could be safe and wanted in Jared's arms. Just for now, she could trust that he wanted her for her. And that had to be enough. She tugged at his belt, eager to get closer.

He groaned and stilled her hand. "When am I going to get enough of you?" he muttered, then swung her over his shoulder.

Michelina yelped. "What are you doing?"

"Doing my duty and hauling you off to my bed to take care of your frustration," he said dryly, striding out of the fencing room and climbing the stairs. With each step, his shoulder jabbed her abdomen.

"Duty?" she echoed, frowning, not liking the use of that term. "Duty is changing a diaper."

"It's a matter of opinion," he said mildly, as he allowed her to slide down his body.

He kissed her again, and although she could feel the evidence of his hard desire against her thigh, she was still bothered that he'd even uttered the word *duty*. She'd come from a world of duty, and that was where she would return. Her stomach turned. She pulled her mouth from his. "I never want you to do *anything* for me out of a sense of duty."

He studied her for a long moment. "What if I consider it my duty as your lover to take care of your frustration?"

The combination of seduction and tenderness in his eyes knocked the breath and the fight right out of her.

His lips lifted in a lazy half grin. "What? Is this a first? Duchess has nothing to say?" He rubbed his thumb over her bottom lip. "There you go, underestimating yourself again."

A lump of emotion formed in her throat. She swallowed over it. "How?"

"I'm gonna show instead of tell this time," he said, sliding his hands beneath her shirt and lifting it over her head. "But before I go any further, there's one question I want you to answer."

He turned toward his bureau, and she spotted her tiara as he picked it up. Michelina's heart stopped. Panic froze her blood in her veins.

Extending his hand, he waved the tiara in front of her. "Leo brought this to me when I came in this evening. It doesn't go with any of my attire." His gaze pinned her with the force of a nuclear missile. "You want to tell me what you're doing with it?"

Nine

Michelina felt as if her brain had locked up and someone had thrown away the key. "Um, it's a, uh…"

"Yes?" he prompted, clearly expecting an explanation.

"Um, it's an accessory," she said. "Like a hat."

"A hat," he echoed skeptically.

"Yes, it's an accessory women wear…to parties." She forced her lips upward in a smile, trying to keep the terror she was feeling from her face.

"Parties," he said, and shook his head. "I have to tell you, I haven't seen any women wear one of these to any barbecues I've attended."

Michelina had no answer to that.

"I've only seen women wear tiaras for three different reasons. One, if she's royalty."

Michelina held her breath.

"You get a funny accent in your voice every now and then, and you like to give orders, but if you were really royalty, I don't think you would have lasted an entire day with my nieces, so that's out." His gaze turned cool. "The second reason a woman might wear this thing is if she's a bride."

Michelina glanced at the tiara and shook her head. This was her ready-to-wear tiara. Her bridal tiara would be far more elaborate. "I've never been a bride."

"That leaves the third possible reason." He sighed, rubbing his thumb over the pearls and diamonds. "Beauty queens wear tiaras."

He looked at her expectantly, and Michelina gave him a blank stare for a full moment before it hit her. He thought *she* was a beauty queen. *Omigoodness.* The urge to laugh hysterically backed up in her throat. She felt her eyes burn with tears with the effort it took to swallow her laughter. "I don't know what to say."

"Don't deny it," he said.

Her stomach twisted. She didn't want to lie to him. "I can't deny that I've been trying to escape the image some people have of me."

"Beautiful, but that's about it," he said.

"Exactly."

He put the tiara on the bed, then turned to her and pulled her into his arms. "You're beautiful, but you and I both know there's a lot more to you than the way you look."

What he said and the way he looked at her made

her feel wonderful and horrible. No one had ever verbalized such belief in her, and right to her face. The power of it rocked through her. Seeing the conviction in Jared's eyes made her feel as if she could do anything, be anybody she wanted to be.

Feeling his belief in her also made her feel like a slug. He deserved the truth about her. She bit her tongue to keep from confessing. She couldn't help believing that once he knew who she really was, he would look at her differently, and she couldn't bear the prospect of that.

He had no idea how desperately she needed what he offered her. With all her family's wealth and position, this was what she had craved her entire life. "Thank you," she said, fighting a sudden urge to cry.

"For what?"

"Just thank you," she said, and stood on tiptoe to press her lips to his. Later, when he learned her real name and was angry with her deception, she prayed he would remember this moment. She knew she always would.

Just a few days later, Jared was preparing for the onslaught of the county celebration. Mimi was checking off items on her to-do list with a calm efficiency that impressed the hell out of him. He suspected most women would have been nervous at the prospect of entertaining three hundred people, but Mimi was unfazed.

He'd been dreading the bill, but she had managed to get businesses and individuals to donate almost all the necessary food and services. He'd caught her on

the phone one afternoon asking a local grocer to donate lemonade, and by the end of the conversation,
he could tell she'd had the guy ready to hand over
the keys to his store. She'd insisted that the owner
post a sign bearing the grocery-store name at the
county celebration.

Mimi was very big on giving credit to everyone
but herself. On the day of the celebration, Jared noticed she kept giving the reporter from the county
newspaper the slip. After one close call, Jared caught
her nearly hyperventilating behind the barn.

"Maybe I should have allowed you to serve champagne," he said. "Roger's harmless."

She shook her head. "He's armed and dangerous—
he has a camera. You're mayor. Can't you expel
him?"

Jared chuckled. "No way. This is one of very few
big local events."

"I beg you to break his camera."

Jared would have chuckled again at her ridiculous
request, but he could tell she was dead serious. "The
circulation for the weekly paper is only a couple thousand." His heart twisted at the hopelessness in her
silver eyes. "Duchess, it isn't the *New York Times*."

She lifted her hand to her throat and took a deep
breath. "I know, but—but—" She took another
breath. "You don't understand. I just—" She shook
her head. "I'll just stay in the background, and,
please, whatever you do, don't send him my way."
She pulled away from Jared and prepared to
dash away.

He snagged her hand, shocked at the temperature of her skin. "Mimi, your hands are ice-cold."

She visibly collected herself, and he watched a transformation before his very eyes. Her hands remained cold, but she lifted her lips in a sexy smile and raised her shoulder in a coquettish gesture designed to distract. It almost worked. "Me? Cold? Then maybe after this is all over, you can help warm me up." She stood on tiptoe and brushed her lips against his. "Pardon me while I check on the book drive. *Ciao.*"

Then she flowed away from him like a fine mist. He had the odd sense that he should be protecting her. She seemed strangely vulnerable, and it was unacceptable to him to allow anything to happen to her. Everything inside him rebelled at the notion that she felt unprotected.

"Hey, Jared."

He heard the familiar voice of his brother-in-law and had to tear his attention away from Mimi.

"Jared," Bob said, still limping from the injuries he'd sustained in the automobile accident. "I know I've thanked you before, but—"

Jared lifted his hand. "Stop right there. You've thanked me enough. I was glad to help with Katie and Lindsey, and Mimi did the bulk of child care duty."

Bob smiled. "They talk about her all the time. Something about how she let them try on her princess crown. Where is she from, anyway?"

"Back east," Jared said, supplying Bob with the same vague answer Mimi had given him. It rankled him that he didn't know more. He knew every inch of her body, but not much more.

He chatted another few moments with Bob, then a neighbor rancher joined in the conversation. A council member complimented Jared on the success of the celebration and tried to persuade him to take on the job of mayor permanently. Jared immediately shook his head. Then just as he was ready to refuse unequivocally, he heard a commotion near the lake.

He quickly scanned the area and caught sight of a feminine blur wearing a pink shirt and low-slung jeans leaping off the pier, her midnight hair flying behind her as she plunged into the water.

His heart stopped, but his feet immediately moved forward in large steps. "What the—" He began to run. Why had Mimi jumped into the lake? She was afraid of the water and had entered it only very reluctantly with himself and the girls. A crowd ran down the pier, obstructing his view. Muttering "Excuse me," he elbowed his way through the throng.

He spotted Mimi clinging to the ladder with a wailing toddler in her arms and felt a surge of relief. Out of the corner of his eye, he saw Roger Johnson snapping photo after photo. Jared couldn't blame him. Great photo op. But Mimi would probably drown herself when she noticed him taking her picture.

Jared made an instinctive decision. He came up behind the local reporter, clapped his hand on his shoulder and took Roger's camera right out of his hands.

Roger gaped at him. "What are you doing? That's the best photo I've ever taken. I could win an award for that."

"Sorry. Gotta respect Mimi's modesty. That water made her shirt transparent."

"I could crop it," Roger argued.

"No."

"No?" Roger echoed, incredulous. "You're tampering with the First Amendment, Jared. You could be stripped of your title as mayor."

"Please," Jared said with all sincerity, "strip me. Do *you* want the job?"

Roger shot him a look of pure disgust. "Jared, this just isn't fair."

"I'll tell you what. I'll save the film and let Mimi decide."

The reporter made a face. "What am I supposed to use in place of that photo?"

Jared shrugged. "I don't know. Romeo's photogenic." Clutching the camera in one hand, he pushed through the crowd. "Anybody got a towel or blanket?" he asked. Someone thrust a couple of baby blankets into his hand. He tossed one to the woman collecting the toddler from Mimi.

Seeing her still clinging to the ladder in the water made his heart twist. He knelt down and extended his hand. "Here, baby. Come on." Her gaze locked with his, and she took his hand. The gesture of trust grabbed at him. As soon as he pulled Mimi up on the deck, he wrapped the baby blanket around her shoulders and urged her down the pier, away from the crowd.

"Wait! I have to thank you!" a woman's voice called out.

Jared reluctantly paused when a young woman ran

toward them with the drenched toddler on her hip. He recognized the excited mother immediately. "Mimi, this is Susan Carroll."

Susan's eyes filled with tears. "I don't know what to say. I thought my niece was watching her. I feel so horrible. Thank God you saw her on the pier!"

"They move so quickly at this age," Mimi said. "I'm glad I could help."

"Thank you so much. I don't think I could have handled it if anything had happened to her," Susan said. "I'm never letting her near water again unless I'm right with her."

"Good plan," Jared said, seeing more of the crowd come toward them. "We should get Mimi back to the house so she can get changed."

Susan nodded, and Jared led Mimi toward the house.

"Thank you," Mimi said breathlessly. "I couldn't believe it when I saw that toddler all by herself on the pier. I would have screamed, but my vocal chords seemed to freeze."

He suspected she had been slammed with the memory of her brother's drowning when she'd looked at that little girl. "You did the right thing. Susan was damn lucky you were in the right place at the right time." Mimi stumbled, and he scooped her up to carry her.

"Oh, my," she said, and wrapped her arms around his neck. "This is insane. It wasn't a big deal, but I swear my knees are weak."

"It was a big deal. That kid could have drowned.

The only problem is, you've just become the county's official heroine.''

She met his gaze in confusion, then she glanced at the camera. Looking slightly ill, she touched the strap. "Did you take this camera away from the reporter?''

He nodded.

"I couldn't let that toddler drown.''

"Damn straight you couldn't. You did the right thing.''

"Could we rest for a minute? I want to stop and catch my breath.''

Filled with fiercely protective feelings for her, he paused beside a tree and gently squeezed her against him.

"I'm getting you all wet,'' Mimi said, clinging to him.

"Do you think I mind?'' he asked, hearing the huskiness in his own voice.

She buried her face in his throat. "No, thank goodness.''

"What do you want to do about the rest of the celebration? Do you want to stay in the house? Do you want me to get one of the ranch hands to drive you somewhere?'' A half-dozen scenarios sprang to his mind.

She sighed, her breath gently tickling his skin. "Right now I don't want to think about it. I want you to kiss me.''

"That I can do,'' he said, and took her mouth with his.

Mimi tried to keep a low profile during the rest of the county celebration, but the combination of low profile and Mimi was like oil and vinegar. Even with her hair pulled back in a low ponytail, sunglasses shading her distinctive eyes, and her wearing jeans and a fitted black T-shirt, she oozed glamour and beauty. The men were tripping over themselves to help her, and the women seemed fascinated by her sophistication. She was a walking billboard for what men wanted and what women wanted to be.

By the time everyone left and the clean-up was completed, she sank down on the sofa in the den with a promise that she would just take a short rest. An hour later, she was sleeping so deeply that Jared suspected the house could fall down around her and she wouldn't wake up.

Restless and bothered, he paced his office and took care of some ranch business. Checking the clock, he decided to give Jack Raven a call.

"How did I rate a call from the top rancher in the state?" Jack asked. "Are you getting married? Do you need a restaurant for your reception?"

Jared rolled his eyes. Jack was always drumming up business. "No chance. I need a favor. I have a friend who is looking for someone by the name of Jack Raven. Do you have any cousins with the same name?"

Jack gave a low, rumbly laugh. "Only about twenty-five. I'm Greek. Half my male cousins are Nick. The other half are Jack. What age Jack you looking for? Who is this friend?"

"My friend is female," Jared reluctantly revealed.

"Is she pregnant?"

"No. She's looking for a man in his late twenties."

"That cuts the list down to five. There's my cousin Jack in Boston. I have another cousin Jack in Roanoke, Virginia. Two in Chicago. The closest one is in Denver, but he's a loner, almost a recluse. He made a lot of money in real estate, and he doesn't come to family gatherings. He has weird-color eyes. Now Jack in Boston, he's a ladies' man and—"

"What do you mean weird-color eyes?"

Jack paused. "They're weird. Very light, almost silver-looking."

The vision of Mimi's face and her distinctive eyes slid through his mind and Jared's instincts went on high alert. "Thanks," he said to Jack. "Where exactly does Denver Jack live?"

Michelina slept in the following day and surprised herself by taking a nap in the afternoon. That evening, Jared insisted on giving her a fencing lesson. As they sparred, she felt the tension hum between them. There was always a sensual, emotional sense of expectation that made butterflies dance in her stomach. But there was also the ticking clock, reminding her that her time with Jared was growing short. She was running out of excuses to stay. She suspected Jared could feel it, too, even though neither of them mentioned it.

The tension between them was so thick, she could barely breathe. Midway through a match, he grabbed her foil and tossed it, along with his, to the side. Cradling her with gentle hands, he took her mouth in a hard claiming kiss that spiraled out of control. Soon their clothes were discarded and they were making love on the floor. He carried her up to bed, and they fell asleep in each others' arms.

Michelina awakened to discover Jared watching her. She lifted her hand to his strong jaw, wanting to memorize how his face looked in the morning. She never wanted to forget how safe yet strong she felt in his arms.

He slid his fingers down a strand of her hair. "Pack a bag. I'm taking you to Denver this afternoon."

Her stomach twisted. Was he so eager to be rid of her? "Why?" she asked cautiously.

"I got a lead on another Jack Raven."

She stared at him in surprise. "How?"

"I talked to our local restaurateur, and he mentioned a cousin by the same name who lives in Denver." He brushed his thumb over her cheek. "Sounds like he might have your eyes."

Michelina sat up. "What? What do you know about him? How old is he? He has my eyes? How do you know? How—"

Jared pressed his finger over her lips to silence her. "I don't know much, but I'll tell you about it on the way. I've got to cram a whole day's work into a few hours right now. It's a maybe, but this guy sounds like he's the right age, and I haven't seen many people with eyes the same color as yours."

Michelina's heart hammered in her chest. "Oh, Jared, if he's my brother, if he's really my brother, this will be fantastic. Amazing! Do you realize I can't remember ever seeing him? The only way I remember him is through pictures. If this is him..." Her voice broke with emotion, and she felt her eyes fill with tears. ''I can't tell you how much this means to me.''

''Try to keep your hopes under control,'' Jared cautioned her. ''I don't want you to be disappointed. It's a big maybe. Remember that. Maybe.'' But he hoped with a fervor that took him by surprise that Mimi wouldn't be disappointed.

Ten

Jack Raven's office in Denver wasn't designed for drop-in visitors. By the time Jared and Michelina reached the penthouse suite, she wondered if Raven Enterprises had more gatekeepers than the royal family of Marceau. Thank goodness Jared had known someone who could get them past the first few barriers.

"Do you have an appointment?" the woman at the desk asked after Jared had given their names.

"No," Michelina said for the umpteenth time to the umpteenth assistant.

"We're interested in learning more about Mr. Raven's resort development in Costa Rica," Jared said smoothly.

Michelina stared at him. "We are?"

He took her hand and gently squeezed it. "Of

course we are. Remember we discussed it after we looked into land development in Arizona?''

"Oh." Michelina nodded slowly at the ruse. "We've looked at so many that I didn't remember if we were looking at Costa Rica or Mexico."

"We have excellent project managers who could help you," the assistant said.

"We prefer to see Mr. Raven," Jared said in a nonnegotiable tone.

The assistant sighed and punched a button on her phone. "Miss Dean, we have some potential investors, Mr. McNeil and Miss Deerman. They insist on seeing Mr. Raven." She nodded and listened, then turned to Michelina and Jared. "Mr. Raven's personal assistant will see you."

Michelina was so frustrated, she nearly stamped her foot. "But—"

Jared squeezed her hand and pressed his mouth against her ear. "This may take more than one visit. If we push too hard, they may not let us in the door again."

Tamping down her impatience, she bit her tongue. A conservatively dressed young woman approached them from the inner office and extended her hand. "Hello, I'm Haley Dean. Please come join me in my office. Maybe I can help you."

"Thank you," Michelina said, impressed with the calm the woman projected as the three of them entered an office decorated in peaceful shades of blue that reminded her of the waters surrounding Marceau.

"Please take a seat. Did I understand that you're interested in the Costa Rica project?" Ms. Dean asked as she pulled a file folder from a drawer next to her desk. "Here is the prospectus. I'll be happy to answer any questions you may have."

"I appreciate your willingness to talk with us, and I'm certain you know the ins and outs of this deal, but I have this quirk about preferring to talk with the person who draws the bottom line," Jared said, sinking into an upholstered chair. "What will it take for us to meet with Jack Raven?"

Haley Dean smiled. "Today it would take an international flight."

Michelina's heart sank in disappointment. "He's not here?"

"No, I'm sorry. He's a very busy man. Sometimes I think I spend more time on rescheduling his appointments than on anything else."

Michelina saw her opportunity to meet Jack Raven slipping through her fingertips. Desperation twisted through her. She glanced around the room. "Will he be back in town soon?"

"Oh, he's usually in this office two or three days a week, unless he finds an opportunity he has to move on immediately." She smiled and clicked the mouse for her laptop computer. "That's what happened today. The soonest I can schedule you would be in two months."

"Oh, that's too late," Michelina said.

Jared took her hand in a comforting gesture. "Are you sure there isn't something sooner? Maybe we could fly to meet him somewhere."

Michelina's gaze fell on a plaque of recognition from a charitable organization hanging on the wall.

"Um, I actually think I may have met Jack before. At a charity function."

Haley Dean hesitated, and some of her warmth seemed to fade. "Really? Where?"

"In New York," Michelina improvised.

Ms. Dean gave Michelina and Jared a long, speculative glance. "I'll give Jack your names when he returns, and perhaps he will be able to see you sooner."

Michelina stifled a groan of frustration. "Oh, I doubt he would remember me. There were so many people at that function," she said. It wasn't exactly a lie—there had been a real function, not a charity fundraiser but her formal christening.

"I think you underestimate yourself. You're quite beautiful, and very memorable, I'm sure."

Michelina looked into Haley Dean's eyes and glimpsed a flash of protectiveness and something deeper in the gaze of Jack's assistant. Realization seeped into her. Haley Dean was a total tiger where her boss was concerned. Michelina suspected Haley was in love with Jack. Best not to alienate her.

She sighed and turned toward Jared. "Well, darling," she said, and forced herself to continue with a straight face despite Jared's uplifted eyebrow. "I believe we are at the mercy of Mrs. Dean."

"Miss," Haley corrected. "I'll do what I can, but you should know that Mr. Raven just doesn't have time for many face-to-face appointments."

Does he have eyes like mine? Is there any chance that he's my brother? Michelina wanted to ask, but she didn't want to blow her chances.

"Maybe a night at the opera will console you," Jared said, his gaze full of tenderness and amusement at her game. She sensed he knew how important this was to her. Handing Haley Dean his card, he informed her, "I can be reached on my cell at any time."

Resisting the urge to beg or demand, because she suspected it would do no good, Michelina allowed Jared to guide her out of the building. He helped her into his truck and climbed in on the driver's side. "'Darling'?" he asked, referring to the endearment she'd called him just moments before.

"Well, I had to do something. I think Haley Dean thought I had romantic designs on Jack."

Jared did a double take. "How in the world did you get that impression?"

She waved her hand in a dismissive gesture. "It's a woman thing. I could see it in her eyes. She's in love with him."

Jared dropped his jaw. "How do you know?"

"I just do. I looked into her eyes and I saw something, and then I just knew. I figured if I called you darling, she might relax and try to get us in to see Jack. For Pete's sake, I think it would be easier to get in to see the queen."

"And have you seen the queen?" he asked, starting the ignition.

She automatically opened her mouth to say yes, then snapped her mouth shut. "At a public appearance once. So, do we go back to the ranch now?"

He shook his head. "Didn't you hear me? We're going to the opera."

Surprise and pleasure rushed through her. "We are? You weren't pretending?"

He shook his head and glanced at her. "I'm the real thing," he said, leaving the car in Park. "What you see is what you get. What about you?"

Her stomach clenched at the expression on his face. He might have asked his question in a casual tone, but he wanted answers. She'd seen the questions in his eyes before, but brushed them aside. He wouldn't always allow her to, though. She sensed the time was coming when Jared would demand answers to his questions. And Michelina didn't know what she would do then.

"You know everything important about me," she assured him. "You know things about me that no one else does."

"I want to know more," he said, the easiness in his voice completely gone. "I want to know where you were born. Where your family lives, and what they do and how all that has affected you."

She bit her lip and held her breath.

Jared reached out and pulled her against him. "I know your body, but I want to know your mind, Mimi. I want to know more."

Michelina felt her throat tighten over a sudden lump of emotion. She wanted him to know her. She wanted to tell him the truth, but she was so frightened....

"Mimi?"

"I'm afraid."

"Why?"

"I'm afraid that once you know about my background, all your feelings for me will change. I just can't stand the thought of that.''

His eyebrows furrowed in confusion. "Is your family in the Mafia or something?"

She gave a short laugh. "No, although they may feel like it at times. No, they're just dysfunctional." She searched for a way to answer some of his questions without telling him everything. "The family business is very demanding. Everyone is expected to contribute to it in some way."

"How do you contribute?" he asked.

Michelina's stomach twisted again. "I haven't really made my contribution yet. That's in my future." She thought of the man her family expected her to marry and felt so trapped she could barely breathe.

"You don't sound happy about it."

"I'm not sure I have a choice."

He cradled her jaw with his hand so she would meet his gaze. "You always have a choice, duchess. The choices may not be perfect and the consequences may not be fun, but you always have a choice."

In Jared's world, she would have choices, she thought. In Jared's world, her life could be different. She could be more than Princess Useless. The relentless sense of family obligation, however, had been drilled into her at a young age, and Michelina didn't know if she was strong enough to completely turn her back on her family. She wasn't certain she could live with the guilt.

"Could we please take a break from this subject?"

He nodded slowly, and she knew the questions would come again.

* * *

When Michelina complained that she had nothing appropriate to wear to the opera, Jared stopped at Denver's Cherry Creek Mall and she selected a dress, bag and shoes in no time flat. Jared was impressed.

Michelina just smiled. Shopping was one of the few skills she'd been allowed to hone over the years. After the shopping expedition, Jared checked them into a suite at Brown's Palace and Michelina marveled over the period decor.

She made no apologies for commandeering one of the large bathrooms. She wanted to look her absolute best. For once in her life—and a secret part of her feared she would only have this once—she wanted to knock Jared McNeil off his feet.

The way her hands trembled slightly as she applied her eyeliner surprised her. Michelina couldn't remember being nervous ever before when getting ready to meet a man. Her heart tripped over itself. She had been on too many chaperoned dates to count, but this was her first real date with Jared. Crazy though it might seem, especially considering the fact that they were already lovers, she wanted him to be impressed. She applied her lipstick, smudging it by accident, and swore.

She brushed her hair and stared into the mirror. She looked the same as she had just a few weeks ago before she'd left Marceau, but she knew she was oh, so different. Taking a calming breath, she smoothed the pink silk dress over her hips and left the bathroom. She turned the corner to the living area of the suite and came face-to-face with Jared.

Oh, wow. She gaped at him. She'd seen him in casual clothes and jeans and…well, nothing, but she hadn't been prepared for how he would look in a black suit. The rancher had disappeared. In his place stood a man sophisticated, confident, devastating to her knees. The only thing that saved her was the fact that he hadn't blinked since he'd seen her.

"Good Lord," he muttered. "I had a hard enough time pulling the men off you when you wore a ponytail, sunglasses and jeans. If you'd dressed like this for the county celebration, you would have caused a riot."

She wanted to cause a riot in *him.* "I'll take that as a compliment," she said, smiling up at him. "You look quite amazing yourself."

His lips twitched and he glanced down at his suit. "You expected me to wear overalls?"

"I don't know what I expected, but this is the first time I've seen you in a suit, and…"

"And?" he prompted.

"And Mr. McNeil-with-the-ego-so-big-I-don't-need-to-stroke-it, you take my breath away."

"Is that so?" he said, looking incredibly pleased with himself. He slid his hand behind her neck and, stroking her nape, lowered his mouth to hers.

She drank in the sensation of the kiss, savoring his flavor and the subtle scent of his aftershave. She could get addicted to the way he smelled, the way he felt, the way he kissed her.

Jared pulled back and sucked in a sharp breath. "We need to go before I try to talk you out of that dress."

Michelina lifted her fingers to his lips to rub off her lipstick. He caught her hand and slid her thumb inside his mouth. She immediately felt a rush of heat. "When does the show start?" she asked breathlessly.

He swore and tugged her toward the door. "Don't look at me that way."

"What way?" she asked, having trouble keeping her steps steady.

"Like you'd let me take you right this minute dressed or undressed," he muttered, punching the button for the elevator.

"Oops. I guess I'd better not look at you then," she said, and stepped into the elevator. "Because you're reading me like a book."

He made a sound of sexual frustration and pulled her into his arms, resting his forehead against hers. "You're going to be the death of me."

"I don't want to be the death of you," she protested. "I just want to make you feel a little...bothered."

He rolled his eyes and pulled her lower body against his, making her intimately aware of his arousal. "If this is bothered, you've succeeded."

He kissed her again and didn't stop until the elevator doors flew open and the guests waiting in the lobby started to giggle. Hot with more than embarrassment, she allowed him to guide her out of the lobby to the arts center where the opera *Carmen* was being presented.

They took their seats in a private balcony box. "Very nice seats. I'm glad I don't have to share you,'' she said. ''How did you manage this on such short notice?''

He shrugged. ''I have a few connections.''

She leaned back in her seat and smiled at the way he didn't try to impress her with his background or *connections*.

He met her gaze. ''Why the smile?''

''I was just thinking that you're very different from the other men I've dated. They often try to impress me with who they know or their titles or—''

''Well, you know my job title. Rancher.''

Michelina had meant other kinds of titles, but she had no intention of correcting him. ''And mayor,'' she said.

He gave a heavy sigh. ''Interim mayor,'' he corrected. ''And that's under duress.''

''Uncle is another of your titles. Brother.''

He nodded.

''Lover,'' she whispered. ''My lover.''

His eyes darkened. ''I thought I told you not to look at me that way.''

''I can't not look at you this way.''

He closed his eyes and shook his head. ''This is going to be a long night.'' He sat back in his seat and slid his arm around her shoulders.

The best singers in the world might have been singing the roles of Carmen and Don José but Jared couldn't keep his hands or eyes off Mimi. The sound of her laughter crawled under his skin and went straight to his heart. He liked the way she leaned into him as if her trust for him were instinctive and total.

The knowledge, however, that Mimi's trust for him was incomplete was like a rock he couldn't remove from his shoe. It bothered him. A lot.

He wasn't sure when it had happened, but somewhere along the way, he'd grown to care for her more than he'd intended. More than her laughter had gotten under his skin, and that was bad news, because as sure as the wind blew in Wyoming, Mimi wouldn't be staying. The thought of it made him feel like he had a case of permanent indigestion.

He had a gut feeling she would be leaving soon, and he was struggling with the need to have more laughter, more fights, more making up, more helping her to see all she was capable of...more of Mimi. She'd been a pain in the butt and caused more than her share of chaos, but she'd also lit up his house, and he wasn't ready to go back to his quiet, peaceful, Mimi-free life yet.

Following an unbidden impulse, Jared reached for her and took her mouth.

She gave a little gasp of surprise before she surrendered to the kiss. He slid his hand to her jaw and savored the texture of her silky hair and velvet skin against his fingers. Her mouth was sweet and responsive. She took him by surprise when she slid her tongue past his lips, taunting him to respond.

He felt his temperature climb as she continued the sexy sweep of her tongue over his. When he returned the caress, she tilted her head to give him better access and drew his tongue into her mouth, as if she couldn't get enough of him. He grew hard.

"You're getting me hot," he whispered against her mouth.

"You started it," she retorted, sucking at his lower lip.

His gaze dipped over the tops of her breasts when he felt her pressing against his chest. He knew how she felt in his hands, in his mouth. "I thought you were excited about seeing the opera."

"What opera?" she asked, sliding her hands beneath his coat to caress his chest.

The strength of his arousal rocked through his veins like gasoline. He wanted inside. He wanted to know all her secrets, all her fears. He wanted her out of her clothes, flat on her back with her legs wrapped around his waist while he sank into her wet, tight femininity.

When she slid one of her hands to his thigh, it was all he could do not to pull her onto his lap. He tore his mouth from hers and sucked in what he hoped would be a mind-clearing breath. Instead, he inhaled the scent of her perfume spiced with her desire. He clamped his hand over hers as it wandered up his thigh.

"We're going to get arrested if we don't stop."

She looked up at him, her eyes nearly black with arousal. "I don't want to stop. I don't ever want to stop with you."

Jared's chest tightened. He wondered how she managed to grab him by the heart and crotch at the same time. "Don't you want to see the rest of the opera?"

The slow shake of her head ripped his restraint. That was it. He wasn't asking again. Standing, he helped her to her feet and ushered her out of their private box to the lobby.

The cool night air did nothing to bring his heat under control. They walked the short distance to their hotel in silence, her hand firmly clasped in his.

As soon as the elevator doors tucked just the two of them inside, they fell into each others' arms. Jared wasn't sure what drove him. The knowledge that Mimi would be slipping through his fingers like water soon? The wildly primitive urge to possess her the same way she had begun to possess him? On her lips, he tasted the same combination of passion and desperation that throbbed inside him.

He lowered his mouth to her throat, then to the top of one of her breasts. She tugged down the strap of her dress, baring her breast to his gaze, to his mouth.

The bold invitation made him want to take her against the wall. He dropped his mouth to her nipple, drawing it deep into his mouth. The sensation of the stiff peak on his tongue drove him crazy.

Her moan tore through him. His restraint evaporated like beads of water on a hot griddle. He slid one of his hands up the slit of her dress and beneath the silk piece of nothing. She was so hot, so wet, so sweet. He plunged his finger inside her and felt her clench around him.

"Jared," she said, her voice pleading.

The elevator doors whisked open, and he instinctively stepped in front of her, shielding her from any potential prying eyes. He adjusted her dress and led her to the suite. The second he closed the door, they were all over each other again.

He pushed down her dress. She pulled loose his tie and struggled with his buttons. She let out a husky litany of frustrated oaths in the sexiest voice he'd ever heard. Jared obliged her by ripping his dress shirt apart, sending the buttons flying.

Mimi blinked. "That was impressive."

"I'm motivated," he muttered, the sensation of her bare skin against his driving him more crazy than he'd been before.

"There is something that I've wondered about," she ventured, unfastening his slacks and sliding her small hand around his erection.

Jared thought he might explode. Taking a quick, shallow breath, he couldn't stop himself from pushing into her caress. "What have you been wondering about?"

Her eyes smoky with desire, she bit her lip. "I wondered what it would be like with, uh, me on top."

An immediate visual of Mimi, her hair flowing over him, her breasts pressed into him, as she rode him seared him. Jared was so hot he knew steam was going to start rising from his body any minute. He kissed her, and the power of his want and need for her was so strong, he felt it in his bones. He wanted Mimi in every possible way. He wanted her so much despite the fact that the end of their relationship was imminent and the fall was going to be rough. Any man in his right mind would take the pleasure and seal off his heart, but for Jared, half measures with Mimi weren't possible anymore.

"You're not saying anything," Mimi said.

"You've fried my brain."

Her lips lifted in a smile that grabbed his heart and twisted. "I keep trying to knock you off your feet."

"Oh, duchess, you did that a long time ago." He kissed her and made her bra and panties disappear. Then his pants disappeared, too. He wasn't sure how. She'd probably melted them. They kissed their way to the large bed.

He touched her body and she touched his, and for once, he made himself totally open to her. He felt her sigh against his chest as she explored his muscles and ribs. He knew he was strong, but she made him aware of it in a totally different way.

She pressed her open mouth against his throat in a caress that he cherished. She was silky, slow-moving, and quiet except for her breath. The silence, however, was the noisiest thing he'd ever experienced. She didn't verbally say she was awed by him, but her hands did. She didn't announce how much she wanted him, but the way her body sought his sang it to him over and over again. She didn't say she loved him, but her eyes shouted it.

And when she rode him with her hair flowing around her shoulders, Jared locked his gaze with hers and knew he would never be the same.

Eleven

Michelina awakened early and drank in the sight of Jared's face. His hard bone structure was barely softened by sleep. She remembered the way he had possessed her last night. And the way she had possessed him.

Her heart contracted. Who would have thought Princess Useless could have such a powerful effect on such a powerful man? The sex between them was more than physical. It was as if what was going on inside them was too big to contain and it had to find expression.

But it was temporary. The unwelcome thought felt like a poison dart in the middle of a beautiful moment. Suddenly too restless to sit still, she slid carefully out of bed, half-surprised she didn't wake up Jared. He was usually awake before her. She padded into the living area and pulled on yesterday's jeans and T-shirt.

Looking down onto the nearly empty street below with her mind full of Jared, she thought of how much he had given her. She'd never dreamed she could feel so confident, so full of possibilities. She wanted to give him something. The man didn't appear to need anything, and he wasn't the type to get excited over a gold watch. She frowned in concentration, her gaze drifting over pots of colorful flowers. An idea came to mind. She dismissed it, then returned to it, fidgeting with the draperies.

He would probably think it was bloody silly, she warned herself, but then again, he might not. Following her impulse, she splashed water on her face, brushed her teeth and hair, skipped her shoes in favor of speed and took the elevator to the lobby.

The gift shop was closed, but she didn't let that stop her. It took a few minutes, but she successfully cajoled the front desk clerk into opening the shop just for her. She made her purchase, paid with cash from her pocket and headed for the elevator with three roses in her hand.

The sound of a familiar foreign accent caught her attention just as she rounded the corner, and she looked over her shoulder. Her stomach fell to her feet. She quickly hid behind the wall and sneaked one more glance at the reception area.

She saw two men talking to the clerk who'd just helped her. Her heart sank as she confirmed her earlier thought that she recognized one of them. He was with Marceau palace security. They were here to col-

lect her, she knew. They were here to collect the prod-
igal princess and take her back to where she belonged.

Everything inside her rebelled at the prospect. Lifting a hand to her throat, she felt herself shake so hard,
she wondered if the floor was moving. But it wasn't.
More like walls crashing down on her. Panic roared
through her. She had to get to Jared, and then she had
to disappear. She pushed the elevator button and
thanked heaven when the doors immediately opened.

Once inside, she closed her eyes to keep from hyperventilating. The sweet scent of the roses combined
with the bitter taste of regret in her throat. She wasn't
ready to go back yet. Sure, it had been nearly a
month, but it had gone by in the blink of an eye. And
she was determined to try to get an appointment with
Jake Raven. How could she accomplish that if she
was forced to return to Marceau?

Her head spinning, she tried to form an explanation
for Jared, but her pitiful brain couldn't put two words
together. The elevator reached her floor, and she
broke into a cold sweat.

Jared heard what sounded like fumbling with the
lock on the door, then a feminine oath. Recognizing
the voice even through the door, he chuckled. Mimi.
He'd heard her leave earlier and had thought about
going after her, but he figured she wouldn't be gone
long, since she'd left her shoes.

Curious and amused, he opened the door. She was
swearing at her key card in one hand and holding
roses in the other. She stopped swearing and met his
gaze. His heart turned over.

"Roses?"

"They're for you," she said, thrusting him into his hand as she swept past him and pulled the door closed.

Jared glanced down at three red roses, floored by the romantic gift. His insides melted, while the rest of him turned stiff. He shook his head, searching for an adequate response. "This is a first. I—uh—"

"That's what I was hoping. I wanted to give you something no one else had."

"You already did that," he said, touching one of the soft petals. It reminded him of her skin. "You gave me yourself."

"It didn't seem like enough."

"It was," he said, then grinned. "But these are lovely, too." He looked at her again and suddenly saw the tightness around her mouth. She was pale. Her frustration with the lock and the flowers had distracted him, but now he recognized her distress. "What's the matter?"

She took a deep breath and bit her lip. "I don't know how to say this."

Jared's stomach sank. There was never good news after the kind of statement she'd just made. "I can't help you if you can't tell me."

Her eyes flashed with anger, and she pushed her hair behind her ear in a savage gesture as she began to pace. "I've been found," she said bitterly. "I saw someone connected with my family in the lobby while I was getting the roses, and I know they're looking for me. They'll probably either be up here any minute, or just lying in wait in the lobby. Jared, I'm just not ready to go back there yet. I can't.''

She looked like a caged animal. ''What do you want me to do?''

''I don't know. I don't know what to do.'' She turned toward him midpace. ''They must know I've been with you or they wouldn't have been able to find me here, so I can't go back to the ranch. I'm just not ready to go back. I need to disappear for a little longer, but I want to try to see Jack Raven.''

Jared ignored the knots forming in his gut and throat. ''You could go to Colorado Springs. It's not that far, but maybe far enough to buy you some time and still give you access to Denver.''

She lifted her fingers to either side of her forehead as if trying to concentrate despite the panic written on her face. ''I'll need a vehicle. And I'm running out of money,'' she murmured to herself.

Shades of his ex-fiancée, Jennifer, floated eerily through his mind, but he tried to push the thought aside. Mimi looked as if she were ready to cry. ''I can give you some money and you can use my truck.'' The second offer caused him some misgivings, which he again tried to push aside.

She looked at him in surprise. ''You'd let me use your truck?''

''Yeah,'' he said with a shrug. ''You'd bring it back, wouldn't you?''

''Of course,'' she said.

''But I think it's about time you told me the real story about your family.'' He gave her a serious look.

She looked away and her shoulders slumped. ''Do

I have to?'' She waved her hand. ''Don't answer that. I know I do.'' She sighed, then turned to face him. ''Would you do one more thing before I tell you?''

''What?'' he asked, thinking she had no idea how much he would do for her. He wondered if his gut would ever feel normal again.

She walked closer to him. ''Would you kiss me?''

The knots inside him tangled again. This scene had all the signs of *goodbye*. He'd known this moment would come sometime, he reminded himself. He'd even known it would come soon. He just hadn't expected to feel as if a ton of bricks had been dumped on his head. Hating the painful knot in his throat, he swallowed hard. ''Sure, I'll kiss you, duchess,'' he said, and pulled her into his arms.

This time she took his mouth and kissed him as if there was no tomorrow. Maybe there wasn't. Her lips were sweet and passionate, full of want and need, desperate. He tasted the same metallic taste of desperation on his own tongue, but tried to focus on how she felt in his arms, her vibrant energy. His heart pounded hard against his rib cage.

The kiss went on and on as if neither of them had the will to end it. Finally they both took a breath. She lifted her hands to his face and looked deep into his eyes. ''I want to memorize the way you are right now, the way you're looking at me, because you'll never look at me that way again,'' she said.

His chest felt so tight, he found it difficult to breathe.

She took a step back and composed herself with effort. His hands burned to pull her against him again.

She sighed and looked away from him. "My family name is Dumont. We live in a small island country named Marceau off the coast of France."

"Okay," Jared said. The name and the country were vaguely familiar, although he couldn't quite place them. That explained the strange accent that crept into her language every now and then. "So Deerman isn't your real name."

"That's right. My given name is Michelina Catherine." She paused, and he saw a look of sheer dread on her face.

Nothing earthshaking so far, though, he thought. She wasn't from a Mafia family, and she wasn't claiming to be an alien from Mars. He started to wonder if she'd overblown the situation in her mind. "Okay," he said. "So you and your family live near France. None of this sounds over-the-top to me."

She winced. "My family doesn't just live in Marceau. We run it," she said. "We rule it."

Rule. Jared's mind slammed into the word at a hundred miles per hour. "Rule?"

She nodded. "My mother is Queen Anna Catherine. My oldest brother, Michel, is heir to the throne. My next brother, Auguste, is military chief. My third brother, Nicholas, is a doctor who advises the Secretary of Health. My fourth brother, Alexander, operates a yacht-building business and lives part-time in North Carolina."

Jared stared at her. He didn't know what he'd expected, but it hadn't been this.

"The plan is for all of us to fulfill a royal role in one way or another."

Jared felt as if his brain was a tire spinning fruit-lessly without progress in a snowdrift. "So you're a princess?"

She sighed and folded her hands together. "Yes."

He scratched his head as he tried to piece together everything she'd told him. "If you don't mind my asking, what is your role?"

Her face flattened to an expressionless mask. "To marry a count from Italy, bear children and provide photo ops for the press."

His heart stopped. "You're engaged?"

She shook her head. "My mother, the queen, has told me that she would like me to marry this man. For the good of Marceau," she said with a slightly ill expression on her face.

"But you don't want to."

"I'm not supposed to think about what I want."

Despite his own raging emotions, Jared couldn't prevent the surge of a feeling of protectiveness for Mimi— Michelina, he mentally corrected himself. He walked toward her and took her shoulders in his hands. "If *you* don't think about what you want, then nobody will."

"But I was born to serve. I was born to fulfill a duty."

"Do you have to serve this way?"

She opened her mouth, then hesitated and closed it. "I always thought I did...until I met you." She closed her eyes and shook her head. "I can't think about this right now. I must go, or I won't even get the opportunity to meet my brother."

Jared could practically see her turmoil bubbling up

from inside her. He despised the helplessness he felt. "If you need something, call me."

Her gaze flashed. "Don't say that!"

"What do you mean?"

"I mean, don't say that! I don't deserve it. I've deceived you and I'm sorry. I don't deserve your generosity." Her eyes filled with tears. "I don't deserve the use of your truck. I don't deserve anything from you." She audibly swallowed a sob. "I can't give you anything back."

Jared's head and chest hurt worse than when he'd gotten a concussion and broken rib playing football in high school. He ground his teeth against the unwelcome emotions ripping at him. Mimi—Michelina, he corrected himself again—was headed for hysteria land, if she wasn't already there. Practicality offered an island of relief from the intense emotions colliding with both of them right now.

"Listen, you've got to get hold of yourself if you're going to be driving my truck."

She sniffed and looked at him in confusion.

"You're not used to driving on the freeway, and your family will likely kill me if anything happens to you while you're driving my vehicle. If you really want some more time before you go back to the royal penitentiary, then you need to focus."

She sniffed again. "On what?"

"On getting your stuff together, following my directions and accomplishing your goals."

She blinked, stiffening her spine before his very eyes. "You're right. I can't wallow over being Princess Useless. That would truly be useless."

He frowned. "Princess Useless?"

She curled her lip in disgust and headed for the bedroom. "My nickname for myself."

While Michelina hastily packed her belongings, Jared shut out all kinds of unwelcome emotions and wrote out the directions to Colorado Springs. As she reentered the room, he detached the truck keys from his key ring.

He reluctantly met her gaze and tried to remain unmoved by the turbulence he saw in her eyes. "Follow the directions, and don't go over the speed limit. If you get stopped by the police, the registration is in the glove compartment. Here's my cell," he said, handing over his mobile phone.

Her eyes widened. "But you need that."

"You need it worse than I do," he said bluntly. "You're traveling in a foreign country without a guide. I wrote my pager and home phone on the directions, in case you get in over your head."

"That's what you expect, isn't it? That I'll get in over my head." She sighed. "That's what I've done so far."

"I'm gonna tell you something, duch—" He broke off and corrected himself, feeling an odd pluck of dry humor. "—Princess, you don't have time to feel sorry for yourself. If you've got the palace hounds nipping at your heels, you'd better get moving."

Her eyes shiny with unshed tears, she bit her lip and lifted her chin. "No such thing as a Wyoming wuss," she whispered.

"Right," he said, determined to keep it light even though he felt as if he had a tennis-ball-size knot in

his throat. He chucked her chin with his forefinger.
"And once you've lived in Wyoming, it never quite
leaves you."

She swallowed audibly. "Thank you for everything."

He crammed his hands into his pockets to keep
from reaching out to her. If he touched her, he knew
she would break apart. It was a kindness that killed
him, but she needed something different than an embrace from him. He handed her his hat, then opened
the door. "Stuff your hair underneath that and try the
service elevator."

She plopped his hat on her head and breezed toward the elevator. "I'll pay you back," she said,
throwing him a kiss.

"Sure you will," he said, though he was anything
but sure.

During the next twenty minutes, Jared told his
mind to stop thinking about Michelina as he went
through the motions of packing his bag. He called a
dealership and made arrangements to lease a truck for
one month. He figured if he didn't see Michelina or
his truck again, that would give him time to buy a
new vehicle. Silly, he told himself. He'd known he
was kissing his truck goodbye when he handed over
his keys to her.

An empty feeling gnawed at him clear down to his
bones as he left the room. He instinctively inhaled,
trying to catch the last of Michelina's scent. *Stop torturing yourself.* He closed the door behind him and
entered the elevator. The ride down to the lobby gave

him time to remember how it had felt to hold her in his arms just last night.

Grinding his teeth, he checked out of the hotel and turned to leave the building. Two men stepped directly in his path.

"Pardon me. Are you Jared McNeil?" one of the men asked.

"Who wants to know?" he demanded, but the man's accent gave him away. He looked like a high-class bouncer.

"Of course," the man said with a stiff nod. "My name is Henri Newport and this is Jean Huguenot. We're looking for this woman." Henri pulled out a photo of Michelina.

Jared's chest tightened, but he'd played poker often enough to hide his reaction.

"We understand she has been seen with you."

Protectiveness roared through him. He covered his tension by giving a low whistle. "She's a babe," he said casually. "Who is she?"

Henri looked affronted. "She is Princess Michelina Dumont of Marceau." Henri narrowed his eyes. "But you already know this. I demand you tell us where she is this instant, or there will be unpleasant consequences."

"I'd like to help you, but I can't," he said with a shrug. "I wouldn't mind meeting her, though, if you can arrange an introduction. I don't think I've ever been formally introduced to a real princess before."

Henri sputtered. "You've met her already. The desk clerk said she was with you last night."

Jared laughed. "I wish. I had a *hired* date last

night,'' he said, and winked. ''If you know what I mean. The woman I was with had long dark hair, but she was no princess.''

Jean frowned. ''You're sure?'' he said. ''You're absolutely sure you haven't seen Princess Michelina? She's been—'' Henri's nudge cut him off. ''We are concerned for her safety and well-being.''

Suffocation cloaked in words of *concern*. Jared visualized a net being thrown over Michelina's head, a cell door slamming closed with her locked inside. ''Sorry, buds, but I told you I've never been formally introduced to a princess in my life.'' And he hadn't, Jared thought, as he left the men staring after him in confusion. He hadn't been formally introduced to Michelina. He'd made love to her, but it would be better for everyone if he could find a way to forget her.

Twelve

Two weeks later, Jared trudged up the porch steps. It was late and he'd skipped dinner again. His stomach protested with a growl. His objective had been simple—to work so hard and so long, he couldn't even think about Michelina, let alone miss her.

Walking through the front door, he felt the familiar ache in his chest and sighed. So far, he hadn't accomplished his objective. He petted Leo before he stopped in the kitchen, where he put together a sandwich and pulled a beer from the refrigerator. In no mood to sit in the den and watch television or do paperwork, he decided to eat his late snack on his way upstairs, then hit the shower.

His contrary mind wandered as he ate half his sandwich without tasting it, and he speculated about what Michelina was doing tonight. He wondered if she had gotten past Jack Raven's gatekeepers, if she'd returned to Marceau, if she'd wrecked his truck. He took a long swig of beer and frowned. *She* wasn't his business.

Everything inside him rebelled at the thought, but he had to get used to it. Eating the other half of his sandwich, he walked into his darkened bedroom and didn't bother to turn on the light as he passed through to the master bath.

As much as he had fought to avoid getting tangled in Michelina's web, even though he'd known she would create chaos in his life, he'd been unable to resist her. Underneath her privileged exterior beat the heart of a female warrior. She'd been determined to overcome her limitations. She'd wanted to fence, accepted his challenge to swim, met him toe-to-toe with her determination. Even though she'd been frightened, she'd jumped into the lake and rescued that toddler. Even though she'd been a virgin, she'd burned up his bed and all his defenses.

She was the most exciting woman he'd ever met, and he felt as if the light had gone out in his life ever since she'd left. Taking another long swallow of beer, he stripped out of his clothes, wondering how long it would take before he felt normal again. How long would it be before he didn't think of her every minute he wasn't working and every other minute when he was working? How long before he didn't reach for her in the morning and wonder what she'd gotten into while he'd been working in the afternoon?

He'd liked the way she'd trusted him with her body and with confidences she hadn't shared with other people, even her family. He'd started to have a strange feeling of destiny about her. It was crazy as hell, but it was as if he'd been intended to come into her life, and she in his. She'd gotten him out of his funk, made him laugh…and made him feel alive.

He turned on the jets of the shower and stepped inside, swearing. Only he would fall head over butt for a princess, for Pete's sake. Talk about impossible! He stood under the spray and tried to focus on anything but Michelina. Romeo's stud schedule. His recent success at finding a new mayoral candidate to replace him. Getting another stud and building another barn. Maybe if Jared crammed his brain full enough, he would fall asleep and dream about the ranch instead of her.

Staying in the shower an extra couple of minutes, Jared savored the hot spray. He reluctantly got out, dried off, wrapped a towel around his waist and walked into the bedroom. He opened a drawer to pull out some boxers.

''Surprise,'' a feminine voice said from behind him.

Jared stopped cold. He shook his head, certain he was imagining things. He swore under his breath. Now he was having delusions. Turning around to confirm his insanity, he saw Michelina sitting on his bed.

His heart tripped over itself, and he blinked repeatedly. An apparition, he told himself, walking toward the bed. He would reach out to touch her and feel air, nothing else.

He extended his hand, and she looked at him uncertainly. "Jared?" She lifted her own hand and enclosed his.

Jared stared down at their entwined fingers in disbelief.

"You don't look happy to see me," she said, tugging as if to pull her hand away.

No chance, Jared thought, tightening his grip. "I'm surprised." He shook his head, staring at her, taking in the sight of the face, the eyes, the woman who had haunted him relentlessly. "I didn't expect to see you again."

She frowned. "I told you I would return the truck. You didn't believe me."

Her pride flashed before him, and he chuckled. If this was a delusion, it was a doozy. "I didn't count on it after Henri and Jean cornered me in the lobby at the hotel."

Her eyes widened. "Oh, no. They didn't hurt you, did they?"

"No, I made up a story about a woman who looked kinda like you but wasn't you, and didn't give them a chance to argue." He sank down onto the bed. "So you brought back the truck," he said, bracing himself for the possibility that she would be leaving again in a few minutes.

"The good news is that I didn't wreck it. But I did change the color."

"The color?"

"Yes, it's no longer green. Now it's black. I was afraid the palace might be looking for a green truck. But I couldn't do anything about the license plate except put mud on it."

Impressed with her ingenuity, he nodded in approval. "Good move."

"You don't mind that I had your truck painted a different color?" she asked.

She could have painted it purple with pink polka dots as long as he got another chance to look at her. "Nah. What about Jack?"

She made a face. "I tried too many times to count, but he was either not there or not available. I even tried dressing as part of the janitorial staff, but they caught me and threw me out. They threatened me with legal action if I didn't stop," she said indignantly.

"I'm sorry, Michelina. I don't know what to tell you," Jared said, surprised at how the sound of her voice made him feel five years younger. "Maybe after you go back to Marceau—"

"That's another thing," she said, interrupting him, squeezing his hand and biting her lip in an obvious display of nerves. "I've had a lot of time to think, and I need to tell you—"

His heart twisted, and he shook his head. "You don't have to tell me anything. I know you've got to go back."

"That's just it. I'm *not* going back. I want to stay with you."

His heart flew at the same time that his mind rejected her words. Unable to stop himself a minute longer, he pulled her into his arms. "Sweetheart, you don't know how much that means to me, but I know you've got to go back. I did a little research on Marceau while you were gone, and you're important to your family and to your country."

"But what about what *I* want? You've always told me I have a choice."

"Yeah, but—"

"Are you saying you don't want me?"

"Hell, no."

"Jared, I've made a decision. I'm willing to give up my title to be with you."

All Jared could do was stare at her. His heart, his lungs, his brain ceased to function. He'd told himself not to expect to see her again. He wondered if he was dreaming.

Her lip quivered. "You're not saying anything." She ducked her head and covered her eyes with her hand. "I just realized I've been a bit presumptuous," she said with a forced chuckle that sounded more like a sob. "I've been so focused on figuring out what *I* wanted that I didn't think about what *you* want, and what you want might not be me."

Jared forced his mouth to work. "You know I want you."

She still didn't look at him. "But you might not want me the same way I want you."

"What way do you want me, Michelina?" he asked, putting her hand aside and guiding her chin upward so she would meet his gaze.

"I want you always," she whispered.

His heart nearly burst. "Aw, hell," he said, squeezing the bridge of his nose.

She ripped her hand away from him. "I was afraid of that," she wailed. "I was afraid you would think that I'm too much trouble, that I was fun for a while, but not—''

He covered her mouth. ''Would you just shut up for a minute so I can catch my freakin' breath? I didn't expect ever to see you again, then I find you in my bed telling me you want to be with me always. I feel like I'm having some kind of out-of-body experience—that I don't want to end,'' he added emphatically.

''I gotta think about this,'' he said, rising from the bed, his mind moving like sludge. ''I can't let you give up your title.'' He shook his head. Everything inside him rebelled at the thought.

''But—''

He held up a hand to silence her, then raked his fingers through his wet hair. ''There's gotta be another way. There's gotta be …'' He sighed. ''Your family. I don't think you've thought this all the way through.''

She sprang to her feet. ''Yes, I have. You told me not to fight my purpose. My purpose is to be with you. I've never accomplished more or felt so useful as I have with you. You make me be a better person.''

Her passionate response tugged at his heartstrings. ''Oh, Michelina, you were always a better person. You just didn't know it.''

''You showed me. I have to be with you. I have never been more sure of anything in my life.''

She was scared, but damn determined. He could read it in her eyes. He took her hand. ''How can you turn your back on your family?''

Her eyes darkened with sadness. ''I don't want to,

but I can't give up my life to marry someone I don't love for the sake of good PR for Marceau." She looked up at him and touched his face. "I always thought love was something giddy and magical, but you've taught me that it's so much more."

She flat-out humbled him. He took her into his arms and kissed her. It was a kiss of promises he made with his heart, promises he would keep. He couldn't believe she'd come back. He didn't know how they would work it all out, but they'd have to. As he felt the fire flare between them and his blood heated, Jared could only think of her. He would think of her family tomorrow.

Michelina made love to him with the force of a firestorm. He should have been dead tired, but he stayed awake all night, trying to decide on the best way to handle the situation. As much as Michelina swore she would turn her back on her family, Jared couldn't allow it. There had to be a better option.

When morning came, so did his conclusion. As he lay propped on his elbow beside her, stroking her hair, he wondered if they were strong enough for what lay ahead.

Her eyes fluttered open and she smiled, lifting her hand to his chin. Jared caught her hand in his and lifted it to his lips. "Good morning, beautiful. We're going to Marceau."

Michelina's smile fell. "I was hoping for Vegas... one of those little wedding chapels they have there."

He chuckled and shook his head. "Don't tempt me."

She sat up and the covers fell, revealing her naked breasts and torso. "But that's what I want to do."

Feeling himself harden, he stifled a groan. "You've succeeded. You are a walking, talking, breathing temptation to me. I'd like to give in to that temptation permanently. I want to be your husband." He took a careful breath, knowing this was the most important moment in his life. "Will you marry me?"

Her eyes filled with tears, and she threw her arms around him. "Yes, yes, yes. Let's go to Vegas and get married before anyone can make things difficult."

He felt a rush of euphoria tempered with the knowledge that they had a bumpy road ahead. "Do you trust me?"

"Yes," she said, pulling back slightly and meeting his gaze.

"Then we have to go to Marceau."

Dread crossed her face. "My family will make things impossible. That's why I said I was willing to give up my title."

"Yeah, but you're forgetting what I told you. Don't fight your purpose. Part of your purpose is to be a daughter, a sister, an aunt and princess. You don't have to choose between being any of those and being my wife."

She let out a sigh of relief, but her gaze was still tinged with uncertainty. "But my family will never go for this."

"If we go to Marceau and tell them our plans, they'll never say they didn't have a chance. I don't want you to have regrets. I could live with a lot, but not that.''

''I would never regret being your wife.''

Lord, he hoped not. ''This is the right thing to do.''

''If you say so,'' she said doubtfully. ''Make sure you pack enough antacids for both of us.''

Jared took in his surroundings as the limo traveled from the Marceau airport to the palace. Marceau was an exquisite jewel of an island, with white sandy beaches and mountains surrounded by blue, blue water. To most observers, it was a paradise no one in their right mind would ever want to leave.

Michelina, with her nails digging into his palm as she recited her family tree, was clearly the exception. ''My father's name was Jules. My mother is Anna Catherine, but you can just call her Your Majesty. I can't predict which of my brothers will be the biggest problem, but Michel is a likely candidate. He's the oldest and since he's first in line for the throne, he has serious control issues. His American wife, Maggie, has really helped, but he still feels responsible for everything. He has a son named Max, from a previous marriage, and he and Maggie have just had another child, a boy with red hair like Maggie.

''Auguste stays busy with the military and his family.

''Nicholas is a wild card. He's a medical doctor, so you would think he might understand a nontraditional choice, but he's very protective when it comes to his own family. He has an American wife named Tara. She's due with their first child any minute. I'm crossing my fingers Alexander and Sophia are in North Carolina at the moment.''

Jared gently pried her fingernails from his palm and stroked her fingers to relax her. ''Will there be a quiz?'' he asked with a grin.

''How can you smile at a time like this?''

''Because I'm with the woman I love.''

She closed her eyes, and some of the tension drained out of her. She took a breath, then met his gaze. ''Promise me you won't let them change your mind about me.''

Jared looked at her in disbelief and pulled her against him. ''No chance.''

''Okay,'' she said. ''We're almost there.''

The limo rounded the corner and pulled into a driveway lined with pots of colorful flowers. The centuries-old palace stood like a proud, beautiful woman. When the driver pulled the limo to a stop, a doorman instantly appeared.

''Welcome home, Your Highness,'' he said with a slight bow as he opened Michelina's door.

''Thank you, Marc. This is Mr. Jared McNeil.''

''Welcome to Marceau, Mr. McNeil,'' Marc said, grabbing the luggage before Jared could.

Michelina took Jared's arm and looked up at him. ''Ready?''

''Whenever you are.''

''In that case, I still think Vegas sounds good.''

He tugged her forward. ''C'mon. Maybe it won't be as bad as you think.''

They walked through the palace door where four men stood waiting. They were dressed in a variety of

clothes, ranging from a business suit to denims, but
they all had the same silver eyes and they all wore
the same facial expressions—frowns. Even Jared
could have been intimidated by the four angry
princes, each of whom almost matched him in height,
but the strength of his feelings for Michelina made
him fearless. Which could be a major mistake. He
suspected he would find out soon enough.

"Welcome home, Michelina," one of the men said.
"Mother is waiting to see you."

Michelina stiffened. "I've just arrived. I want to
make sure my guest is made comfortable."

"We will make sure that Mr. McNeil is comfortable," her brother said smoothly. "Run along."

Jared covered a wince. Patronizing Michelina
wasn't a good choice at the moment.

She stiffened further. "I'm not quite ready to run
along. Jared, I'd like to introduce you to my
brothers—Michel, Auguste, Nicholas and Alexander.
They all answer to Your Highness," she said, smiling
with effort.

"Your Highnesses," Jared said with a nod as he
tried to put the best foot forward. "Nice to meet
you."

Each of the men gave a brief curt nod, but said
nothing.

Michelina sighed. "Where are your wives?"

"We thought it best to leave them at home."

"I disagree," she said with a sweet smile. "They
civilize you."

The one she'd introduced as Nicholas unbent a
smidgen and cut his eyes at her in amusement. "I

can't disagree there, but Mother is waiting to see you.''

"Yes, but Jared civilizes *me*.''

Jared felt all four of their speculative gazes hone in on him.

"We'd like to learn his secret,'' Nicholas said dryly, then moved toward Michelina and embraced her. "Go on and take your guilt trip. It's already booked. We'll chat with your new friend.''

"I don't trust you with him,'' she said bluntly.

"Afraid he can't handle us?'' Nicholas goaded her.

Jared almost rose to that challenge, but he saved his firepower. He figured he would need it later.

Michelina rolled her eyes. "Okay, I'll go see Mother, but if you treat my guest with disrespect, I won't speak to any of you ever again.''

"Tough threat,'' Nicholas said, raising his eyebrows.

"I mean it. You have him to thank for me being here right now. I wanted to go to Vegas.'' She turned to Jared and pressed her audacious mouth to his. Jared steadied her with his hands even as he knew she was kissing him to put her brothers on notice. At the same time, she was girding herself for her visit with her mother.

"Don't worry about me,'' he murmured to her. "I can handle them and ten others for you.''

"My mother is the equivalent of ten others,'' she warned him.

He smiled and adjusted a stray strand of her hair. "So let's do the dirty work, and you can take me to the beach later.''

She finally smiled, a genuine lifting of her lips that made his heart turn over. "It's a date." She strode down the hall with a world of purpose in her walk. His gaze was glued to her until she turned the corner and left his sight.

Then he turned to the four angry princes and clapped his hands together. "Show me to the rack."

Alexander, the youngest brother, almost chuckled. "No rack, but we heard you enjoy fencing, so my brothers and I thought you might enjoy a match. This way," he said, and the four of them led the way downstairs.

Jared hoped he could shake off his jet lag, or he had the uncomfortable feeling he was going to end up wearing a foil in his gut. "I'm game."

"All of us wanted to spar with you, but we knew time wouldn't permit a fencing marathon. So we drew straws, and Michel won."

Jared nodded, following them through a walkway where a beagle scampered toward them, barking and wagging his tail.

"Elvis, you scamp," Michel said, bending down to rub the dog. "My son Max's dog."

Jared knelt down to pet the squirmy animal. "Elvis?"

"My son named him," Michel said. "He drives the advisors crazy."

"Your son or Elvis?" Jared asked.

Michel threw him a sideways glance. "Elvis. Do you prefer foil?" he asked, as they entered a well-equipped fencing room.

"Yes."

"We have several changing rooms. Choose your weapon and dress out, and we can get started."

Feeling the men stare at him, he picked up a couple of foils, chose one, grabbed a suit and headed for the changing room. He knew he would need to be on guard for more than fencing. He was being tested and probed, and judging by her brothers' expressions, they hoped he'd be shipped off without Michelina. He hated to rub them the wrong way from the get-go, but if they were half as astute as Michelina, it wouldn't take them long to see that he was rock-solid set on their sister.

Minutes later, Jared stood across from Michel, his mask in place. He saluted, and the foils began to fly.

"How did you meet my sister?" Michel asked, winning a point right off the bat.

Jared instinctively protected Michelina. She already suffered from a lack of respect from her brothers—he didn't need to exacerbate that. "Her truck broke down one night near my ranch. She was stranded and was concerned about money, so I let her have one of my extra rooms for the night. When my housekeeper broke her foot the next morning, Michelina offered to help take care of my sister's daughters."

Michel faltered and Jared took advantage, tapping the prince's chest with his foil. "Michelina offered to take care of children?"

"She did a good job, diaper-changing and all."

Jared heard a roar of laughter from the sidelines, and Michel lifted his hand and called, "Time." He pushed back his mask and dipped his head in disbelief. "Michelina changed diapers?"

"Yep," Jared said, pushing back his mask. Taking a quick breath, he hazarded a glance at her other brothers. He swallowed a grin at the varying degrees of amazement he saw on their faces. "She jumped into a lake and rescued a toddler during a county celebration, which she planned, and organized a book drive. And took a few fencing lessons from me, because I understand her lessons were interrupted when she was younger. That right, Nicholas?"

Complete silence filled the room. Nicholas gave Jared yet another assessing glance, as did Alexander, while Michel and Auguste were staring at him in shock.

Michel walked toward him. "She jumped into a lake to rescue a child?"

Jared nodded. "Sure did."

"A book drive?" Auguste echoed.

"The county library was running low. She has a way of making people want to help at the same time she gives a lot of credit, but you've known her a lot longer than I have, so I'm sure you already know that," he said, making a point without the use of his foil. He suspected most of the important points he would make today wouldn't involve his foil.

"You say you gave her fencing lessons," Nicholas said. "What else did you teach Michelina?"

"I hope to believe in herself," Jared said.

"Did you take her to bed?" Michel asked, and a dangerous electricity immediately crackled in the air.

Jared chose his words carefully. "It wouldn't be appropriate for me to discuss something like that with

Michelina's brothers. It should be her choice when and if she discusses that subject.''

''I'm her oldest brother,'' Michel said with a hard glint in his eye. ''It's my right to know.''

''I'm not arguing with you,'' Jared said. ''It may be your right to know, but it's not my right to tell.''

Michel wasn't at all satisfied as he returned to his former position. ''Let's resume the match.''

They saluted, then began again.

''My brothers and I don't believe you are the right man for Michelina,'' Michel said. ''What would it take to gain your agreement?''

Jared's stomach turned. He had been willing to give the benefit of the doubt to Michelina's brothers. He understood their desire to protect her. She was damn well worth protecting. ''I'm not sure what you mean,'' he said, his foil clashing with Michel's.

''To put it bluntly, how much would it take for you to go away? Permanently,'' he added, tapping the area just above Jared's heart.

''There isn't enough money,'' Jared retorted, going on the offensive.

Michel successfully deflected Jared's thrust. ''Every man has his price.''

''I'm sorry you haven't met one that can't be bought,'' Jared said, going after him again.

Michel named a sum.

Jared shook his head, fighting his temper, trying to keep his focus on the match.

Michel named a higher sum.

Jared shook his head and took another hit just below his heart.

Michel named a still-higher sum.

Jared's foil clashed with Michel's. "You're wasting your breath. You could offer me all of Marceau, and the answer would be the same."

"You're not good enough for her. She deserves a husband with a title," Michel said. "She'll change her mind and regret being with you."

Unmoved, Jared continued to parry with Michelina's brother.

"You must see that she doesn't know her own mind. She can't be counted on to make such an important—"

Fury raced through Jared, and he turned his foil on Michel with such force that he knocked the prince's weapon out of his hands. His heart hammering a mile a minute, Jared balled his hand into a fist and itched to give Michel what he was asking for.

Instead, he tossed his own foil on the ground. "You can insult me all you want, but lay off your sister. I don't care if you go by Your Majesty, Your Highness, billionaire or brother, if you insult Michelina, then I will cheerfully rip your face off." He pulled off his mask and glove in disgust. "I've had enough of this tea party," he said, and strode toward the changing room.

"Jared," Nicholas called after him.

Taking a deep breath, Jared turned and cocked his head.

"Join us for a beer," he said.

Michel walked toward him. "The duel was a test— unpleasant, but necessary. Michelina is a prize."

"More than you realize," Jared said, the light

dawning as he realized how he'd been set up. He couldn't fault them for wanting to protect her, but it still left a bad taste in his mouth.

"Come, let us make it up to you," Auguste said, extending his hand.

"Please," Alexander said. "Or I'll never hear the end of it from my wife."

Nicholas winced. "Or mine."

Michel gave a heavy sigh. "Or mine."

Jared began to regain a shred of his sense of humor. "Based on how you try to keep Michelina from pursuing any sort of adventure, I would have thought all of you would have chosen utterly docile, agreeable women for your wives."

The Dumont brothers exchanged glances. "It's a fatal flaw among the Dumont men," Nicholas said. "We're drawn to spirited women. But don't laugh," he said, pointing a finger at Jared. "If you've decided to take on Michelina, then you must have the same flaw."

Thirteen

"No, Mother, there is nothing you can say to persuade me to marry Count Ferrar," Michelina said for what felt like the fiftieth time.

"But he would be such an enhancement for Marceau," Queen Anna Catherine said for the fifty-first time. "The advisors are convinced he is the perfect match for you."

Michelina was starting to lose patience. No, that wasn't quite true. She'd had very little patience *before* this meeting had begun. "The advisors are wrong. If they're that crazy about Count Ferrar, then perhaps one of *them* should marry him."

"There's no need to be impertinent," Anna Catherine said with a frown.

"There's no need to continue talking about the count. He's out of the picture."

''Michelina, you've lived a very sheltered life. You should be willing to accept the good advice being offered to you.''

Michelina set down her cup of tea. ''I'm not as sheltered as I was.''

''Your disappearance terrified the entire family,'' the queen said, and at the drawn expression on her still-lovely face Michelina felt a stabbing pain between her ribs.

''I'm sorry all of you were terrified, but I'm not sorry I disappeared. It gave me a chance to do things I haven't been permitted to do. I learned a lot about myself, about what I want and what I can do.''

''And what you think you want is this rancher,'' her mother said with distaste.

Michelina resented her mother's tone. ''I *know* I want him, and I *will* have him.''

''You say that as if you have no need to consult your brothers, the advisors or me.''

''I don't mind consulting, but it won't change my decision. I'm going to marry Jared, Mother. Nothing will stop me. We can either have the wedding here or in Las Vegas. You choose.''

Her mother blinked in disbelief, then shook her head. ''This man is totally unprepared to be married to a royal. He has no idea of what is required of you and what will subsequently be required of him.''

''Maggie didn't know. Neither did Sophia or Tara.''

''Yes, but they're wom—'' The queen broke off as if she'd caught herself before making a sexist statement. "Why are you so convinced that this Jared is the right man for you?"

"Because he makes me believe I can do things. He wants me to be true to myself. He loves me, not my position, but he respects my family. Even though I've told him how dysfunctional we are—"

Anna Catherine's eyes widened in horror. "You told him the Dumonts are dysfunctional?"

"Of course. That was why I didn't want to come back. I wanted to go to Vegas, but Jared insisted that we come here because he knew that even though my family can be a pain, you're terribly important to me."

Her mother squeezed the bridge of her nose. "I'm getting too old for this."

Feeling a twist of sympathy for the queen, Michelina reached for her hand. Their relationship had been volatile for years, but she would never forget how her mother had often traded sleep to read to her during her early childhood.

"Mother, whoever I marry has to be strong enough to love me and accept my position. Jared is the strongest man I've ever met."

"But you'll live in Wyoming, of all places!" her mother protested.

"He's going to hire extra help at the ranch so we can come back to Marceau frequently. He thinks our island is beautiful."

"Well, of course he does," Anna Catherine said with pride, then let out a sigh. "I will meet him," she said grudgingly.

"Thank you," Michelina said, bounding around the table and kissing her on the cheek.

The queen gave a start at Michelina's impulsive act of affection. "I'm not promising anything."

"You're going to love him," Michelina promised.

Michelina had been right. The queen had loved Jared. In fact, she thought so much of him that she talked him into building a second, smaller ranch on Marceau with one of the prolific Romeo's superstud offspring. The Marceau ranch served dual purposes. It meant Jared had a reason to visit Marceau and it also provided jobs.

A quickie Vegas wedding was ruled out by everyone except Michelina, but she'd been able to negotiate the one-year engagement her mother had insisted on down to four months. Four months during which she and Jared had not more than fifteen minutes alone. If she'd known her mother had planned such constant supervision, Michelina thought, she would have definitely insisted on Vegas. And she suspected Jared would have been quick to agree.

On the morning of her wedding, the cathedral was packed with dignitaries and celebrities from all over the world, and the ceremony was being televised by satellite to Marceau, Europe, the United States and beyond.

"You look beautiful." Her brother Michel extended his arm and patted her hand. "You're completely calm," he said, surprise in his voice. "You don't mind this media circus?"

"Jared helped me with it," she said, eager to see her groom. Her heart kept flying into her throat.

"How did he do that?"

"He said if the cameras got too much, just to look at him and remember that we don't have to invite the world into our honeymoon suite."

Michel chuckled. "Thank God for that." He looked at her again, searching her eyes. "You found a good man."

"Yes, I did," she said, still pinching herself at the way her brothers had so quickly accepted Jared into the fold.

"He found a good woman."

The compliment warmed her from the inside out. She couldn't help smiling. "Yes, he did."

The organ began the introduction to "The Wedding March," signaling the time for Michelina to walk down the aisle. "Time to go," she said, so eager she could have skipped instead of walked. She entered the crowded cathedral to the flash of a thousand cameras and the murmured approval of the throng. She saw her brothers in their tuxes on one side and her sisters-in-law in their bridesmaid's gowns, dabbing at tears, on the other side. Her gaze latched on to Jared's, and the love she saw in his eyes overshadowed everything else in the room.

Twenty minutes later, they were pronounced husband and wife. Ten hours after that, she was ripping off his tux in the bedroom of a lovely guest house overlooking the ocean.

"I've been wanting to get you out of these clothes since I first saw you this morning," she said, impatiently shoving down his jacket and tugging at his shirt.

Jared helped by shrugging off his shirt. "It might have provided some interesting film footage if you hadn't been able to restrain yourself from stripping me during the ceremony."

She giggled. "Unforgettable."

"You already are," he told her, lifting his hand to her hair.

She pressed her cheek against his chest and sighed. "Do you realize that I get to spend every single night of my life with you from now on?"

He nodded. "You're stuck."

"You've always told me I can do anything I want to, right?" she asked as she unfastened his slacks and slid her hands inside his briefs; he was already hard.

"Yesss," he hissed, his eyes growing dark with arousal.

"There's something I've wanted to do for a long time," she told him. "But I haven't had the opportunity because there have been too many people around."

"What would that be?" he asked, moaning as she stroked him. "The last time you wanted to do something you haven't done, it involved sexual positions. Michelina, I've been patient, and I somehow managed to deal with the chaperons your mother insisted on, but if you keep rubbing me like that, I can't make any promises about how long I'll last."

"Well, we don't have to do it just once, do we?" she asked, pushing down his briefs and slacks.

Jared swore under his breath.

She pressed an openmouthed kiss to his chest, then slid her tongue down the center of his torso to his belly button. His flat abdomen quivered beneath her attention.

"What are you…"

She lowered her lips still farther, kissing him intimately, taking him into her mouth.

He swore again and again, but his curses of pleasure sounded like music to her ears.

He pulled her slightly away. "*What* are you doing?"

"You've put up with so much insanity for the past four months…. I just wanted to thank you."

"And this is the way you plan to express your gratitude for the rest of our marriage?" he asked, pulling her to her feet.

"Yes."

Jared groaned. "I have just died and gone to heaven." He swept her up in his arms and carried her to the lavish bedroom in the back of the guest house. She would look at the room more closely some other time, when she didn't feel so wanton and needy. As he stripped off her dress, Michelina looked into Jared's eyes and felt herself sinking.

"I know what you do for me," she whispered to him. "You make me believe I can do anything, and you've even promised to help me find Jack now that the wedding craziness is over."

He nodded in agreement.

"What do I do for you?" she continued. He was so strong sometimes it was hard for her to believe that he could need her for anything.

"Besides the obvious..." he said, with a sexy grin that made it difficult for her to breathe. He lifted her hand to his chest, and she felt his heart pound against his rib cage. "You turn a light on inside me. When I'm with you, it never goes out."

And as Michelina sealed her wedding vows with her husband, she knew the light between them would burn forever.

*   *   *   *   *

0807/009/MB103

Mediterranean Men

Let them sweep you off your feet!

Gorgeous Greeks

The Greek Bridegroom by Helen Bianchin
The Greek Tycoon's Mistress by Julia James
Available 20th July 2007

Seductive Spaniards

At the Spaniard's Pleasure by Jacqueline Baird
The Spaniard's Woman by Diana Hamilton
Available 17th August 2007

Irresistible Italians

The Italian's Wife by Lynne Graham
The Italian's Passionate Proposal by Sarah Morgan
Available 21st September 2007

M&B

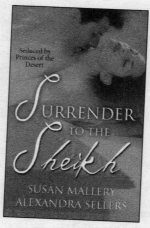